Paul and James's Naturist Adventure

Nigel Keer

Published by Nigel Keer

Publishing partner: Paragon Publishing, Rothersthorpe

First published 2012

ISBN 978-1-908341-69-3

Book design, layout and production management by Into Print

www.intoprint.net

+44 (0)1604 832149

Chapter 1

Paul Jessop and James Handle are two fourteen-year-olds who have known each other all their lives. They live next door to each other and have something quite significant in common; both of them are only children. As a result of this they get on extremely well and are often mistaken for twin brothers. Their parents also know one another too and both families have enjoyed holidaying together many times. Paul and James also enjoy holidaying together very much; sometimes it would be the seaside and other times elsewhere. Paul and James preferred the seaside and weren't over keen on holidays which involved a lot of walking; however, this was to change.

In the May half term holiday they'd agreed to help on a neighbour's garden. Mr. and Mrs. Hope, a couple in their late seventies, had promised them a treat for cutting the grass, weeding and generally tidying up. So at about ten thirty on Tuesday morning they went over to see them. Paul and James worked well, and by half four they'd finished and were sat down on the grass talking. Mrs. Hope invited them in for a cup of tea and a slice of cake, during which time Mr. Hope gave them a tenner each. "Thanks very much Mr. Hope," smiled Paul and James.

"Worth every penny boys; you've both done a great job with the garden, it looks lovely now," said Mr. Hope. Paul and James carried on chatting with the Hopes and were nearly late home for their tea.

The next day Paul and James went out, and around midmorning, found themselves walking along a pretty deserted path which lead up to and through the woods. They weren't that far from home, no more than a mile or so when they saw someone that made them stop and stare. A man was walking towards them in the distance. They couldn't quite decide what this man was wearing so moved off the path and into the trees out of sight. He gradually got closer and as he did so Paul said; "I don't think he's wearing any clothes is he?"

"He looks to have a rucksack on his back," said James.

"Yeah I know, but what else, just trainers?" At that point the man stopped and turned to take a photograph of the surrounding countryside. Paul and James waited to see what would happen next. The man carried on walking towards them and was now about three to four hundred yards away.

"Do you know, I think you're right," said James. The man stopped again and took off his rucksack. He took out a bottle of what looked like Coca Cola, had a drink then promptly put the bottle back. He stayed where he was, and after taking another photograph, he picked up his rucksack and continued to walk towards Paul and James. Suddenly a cyclist appeared from nowhere and headed straight for the apparently naked man at some speed. Paul and James thought the cyclist would frighten the man away if he really was naked, but curiously, this didn't happen. The man kept walking along the path and past very close to where Paul and James were hiding. There was of course no mistaking it now; this man was completely naked save for his rucksack and trainers. Paul and James smiled at one another and could hardly believe what they'd just seen; a man, almost as old as their parents, just walked past them completely naked. Once the man had past them, Paul and James carefully got out of their hiding place and continued to observe him as he walked away, stopping occasionally to take the odd photograph. They quickly decided to follow him, but at a safe distance.

"Why do you think he's naked?" asked Paul.

"How should I know," replied James. "He can't really have gone out of his house like that and forgotten to put his clothes on surely."

"Damn! We've lost him," said Paul suddenly. "Quick, this way!" James quickly followed Paul along a very narrow and somewhat overgrown path. "Ouch, damn Nettles!" exclaimed Paul rubbing his leg.

"I bet the naked man didn't come this way," laughed James. "He'd have stung himself to death." The path the naked man had apparently taken descended and curved round to the left. Paul and James could now look over to where they thought he might go. Sure enough they weren't wrong and after a few minutes they saw the naked man again. They watched him continue towards the railway line. "He's still naked isn't he," said James.

"Yeah I think so," replied Paul.

"If he gets too close to the railway line train passengers might see him." The man stopped a good hundred yards short of the railway line and took off his rucksack. He had another drink of Coke and then put the bottle down. He then took a bright orange towel from his rucksack and spread it out on the grass. Paul was wondering if he might be some kind of eccentric trainspotter, but didn't say anything. With nobody else in sight the naked man laid down on his towel. To anyone casually observing him it now looked as if he was sunbathing. Paul and James stayed where they were for quite a while and it was getting hotter as the day went on, more so than yesterday when they were tidying the Hope's garden. The man was sunbathing and was applying sun cream when Paul and James looked over again a few minutes later.

After a good hour or two sat watching the naked man Paul and James were starting to feel hungry. "He's pretty settled don't you think?" said James. "Why don't we go and get something to eat, fish and chips say, then come back and see if he's still here."

"Hmm," Paul thought for a moment; he just fancied some fish and chips. "Hang on a minute, I've got a better idea; one of us can go to the chippy while the other stays here and keeps watch."

"OK then, I'll go. Would you like a drink as well?"

"Yeah, Cherry Coke please," replied Paul. So James went to get some fish and chips and left Paul observing the naked man.

Paul had never before seen anyone walk about fully naked, except of course in changing rooms and showers, but this was very different because it was outside in the open air, and it aroused Paul's curiosity a great deal. As Paul continued to observe him the naked man turned over and laid on his back face up. The naked man looked around, stretched out his arms and then laid quite still. Even though Paul was a good hundred yards away he could clearly see this man's privates. How could he possibly be so unconcerned, thought Paul. What would happen if someone saw him? After just over two hours sat watching him Paul felt sure there was no one else about and was beginning to wonder what being naked outdoors might feel like. Paul looked at himself. He was only wearing a T-shirt, shorts, boxers, socks and trainers. He stood up and took off his T-shirt. There was a gentle breeze which Paul liked the feel of on his skin. He looked around again and moved back a few feet. He couldn't see anyone at all and his friend James had only been gone a few minutes. It must be fifteen to twenty minutes walk to that chip shop and back thought Paul; so he figured James wouldn't be back for a while. From where he was now standing Paul could just see the naked man lying down on his orange towel. He paused for a moment, looked around again, still nothing. A train went past in the distance tooting for the foot crossing then quickly disappeared from view. It was all quiet again, save for the odd bird or insect. Paul then took off his trainers and socks. The grass was warm under his bare feet. He sat down on his T-shirt and continued to observe the naked man, who was now sat up reading a magazine. He looked around again; still no sign of anyone. Just then Paul was suddenly startled by his mobile phone. He'd received a text message from James and it read: [Cud b a while - long Q at chip shop]. Paul replied straightaway with: [OK naked man is still here]. Paul put his phone down on the grass next to him.

By now the sun was at its highest and there wasn't a cloud for miles; it felt really hot. Paul stood up again and bravely pulled down his shorts. As he did so he was somewhat unnerved by another train passing by in the opposite direction, then all was quiet again and the naked man was still reading his magazine. It's now or never, thought Paul. So after yet another look round Paul gingerly pulled down his boxers. He now felt very exposed and vulnerable, not at all like the confident fourteen-year-old he was. Paul risked taking his boxers right off and stood up completely naked. The gentle breeze had almost gone, but there was still a very slight movement of air. Paul thought this felt very nice on his naked body. This was his first ever outdoor naked experience and he quite liked it. Looking across Paul was surprised to see that the naked man had gone, but his orange towel and rucksack were still there. He can't have gone far, thought Paul as he sat down on his T-shirt. Just then his phone beeped again making him jump. Another text message from James, he thought; it was. James was now on his way back with the fish and chips. Paul thought he'd better put his shorts back on at the very least so as not to freak James out upon his return, but feeling the way he did Paul risked another five minutes in the nude. Even in this relatively short period of time Paul had clearly made up his mind about being naked outdoors, and the only thing causing him any concern was someone seeing him and informing his parents. Paul was about to put his shorts back on when he had a thought. He wondered if his trainers would fit through them; so put his socks and trainers on first. Paul then picked up his shorts and tried to put them on over his trainers. This wasn't particularly easy, but he managed it without falling over. Then, as Paul picked up his T-shirt, James arrived back with the food and drink. "Sorry it took so long. They were queuing out into the street!"

"Never mind, you're here now. Did you get any scraps?" asked Paul.

"Yeah, here, help yourself." Paul and James sat down on the grass and enjoyed their fish and chips together. James couldn't help noticing that Paul had taken off his T-shirt. He simply assumed Paul was rather warm and had taken off his T-shirt in an attempt to cool down.

"Mmm, nice fish from that chippy don't you think," said Paul.

"Yeah, great; chips are nice too," smiled James. While he was eating Paul couldn't help wondering if James had seen him before he'd got dressed. The not knowing caused him to feel a little uneasy.

"Is the naked man still there?" asked Paul as he was finishing his last mouthful.

"Yep," replied James turning round to check. At this point James decided to take his T-shirt off as well. "Phew, it's pretty hot here isn't it."

"You're not wrong there," replied Paul. James got up and collected all the fish and chip papers. He pushed them into the bag he'd been given by the woman in the chip shop and as he did this James noticed a pair of boxers a few yards away.

"Hey what're these?" smiled James, holding up the pair of almost new black boxers. "They're very like yours Paul." Paul was immediately struck dumb and went red in the face. How could he tell James what he'd done while he was away? Paul muttered incoherently at first, but then decided to be honest. After all, James was his best friend and they'd been in more embarrassing situations at school.

"Yes, they are mine," said Paul. "Thanks for finding them for me." Paul knew James was going to ask why he wasn't wearing them, and, of course, he did.

"Why have you taken them off?" James asked cautiously, trying not to embarrass his best friend too much. Paul looked over at the naked man who'd gone back to lying face down on his towel.

"You see the naked man don't you?"

"Yeah," replied James.

"Well, I was wondering what he might be feeling like; you know, naked, in the open air."

"Oh, right; so you thought you'd find out."

"Yes," said Paul rather bluntly.

"What did you think about it?" asked James.

"I felt very exposed and vulnerable at first; if someone else saw me fully naked, just how embarrassing would it be; but it did feel kind of relaxing in a way, know what I mean?"

"Hmm; I think so," said James. "Did you stay right here or did you er, walk about a bit?"

"I just stood here and looked around. When you sent me that second text it made me jump, I couldn't help it!"

"Sorry about that, but I couldn't have known what you were up to could I?" smiled James.

"No, I s'pose not." This was followed by a brief pause in conversation. "If I'd have gone for the fish and chips and left you here, would you have been tempted to do the same?"

"I don't think so. The thought hadn't occurred to me, but I must say if I had I think I'd have put my boxers back on before you got back," smiled James.

"Yeah yeah, OK," said Paul, trying to forget about the fact he didn't have his boxers on under his shorts.

There was another moment of quiet which was unexpectedly disturbed. Paul and James heard a deep throbbing sound in the distance similar to a motorbike, but this became far louder. Two big diesel locomotives came into view struggling with a very long train of oil tankers. It blasted its horn for the foot crossing and very slowly disappeared as did the sound of it, then all was calm again. "If I'd have come back a bit sooner and found you naked would you have been angry with me?"

"Well, to be honest I think I'd have grabbed my clothes and tried to hide," said Paul defensively. "Why are we still talking about this anyway?"

"Well, seeing as it's a hot day, and, we're alone."

"Yes?" said Paul slowly and with considerable interest. James suddenly side stepped and changed the subject.

"Is the naked man still there?" They both moved over to get a better view. No, the naked man had gone. Paul and James thought for a moment. "Where do you think he's gone to?" asked James.

"How should I know?" replied Paul. "Anyway, what were you about to say before you suddenly changed the subject?"

"Nothing much," shrugged James. "I just wondered what er…" James left the sentence unfinished and looked away from Paul's direction. Paul felt uncomfortable after trying to get a straight answer out of James.

"Sorry, I er…"

"What?" asked James.

"Why don't we walk round to where the naked man was?"

"Yeah, come on then." Paul and James got up and began to walk down the path to where the naked man had been. Paul had again forgotten his boxers.

"Hey, wait a minute! Where's my boxers?" exclaimed Paul after a few yards.

"Oh, you must have left them up there where we were," replied James. "I'll go and fetch them for you." Paul waited with his T-shirt in his hand as James reappeared with his boxers. "Are you gonna put them back on?" asked James with a bit of a giggle.

"Not right now, thank you!" snapped Paul. They continued to the spot where the naked man was last seen. All they could see was an area of grass flattened by him lying down. Another train came past tooting as usual for the foot crossing. Paul and James looked around where the naked man had been, and apart from finding fifty pence, didn't see anything particularly interesting.

The time was now nearly six o'clock and the heat of the day was beginning to fade. Paul and James put their T-shirts back on.

"Do you think we should be heading home now?" asked James. "Our parents might be wondering where we are."

"Yeah why not. We haven't seen the naked man for well over an hour now have we?" Still keeping their eyes peeled for anything unusual, Paul and James walked home. As they got to within sight of their homes Paul realised he was still carrying his boxers in his hand. How was he going to explain this to his mum or dad if they should happen to see him enter the house. Paul's dad's car wasn't there. Well, dad's out, thought Paul, just mum to worry about. Just then Paul had a thought. "Do you fancy watching TV with us?" he asked.

"Yeah OK," replied James. "I'll just get something to eat and I'll come round in half an hour or so."

"OK then, I'll see you a bit later." Paul and James went inside their homes. Paul's mum was in the kitchen getting the dinner ready. Paul threw his boxers behind a chair hoping he'd be able to pick them up later when nobody was looking. "Something smells nice," said Paul showing interest in what his mum was cooking.

"Pizza, salad and garlic bread love, OK? It'll be ready in less than five minutes so you might as well help yourself to some salad." Paul helped himself to a couple of leaves of lettuce, some cucumber, a piece of tomato and a few onion rings. "You can put the TV on if you like," called his mum. "I'll bring you a slice of pizza through in a minute." Paul switched the TV on and sat down on the sofa. His mum came in with a slice pizza for him.

"Mum, I've asked James round later; it's OK isn't it?"

"Yes love fine; only I'll have to leave you both for an hour or so. I said I'd help your grandad with his cleaning and what not."

"Oh that's OK," said Paul. Paul finished his dinner and took his plate and knife and fork into the kitchen. He helped himself to a glass of orange juice from the fridge and then went back into the front room and sat down. He wasn't sat down for long when

James knocked on the front door. Paul got up and let James in just as his mum was coming downstairs.

"Right, I'm going out now," she told them. "I should be back around quarter to nine give or take. Oh, and your dad's been held up at work. He doesn't expect to be home until after ten. See you when I get back."

"OK, bye mum." Paul's mum left the house and closed the front door. Paul locked it behind her.

"Right then," said James. "What you watching?"

"Not a lot really, let's go upstairs and play a game." Paul and James went upstairs to Paul's bedroom.

"You got Monopoly?" asked James.

"Yeah sure, it's under my bed, hang on a minute I'll just get it." Paul reached under his bed and brought out his Monopoly. "Here, you set it up; I've just remembered something." Paul left the room and went downstairs to retrieve his boxers. He picked them up and went back upstairs. "Didn't want to leave these where my folks could find them," smiled Paul.

"I take it you got in without being seen with them in your hand then."

"Yeah I did, I hid them behind a chair." Paul and James continued with their game of Monopoly; neither of them mentioning the naked man. James eventually won the game with hotels on the Trafalgar Square set being Paul's unfortunate downfall. They put the game away and sat still for a while. Paul then brought up the subject of the naked man. "I know it might be a bit of a tall order, but shall we go out tomorrow and see if we can see the naked man again?"

"Yeah, I s'pose we might as well," replied James. "By the way, where's your mum? It's nearly half nine." Just then Paul's mum came back in.

"Sorry I'm later than I said; everything OK?"

"Yeah fine," replied Paul. "James is going home now anyway." Paul saw James out then went back upstairs to his bedroom. He kept thinking about the naked man. Paul decided to get a shower before going to bed so grabbed a towel from the airing cupboard and went into the bathroom. He took off his socks and T-shirt, and slipped out of his shorts. Paul turned the shower on and stepped in. As he washed himself he looked closely at his skin; it felt soft and smooth. He noticed his arms were beginning to tan ahead of the rest of his body. Paul finished showering and turned the shower off. He stepped out, grabbed his towel and began to dry himself. A couple of minutes later Paul heard his dad arrive home.

"Evening," said his dad on entering the house. Paul could hear his parents talking downstairs. He finished drying himself, put on a clean pair of boxers and his dressing gown, and then went downstairs to join his parents in the front room.

"Good day son?" asked his dad.

"Yeah, not bad thanks," replied Paul. "Dad, while James and I were out we er..." Paul left the sentence unfinished.

"We er, what son?" asked his dad.

"Er, nothing really."

"It's OK love you can tell us," said his mum. "Is someone bothering you?"

"No no, not at all. I was just wondering where we were thinking of going on holiday this year." Paul evaded the issue of the naked man.

"We haven't decided yet have we Maureen," said his dad.

"What about North Wales, or Devon and Cornwall?" suggested Paul "Or can we go abroad this year? James and I were talking about this yesterday." This was a bit of a lie as Paul wanted to throw his parents off the scent of anything untoward.

"We'll see love," said his mum. "Are you going up to bed now? It's nearly half ten."

"Yeah, night dad, night mum."

"Night love," said his parents. Paul went upstairs to bed and took off his dressing gown. It was still on the warm side so he opened his bedroom window a couple of inches. Paul then laid down on his bed and thought again about the naked man. What if someone saw him; wait a minute, someone did see him; there was the cyclist for a start, he didn't seem to care and neither did the naked man himself, he just kept on waking and taking photos; and, generally speaking, was minding his own business.

At first Paul couldn't understand why a fully grown man would want to go about completely naked, but he now had some understanding after trying it for himself and liking it. Paul thought again about the time he was alone. He remembered taking off his clothes and in particular the moment when he took off his boxers and stood up as naked as the day he was born. Paul decided to do something he'd never done before and that was to sleep naked. He set his alarm clock for 08:30. He wanted to be awake before 08:45 which was usually the time his mum would get him up. Paul turned out the light, got into bed and slipped off his boxers under the duvet. After a few minutes he felt the need to go to the toilet. Damn, how can I go to the toilet like this? Hmm, very easily I suppose if I was alone, thought Paul, but he wasn't. Paul got out of bed, stumbling slightly in the dark, and went over to turn his bedroom light on when he heard his dad come upstairs. Oh no! Please, please don't come in dad, Paul said in his mind. His dad walked past his bedroom door. Paul found the light switch and turned it on. He quickly picked up his boxers and put them on. Paul nipped across to the toilet and then back to his bedroom. He turned out the light again and carefully got back in to bed. He risked taking his boxers off once again, but this time he put them under his pillow. Just in case, he thought. Paul felt very comfortable and snug in bed naked and he soon drifted off to sleep.

Chapter 2

Next morning Paul woke to his alarm clock bleeping. He stopped it immediately so as not to alert his mum. His dad usually set off to work at quarter to eight. For a minute or two Paul laid quite still in bed. He'd had a good night's sleep. Maybe I'll sleep naked more often, he thought to himself.

"Paul, are you up yet?" called his mum from the bottom of the stairs.

"Yes mum, I'll be down in a few minutes." Paul got out of bed and stood naked in front of his mirror. He had a good look at himself. At fourteen years old his body was beginning to develop into that of a young man. He was starting to grow hair under his arms and around his privates; however, the rest of his body remained completely hairless. I do hope I don't end up growing too much hair, Paul thought to himself. I really like the way I am just now. Paul continued to look at himself in the mirror. He knew he wasn't over-weight, in fact he thought he was on the skinny side. His friend James was a couple of inches taller and of slightly larger build, but Paul didn't mind. Paul got dressed and went downstairs. He had some breakfast and then went back upstairs to his bedroom.

"Are you going out again today with James?" asked his mum.

"Yeah, I'm gonna call for him in a few minutes," replied Paul. Paul remembered he'd left his boxers under his pillow so promptly went upstairs, removed them and put them in the laundry basket. Whilst doing this Paul had an interesting thought, and after yesterday's encounter with the naked man, was thinking about being naked outdoors again, but wasn't quite sure how to introduce the idea to James. Paul had a look through his chest of drawers and found a pair of shorts he always said were a bit too big for him. He took off the shorts he was wearing and tried them on. Paul pulled the cord around his waist and tied it in a bow. He'd had these shorts since he was twelve, but had rarely, if ever, worn them. He looked in the mirror again. Hmm, not bad, he thought, better than they were two years ago. Paul paused for a moment then went to the top of the stairs.

"Mum," he called, but there was no answer. Paul looked

out of his bedroom window. His mum was outside talking to the postman. Great, thought Paul. He quickly took off both his shorts and boxers, and then put his shorts back on. Paul thought he could take these slightly larger shorts on and off fairly easily over his trainers, should the opportunity present itself. Paul went downstairs and put his trainers on. His mum came in with a letter she'd signed for.

"Are you off out now?" she asked.

"Yeah, gonna call for James," replied Paul.

"OK love, I'll see you later."

"OK, bye Mum." Paul went next door and knocked on the front door. James's mum answered it. "Hi Mrs. Handle."

"Oh hello Paul. James, Paul's here," she called.

"OK, just a minute," replied James from somewhere upstairs.

"Come in a minute Paul," said James's mum. "He shouldn't be long." Although Paul wasn't yet aware of it, James had been having similar thoughts about being naked outdoors. Yesterday's encounter with the naked man had given him ideas as well. Add that to the fact that Paul had told him he'd been naked, even if it was only ten minutes or so, interested James. James came downstairs wearing a T-shirt and shorts very similar to Paul's.

"Oh James, are you going out like that?" said his mum.

"What's wrong mum?" asked James.

"Those shorts are too big for you, I've told you before."

"Don't worry mum, I'm fine." With that said Paul and James went out.

It was another warm day just like yesterday. "Shall we go to where we last saw the naked man?" James suggested.

"You took the words right out of my mouth," replied Paul. "Did you tell your mum and dad about seeing a naked man yesterday?"

"No I didn't, I thought it best not to," said James. "And in any case, do you think they would've believed us?"

"Yeah, I guess your right there; they'd have probably thought we were being silly." Paul and James walked to where they'd last seen the naked man the previous day.

The sun was rising higher in the sky, and although it was only ten o'clock, it was starting to feel very warm indeed. They got to the same spot where they were yesterday, stopped and looked around. Needless to say - no naked man.

"Do you think we'll see him again? After all he might not live round here," said James.

"That thought had crossed my mind," replied Paul. They waited about an hour, but didn't see anyone, not even anyone clothed. A train went past, tooting as usual for the foot crossing. A few minutes after the train had gone Paul pointed at the foot crossing and said; "Look!" Sure enough a man carrying a rucksack was walking across the railway line, but he certainly wasn't naked. He was wearing a white sleeveless T-shirt, dark blue shorts, socks and trainers. Paul and James wondered if this was the naked man they'd seen before, but was now clothed. They observed him as he continued to walk across the railway line and though the gate. The man then stopped and sat down, but he was only sat down for a couple of minutes while he looked at his map. He quickly got up again and walked back towards the crossing. Paul and James were still watching him as he re-crossed the railway line and disappeared from view. "I doubt that was the same man we saw yesterday," said Paul. "And besides, he didn't have a map."

"Yeah, I guess so," said James. However, unbeknown to Paul and James, this man was indeed the same man they'd seen yesterday. He'd spotted both of them and had simply decided to go elsewhere. Paul and James had no idea they'd been seen so continued to wait. They waited and waited, but still, nothing.

"I'm getting bored waiting here," said Paul. "Why don't we walk about a bit, you never know."

"Yeah, OK then," said James. They walked around for a few minutes and when they got to the spot where they'd seen the man, who'd crossed the railway line, checked his map and then quickly re-crossed, Paul spotted a piece of paper folded up. He picked it up and unfolded it carefully.

"James!" said Paul suddenly.

"What?"

"Come here and look at this." It was a flyer for a naturist swim at their own local leisure centre. Paul and James could hardly believe what they were reading.

"If that's what I think it is; that man must have been the naked man we saw yesterday after all," said James.

"Yes, and I bet you anything you like this fell out of his bag when he checked his map." The swim was for the coming Saturday evening commencing at seven o'clock. Paul and James looked at each other.

"Do you think the word naturist means the same as naked?" asked James.

"I've a feeling it could do," replied Paul.

"We could look it up in the dictionary when we get home to make sure."

"Yeah, that's a good idea; or we could type it into an internet search engine and see what comes up," smiled Paul.

"Supposing it does mean the same. Do you er..." James stopped mid-sentence again.

"Do what?" asked Paul.

"I mean go there and look through the window and see if everybody is naked."

"Hmm..." Paul thought for a moment about what James just suggested. "We could do that, but do you really think if it is some kind of naked swimming session we'll be able to look through the windows at everyone? They'll block them out for sure."

"Yeah, I s'pose so. What do you want to do then, sneak in somehow before it starts," suggested James with a smile.

"How on earth would we get away with that?" asked Paul. "We would have to be naked to blend in, just how exactly would you cope with that?"

"Hmm, you've got a point there; it could be embarrassing, especially if we were found out; and in any case, we've never even been naked together ourselves, let alone with anyone else." Whether or not it was James's intention to say just what he did Paul wasn't sure, but it did give him the cue he wanted.

"Well, let's just think about that for a moment. If we find somewhere quiet and out of the way, why don't we give it a try? Just a few minutes to start with if you like."

"Oh yeah, where?" asked James with interest.

"Follow me," said Paul. Paul suspected right, wearing those slightly bigger shorts was about to pay off. He led James down a steep embankment to a clearing between the trees. With nobody in sight they were very much alone. There were tall trees nearly all the way around them. It was very warm and calm, and they were far enough away from the railway line so as not to be disturbed by the noise of passing trains.

"Right," said Paul. "What about here?"

"Do you think it's safe enough for us to take all our clothes off here?" asked James.

"Well, I think it's about as safe as we're going to get. Why don't we start by taking off our T-shirts." Paul took off his T-shirt and dropped it on the grass by his feet. James took off his T-shirt as well. So far so good, thought Paul. "Have you got any boxers on under your shorts?" asked Paul.

"Yeah, why?"

"Well, I haven't."

"Why don't we take off our trainers and socks next," suggested James.

"OK, go on then," said Paul. So both of them sat down on their T-shirts and took off their trainers and socks. There was a brief pause in conversation then Paul said; "If you've got boxers on under your shorts, could you take your shorts off first?"

"Er, OK then." James stood up and had a good look around. There was nobody to be seen anywhere and it was still very quiet where they were. James slowly undid the cord in his shorts and took them off. He was wearing a dark blue pair of boxers. Paul could clearly see that James felt uneasy at removing his shorts out in the open.

"Are you OK?" he asked, trying to reassure him.

"I think so," replied James as he sat back down.

"We must be able to do this," said Paul. "If we wanna get into the leisure centre that evening to see what's going on the best disguise is surely going to be our birthday suits, wouldn't you agree?"

"Yeah I know, but didn't that letter or whatever it was say anyone under eighteen had to have permission from their parents to attend." Paul hadn't read that bit so looked again to check.

"Damn! It does," said Paul. "How we gonna get round that?"

"Don't know," replied James. "If I asked my mum or dad

they'd hit the roof for sure. What about your folks?"

"Yeah, I suspect they'd probably do exactly the same. However, there's nothing to stop us doing it here, is there?" continued Paul, as he stood up in just his shorts.

"No, I guess not," said James still feeling somewhat uncomfortable. "Why don't you do it first, I promise I won't laugh." James had been waiting for this moment to happen, but now it was here it scared him.

Both Paul and James were very introverted boys. Neither had seen the other with anything less than shorts or swimming trunks on and they'd always shied away from communal changing rooms. However, it would have been very unlikely for them to have seen each other while at school because they weren't just in different classes, but different years as well. Although they were the same age, fourteen, Paul would turn fifteen on the nineteenth of August, usually making him the youngest in the class. James's birthday was the third of September and was just over two weeks after Paul's. This meant James was in the year below Paul, but was always the eldest in the class.

Paul finally decided he must do it and take off his shorts. He hoped James would have enough courage to do it as well. He looked around again and took a deep breath. His heart was beating much faster than normal. Paul undid the cord in his shorts, and then, because they were too big for him, they suddenly dropped to his feet. He quickly sat down again and took his shorts right off. For the second time in as many days Paul was now completely naked outdoors.

"Come on then, your turn," smiled Paul looking across at James. James's heart was beating very fast as well. He'd just seen his best friend naked for the first time in his life. James knew he must face his fears and take off his boxers. He stood up, paused for a moment, then after a good look round, he finally found the courage to do it. He took a deep breath, and, although he was still feeling nervous, he pulled down his boxers. When he had James quickly sat back down.

"Come on, right off," said Paul with a wry smile. James took his boxers right off. Both boys were now completely naked, but they were sat down. "I think we should stand up," said Paul.

"Er, after you," said James nervously.

"I think we should to stand up together, and walk about a bit," said Paul. "If we look straight ahead and not at each other we can feel what it is like to be naked in the open air. Paul and James slowly stood up and looked ahead. There was a slight breeze through the trees. Paul had briefly enjoyed this before while alone and he was hoping James would like it too. "What do you think?" asked Paul.

"Er... OK... er... I think," stammered James feeling very vulnerable and exposed. "What about you?"

"Fine," replied Paul. "Let's walk a few paces. Be careful where you tread there might be thistles and sharp stuff."

"Can't we put our trainers back on?" asked James.

"Yeah, OK then. I suppose that would make sense. Just our trainers mind, nothing else." They both sat down again and put their trainers back on. "Right, are you ready?"

"I'm as ready as I'll ever be I s'pose," replied James still feeling nervous. "Where we gonna walk to?"

"What about that tree over there?" suggested Paul pointing at a large oak tree about a hundred yards away.

"That's a bit far isn't it," said James.

"Well, let's walk about half way and see how we feel," suggested Paul.

"OK then." While still trying not to look at each other, Paul and James stood up and began to walk towards the tree Paul had suggested. They got just over half way and stopped. "Now what?" asked James.

"Nothing; are you OK to keep going?"

"Yeah, I think so; let's keep going." They got to the tree Paul had set as a target.

"Right, let's walk back," said Paul. Paul and James walked back to where they'd left their clothes and promptly sat back down. "Hmm, this is not how I'd hoped we could be together," sighed Paul. "It's as if we're scared to death. We need to be more relaxed and confident. Why don't we walk over to the tree again, but separately this time; you know, one at a time."

"Er... OK then. Who's gonna go first?" asked James. Paul felt uncomfortable again because he quickly realised it would be him going first, but he gave James the choice.

"Would you like to go first?" he asked.

"Er; well, I..." James found it difficult to answer.

"Look, it's OK, I'll do it first," said Paul, feeling as if he'd backed himself into a corner. "And then you can do it when I come back."

"OK." Paul stood up; and with his arms by his side, he began walking towards the tree openly naked. Although he was nervous, Paul tried to appear as relaxed as he could. He felt reasonably OK walking away from James because he knew he could only see his back, his bottom and the back of his legs. Paul was more concerned about walking back 'cos he knew James would be able to see him full frontal. As he continued walking towards the tree Paul kept thinking; I've got to walk back as if I don't have a care in the world, it will help James if I do. How can I expect him to do something I'm not prepared to do myself. Paul stopped at the tree, his heart really pounding. I must do this as relaxed and as carefree as possible, he thought; here goes. Paul turned round and faced James. He walked back slowly, arms again by his side. Paul made no attempt to hide his privates. He looked straight ahead for a few moments then at James, but quickly turned away. No, thought Paul, I must act as relaxed and as normal as possible for James's sake as well as my own. Paul stopped about half way back. He'd now made up his mind to really go for it. So he bent down and picked up a dandelion clock. He looked across at James and carefully blew the seeds away. Paul dropped the stem and continued to walk towards James. He stopped again about thirty yards from where James was sitting and reached up with both his arms. Paul stretched his body as much as he could in the warm sunshine. James looked on in amazement, his mouth wide open. Paul walked back and sat down beside him.

"Did you er... enjoy that?" asked James.

"Yes, I'd like to think I did. I felt uneasy at first, but I felt free and liberated. What did you think when I picked up that dandelion clock, and also when I stopped and had a good stretch?"

"I can't believe you just did that," replied James, his heart really pounding now knowing he was going to have to walk over to the tree completely naked, and, on his own. Paul waited for James to stand up.

"Can you do it?" he asked.

"I'll give it a go," replied James nervously. James stood up and slowly walked towards the tree, but did so far more surreptitiously than Paul had done. James was looking around all the time and was terrified someone was going to see him while he was naked. James got to the tree and stopped. He felt his heart rate was off the Richter scale. If Paul can do it, I can do it, he thought trying to feel more positive. James turned round and started to walk back. He too managed to resist any temptation to hide his privates, and as he got closer Paul stood up.

"Just stop there a moment," said Paul. Paul walked forward so he was about ten to twelve yards away from where James was standing. "Look at the pair of us!" said Paul firmly. "We've known each other all our lives, so just what is there to be embarrassed about? We're two fourteen-year-old lads with healthy bodies and all the bits in the right places, don't you agree?"

"Yeah of course I do; so why is it we feel so stressed then?" asked James

"Well it's something new, something we've never tried before," continued Paul. "It might be a bit like having an aversion or phobia. We have to face it so that we can eventually overcome it."

"How long have we been naked?" asked James.

"Only twenty minutes or so, if that," replied Paul, but James thought it felt longer.

"Can we put our shorts back on yet?" asked James hopefully. Paul was thinking about what they could do next and took no notice of what James just said.

"If we're gonna try and get into that swim on Saturday evening we must be more relaxed while we're naked," insisted Paul.

"I know that, but, I'm finding it, well, difficult," said James still looking around. "Are you sure there's still no one about? If we're seen here like this we'll be in big trouble for sure." Paul looked around and tried to reassure James that everything was going to be fine. However, the naked man they'd seen yesterday, and earlier this morning while clothed, had walked past a gap in the trees. He didn't see them at first because he was admiring the view, but then he heard voices. Although they weren't aware of it Paul and James had indeed been seen, but thankfully for them, only by the naked man, who was also naked himself now.

"Why don't we walk over to that tree again," suggested Paul, "But this time when I get there I'll stop. At that point I'd like you to walk over to me, OK?"

"Yeah, OK. Go on then," said James. Paul got to his feet again and walked over to the tree. He began to feel more relaxed the longer he was naked. The naked man was watching as Paul walked over to the tree and was surprised to say the least! Paul stopped at the tree and signalled to James. James stood up and walked over to him.

"Slowly, there's no rush," said Paul. James stopped when he got to where Paul was.

"Right, let's walk back together," said Paul, his confidence further increasing. "How do you feel now?" he asked. "And be honest."

"Er... not too bad actually," replied James. "Being naked is kind of relaxing and liberating isn't it."

"Yes it is, and that's just how I feel as well," said Paul. "It's a pity we haven't got..." Paul stopped, but then continued. "...a tennis ball, or something we can throw and catch." Suddenly James felt something hard under his left foot. He looked down and saw that it was a golf ball. James picked it up and knocked off the bits of dirt.

"Will this do?" he asked holding out the golf ball."

"Yeah OK, I s'pose it's a start," replied Paul. "Right then, if you stay where you are I'll move back a bit." They were now about thirty yards apart. Paul threw the golf ball to James who promptly missed catching it, a golf ball being rather small. James picked it up and threw it back to Paul. Paul managed to catch it, but only just. They moved a bit closer together and then Paul threw it for James to catch and so on. They kept this up for a good ten minutes. All this time they were being observed by the naked man, who was suitably impressed. He walked off after a few minutes and left them to it.

It was now just after quarter to two and Paul and James

decided to go home and get something to eat. "I assume we're going to put our clothes back on to go home," said James.

"Well of course we are; unless you want to go home like this!" smiled Paul.

"I don't think so!" replied James sharply. "I mean, can you imagine the look on our mums and dads faces if we walked into our homes like this; they'd kill us!"

"OK don't panic, I was only joking; here's your shorts," said Paul as he past James his shorts. "This is why I was wearing these larger shorts. I can put them on over my trainers easily." James was trying to put his boxers on over his trainers when Paul interrupted him. "Leave your boxers off; just put your shorts on and see how you feel. The air will be able to pass round your er..." Paul paused.

"Privates?" James finished the sentence for him.

"Yeah. After doing it yesterday I got use to it and I think it feels nicer, like your only one step away from being naked." James put his shorts on and stood up. "What do you think?" asked Paul hoping James would like the absence of his boxers under his shorts.

"OK fine," replied James. "It's like you said; I feel like I've got more room for my er..."

"Privates?" Paul said the word this time.

"Yeah, you're right," smiled James. "I think I'll wear my shorts without boxers all the time from now on. Paul and James picked up the rest of their clothes and walked back home. Paul's parents were both out and so was James's dad. James's mum was cleaning and tidying up when they went in.

"Hi mum."

"Hi Mrs. Handle," said Paul and James as they entered.

"Where've you two been all morning, it's ten past two?"

"Out," said James trying to avoid saying anything that might incriminate the pair of them.

"We've been over by the railway line," said Paul more honestly. "We just walked around, watched a few trains and sat in the sun." This wasn't far from the truth, the only thing Paul left out was the fact that they'd been naked for the best part of two hours.

Paul and James helped themselves to a few things out of the fridge while James's mum buttered some bread for them. They took their lunch outside and sat down on the front lawn.

"Are you two going out again when you've finished? Only I could do with a hand with the shopping," asked James's mum. "Paul can come too I don't mind."

"Yeah OK mum, we'll both come with you," replied James. Paul and James finished eating and went back inside. "Are we going shopping right now?" James asked his mum.

"In a few minutes; I need to get my purse, shopping bags and the car keys. Could you put your T-shirts on if you're coming. I don't think it's seemly you both going into Morrisons in just shorts."

"Yeah, OK mum." Paul and James put their T-shirts back on and waited for James's mum. They got in the car and set off. Morrisons was opposite the leisure centre where the naturist swim was to take place the coming Saturday evening. "There's the leisure centre," said James without thinking. Paul glared at James.

"Are you two thinking about going swimming?" asked James's mum.

"Er, yes, perhaps," replied Paul while elbowing James in the ribs.

"Sorry," said James quietly.

"I can't remember the last time we went swimming James. You should go more often, it's good exercise. Take Paul with you, I'm sure you'll enjoy it." Paul and James looked at each other and smiled.

They arrived at Morrisons and got out of the car. "If you want to go in I'll catch you up in a few minutes," said Paul. "I might as well find out what time we can go swimming."

"OK fine; we'll see you inside Morrisons," replied James. Paul walked across to the leisure centre. He noticed there were a lot of windows and couldn't help wondering if they'd block them all out. Paul went inside and asked the woman on reception for the opening times of the swimming pool. She pointed him to a leaflet in a rack on the opposite wall. Paul took one out and said; "This one?"

"Yes that's right."

"How much does it cost to go in?"

"It's usually £2:90 for adults and £1:45 for children. How old are you?" asked the receptionist.

"Fourteen," replied Paul.

"If your mum or dad comes too you go in free. It's one free child per adult."

"OK then, thank you," said Paul as he left. Paul walked back across to Morrisons and went in. He found James and his mum by the fish counter. "Ah, there you are," said Paul.

"Did you get what you wanted?" James's mum asked him.

"Yes I did thanks," replied Paul showing James and his mum the leaflet he was given.

The three of them continued with the shopping trip and then went home. Once they arrived home Paul and James helped unload the shopping.

"Thanks very much boys," called James's mum. "Are you two going back out now or waiting till after tea?"

"We'll wait till after tea," replied James. Paul and James went upstairs to James's bedroom. Paul had been reading the leaflet on the way home and now gave it to James pointing out the opening and closing times for Saturdays.

"Look at the times for Saturdays," said Paul. "It's 7:30am until 6pm."

"So does that mean the swimming pool is normally closed on a Saturday evening?"

"Yes it does," said Paul. "All we need to do is stay in after the pool closes at six on Saturday."

"Yeah, but how we gonna do that?" asked James.

"I don't know yet," replied Paul. "Maybe we could hide somewhere. It'll be for an hour because the pool shuts at six and the naturist swim starts at seven."

"I s'pose the changing room toilets might be a possibility, but for an hour. We'd be doubled up like a pen knife," said James. "And what if we were spotted; wouldn't you feel embarrassed standing there totally naked? 'cos I'm pretty sure I would be."

"Yes well, er... tell you what; why don't we go for a normal swim tomorrow, the day before? That way we can check the place out," suggested Paul.

"Good idea that," smiled James.

"Oh, and just one more thing; I don't think our parents suspect anything, so let's keep it that way, OK."

"Fine," replied James starting to feel more at ease about it all.

Paul and James had their tea and went out again, but this time they kept their clothes on. They weren't gone long because the weather suddenly changed. They saw a huge flash of lightning followed by a loud crack of thunder. Dark clouds quickly filled the sky. Paul and James went inside Paul's house this time with only a few minutes to spare. A sudden downpour nearly soaked them to the skin. "Good job we decided to go home when we did," said Paul.

"I know, imagine being stuck outside in this!" It continued to rain quite heavily but gradually reduced to a fine drizzle after about twenty minutes. Paul and James stayed inside and it wasn't long before they went upstairs to Paul's bedroom. "Why don't we have a look on the internet and see if the word 'naturist' really does mean being naked.

"OK then," said Paul. Paul plugged his computer in and switched it on. "What do you think we'll see when I type in the word 'naturist'?"

"Let's find out," replied James enthusiastically. So Paul carefully typed the word 'naturist' into the Google search engine. It threw up a vast amount of information. They were amazed at what they had discovered, but in short Paul and James had made the connection they suspected from the start. A naturist was someone who would happily go about with no clothes on. Paul and James were checking out a few of the many links which Google had thrown up and were happily doing this when Paul's mum called up to them.

"Paul! James! I'm just popping over the road to see a neighbour. I won't be long," she called.

"OK mum," replied Paul.

After a good hour or so looking at various naturist websites Paul and James decided they'd seen enough and Paul turned his computer off. They went downstairs and into the front room.

"Would you like a drink?" asked Paul.

"Please," replied James.

"Tea or coffee? Or would you prefer a cold drink?"

"Tea's fine thanks." Paul went into the kitchen and put the kettle on. While he was waiting for it to boil he came back into the front room. He told James that he'd slept naked the previous night.

"Did you sleep better like that?" asked James.

"Yeah I did," replied Paul. "I felt more relaxed, but also a bit worried in case my mum or dad came in. I set my alarm clock so I could wake up a few minutes before the time my mum would normally get me up."

"Are you gonna sleep naked again tonight?" asked James.

"Why certainly," replied Paul. "If it's warm enough, which it usually is. Why don't you try it?"

"Er... I could do, but it's a bit risky; although my mum does usually let me sleep in when it's school holidays. Tell you what; I could go to bed as normal and then take my boxers off once I'm in bed."

"Do you know that's exactly what I did," laughed Paul. There was a 'click' from the kettle which had now boiled and switched itself off. Paul nipped back into the kitchen and made James and himself a mug of tea. Just as Paul returned with two mugs of tea his mum came back from where she'd been. An elderly neighbour had caught a mouse in a trap, and, even though it was dead, was terrified of it! Mrs. Jessop had offered to get rid of it.

"Oh, is one of those for me love?" asked Paul's mum as she sat down.

"No but I'll make you one mum," replied Paul.

"Thanks love. I said I'd get rid of a mouse for Mrs. Woolston. She can't stand mice, poor woman." Paul's mum switched the TV on and they sat together for a while until James thought it was about time he went home.

"I'll come round tomorrow morning; night," said James. Paul saw James out then joined his mum in the front room watching some sort of documentary, the subject of which suddenly changed to naturism. Paul suddenly froze, and for a minute or two didn't move a muscle. Having just seen a number of people naked on TV he quickly glanced across at his mum in order to see her reaction; there wasn't one.

"Are you OK love?" she asked as she looked across at him. "You look like you've seen a ghost." Paul quickly snapped out of his brief but 'trance-like' state.

"Er; yeah, sorry mum, I'm fine, really I am," said Paul rather nervously.

"They're only nudists love and I think they're harmless enough; do you want to watch it?"

"Er, no not really. I think I might get an early night actually."

"OK then, good night love."

"Night mum." Paul went upstairs to bed feeling a bit shell shocked at what he'd just seen on TV. He was concerned his mum might make some sort of connection to him and James being naked. If Paul had been in the house alone, or perhaps with James, he would certainly have enjoyed watching that documentary about naturism, but he felt he couldn't with his mum present in the same room. Paul took off his dressing gown and got into bed. He risked taking off his boxers once again and went to sleep the way he now liked - naked.

Chapter 3

It was now Friday morning and was the day before the naturist swim. Paul and James woke to another bright sunny day. They had their breakfasts and then, at about ten past nine, James called for Paul.

"Morning Mrs. Jessop," said James.

"Oh hello James. Paul, James is here," said Paul's mum turning towards the staircase and looking up.

"OK mum; tell him to come up here," replied Paul from his bedroom.

"He's in his bedroom if you'd like to go upstairs." Paul's mum closed the front door and went into the kitchen.

"Hi," said James as he entered Paul's bedroom.

"Did you do it last night?" asked Paul.

"Do what?"

"Sleep naked," said Paul quietly.

"Oh that," replied James. "Yeah I did, and it felt very comfortable."

"Thought you'd say that."

"Well, it was until my mum came in to get me up." Paul's heart sank at the thought they'd been rumbled, but was relieved to hear James hadn't actually been seen naked in bed. "About ten minutes before my alarm went off my mum came in to get some of my washing and said; 'Come on, I think it's time you were getting up,' and then she left. I jumped so much in bed it's a wonder I didn't hit my head on the bed head."

"Phew, that was close," said Paul as he continued packing a large sports bag.

"What are you packing your sports bag for?" asked James.

"I'll tell you later," said Paul as he zipped up the bag. Paul got James to go in front of him as they went downstairs. "Is my mum in the kitchen?" asked Paul quietly.

"No, she's in the back garden talking to my mum."

"Excellent," said Paul as he overtook James at the bottom of the stairs. Paul took his sports bag outside and hid it behind a bush in the front garden. They went out the back to where their mum's were talking.

"We're going out now, OK?" said Paul.

"OK boys, don't do anything I wouldn't do," laughed Paul's mum as they left. James smirked at Paul.

"Don't do anything I wouldn't do," he sniggered. Paul giggled as James repeated what his mum has just said. "Do you think your mum would go naked then?" James asked with a wry smile.

"I very much doubt it; I bet her only naked activity is taking a shower, other than sex of course," replied Paul. Paul picked up his sports bag on the way out and they set off. Paul and James were heading to where they'd been before. On the way James asked Paul about the bag he'd packed.

"What have you packed in your sports bag? It looks pretty full."

"It is," replied Paul. "Here, feel the weight of it." Paul passed his bag to James who, for a moment, struggled to carry it.

"Oh my word!" said James. "What on earth have you brought with us?"

"You'll see," replied Paul still keeping James wondering.

"Right, here we are; put the bag down there, unzip it and look inside." James did as Paul said. He unzipped Paul's sports bag and inside were two large towels, a large size carton of Tropicana orange juice, two bottles of water and a bottle of sun cream. In the side pockets Paul had packed a tennis ball, two packets of crisps, a chess board and a set of dominoes.

"What's all this for?" asked James.

"Well, we're going to go 'naturist' again, you know, naked, aren't we?"

"S'pose so," replied James.

"Well, we can lie down on the towels, one each, see," continued Paul holding a towel out for James. "Here you are." James took the towel from Paul and watched as he spread his towel out on the grass. "Right, now you spread your towel out next to mine." James did as Paul said and spread his towel out a couple of feet away.

"Now what?" asked James.

"We take our clothes off again and lie down on the towels. Haven't you ever heard of an all over tan?"

"That's what the naked man was doing when we first saw him

here wasn't it?"

"Yes," said Paul taking off his T-shirt. "Well, apart from our arms," continued Paul holding out both his arms. "We are, well, rather pale aren't we?"

"Hmm, yeah; I must say you're right there," replied James looking at his own body.

"Right then, are we gonna go naked? We should be fine with our bodies now shouldn't we," said Paul confidently. James was still on the nervous side. He took off his T-shirt and sat down on his towel next to Paul. "Come on then, let's take off our shorts, lie back and enjoy the sun." Even after yesterday James couldn't help feeling slightly wary about being naked again outdoors.

"Can you go first?" asked James. "I think you're better at this than me."

"Come on, we've done it before, haven't we," said Paul encouragingly. "...and we know what each other looks like naked now, don't we."

"Yeah I know, I just can't help feeling a bit worried. You know, in case we're seen."

"Hmm, I think it's unlikely right here, and we were undisturbed yesterday weren't we?"

"Yeah I know we were."

"Look, if it makes you feel happier, I'll go naked first," said Paul. "I don't mind."

"OK, go on then; I'll do it after you." With that said Paul stood up, and, even though he was a little apprehensive himself he remained as relaxed as he could. Paul pulled down his shorts and took them right off in full view of James; after which, he sat back down on his towel openly naked. Still feeling a bit nervous, James got up, pulled down his shorts and took them off.

"Seeing as we're not going to be walking around for a while we can take off our trainers and socks, that way we're totally nude," said Paul. So Paul took his trainers and socks off and then laid back on his towel as naked as the day he was born. Looking at how relaxed Paul now was, James took off his trainers and socks too and laid back.

Both Paul and James were now completely naked and were laid back on their towels face up. "I think I could get used to this very easily." said Paul. "What about you? Can you honestly say you don't like the warm sun on your naked body?"

"Hmm," For a few moments James pondered what Paul just said. He was sure it felt relaxing, and yes; he did like the warm sun on his naked body; however, there was one issue that bothered him. It was the fact that everyone else could see his privates. "Well, I have to admit; if it's just you and me with nobody else for miles, I think I can cope with it; but do you honestly think we'll actually be able to be part of a naked swim at the leisure centre tomorrow evening and not feel embarrassed or stressed out? What I mean is; how many other people will be there?"

"Well, I'd guess it could be around twenty or thirty," suggested Paul. "Or may be more; I'd suspect it really depends on how many people know about it."

"Twenty or thirty!" said James in surprise.

"Well think about it; it would have to be worthwhile them opening the leisure centre wouldn't it, and in any case, the more there are the easier it will be for us to blend in." James was starting to feel very uneasy at the thought of being naked among thirty or more other people.

Paul and James had now been laid on their towels for over an hour and James was feeling like he was burning.

"It's pretty hot here isn't it?" said James. What happened to that sun cream you brought? Do you think we should put some on?"

"It's in my bag, and yes, we should get some on otherwise we'll burn, and how would we explain that to our parents, hmm?" replied Paul.

"Yeah, I see what you mean," said James. "Imagine going back home with a sunburnt bum or worse, a sunburnt er..."

"Penis," Paul chipped in.

"Yeah exactly," said James as Paul handed him the sun cream. James opened the bottle and started to apply some to his body.

"Don't be afraid to slap plenty on," said Paul. This was something James wasn't use to doing. He began with his arms and shoulders then moved on to his chest, legs and feet. "When you've finished, if you wanna lie on your front I'll rub some into your back for you."

"Yeah OK, thanks," said James. So when James was ready he handed Paul the sun cream and laid flat out on his front. He squeezed some sun cream directly on to James's back causing him to flinch slightly as it made contact with his skin. Paul then used both his hands and slowly massaged the sun cream into James's back.

"You OK?" asked Paul.

"Fine; I'm really enjoying this," smiled James. Paul had a wonderfully gentle touch. He wanted James to feel as relaxed as possible and was certainly succeeding.

"There you are then," said Paul.

"Can you go a bit lower and do my bum?" asked James.

"Er..." Paul thought for a moment; he was a bit concerned as to how he might feel rubbing sun cream into James's bottom, but Paul didn't want to spoil things, so he quickly agreed. "OK then, stay where you are." Paul then squeezed some sun cream into his hand and began to massage it into James's bottom. Paul felt mildly uncomfortable doing this, but James was certainly enjoying it. Thinking about Saturday evening and what they faced, Paul did his best to help James feel as relaxed as possible while he was naked. "Right then, you're done," said Paul.

"Thank you," replied James softly, and with a smile Paul didn't quite understand. Paul wasn't sure whether James had got him to rub sun cream into his bottom deliberately to make him feel awkward.

"When I've done myself, can you do the same for me please?" asked Paul.

"Yeah sure," replied James while still lying face down on his towel. Paul applied sun cream to all the parts of his body he could reach and then he too laid face down on his towel.

"Ready," he said.

"OK, just a minute," said James as he reached over for the sun cream. He squeezed some out on to Paul's back as he lay on his towel. James gently rubbed it in. "How does this feel?" he asked.

"Lovely," replied Paul. "I think I could get used to this too. When you've done my back can you do my bum as well?"

"Yeah sure," replied James. James applied more sun cream

to Paul's back and then moved down to his bottom. "Right you're done." As Paul put the sun cream back into his bag James suddenly said; "Wait a minute, I haven't done my privates. Is it OK to use this sun cream on your privates?"

"Yeah I think so," replied Paul. "Which reminds me, I didn't put any on mine either."

"OK then, roll over." Paul rolled over on to his back.

"Hey, wait a minute! I think I can do this myself," said Paul suddenly realising what James was about to do.

"Ha Ha, just testing," laughed James. Paul took the sun cream from James and started to apply some to his privates. James was curious and was watching Paul with considerable interest. He'd always wanted to see Paul's privates, preferably without him knowing; however, Paul was very much aware of where James was looking, but decided to remain confident and didn't do anything about it; and in any case, he was thinking about doing the same thing himself assuming James let him.

"Right, that's me done," said Paul handing the sun cream back to James. James assumed Paul would do just what he'd done so decided to give him a bit of an eyeful. James cheekily opened his legs wider than was strictly necessary. Paul noticed this with considerable surprise, especially after James was slow to take his shorts off when they first got there. Paul simply couldn't resist the open invitation James was giving him as he applied sun cream to his privates.

"Right, that's me done as well," said James and he past the sun cream back to Paul. Paul and James had only seen each other naked for the first time the previous day, and that was only after some friendly persuasion from Paul. James was now laid flat on his back on his towel soaking up the sun, and showed no sign of being bothered by the fact he was doing so completely naked. Paul felt James's confidence was level with his and was now really looking forward to tomorrow evening's naturist swim.

By now it was early afternoon and Paul felt like doing something other than lying about on towels all day. He sat up, looked in his bag and took out the carton of orange juice. He had a drink and then offered it to James.

"Would you like a drink of orange juice?" he asked.

"Yeah, thanks," replied James taking the carton of orange juice from Paul. Paul put his trainers on and took the tennis ball from his bag.

"Do you wanna play throw and catch again?"

"Yeah, OK then."

"You'd better put your trainers on then," said Paul. James put his trainers on and stood about ten to twelve yards away from Paul. Paul and James threw the tennis ball back and forth. This was easier to catch than the golf ball they'd used before and after a few minutes they moved further apart so they could put more energy into throwing the ball. They were now a good fifty to sixty yards away from each other and were playing happily; it was almost as if they'd forgotten they were naked. After half an hour or so playing with the tennis ball Paul and James gave up and sat back down on their towels. "I've got Chess and Draughts in my bag," said Paul. "Which do you prefer?"

"Draughts please, I always lose at Chess." Paul took out his Chess and Draughts board, but had forgotten all the pieces.

"Damn! I've forgotten to pack the playing pieces," said Paul. "I've got dominoes."

"OK then, let's play dominoes." Paul and James spent the best part of an hour playing dominoes. They lost count of the number of game they'd played, but Paul seemed to think James had won more than he had. They continued to share the crisps, orange juice and water Paul had brought with them.

"Let's put the dominoes away and do something else," suggested Paul.

"What did you have in mind?" asked James.

"I was thinking about a naked runabout. We can leave our things here, I wasn't thinking of going out of sight of them. Let's walk over to that tree again and I'll race you back here."

"Yeah, OK then," smiled James. They walked over to the tree and stopped.

"On my word," said Paul. "Three, two, one, go!" Paul and James ran back to their towels as fast as they could. This was quiet some achievement for both of them, and they were now really enjoying running about and playing together naked. From a distance the innocent sight of them enjoying naturism would have surely melted the hardest of hearts.

Paul and James, now somewhat out of breath, eventually sat back down on their towels. With the orange juice all gone and very little water left, James asked Paul what time it was. "Twenty-five past four."

"Should we be heading home soon if we're going to go for a swim this evening?"

"Yeah OK," replied Paul. "Let's pack the towels and things away. Do you fancy walking part of the way home naked?"

"Er, OK then; but let's keep our shorts to hand and walk slowly." James suddenly realised he was still naked and moving away from the area they'd seen as safe was starting to unnerve him. Paul and James walked round to the path and continued slowly for a few hundred yards. In the distance Paul saw a couple walking their dogs.

"Time to put our shorts on," said Paul. "There's someone up ahead." Paul and James stopped and put their shorts on. They set off walking again and James said something Paul never expected.

"It's a pity we've had to put our shorts on 'cos I'm beginning to like being naked. You can move around a lot easier; clothes restrict you, even shorts do."

"I know; it's nice being naked isn't it?"

"Yeah, I rather think it is."

When they arrived home Paul hid his bag in the front garden again. They went inside Paul's house and his mum was in the front room reading the paper.

"Oh hello you two," she said as they came in. "Where've you been all day?"

"We've been over by the railway line again, walking around and seeing what we could find. James found a golf ball yesterday," said Paul showing his mum the golf ball he'd had in his pocket from yesterday. James looked at Paul and mouthed 'swimming'. "Oh, is it OK for me to go swimming this evening with James?"

"Yes if you like. How much money do you need?"

"It's £1:45 each plus bus fare there and back. I'd say £8:00 should be enough."

"OK, wait there a moment, I'll get my purse." Mrs. Jessop left the room for a few moments leaving Paul and James alone.

"How we gonna explain our sudden interest in going swimming?" asked James. "I've not been since I left junior school, that'll be at least three years ago!"

"Don't worry, I'm sure we'll think of something; I'm in the same position myself actually," said Paul. Paul's mum came back into the front room.

"Here, I haven't any change, take £10:00 and get yourselves a can of pop each on the way out if you like. What time do you think you'll be home?" asked Paul's mum.

"About half nine, give or take a few minutes," replied Paul.

"OK then love," said Paul's mum. Paul and James went upstairs to Paul's bedroom.

"I haven't any swimming trunks," said Paul. "I outgrew my last pair."

"What about taking your football shorts from school?" suggested James.

"Oh yeah, good thinking; now where are they?" said Paul as he started searching for them. Just then Paul heard his mum come upstairs and go into the toilet. "My bag! I've just remembered." Paul ran downstairs and picked up his sports bag from where he'd left it in the front garden then ran back upstairs to his bedroom. He unpacked it and threw the towels they'd used into the laundry basket. Paul helped himself to two clean towels from the airing cupboard and put them into his sports bag along with his black school football shorts which were in his top draw right at the back. As his mum was washing her hands in the bathroom, Paul asked her if he could take a bottle of shower gel with them.

"Yes of course you can love. There's a couple of bottles on the top shelf in the shower, take which ever you like." Paul took one and put it in his bag. "Are you having a sandwich or something to eat before you go swimming?" asked Paul's mum.

"Yes please," replied Paul and James. Paul's mum went downstairs and made them some sandwiches.

"Ready," she called. Although Paul and James weren't over keen on it, Paul's mum had made them a bit of salad as well.

"There's orange juice in the fridge if you want to help your-selves. Give me a shout when you go won't you."

"Yeah OK mum, will do. We need to go next door anyway to get James's swimming trunks," added Paul. Paul and James finished their tea and went next door to get some swimwear for James. "Mum; we're going," Paul called to his mum as they left.

"Right, OK then. I'll see you when you get back, bye." Like Paul, James took his black school football shorts.

They walked over to the bus stop and waited for the bus. They only had to wait four or five minutes and got on when the bus arrived. It took them approximately twenty minutes to get to there, and Paul and James thanked the driver as they got off. They walked across the leisure centre car park and went in. Paul paid the receptionist and they continued through to the changing room. When changing for swimming in the past, Paul and James would normally only do so in cubicles with a door or curtain, but Paul suggested they use the communal area behind the lockers to get changed. "Let's go round here to get changed," he said. "We have to get used to being less concerned about anyone seeing us naked."

"OK then," said James starting to feel a bit uneasy again. Paul and James got undressed and put their shorts on. They put their clothes in a locker and went through to the pool. It was on the quiet side for a Friday evening. There were only a dozen or so other people in the pool, however, this did increase in the next half hour. Paul and James were enjoying swimming and splashing about in the water. The slide was good fun too.

"What do you think it'll be like doing this naked tomorrow evening?" asked Paul.

"Er... I'm not really sure actually," replied James. "I s'pose you'd go down the slide quicker."

"Yeah, that's what I was thinking; our shorts hold us back and create drag. Let's get out for a few minutes and check this place out. Don't forget, we need to find somewhere to hide." There was nowhere to hide around the side of the pool so Paul and James went back into the changing room. As they were looking around they saw a disabled toilet. The lock was broken so Paul initially dismissed it, however, James had noticed an ordinary toilet with an 'out of order' sticker on the door.

"Why don't we take that sticker off and stick it on the disabled toilet," he suggested.

"Hmm, not a bad idea that," replied Paul. "Will it come off without tearing?"

"Why don't you have a go, there's no one about." Paul reached up and peeled the sticker off the toilet door. It came off easily as it wasn't really a sticker; it was more like a window decal. James looked at Paul with the 'out of order' sticker in his hand and smiled. "Now see if it'll stick on the disabled toilet door." It did, but Paul took it off again. "Why've you taken it off?" asked James somewhat surprised.

"There's almost twenty four hours to go before the start of the naked swim. Supposing someone sees it, and perhaps, repairs the lock; no sticker. We'll hold on to it until tomorrow, then we'll be able to stick it on the door a few minutes before normal closing time."

"Brilliant plan!" smiled James. James was starting to feel excited now at the possibility of success. This in turn made Paul feel happier too. Paul and James went back to their locker and Paul put the 'out of order' sticker in a side pocket in his bag.

"It's only five to eight, let's go back into the pool for a while; we've still got a good hour to kill before it shuts at nine," said Paul. They continued having fun swimming about and sliding down the slide.

At about quarter to nine Paul said; "Why don't we get out now so we've got time for a shower."

"Yeah, OK then," replied James. They both got out of the pool and went into the changing room. Paul got the shower gel from his bag and they walked over to the shower area. As they approached they saw man and his ten-year-old son showering. Paul and James couldn't help but notice that they were doing so without their swimming trunks on. They moved a discreet distance away from the showers.

"We should shower like that," said Paul glancing in the direction of the showers.

"B-but what if an attendant or someone walks past?" asked James with a slight stammer.

"I don't think it matters in the changing room showers, otherwise, they wouldn't be like that; and if a young boy that age can use a communal shower completely naked and not appear to be bothered, why should we?" replied Paul raising his shoulders in a carefree sort of way.

"Well, I s'pose we would look a bit silly if we let him get the better of us at his age," said James trying to sound positive about the impending situation. After a few minutes the young boy and his dad finished showering and left.

"Right," said Paul. "In we go." James felt nervous and not really ready for this, but he did not want to let Paul down. He knew in his mind he had to conquer his naked fears. Paul and James started to shower, the odd person walked past as they did. After a couple of minutes Paul said; "Come on then, there's no one about now. Let's just go for it and take off our shorts; I don't think anyone will mind."

"Can you go first?" asked James still slightly anxious about voluntarily showering naked in a communal shower.

"No, wait; look, we're in this together. Why don't we do it together, simultaneously, OK?"

"OK then."

"After three," said Paul. "One, two, three, off." Paul and James both took off their shorts and continued to shower naked. An attendant walked past and said nothing. He didn't even look in their direction. "We can relax," said Paul confidently. "There's no need to worry. I bet lots of people shower like this here." Paul's words were a good guess for what happened next. They'd been showering naked for a few minutes when two other lads, one aged about twelve and the other about fifteen, joined them. They entered the shower area wearing their swimming trunks, but on seeing Paul and James showering naked, the younger boy immediately took his off. Barely a minute later, and presumably not wanting to be the odd one out, the older boy took his swimming trunks off as well. James was considerably surprised at this and looked at Paul. "Well, what did I tell you," said Paul quietly. "It's much easier to shower like this, isn't it?"

"Yeah, I have to admit your right there," said James. James was starting to feel much more relaxed now as there were four of them all showering together naked.

"Excuse me," said the older boy. "I hope you don't mind me asking, but do you always shower here without your swimming trunks on?"

"Oh yes, absolutely," replied Paul with a wry smile.

"No we don't," said James rather bluntly. "This is our first time and we're trying to get used to being naked. What about you?"

"Well, as soon as we saw you two showering naked we couldn't resist doing the same. We're here because our local swimming pool is closed until Christmas for a complete rebuild."

"Oh, right," said James.

"Couldn't you shower naked there before it was closed?" asked Paul.

"No. There was a big sign in the shower area which clearly stated in capital letters; 'SWIMMING COSTUMES MUST BE WORN AT ALL TIMES WHILE IN THE SHOWER', so we never did. Mind you, even if we could've done I'm not so sure we would, unless of course there was someone else there to help us feel less alone."

"That's a pity," said Paul. "I think it's really good to be able to shower like this and not be worried about what anyone else thinks."

"We have to do it at school after PE," said the younger boy. "But it's chaos more often than not 'cos there's so many of us trying to shower at once."

"Yeah, he's right there. Anyway, my name's Ben, and he's my younger brother Harry. What are your names?" asked Ben.

"I'm Paul and he's James. We've been friends all our lives, fourteen years" replied Paul.

"Well I'm sixteen and I'm in year eleven at school," said Ben. "I'm partway through my GCSEs. Harry's in year eight and will soon be thirteen. If you're both fourteen I s'pose you'll be in year nine won't you."

"Yeah, I'm in year nine," said James.

"But I'm in year ten," said Paul. "We were born just over two weeks apart. I was born in August and James was born in September. Although we're the same age for most of the year our dates of birth mean we're in different years at school."

"That's interesting," said Harry. "There's really only two weeks in your ages and you're in different years?"

"Yep, that's right," replied James.

"We were even at different schools three years ago until James moved up to year seven the following year," said Paul. "Anyway, I think it might be time to get out now. It must be after nine."

"It is, it's nearly ten past," said Ben. "But we can stay in here longer. The pool shuts at nine, but the gym stays open until ten-thirty and those using the gym may want to shower before they leave."

"Oh of course, I never thought about that," said Paul.

"So what time were you thinking of going home?" asked James.

"We normally get out at quarter to ten," said Ben. "That gives us fifteen minutes to get dried and dressed so we can leave at ten."

"Our dad works near here and he gives us a lift home," added Harry.

"Yeah he does." Ben paused, but then continued, "What was it you said earlier about trying to get used to being naked? Do you find it difficult or embarrassing to shower naked at school after PE?"

"Yeah we do. I once walked home just before the farce of a PE shower session and missed my last lesson," said James.

"Ha, I seem to remember you getting a detention for that," giggled Paul.

"Yeah you can scoff," snapped James. "You've done it as well, more than once."

"Yeah, I know, but PE was my last lesson of the day back then, so no one ever found out."

"Are you both OK with it now?" asked Harry. "'Cos you seem to be relaxed enough to me."

"Yeah, I s'pose so; we're working on it," said Paul.

Just then Ben stepped out of the shower area and looked around the corner. Paul, James and Harry looked puzzled and were wondering what he was up to. Ben came back a few moments later and told them; "Just stay here, I've had an idea." Ben walked off without his swimming trunks and came back into the shower area about thirty seconds later. "The cover has not been pulled over the small pool yet," smiled Ben.

"So," said Paul.

"Well; haven't either of you ever been tempted to skinny dip," said Ben quietly. Paul and James were absolutely 'gobsmacked', and neither knew what to say in response to what Ben just said. "I take it you know what skinny dipping is," continued Ben.

"Er, swimming naked?" suggested James lightly, while trying his best not to let on he knew exactly what skinny dipping was.

"Yep," replied Ben.

"B-But we can't do that now," said Paul looking slightly shocked at what Ben was hinting at.

"Why not? It's as quiet as a mouse out there," said Ben.

"But we'll never get away with it," said James.

"Only one way to find out, if you're up for it that is," smiled Ben. "Are you gonna come too Harry?"

"Er, yeah, go on then. It sounds pretty daring actually," smiled Harry. So the four of them abandoned their swimwear in the shower area, and with Ben leading the way, they slowly walked through to the pool. Ben poked his head out first to check the coast was clear and then beckoned the others forward. Then, with barely making a sound, Paul, James, Ben and Harry carefully got into the small pool. The lights had been turned off so it was on the dark side. The four of them stayed close together in the pool and continued talking.

"Well, what do you think?" asked Ben quietly.

"Not bad," replied Paul.

"Have you done this before?" asked James.

"No, but I've always been tempted to. Harry and I skinny dipped for the first time in a river last summer, but like now, it was almost dark."

"Are we gonna swim about a bit in the nude then, seeing as we're in here," suggested Harry. With Harry swimming away from the group first it wasn't long before Paul, James and Ben followed suit. All four of them were enjoying their sly skinny dip, and one couldn't help but imagine the wonderful view they were forming to anyone looking down from the balcony.

After a few minutes, and with all four of them still leisurely swimming about in the nude, they heard a door slam shut followed immediately by what sounded like glass being smashed. This sudden sound frightened them and consequently caused them to stop swimming and regroup. "W-what on earth was that?" asked Paul who was beginning to think a sly skinny dip might not have been such a good idea.

"It sounded to me like a door slamming and a window breaking," replied Ben.

"Do you think it might be a good idea to get out now," suggested James.

"Just hang on a minute," said Ben. All four of them were close together in the far corner of the pool. "Listen!" They couldn't hear anything initially, but a few moments later another door slammed shut, but this time there was no smashing sound.

"I really don't like this," said James. He felt as if all the hairs on his back were standing on end.

"Stay still," said Ben. "We're less likely to be seen if we keep still and stay quiet." There was the sound of another door opening and it was coming from the balcony.

"Look, on the balcony," said Harry. A cleaner had made her way on to the balcony and was about to start using one of those floor cleaning machines on the balcony floor above the small pool. Paul, James, Ben and Harry stayed where they were for a couple more minutes until Paul noticed she was listening to music through earphones.

"I think were safe enough," smiled Paul. "Look, she's wearing earphones. I bet we could all jump in here and she wouldn't her us!"

"Wow, that's a relief," said James. "I was getting really worried there for a minute."

"Anyway, perhaps it is time we got out now," suggested Ben. "It's nearly twenty-five to ten."

"Yeah OK c..." Paul suddenly stopped mid-sentence. "Hang on a minute, I've just had an idea. Would you be up for something even more daring?"

"Such as?" asked Ben with interest and not usually one to refuse a dare, unless of course it was downright dangerous.

"Why don't we all get out of the pool here in this corner and walk right round the pool and then back into the changing room. I doubt 'Mrs. Mop' will see us 'cos she's busy cleaning."

"OK then, you're on," said Ben.

"Yeah, we can do that no sweat," added Harry.

"James?"

"Yeah, OK; I wouldn't want to disappoint anyone." With moonlight now shining through the windows and glistening on the water, Paul, James, Ben and Harry climbed out of the pool and sat on the side.

"Right, who's going first?" asked Ben.

"Does it matter?" asked James.

"No not really," replied Paul. "I'll lead the way. Come on, before 'Mrs. Mop' up there sees us." The four of them stood up, and with Paul leading the way, they slowly walked around three sides of the pool, then went back into the changing room and into the shower area.

"Well," said Paul. "How did we all feel doing that?"

"OK," replied Ben.

"James?"

"Yeah, it was OK."

"Harry?"

"Fine; I'm not scared to be seen in the nude if that's what you were thinking."

"Same here," added Ben. "I don't think there's any shame in being seen naked, is there?"

"No I s'pose not," said James.

"So has anyone got any fears or worries about nudity now?" asked Paul.

"No," replied Ben and Harry.

"James?"

"No, I s'pose not; but without meeting Ben and Harry here I think I might still be a bit uneasy. I'd really like to thank both of you for being here this evening and helping me like you did."

"No problem," smiled Ben. "You both helped us as well. While we're not really er... what's the word? 'Naturists', I think. We would like to go skinny dipping more often, especially in the summer when it's nice and warm, and we can do it outdoors."

"Did you know there's naturist swim here tomorrow evening?" asked Harry.

"Oh, really?" said Paul trying to sound surprised.

"Yeah, there is," said Ben. "But our parents won't let us go. Our mum's hydrophobic which means anything more watery than a shower is a very unpleasant experience and because of this she never learnt swim."

"And our dad's not really interested in swimming either," said Harry. "He kept an eye on us when we skinny dipped in that river, but I'm not sure he'd have jumped in to save us if we got into difficulties. I think he'd have yelled at some else!"

"Yeah, Harry and I can swim far better than our parents."

"What time is it now?" asked James.

"It's just after twenty to ten," replied Ben. "Are you two getting out now?"

"I think we'd better," replied Paul. "We said we'd be back home by now!"

"If you're late back just say the bus broke down," added Harry with a smile.

"Yeah right," said James. "Knowing us it probably will do now."

"Anyway, if you're getting out now we might as well join you," said Ben.

The four of them finished showering, and after retrieving their swimwear, they walked to their lockers to get their clothes. They got dried and dressed and went through to the reception area.

"I've really enjoyed meeting you this evening," said Paul.

"Same here," said Ben.

"Are you coming here again?" asked James.

"We'll be here every Friday evening until our local leisure centre reopens, 'cos we have a swimming lesson first, but as it's half term this week there's no lesson."

"Oh right," said Paul.

"Yeah, we just came here for a general swim this time," added Ben.

"I thought the best bit was skinny dipping in the small pool," smiled Harry. "It was daring alright, but I loved it."

"You're not wrong there," said James. "It was quite daring

swimming naked in the dark like that."

"I know. I'd love to do it again," smiled Paul.

"Me too," said Ben. "But keep what we did tonight to your-selves won't you. Look our dad's arrived now so we'll have to say good bye."

"We'll look forward to seeing you again sometime," said Harry.

"OK then. Bye for now," said Paul and James.

With Ben and Harry now gone, Paul and James walked over to the bus stop.

"When's the next bus," asked James.

"22:28. We've just missed one by a few minutes," replied Paul. "Why don't we get a takeaway?"

"Good idea, I'm starving," said James. Paul and James bought a pizza and shared it.

"Mmm…, this is very nice," said Paul, as he tucked in.

"Same here; we must make a mental note of that pizza shop," replied James. "It's really good." Paul and James finished their supper and then walked back to the bus stop. The bus was already there, stopped at the bus stop with the left indicator flashing.

"Come on, run!" said Paul. "We might just make it." They ran over to the bus and found the driver standing on the pavement talking on his mobile phone. He broke off conversation momen-tarily to speak to them.

"I'm sorry lads, this bus has broken down," he said.

"Oh no, that's another half hour we're going to have to wait," said Paul.

"No," said the bus driver. "I'm late, I should've been here a good twenty minutes ago. The next one should be here just before half past ten."

"Oh, right. What's happened to your bus then?" asked Paul.

"I'm not exactly sure," said the bus driver. "The door won't close properly. I've been having trouble with it for the past hour or so which is why I'm late."

"Do you think you'll be stuck here a long time?" asked James.

"It could be an hour or two. It depends how busy the service team are. I've been told they're on their way." At that point the next bus came into view. Paul and James bid a good night to the driver whose bus had broken down. They got on the following bus and went home.

Paul and James were over an hour late and Paul was concerned his parents might be wondering where he was. "I'll come round tomorrow morning," said Paul.

"OK then. We'd better get inside now, night."

"Yeah, night James." Paul went indoors at the precise moment his mum picked up the phone. She was about to ring the leisure centre, because as Paul rightly thought, she was beginning to wonder where he was.

"Oh at last, you're back! I was just about to ring the leisure centre. You forgot to take your mobile."

"Sorry mum," said Paul. "We got talking to two other lads while we were in the shower and forgot about the time. Then the bus broke down."

"Oh, OK then love. Are you going straight up bed?"

"Yeah, it's been quite a long day mum. Is dad home yet?" asked Paul.

"No not yet love, but he shouldn't too be long."

"OK, night mum."

"Good night love." Paul went upstairs, he dropped his bag on the floor and quickly got undressed. With his dressing gown carefully positioned by the side of his bed he slipped off his boxers and got in. Paul thought being naked in bed was lovely, especially after swimming. He felt 'super clean', and was asleep in a matter of minutes.

Chapter 4

This was the day Paul and James had been looking forward, Saturday, the day of the naturist swim. Even though it wasn't a school day Paul got up fairly early and was downstairs by about twenty past eight. He'd slept naked for the third time and had had a good night's sleep. Paul helped himself to some corn-flakes and milk in the kitchen and sat down. While he was eating his mum walked in. "Oh, you're up early," she said in surprise considering how late it was when Paul went to bed. "Are you and James going out somewhere special today?"

"No; not unless James has thought of somewhere to go. We might go swimming again. We both enjoyed it yesterday evening; do you mind if we go again so soon?" asked Paul hoping his mum would agree and let him go.

"Hmm, I don't see why not, but please remember to take your mobile with you this time."

"Yeah, OK mum. I think James's mum will pay for us this time if we ask nicely."

"OK then enjoy yourselves."

"Thanks mum, I'm sure we will. I'm going to call for James in a few minutes. I hope he's up," said Paul. Paul looked out of the living room window. It was another lovely sunny day and there was very little in the way of cloud.

Just before nine o'clock Paul went next door and called for James. "Hello Mrs. Handle," said Paul.

"Morning Paul," said James's mum "James, Paul's here."

"OK mum, I won't be a minute," replied James.

"Come in a minute Paul, he's just finishing his breakfast."

"Morning," said Paul.

"Oh hiya," replied James. "Have you got anything planned for today?"

"No not really, I was just thinking of our usual place if you like. That is until we go swimming again," said Paul with a notable smirk across his face.

"Well, I've been looking at this map. I know you're not that good with maps, but if you look closely there's this area here where the river curves and twists its way through the hills.

There's a footpath quite close most of the way."

"Are you suggesting we go there and see what it's like?" asked Paul.

"Yes I am, and I think there's a good chance we might be able to swim in the river," replied James.

"Do you think it will be safe enough for us to swim naked?"

"I hope so," said James with wry smile. Paul now got the distinct impression James was actually wanting to go naked.

"How we gonna to get there?" asked Paul. "It must be some distance away."

"We can get the train. Look, here's the station, and here's the footpath," said James, pointing at the map. "It shouldn't take us much over half an hour to walk from the railway station to that point just there. It'll only be a mile or perhaps a mile and a quarter," said James, pointing at the map again. "It takes about an hour to get there by train. My mum's going into town so she's going to give us a lift to the station. The train we need to get leaves at 09:51."

"Do you think we'll make that? It's nearly quarter past nine now," said Paul.

"I think so; my mum's done us some sandwiches and drinks and I've put them in my rucksack already along with a couple of towels, my school shorts and a bottle of shower gel. My mum's given me thirty quid for our train fares and for swimming. I've told her we're going for a walk in the countryside, which isn't that far from the truth," replied James with a smirk. "You got your mobile?"

"Yeah sure," replied Paul.

"Great! I've got two towels for now, but we might need another two for this evening's swim."

"Do you think we'll be back in time?" asked Paul.

"I hope so," said James. "Is there any chance you could get two towels just in case we have to go straight to the leisure centre?"

"I'll nip back home and ask my mum. Hang on a minute." Paul went back home and asked his mum. "Mum, can I have a couple of towels please?"

"Yes love help yourself; you can't really go swimming and not have a towel can you. There in the airing cupboard along with your school shorts."

"Thanks mum," said Paul as he helped himself to two clean towels and his shorts. "I'm going now. I'll see you later."

"OK, bye love."

Paul went back next door just as James and his mum were leaving. They all got in the car and set off. James's mum dropped them off at the railway station with about ten minutes to spare. They bought tickets from the self-service ticket machine and then quickly walked over to the train. The train took just over an hour to get to where they wanted. Paul and James alighted and walked over to a seat so James could check the map. "Right, follow me," he said. James led the way along the path towards the river. It took them a good half an hour to walk to the spot James had suggested. "Well, here we are then." They were now in a narrow valley with thick trees on either side. "What do you think?" asked James.

"Well, I have to admit it's very nice and secluded," replied Paul.

"The river should be deep enough to swim in here, but lower down it becomes much shallower. There looks to be a bit more space up ahead where we can spread our towels out and sit down." Paul and James continued to walk another hundred yards or so then stopped, spread their towels out and sat down close to the edge of the river. There was an area of firm ground here a bit like a beach leading into the river. "We've got a good four hours here. Our train back leaves at 15:55, so to be safe, we need to be making a move no later than quarter past three. We can walk back a different way, if you like, but it'll take longer."

"How much longer?" asked Paul.

"About twenty minutes to half an hour," replied James.

"Oh that's OK. Look, I can't see anyone else about," said Paul looking around. "Why don't we go naked now?" Just as Paul said this he turned round, and, to his surprise, saw that James had stripped off already. This time without a word of encouragement. Paul quickly took off his clothes as well and joined James walking towards the river. As he was about to put his foot into the water Paul said; "I bet this is freezing cold. Arrrh! Yes it damn well is."

"Well what did you expect? The sun's not been up that long and we're in a deep valley," laughed James. "Let's sit down, we've got plenty of time." Paul and James sat down on their towels and decided to have their sandwiches.

It was slowly getting warmer as the day went on and after having their picnic lunch they spent the next hour lying down on their towels enjoying the sunshine.

"Did you bring your sun cream?" asked James.

"Sorry no, I didn't think to," replied Paul.

"Oh well, if we get too hot I s'pose there's always the river to cool us down."

"I doubt we'll be swimming in there, it's way too cold."

"Don't be daft, it'll warm up a bit later on; and in any case, are you going to admit to being a wimp?" smiled James.

After an hour or so soaking up the sun James decided to test the river out. After all it was his idea to come here. He slowly walked into the river cringing at the cold.

"Ha ha," laughed Paul. "Told you it was cold."

"OK OK," said James. "It's just going to take a bit of getting used to." To Paul's surprise James was now walking knee deep in the river and was shivering because of the cold, but still James went on. "Aren't you even going to try it?" called James. "Come on."

"OK coming," replied Paul. Paul got up from his towel and walked to the edge of the river. He dipped his foot in the water again and cringed.

"Come on in!" shouted James, from water almost covering his privates. "It might be on the cold side, but it's very refreshing." Paul wasn't aware of this, but James had taken to having a cold shower at home most mornings to freshen up after his dad said it was good for him and he was now happily swimming about in the river. James appeared to have completely forgotten he was naked. Paul continued to walk slowly into the river. Then, all of a sudden, he ran forward and gave a slight scream at the cold. "Wow, you didn't need to do that," said James.

"I d-did, look over there," stammered Paul pointing towards the river bank and down stream. He'd seen a man walking towards them carrying a large black wooden box and a fishing rod. For once it was James who had to reassure Paul.

"Get over here quick," said James. He was standing in deeper water which more than covered his privates.

"Hi lads, nice weather for a swim?" asked the man as he walked past.

"Lovely," replied James.

"Ah well, watch you don't end up feeding the fish."

"Eh? What fish?" asked James with a puzzled look on his face. "We've not come here to feed fish."

Thinking that Paul and James might be swimming about in the nude the man said; "Think about it, fish will eat anything that looks tempting and hangs down." Just as the man finished saying this a sizable fish swam between Paul's legs. Paul panicked and splashed about hoping to frighten the fish away. "Told you," laughed the man as he walked off up stream. Paul looked across at James with a look James didn't much care for.

"Sorry; it never crossed my mind there'd be fish swimming about. My dad went fishing a couple of years ago with a friend of his and caught nothing."

"Well I'm getting out," said Paul. "I want to keep my privates in tact." Paul got out of the water and went to lie on his towel. James carried on swimming about for another few minutes then he got out too. After a further half hour or so Paul and James decided to move on and walk back to the railway station. As it was only half past two James suggested they go back the longer way thus making the walk circular.

"Why don't we walk back to the station naked and see how far we can get before we have to put our shorts on," suggested Paul.

"Yeah, OK then," replied James. Paul and James put their trainers on and then packed their T-shirts, socks, shorts and other items, except for the map of course, into James's rucksack. After checking they hadn't left anything behind Paul and James set off walking back to the station. James was leading the way, him being the one with the map. They were walking somewhat slowly because they were still naked. It was as if James felt better carrying the rucksack, like he was less naked, but his privates were still on view to anyone facing him. Considering the way Paul and James were now it would be hard to imagine them being prudish. They were walking about in the open countryside fully naked and not even James appeared to care.

"How long have we got left before the train leaves?" asked Paul.

"It's just after three now so I'd say about fifty minutes. We're about a mile away from the station so we'll probably have to put our shorts on soon. Do you wanna carry my rucksack for a bit?"

"Yeah OK, I don't mind," said Paul. They stopped for a couple of minutes, had a quick drink of water and then Paul carried James's rucksack. Paul was again a bit surprised to see James continue to walk openly naked. Maybe James had finally overcome his naked fears, thought Paul.

While still walking towards the railway station, Paul and James found themselves facing a situation neither had thought of. Walking towards them in the distance was a blonde girl aged about seventeen. She was wearing a bright yellow T-shirt, green shorts and trainers. As they approached James suddenly stopped in panic. Paul looked ahead and saw the girl. "Just keep going," said Paul quietly. "I don't think she's seen us." The girl was reading a magazine and paid no attention to either Paul or James. They past each other and incredibly nothing happened.

"I don't believe it!" said James in amazement. "We just walked past a teenage girl while fully naked and she didn't even notice!"

"Well; what did you expect from a blonde female with her nose in a magazine? If we'd have said 'Hi' I doubt we'd have got a response," said Paul in a rather laddish way. This set James off laughing so much he had to stop and sit down for a few minutes. They each had another drink of water and then continued walking to the railway station.

They got near to some houses on the edge of the village. "I think we should put our shorts on now, it's only a hundred yards or so to the station. There's no rush though, we've still got a good ten minutes before the train leaves," said James. Paul and James put their shorts on and walked the last few yards to the station. The train arrived almost on time and they got on. The train journey back was slower because it called at all intermediate stations. When they finally got back Paul suggested it would be better to go straight to the leisure centre rather than risk going home and being late back and not being able to get in, however, there was a slight problem with this. Paul had left the 'out of order' sticker in his bag at home.

"Damn!" he said. "I've left that 'out of order' sticker in my bag at home."

"Well I think we should go to the leisure centre now. We'll never make it otherwise. It's almost five o'clock as it is," said James. They arrived at the leisure centre at ten past five, paid and went in. Paul and James quickly got changed, but instead of going in straightaway, they decided to have another look round. The lock on the disabled toilet door had been mended so access wasn't going to be easy. Just then Paul noticed a door with the words 'group changing room' on it. He tried the door and it opened.

"James, in here," he said. They both went inside and found the room empty. On the right-hand side of this changing room there was a toilet. Paul tried the door and it opened. It wasn't a disabled toilet, but there was plenty of space for both of them to hide and the door came right down to the floor so there was no chance of anyone looking underneath it and seeing them.

"Do you think we'll be safe enough in here?" asked James.

"I hope so," replied Paul. "I don't think we've got an alternative. Let's go through to the pool now. We've got nearly three quarters of an hour to kill before we need to hide."

"OK then." Paul and James walked through to the main pool and jumped in. It was very quite; Paul counted just seven other swimmers.

"I hope there's a better turn out to the naturist swim, otherwise we're gonna stick out like a sore thumb," said James.

"Hmm, you've got a point there," replied Paul.

"How on earth are we gonna get away with this? Ten minutes in the dark is one thing, but..."

"Let's not panic too soon, I think there could be quite a few attending this swim. We'll just have to hope no one notices us."

At about ten to six the leisure centre staff started putting up black plastic sheets to block out the windows. "They're preparing for the naturist swim," said Paul. "Look, they're blocking out the windows to stop people looking in."

"Well at least we're going to be safe from people outside," said James, now feeling the butterflies in his stomach more than ever. It was now five to six.

"Only five minutes left," said Paul his heart rate starting to increase as well. "Come on, let's get out now."

"OK then."

"We can shower for a few minutes if you like." Paul and James got out of the pool and went through to the changing room. They showered for a few minutes, but kept their shorts on this time.

Just after ten past six Paul got his mobile phone from their locker, they entered the group changing room toilet, closed the door and sat down on the floor. They waited and waited, it was exceptionally quiet. Half an hour past by and they heard nothing. Then a few minutes later they heard voices. "It sounds like someone's moving about. It must be nearly seven by now," said James.

"It's five to by my phone, but I think it's a bit fast. We'll give it another ten minutes, best be on the safe side," replied Paul. Just under ten minutes later they heard voices again, more of them this time. Paul slowly opened the toilet door and looked out into the changing room. There was nobody there. "Right, come on. Let's get out of here." They both got out and walked over to the group changing room's main door. Paul very carefully pulled the door open and looked through the gap before quickly closing it again. "We've done it! Everyone out there is naked," said Paul triumphantly.

"What now?" asked James.

"Isn't it flaming obvious," said Paul beaming with delight. "We take off our shorts and join in. We just have to pretend we're part of the group. Come on, get your shorts off!" Paul and James quickly took their shorts off.

"Are you sure we're gonna get away with this?" asked James standing there completely naked with his shorts in his hand.

"Well let's hope so," replied Paul. "We can't exactly back out now." Paul and James, now naked, left the group changing room. They put their shorts in their locker and continued through to the pool. They passed a young family on the way; mum and dad mid-thirties, son and daughter, nine and eleven.

"Hello," said the daughter. "Nice here isn't it? Have you been before?"

"Er; no, this is our first time," replied Paul nervously.

"Trust us you'll love it after a while. Everyone's so friendly here aren't they mum?"

"Yes of course darling. Do let the boys pass."

"Sorry; I'm Alice, and my brother's Craig. What are your names?"

"I'm Paul and this is James," said Paul.

"Where's your mum and dad?" asked Alice.

"They're in the pool," replied Paul quickly.

"Oh well, we'll see you later perhaps. Nice to have met you both." Paul and James had, rather quickly, made two new friends; but naturist friends this time. Alice and Craig had been brought up as naturists from birth by their parents and grandparents.

Even allowing for last night's sly skinny dip, Paul and James were still a bit apprehensive about being naked in their local leisure centre, and after slowly walking through to the pool, they could hardly believe the sight that greeted them. There was about sixty to seventy people all swimming about naked and enjoying themselves. Paul and James looked at each other. "I don't believe it!" said James in amazement. "Just look how many there are." To add to the fun the staff had brought out an inflatable.

"Well, what on earth are we waiting for," said Paul. "Let's get in." They jumped in and swam straight to the inflatable. Suddenly they were having the time of their lives, and after a while, it was as if they'd completely forgotten they were naked.

Paul noticed a wide age range among those present; there was a young mum with a baby and toddler, and there was a couple who appeared to be much older than Paul's grandparents. However, Paul noticed something else; there weren't many, if any at all, his age, but he didn't say anything. After a good twenty minutes playing on the inflatable Paul and James took to the slide, and Paul was right, you do go down the slide faster naked!

About halfway through Paul and James swam to the shallow

end of the pool and had a few minutes rest. "What do you think then?" asked Paul.

"Great fun," replied James smiling broadly.

"No, I meant; how do you feel about being naked among so many other people?"

"OK, I think. Everyone else is naked aren't they, and they're OK with it. What about you?" asked James.

"I feel totally liberated," said Paul suddenly stretching out his arms and legs before falling backwards into the water. "Swimming before with shorts on is totally different to now. Don't you agree?"

"Yeah, I do now," smiled James.

"I simply couldn't careless who sees me naked now, I love it!"

"Same here; anyway, don't you think you'd better find a way of getting us out of here without anyone noticing."

"Well that's easy. We just get out and get dried and dressed with everyone else." Just then a man approached them.

"Hello boys; I've not seen either of you here before. Where's your parents?"

"Er; over there, I think," replied Paul, pointing at the deep end of the pool. This man was one of the organisers of the naturist swim and was concerned Paul and James were here alone and without permission. The man swam away. Paul and James got out of the pool and went into the changing room. "This could be a bit difficult," said Paul. "But let's not panic yet. Chances are he'll be looking for our mums and dads."

"Yes, I know that, but he's not going to find them is he!" said James starting to panic. Just then another man spoke to them.

"Hi lads, not seen either of you here before." This was the naked man Paul and James had encountered at the start. "Hang on a minute though you do look familiar. Where've I seen you two before, let me think. I think it was last Wednesday or Thursday. I was walking around myself and I noticed two boys about your age also walking around naked just like me. Then you were throwing something, a ball I presume. Am I right?" James went red in the face and glared at Paul.

"Did you see us earlier this week running about and playing throw and catch naked?" asked Paul his voice trembling slightly.

"Yes I did," smiled the man. Paul coughed and nearly choked. "But don't worry in the slightest. Your secret is safe with me. I wouldn't dream of jeopardizing your enjoyment of naturism by gossiping. Enjoy lads, see you next time."

"OK er, thanks, thanks very much," said Paul as the man walked away.

Paul and James went back into the pool, inflatable now gone, and were swimming about when Paul suddenly saw someone he knew from school.

"Mum, mum; look over there. It's Paul Jessop and James Handle from school."

"Oh no," said Paul. "It's her, Katie." James glanced across at Katie then suddenly ducked under the water. "Oh no you don't!" snapped Paul and he dragged James out from under the water. "We're in this together." Katie was a rather annoying friend from school. She was in James's year, but Paul knew her only too well.

"How we gonna live this down?" asked James. "When we get back to school on Monday we'll be a laughing stock!"

"Don't worry," said Paul. "I don't think Katie will say anything, not about this. She'll drop herself in it as well if she does."

"Hi there," said Katie.

"Hi Katie," said Paul.

"I didn't know you two were naturists."

"Well, this is our first time, and we really like it, don't we James," said Paul giving James a slight kick under the water.

"Yeah, great fun," added James quickly.

"Are your mums and dads here?" asked Katie.

"Er, no. They got out a few minutes ago," replied Paul.

"Oh right," said Katie. "Perhaps they've gone to play badminton. Anyway, don't worry about a thing; you'll enjoy naturism. Just one thing though."

"What's that?" asked Paul cautiously.

"Don't tell anyone at school. You might be looked on as being a bit, well, weird."

"Don't worry Katie, we won't tell anyone we've seen you," said Paul with a notable smirk. Paul and James looked at each other and smiled. "Fancy playing badminton?" asked Paul.

"What, naturist badminton?"

"Of course; they must have hired the whole leisure centre not just the swimming pool." With about forty minutes left Paul and James got out of the pool and went upstairs to the gym. They each picked up a badminton racket, Paul picked up a shuttle cock and they played badminton naked for the first time in their lives. They really enjoyed this and kept it up for a good twenty minutes, after which, Paul suggested they go back to the pool. "Let's go back to the pool for the last few minutes. It could be a long time before we swim like this again," continued Paul pointing out the fact that they were still completely naked. They put down the badminton rackets and went back downstairs to the pool. It was now ten to nine and Paul and James jumped into a much quieter pool. The organiser saw them again and went over to speak to them.

"Are your parents still here?" he asked.

"They've got out," replied James quickly.

"No, come on, admit it. I don't think your parents have been here all evening have they; and I'd very much like to know how you two got in."

"Er..." James panicked.

"I think we're er, gonna have to come clean," said Paul nervously.

"Yes, I think that would be a good idea."

"B-but, my mum and dad, they'll kill me!" spluttered James.

"Oh, don't worry, I'm sure they won't," said the man suddenly seeing James's happy face drop and tears well up in his eyes.

"We came here for a normal swim just after five o'clock, and then we hid in the group changing room toilet while we waited for everyone else to go in. We then simply took off our shorts and joined in," said Paul.

"Well I must admit I'll give you full marks for getting in, but I'm afraid I'm going to have to speak to your parents. If you're under eighteen you need parental permission to attend this swim. Look, it's nine o'clock now, get out and get dried and dressed. Would I be correct in assuming you'd like to come again?"

"Oh yes please!" said Paul and James excitedly.

"Right, OK then. Wait for me by reception." Paul and James got dried and dressed then waited by reception as instructed.

After a few minutes the man came out and met them.

"How are you two getting home?" he asked.

"We were gonna get the bus, or may be ring my mum if we'd a long time to wait," replied Paul.

"So your parents know you're here?"

"Yeah, I think so," said Paul. Just then Paul's mobile phone rang. It was his mum and she sounded concerned, especially after he was late home last night, but was quickly relieved when he answered his phone.

"Where are you both?" she asked.

"We're at the leisure centre and we're just about to leave," replied Paul.

"Oh; I thought the leisure centre closed at six o'clock on a Saturday not nine."

"We er... stayed later. There was something else going on this evening. I was going to ring you to ask you to pick us up, but we've got a lift if it's OK."

"Who with?" asked his mum. Paul looked at the man and he quietly said; 'member of staff.'

"A member of staff from the leisure centre, and he wants to see you and dad."

"Oh, OK then. I'll see you when you get home, bye love."

"Bye mum." The man led Paul and James to his car and they got in. Paul sat in the front passenger seat and directed the man to where they lived. It only took them ten minutes or so to get there and they arrived just as James's parents were arriving home.

"Uh oh," said James. "This is gonna be interesting." They got out of the car and walked towards their homes.

"Good evening; are you Mr. and Mrs. Handle?" asked the man.

"Yes we are," said James's mum.

"Let me introduce myself, my name is Peter Simpkin and I'm from the leisure centre. Could we go inside please, we need to talk."

"OK, but why have you given my son and his friend a lift home? Is there something going on we should know about?"

"I'm afraid so, but there's no need to be overly worried. However, we do need to discuss it and I think it would be best in front of both sets of parents."

"OK then. Let's go and see the Jessops," said Mrs. Handle. So everyone went to the Jessop house. Mr. Simpkin rang the doorbell. Mrs. Jessop opened the front door and was slightly taken aback to see so many people standing there.

"Oh hello," she said.

"Good evening; I'm Peter Simpkin and I'm from the leisure centre."

"Oh yes, come on in everyone and go through to the front room."

"We need to talk about why your son's Paul and James went swimming this evening."

"Why, has something happened? Paul and James are very well behaved boys."

"Oh it's nothing like that, please be assured," said Mr. Simpkin raising his left hand slightly. "They went swimming twice in effect. They went in as normal at around five o'clock, but then stayed in past closing time at six by hiding in the group changing room toilet.

"What on earth made you do that Paul?" asked his dad with no idea where this was leading. Paul felt embarrassed and didn't say anything. He just shrugged and looked at the floor.

"Let me explain; your sons Paul and James had knowledge of a private swim between seven and nine o'clock this evening. This private swim is naturist; that means nobody wears any costumes. Just how your sons discovered this I don't know, but they appeared to enjoy every minute of it." Paul's parents looked at each other and, although they were stunned, couldn't help but laugh. James's parents were equally surprised too.

"You actually went swimming fully naked in front of everybody else." said James's mum.

"Yes they did," said Mr. Simpkin. "Everyone else was naked too, it wasn't just your sons. I myself am not actually a member of leisure centre staff, but the primary organiser of the naturist swim. If they want to go again they need your permission because they're under eighteen."

"Oh I'm not sure they'll be going again," said James's mum. "We'll discuss this further when you've gone."

"Right, OK then. That's all I have to say on the matter, so I'll be on my way. Good night to you all." Paul's mum saw Mr. Simpkin out and then rejoined the others in the front room.

"Well," she said. "If anyone else had told me you'd done this I'd have to say I don't believe you. My son and his best friend swimming naked. Whatever next?"

"I bet I'm grounded for a month now aren't I," said James turning towards his parents with tears in his eyes.

"Hmm, I'm not really sure we should in this instance," replied James's mum. "It's not as if you've done anything seriously wrong is it. It's only er, what's it called; skinny dipping, isn't it?"

"How did you know about this naked swim anyway?" asked Paul's dad.

"It was last Wednesday morning," said Paul. "We saw a naked man walking in the woods and decided to follow him, but it was the next day when we saw him again near the railway line, while he was clothed, that he must have dropped this when he checked his map." Paul showed his dad the flyer for the naturist swim. "We worked out that if we hid somewhere for an hour after six o'clock we could come out without our shorts on and simply blend in with everyone else. I'm really sorry dad, we never expected any of this."

"What did it feel like swimming about naked?" asked James's dad. "Was it better than swimming with shorts or swimming trunks on?"

"It was great, really free and liberating," replied James while still slightly upset. "We didn't just swim though we played badminton as well, didn't we Paul?"

"Yeah we did."

"What badminton? Naked? I don't believe it! This just gets better and better," said James's mum.

"Look it's getting late now and we're all tired I'm sure. Let's get to bed and we'll talk again tomorrow, OK?" said Paul's dad rather quickly.

"Yes OK then. Sorry if I sounded a bit shocked," said James's mum.

"Night everyone," said Paul's dad.

"Night Paul," said James.

"Night James," said Paul. The Handles left the Jessop's house and went home.

Chapter 5

Next morning, Sunday, Paul and James both slept in. At about quarter past nine Paul got up, and after having a quick wash, he got dressed and went downstairs for his breakfast. His dad was in the kitchen and offered to cook his son a full English breakfast. "Would you like a full English after your cereal Paul?"

"Yes please dad, I'd love a full English breakfast, thanks. What about mum?"

"Don't worry son, I'll clean up before she gets back!"

"No dad, I meant, isn't she gonna want some breakfast too?"

"Your mum and fried food don't go in the same sentence do they son?

"No, I s'pose not. Where's she gone to anyway?" asked Paul.

"She's gone over to that Mrs. Woolston's again, another mouse I think. Honestly, a woman her age being frightened of a mouse."

"Yeah, I know what you mean dad. It is a bit daft," smiled Paul.

"Right, you ready for this son?"

"Sure am."

"There you are then," said his dad as he gave his son a plate of bacon, egg, sausage, mushrooms, baked beans and a slice of fried bread. "You enjoy that son while I wash up then evidence." Just as Paul was finishing his last mouthful his mum walked back in.

"Have you two been having a fry up? Honestly, you can smell bacon halfway down the street, and you know as well as I do that certain neighbours across the road don't like it."

"Oh come on Maureen, the odd fried breakfast isn't go to do us much harm. We haven't had one for over a month have we son?"

"I can't remember dad," replied Paul getting up and putting his plate and knife and fork in the sink.

"Well if they don't like it they can damn well lump it. We've had to put up with their foul smelling food on more than one occasion haven't we?"

"Yes, well, maybe so. Please make sure you clean everything you've used both of you. I'm going to sort out the washing now." After she said this Paul's mum went upstairs. His dad finished the washing up and then joined his son in the front room.

"What were you thinking of doing today Paul?" asked his dad.

"Not a lot. I was gonna call for James soon seeing as he hasn't come round yet," replied Paul.

"Well, going back to last night, your mum and I had a look on the internet about naked, sorry, naturist things and I have to admit it opened our eyes. We swam naked in the sea many years ago while on holiday abroad, before we were married. We only did it once, but I do remember how good it felt. We didn't know James's parents back then. In fact, I'd only known your mum a few months."

"Oh, right," said Paul with a puzzled but interested look on his face, wondering where this could be leading.

"We were very much younger then and we never did it again, so it was just a one off. However, your swim yesterday evening prompted us to look on the internet, something we didn't have in the 1980's." Paul's mum came back downstairs and into the front room with a load of washing she'd sorted. "Ah, there you are love. I've been talking to Paul about what we discovered on the internet last night."

"Oh have you. Are we going then?" asked Paul's mum not giving any clue as to what it actually was.

"Going where?" asked Paul showing a keen interest in what appeared to be something very secretive. Paul's mum had jumped the gun.

"Thanks a lot love. I haven't told him yet."

"Told me what dad?" begged Paul looking directly at him.

"Well, there's a naturist swim this afternoon at Smithfield Leisure Centre. Two till half five. Would you like us to go, as a family that is?"

"Er; yeah, I'd love to go," said Paul with some considerable surprise. "But what about James? Can he come too? Please dad, it wouldn't be the same without him."

"Well, we haven't spoken to the Handles, not since last night anyhow," said Paul's dad. "I was thinking of going next door now actually. You can come with me if you like."

"OK dad; let me get my trainers on and I'll be right with you," said Paul. Paul couldn't get his trainers on fast enough and quickly darted out of the front door after his dad.

"Morning Paul, Tony," said Mrs. Handle.

"Could we come inside for a few minutes," asked Paul's dad.

"Yes of course, go through to the front room. I'm assuming this has got something to do with last night."

"Yes it has, is Andrew about?"

"No, he's just popped out to post a letter. He shouldn't be more than a few minutes."

"Well, you're right, it is about what our lads got up to yesterday evening," smiled Paul's dad. "Maureen and I had a quick look on the internet last night, and, to cut a long story short, we've found out there's a naturist swim taking place this afternoon at Smithfield Leisure Centre."

"Oh have you," said James's mum. "I was a bit mystified by your rather swift departure last night."

"Yes, well, Maureen and I have decided to find out for ourselves what naturism is like. Paul would very much like it if you'd allow James to come with us."

"Oh well, er, I'd have to speak to Andrew." Just then James's dad came back in.

"Oh hello," he said. "Is this about yesterday?"

"Yes," replied Paul's dad. "There's a naturist swim this afternoon at Smithfield Leisure Centre, two till half five. Maureen and I have decided to take the plunge and find out what naturism is like for ourselves. Paul is keen to go too, but what he really wants more than anything is James to come with us." This was followed by a short pause in conversation. Then James's mum got up and went to the bottom of the stairs.

"James, can you come down here a minute please." James came downstairs and into the front room.

"Oh hiya Paul, I wondered if it was you."

"Hi James."

"What did you want me for?" asked James cautiously, while still feeling the emotional scars of last night. "Are you still annoyed with me for swimming naked with Paul?"

"No love, come over here and sit down. Paul and his dad would like to take you swimming again today, if you'd like to go that is."

"Hmm; I don't really feel like going swimming if I have to wear my shorts. It was really nice naked and everyone was so friendly."

"Sorry love, I didn't say did I. It's another naturist swim, this afternoon, at Smithfield Leisure Centre." James's face suddenly lit up.

"Oh brilliant," said James. He remembered Smithfield Leisure Centre being very good. "Can I go, please, please," begged James.

"I don't see why not," said his dad. "There's no funny business at these places is there?"

"Well that's one of the reasons why we're going to give it a try and go with them."

"Oh, fine," said James's dad slightly surprised. "What's the other reason then?"

"We're not letting the kids have all the fun and us miss out!" replied Paul's dad with a wry smile.

"Mum, dad, why don't we all go, as a group of six? I'm sure you'll enjoy it and you've known Paul's mum and dad for years." James's parents looked at each other.

"What do you think Helen? Would you be happy for us all to go?"

"Oh er, I'm not sure about that," said James's mum cringing somewhat. "I mean, swimming about with nothing on at all."

"Oh come on Helen, what have we got to worry about. If it's not for us we'll just not go again, and it's thirty odd miles or so from here. Who's going to see us that knows us? I suppose it is a bit unusual for the kids to introduce us adults to naturism and not the other way round."

"One thing I'd like to know James, is how did you actually manage to blend in without being noticed until the end? I mean, let's be honest here James, your normally very reserved and always cover up. It's as if you've gone from one extreme to the other and pretty quick as well." James went red in the face and felt embarrassed again. "Don't tell me there's more."

"We're going to have to tell," said Paul looking at James. "It won't be easy to hide our nicely tanned bodies will it?" Paul and James told their parents what they'd been doing by the railway line and how they'd copied the naked man they'd seen at the beginning of last week.

"Although Paul was nervous himself, he helped me get over my fears. We showered naked after Friday's normal swim which is why we were late home, if you remember. We got talking to two other lads while we were in the shower and they joined us showering naked. Being part of that felt OK, so it's no big deal now, I'm not that bothered who sees me naked. I've found it relaxing and quite enjoyable. Can we all go, please?" asked James hopefully.

"Oh, go on then. Let's throw caution to the wind. I just hope we don't end up regretting it," said James's mum.

"Our car or yours then," said James's dad. Paul's dad offered to drive everybody in his car.

"Thirty miles, that's a good half an hour to three quarters. Shall we set off just after one o'clock then, allowing for any hold ups?"

"Yeah fine, great," replied James's mum and dad.

"OK then, we'll see you just after one."

Paul and his dad returned home and they continued talking about recent events and why Paul and James decided to go naked. Paul told his mum and dad again about the first time they saw the naked man and also about when James went to get them both some fish and chips. Paul told them he took all his clothes off to feel what the naked man was feeling. "It was a very warm day, and although I felt vulnerable at first, I did actually enjoy the experience," said Paul. "When James came back he found out because I'd forgotten to put my boxers back on. I was honest with James as I always am and we talked about it and what it felt like. Later, when I suggested we both take off our clothes and go naked, James was very nervous, understandable I suppose, but as you now know, he gradually got as he enjoyed it."

"Well I must admit, it's not something I'd ever have guessed you'd do, but if you enjoy it it's fine with us, isn't it Maureen?" said Paul's dad.

"Yes, I suppose so, but you must tell us if any adult takes an unhealthy interest in you," added Paul's mum.

"Mum I'm fourteen, nearly fifteen. Don't paedophiles usually go for younger kids?"

"Just be careful that's all we ask of you."

A little later Paul and James decided to sit outside in the sunshine in the Jessop's front garden. They were enjoying the sun lying down on car rugs with their shorts on this time. However, time was getting on and Paul's mum suggested having a bite to eat before going swimming. She did them beans on toast and a poached egg each. Paul and James enjoyed their lunch while in the front garden.

At quarter to one James went inside to get ready and reappeared with his parents just as it was turning one o'clock. "Right, are we ready for this then?" asked Paul's dad.

"As ready as we'll ever be," replied James's dad. Everyone got into Mr. Jessop's car and they drove to Smithfield Leisure Centre. When they got there they all noticed the name had changed to Smithfield Water Park. There were a lot of other people outside the building because it wasn't quite two o'clock. The Jessops and the Handles got out of the car and walked over to join the queue. While queuing they were given a slip of paper which informed them of what was available. Paul and James were really excited to be here. They'd not been for well over five years, and had certainly never been here naked. They opened the door for everyone to go in on the dot of two. It was pay on entry so it took a good few minutes for everyone to get through. Once inside everyone stripped off without a word. Most people took their towels with them to the pool side. Paul, James and their parents were no exception. The six of them chose a table close to the pool and put their towels down on the chairs.

This swim was of course considerably busier than the one Paul and James had been to the previous evening. There was well over four hundred people attending this one, and after a quick dip, Paul and James headed over to the slides paying no attention whatsoever to the fact that they were completely naked. Their parents found the whole thing amazing, especially the Handles, who'd never ever considered doing anything like this before. "Do you know, I think I could get used to this very quickly," said James's dad. "I feel totally liberated."

"Although I was somewhat apprehensive at first, I've got to agree with that. It is very pleasant and relaxing just being in your own skin," said James's mum. "How do you both feel?"

"Pretty much the same actually," said Paul's dad. "But we must confess, this isn't actually our first time in the nude."

"Oh yeah, come on spill the beans," smiled James's dad.

"Well, we both swam naked in the sea while on holiday twenty years ago. It was just a one off because we never did it again, until now that is. We were in our early twenties and there were a few other bathers of a similar age who were larking around and daring each other to run into the sea and swim naked. After seeing some of them strip off and do it we decided to give it ago as well. It was only a few minutes, but I do remember how good it felt."

"I don't believe it," gasped James's mum. "Tony and Maureen Jessop on holiday and swimming naked, whatever next?"

Just under an hour later Paul and James rejoined their parents. They told them they'd found a passageway which led outside.

"Mum, dad. If you go round the back of the Space Bowl slide there's a passageway which leads outside," said Paul pointing towards the passageway he and James had found.

"OK son, show me." Paul's dad followed them and they went outside. "Hey, this is really good. It's almost like being abroad. Come on, let's go back and tell the others." James stayed outside in an attempt to safeguard a table while Paul and his dad went back to tell the others. "Fancy going outside for a bit? The sun's very warm and welcoming."

"Yeah OK," replied James's dad. "Are we all going to go outside for a bit then?"

"Yes, OK then, why not," said Paul's mum. "Let's get some fresh air." Paul led the way and his and James's parents followed. The six of them enjoyed the outdoor pool for ten or fifteen minutes after which they got out, laid down on their towels and soaked up the afternoon sun. At a rough guess they were joined by at least a hundred other naturists of various ages, all of whom were enjoying the sun too.

After half an hour's lying in the sun Paul and James went back inside. They were enjoying naturism to the full. James couldn't believe how the change had helped his confidence. He only wished he'd started sooner. PE at school would now be much easier as well, especially the showers afterwards he thought. This was something James had always tried to dodge in the past.

"Do you fancy getting something to eat and drink?" asked Paul.

"Yeah OK, let's go and ask our mums and dads." Paul and James went back outside and asked their parents if they could get something to eat from the café. Everyone felt like a bite to eat so picked up their towels and went inside to the poolside café. Paul, James and both their mums queued up, their dads remaining at the table they'd got. They'd decided on just a snack so came back with tea, coffee, hot chocolate, cakes and biscuits. Paul and James didn't take very long eating and drinking and were soon back on the slides.

"I must say I'm really enjoying this experience," said James's mum.

"I thought you would," replied James's dad with a cheeky smile.

"Andrew, really! I didn't mean anything like that. I know I'd reservations at first, but I think it's really quite pleasant to relax in the nude occasionally. And as you can see it's obviously a very popular pastime seeing as there's so many people here." Just then a man approached both families and reintroduced himself. It was Peter Simpkin from the swim yesterday; the one Paul and James had sneaked into.

"Oh hello again," he said a bit surprised at who he'd suddenly seen. "It's Mr. and Mrs. Jessop and Mr. and Mrs. Handle, am I correct?"

"Yes that's right. I'm sorry, do we know you?" asked Paul's mum.

"I'm Peter Simpkin, from the swim yesterday, and I brought your sons home after they cleverly sneaked in and swam naked!"

"Oh yes of course, sorry."

"I must say it's very nice to see you all here. I'd never have thought for a moment that you'd all give naturism a try, and so soon as well. What do you think about it so far?"

"I feel relaxed and liberated," said James's mum.

"Likewise," said Paul's mum. "I think we've found a new interest we can all enjoy."

"Do you know it's great to hear you say that. What do you think about the new health spa?"

"Health spa?" asked James's mum.

"Oh yes there's health spa upstairs now. You know, steam room, sauna, jacuzzi, that sort of thing; and there's a cold plunge pool if you're brave enough!"

"That sounds tempting," chipped in James's dad.

"Also, before I forget; I don't know if you're aware or not, but there are a number of naturist beaches around Britain. Would you like some information on these?"

"Yes that would be nice, thank you."

"And if you'd like to attend the swim near to your home please let me know. It's the second and last Saturday of the month."

"Thank you very much Mr. Simpkin," said Paul's mum.

"Please call me Peter."

"OK, thanks Peter."

"You can find out other information on naturist comings and goings by visiting www.bn.org.uk, British Naturism's website. I'll see you around no doubt."

With about an hour remaining Paul and James went back to their table. Their parents weren't there as they were sat chatting in the shallow end of the wave pool.

"Paul! James! We're over here," called Paul's mum. Paul and James's parents got out of the pool and went over to their sons. "We're going to check out the health spa now. Do you want to come too?"

"Er, what's a health spa?" asked James.

"It's a combination of a steam room and sauna isn't it," said Paul.

"Yes that's right, and there's a jacuzzi there too; are you coming?"

"Er, yeah OK," said James while still not quite sure about what he was getting into. All six of them picked up their towels and headed upstairs to the health spa. This was a very recent addition and had only been open a week. With its shiny black and white tiles, tactile floor and polished silver metalwork they all thought it looked very impressive, and expensive. They each threw their towels on a chair. "What do we have to do," asked James.

"Let's try the steam room first shall we," suggested James's dad. James opened the glass door and went in followed by the rest of them. The steam room was very spacious and could easily take around thirty to forty people. It was lovely; nicely hot and very relaxing.

"Ah, now this is nice," said James after just a few moments. He stood up and moved nearer to the steam outlet.

"Don't get too close James," said his mum. As there was plenty of space James decided to lie down on the marble bench. To say he didn't know what a health spa was James was clearly enjoying his time in the steam room. After a good ten to twelve minutes they got out. Paul and James's parents went over to the showers.

"Do you know what to do next?" Paul asked James.

"Shower?" replied James.

"No, you jump into that small pool over there first," said Paul trying not to giggle, and not actually expecting James to do so, but he did.

"Arrrhhh!" shrieked James. "This is freezing!" James quickly realised he'd been conned by Paul and was plotting his revenge. After all, revenge is a dish best served cold, thought James. Although James regularly had a cold shower at home, this pool was somewhat colder. "P-Paul, g-give us a hand out of here, I-I can't f-feel my f-fingers they're so c-cold." Thinking he'd overstepped the mark Paul took pity on James and walked over to the cold pool to help him out. However, as soon as James got hold of Paul's hand he yanked it and pulled him in. Paul screamed at the cold.

"My word you two are keen to get things right aren't you," laughed James's dad.

"Eh?" replied James shivering as if he was having a seizure.

"The cold pool I mean. As soon as you leave the sauna, or steam room, you're supposed to jump in there, that's the etiquette." Paul and James climbed out of the cold pool and didn't say anything. They went into the sauna while their parents sat down in the rest area. Paul and James were alone in the sauna and both were laid on their backs on the upper seating area.

"Look, I'm sorry for telling you to jump into the cold pool. I didn't really think you'd do it," said Paul. "And you got me back fair and square, which I suppose I deserved."

"Yeah, OK then, apology accepted," said James. "Why are we supposed to jump into the cold pool after this anyway?"

"I'm not sure really, but I think it's what they do in other countries," replied Paul.

"Well, why don't we try it again then in a few minutes and see if we can take it like men, instead of screaming like a couple of girls. We can warm up again in the jacuzzi afterwards."

"Hmm, alright then." After ten minutes relaxing in the sauna Paul and James got out and walked over to the cold pool again.

"Let's ease ourselves in so it's less of a shock," suggested James. They sat on the edge and slowly lowered themselves in. "Ooooo...," muttered James through gritted teeth. Paul eased himself in and then let go of the side of the pool. He ducked right under for a few moments then swam to the surface.

"Oooooo - how long - have we - got to stay - in here?" asked Paul while trying not to shiver like a nervous wreck.

"I'm getting out now, but you can stay in longer if you like," smiled James.

"No thanks!" replied Paul sharply. "I'm going warm up again in the jacuzzi. Are you coming?"

"Sure am." Paul and James walked round to the jacuzzi, but they couldn't get in because it was full. There was a shower area opposite the jacuzzi so they made for that in order to warm up quickly. "Ah, this feels better. I can feel my fingers and toes again now."

"Same here," said Paul. "Well we did it didn't we, and without the girly screaming. May be we need to get used to it. You remember what you said yesterday when we were by the river?"

"Yeah, I know. I'm not going in the cold pool again now," replied James.

"Oh I didn't mean now, I just meant more often in general. I know there wasn't a cold pool at the swim yesterday evening, but I did notice a cold shower, and if we're going to be attending regularly we could use that," said Paul.

"Yeah OK. It'll probably be easier to take than a cold pool in any case, you know not being completely submerged in cold water."

"Yeah, that's what I was thinking as well." While they were busy talking Paul and James failed to notice people leaving the jacuzzi and by now there were only three other naturists in it.

"Hey look, we can get in the jacuzzi now," said James. James carefully stepped into the jacuzzi closely followed by Paul.

"Ah; now this is what I call relaxing," said Paul lying back with his hands behind his head. "What do you think?"

"Same here," smiled James. "It's lovely and warm." Just then the water jets and bubbles stopped.

"Aw; I was enjoying that."

"Me too."

"Don't worry," said a man getting up to leave. "It goes on and off quite a lot. I think it's on some kind of timer." With the jacuzzi now just a hot pool the two other remaining naturists got out as well. Paul and James now had it to themselves and could stretch out to their heart's content.

"Even without the bubbles it's nice and relaxing, don't you think," said James.

"Yeah, I s'pose so. It's great being naked in here though isn't it," added Paul with smile.

"Oh yeah without a doubt. I'd hate to have to do this wearing shorts. You wouldn't be able to feel the bubbles round your... well, you know."

"Yeah, I get the picture," laughed Paul. At that moment the jacuzzi burst back into life. The jets and bubbles started up again with rumbling sound. Paul and James sat as low as possible in the jacuzzi. Only their heads were visible above the water. They really enjoyed this and stayed in undisturbed for quite a while.

With about ten minutes to go before closing time Paul and James's parents left the rest area and headed for the jacuzzi.

"Oh, I was wondering where you two were," said Paul's mum. "Are you gonna let us in then?"

"Sorry," replied Paul moving out of the way.

"I thought you'd both gone back downstairs," said James's mum.

"Oh no. We've been up here a good half hour I'd guess," replied James.

"It's really good is this health spa, isn't it. I can't wait to come again," said Paul.

"We'll see," said his dad. "Anyway, isn't it almost time to jump into the cold pool again?"

"I'm not going in there again," said James quickly.

"Well you'll find it difficult to get dry," said his dad. "If you jump into the cold pool for a few moments all the sweat glands on your body will close up and you'll be able to get dried a lot easier, trust me." Paul, James and their parents got out of the jacuzzi and walked over to the cold pool. James's dad was first to jump in. Paul decided to go for it again and jumped in too. Although cold and a shock to his body he didn't scream. He climbed out and encouraged James to jump in again. James's mum beat him to it, but then he plucked up the courage and jumped in as well. Paul's mum was last and jumped in as James and his mum were climbing out.

It was now half past five and time to get out. Some had gone earlier, but this was the end of the naturist session. Everyone went through to the changing room and got dried and dressed; commonly called 'going textile'.

The Jessops and the Handles drove back home and decided to round the day off with a barbeque in the Handle's front garden. James's dad got the barbeque out and set it up. He lit it fairly easily and then left it for a while to help prepare the food for cooking. He came back outside with a tray of sausages, steak, beef burgers, chicken pieces and half a dozen skewers. The women were preparing salad inside when James walked in. James had forgotten about a bar of chocolate which he'd left in his pocket. It had melted and seeped through to his skin so whilst waiting he decided to shower and get cleaned up. He came back downstairs wearing his sandals and a towel. James went outside to see how his dad and Paul were getting on cooking the food, when his dad accidentally moved his chair on to a corner of his son's towel.

As James turned towards Paul his towel was pulled from him leaving poor James completely naked in the front garden.

"Dad, my towel!" exclaimed a rather embarrassed James.

"Oh I'm so sorry love." But before his dad could move his chair, James ran back inside the house naked hoping no passers-by had seen him. A few minutes later James reappeared wearing a T-shirt and a clean pair of shorts.

"I bet you did that deliberately didn't you?" said James with a huff. His dad and Paul were trying their best not to laugh, but couldn't help it.

"Sorry again love. I'll give you the biggest sausages."

"Thanks dad. I hope you both had a good laugh anyway," replied James starting to see the funny side of what just happened.

The Handles and the Jessops all enjoyed the barbecue and stayed up quite late talking about their new interest and where they could go with naturism from here.

Chapter 6

It was now Monday morning and Paul and James were back at school for the last term of the school year. At morning beak they saw Katie and went over to talk to her.

"Hi Katie," said Paul.

"You haven't said anything to anyone here have you?" asked Katie.

"No we haven't," replied Paul.

"Are you trying to tell us you're embarrassed about being a naturist?" asked James.

"No not really; but I do think it would be easier in school if only close friends, like you two, know. My mum tells me we, as naturists, shouldn't gossip about other naturists. I would like to tell everyone I am a naturist and swim naked 'cos I really love it, but I fear most other kids wouldn't understand. Are you both coming again a week on Saturday?" asked Katie somewhat cautiously.

"Too right we are, aren't we James," replied Paul.

"Oh yeah, we've never swum anywhere naked before in our lives and we really loved it, apart from when we were spotted by Mr. Simpkin that is," said James.

"Yes, that was embarrassing and perhaps inevitable, but it has made it so we can go regularly without the need to sneak in," added Paul. "It was as if he was on our side, but he still had to see our parents to cover himself in case anyone asked. Now both our mums and dads have joined in as well."

"Oh have they."

"Yeah they have. We got talking yesterday morning after my mum and dad had a look on the internet and found out about the swim at Smithfield Water Park," said Paul.

"Smithfield Water Park?" said Katie.

"Yeah, it was really good."

"I know it is, and they've just opened a health spa. I wanted to go to there, but my mum said it was far too difficult 'cos there's no bus, or train, anywhere near it."

"Yeah, it did look a bit out of the way now you mention it," said James.

"Still, I'm sure there'll be other times. Somewhere like that isn't going to do just one naturist session and never again is it, and you could always get a taxi next time." said Paul, trying to reassure Katie there'll be other naturist times."

"Or maybe you could come with us, if we go again that is," said James.

"Yeah well, I wish my dad would come with us now and again, and my older sister Jenny," said Katie.

"Don't they like naturism then?" asked James.

"My sister did it a couple of times about three years ago before she went off to university. She's eighteen now, but my dad's never done it. He thinks it's just perverse and shouldn't be allowed," said Katie.

"Have your parents split up?" asked Paul.

"Yes, but that was quite a while ago and long before my mum got talking to a friend of hers and found out about naturism. She tried it on her own the first time 'cos she didn't think kids would be allowed in, but when she came back she told me and my sister kids were allowed in with their parents, and we could go with her if we wanted to. A few weeks later my mum fancied going again and asked us if we'd like to go with her, so we did, and I took to it like a duck to water straightaway, but my sister Jenny said she felt uncomfortable not wearing her costume."

"Really? She actually said she felt less comfortable not wearing her swimming costume?" asked James in surprise.

"Yes she did, but my feelings are entirely the opposite of hers. I love swimming naked and don't like it when we go with school 'cos we have to wear our costumes."

"Yeah, I know exactly what you mean there," said Paul. "I doubt we'll ever be able to swim naked when we go as a school group." Paul and James felt a bit sorry for Katie. They weren't aware her parents had split up.

At the next swim two weeks later they saw Katie and her mum again and went over to talk to them. "Hello Mrs. Finch, Hello Katie," said Paul and James.

"Oh Hello, would you two be Paul Jessop and James Handle by any chance?"

"Yep, that's us," replied Paul. "We came two weeks ago and sneaked in by hiding in the group changing room toilet."

"Oh is that how you both got in without your parents being here, I did wonder," said Mrs. Finch. Paul and James continued talking to Katie and her mum about how they'd found out about the naturist swim and also how they'd practiced being naked near to where they lived. Katie and her mum were a bit surprised to hear this, especially the bit about the naked man; however, Paul and James insisted it was the truth.

"We just did what he did and we really liked the feeling of not wearing clothes," said Paul. "We later bumped into him in the changing room about halfway through the first time we were here, and he told us he'd seen us running about and playing throw and catch naked."

"Yeah, we thought we were gonna be for the high jump, but we couldn't have been more wrong," said James.

"I must admit though, we were both very nervous to start with. We'd never ever seen each other naked before, so it took a bit of getting used to," said Paul.

"We like it so much now we'd live naked given half a chance!" added James with a smile.

"Oh that would be so nice wouldn't it, if only it were possible," said Katie.

"Why don't we have a go at playing badminton again," suggested Paul. "Does your mum fancy a game Katie?"

"I'll ask her just a minute." Katie swam over to her mum who was now taking to another woman. "Mum, would you like to play badminton with us?"

"Oh go on, don't disappoint your daughter. I'll catch up with you later," said the other woman.

"Yes OK, go on then, why not," replied Katie's mum.

"Paul and James would like to play too, can they join us?" asked Katie.

"Yes love of course they can." So the four of them got out of the pool, grabbed their towels and went to the gym. There were a number of other naturists also playing badminton so space was very limited, but after a few minutes wait, one couple left the gym and gave their rackets and shuttle cock to Paul and James.

Katie and her mum acquired a racket each and they enjoyed the next ten to fifteen minutes leisurely playing badminton together naked, after which Katie's mum said she fancied a rest and a drink. As three was an awkward number for playing badminton, Paul decided to let James and Katie play on while he went to the toilet.

"I'm just going to the toilet, I won't be long," said Paul as he left. Paul went to the toilet and came back a few minutes later with a rather childish grin on his face.

"What's so funny?" asked Katie.

"Yeah, you've only been to the toilet; so what's the big joke?" asked James.

"Well, while I was peeing down one of the urinals there was a little boy of about two or three stood next to me with his dad. His dad had to lift him up so he could pee down one of the urinals, and while he was peeing he said, [In a high pitched childish voice] 'It's a lot easier to pee like this, isn't it daddy.' I couldn't help but laugh. The little boy's dad also saw the funny side of what his son said. It's a wonder I didn't pee on my feet for laughing," said Paul still trying not to laugh too loudly. James and Katie also had a good laugh at what Paul told them.

"Was that really so funny?" asked Katie's mum. "You three really are easily amused aren't you."

"Sorry mum," said Katie. "It was the way Paul said it which made it sound so funny."

"Well, be that as it may. Look, I'm going back to the pool now. Are you staying here with Paul and James?"

"Yes mum, we'll stay here a bit longer."

"It's just after eight o'clock now. Come back to the pool in about half an hour."

"OK mum, we'll see you in the pool later," said Katie. Katie's mum walked back through to the pool while James decided to sit down for a while and let Paul play badminton with Katie.

While they were playing James found a magazine underneath the bench on which he was sat, the cover of which had been torn off. He picked it up and began to flick through it when it suddenly fell open at a particular page. There was an article on this page which was headed with the words 'Overcoming Your

Phobia - Gymnophobia'. James was intrigued, due primarily to there being a small picture of a naked boy and girl. As he began to read the aforementioned article it immediately struck a chord with him. James quickly realised that gymnophobia was the fear of being seen naked. That's just like I was, he thought to himself, and Paul helped me in a similar way to what it says here. "Paul!"

"What?"

"Come here a minute, I want to show you something." Paul and Katie stopped playing badminton and put the rackets down. They walked over to where James was sat and he showed them the article in the magazine he'd been reading.

"This is very uncanny," said Paul looking intently at page he was reading.

"I know. I was thinking exactly the same," said James.

"B-but that picture of the boy and girl, it might just as well be you and me."

"What's it about?" asked Katie.

"Gymnophobia," replied James feeling somewhat proud at learning a new word.

"What on earth does that mean?"

"If you have it, it means, you wouldn't be seen dead here like this," said Paul trying to keep a straight face. "Let's see if your mum knows what gymnophobia is Katie."

"OK then. It's almost half eight now anyway, so she'll be expecting to see us back in the pool very shortly." Paul, James and Katie walked back through to the pool. They found Katie's mum talking to the same woman she'd been talking to before going to play badminton. "Hi mum," said Katie as she sat down on the edge of the pool with Paul and James.

"Oh hello you three."

"Mum, do you know what gymnophobia is?"

"Oh er... no love I don't. Are you going to tell me or do I have to guess?"

"I know what it is," said the other woman with a smile.

"Oh, right; what is it then?" asked Katie's mum still looking slightly puzzled and feeling like she should already know.

"Why don't we see how your daughter puts it first?"

"OK Katie put us out of our misery."

"It means; you wouldn't be seen dead here like this, or at least that's what Paul said a few minutes ago after reading that magazine." This was followed by some rather childish laughing from Paul, James and indeed this other woman.

"What magazine have you three been reading to come out with a line like that?"

"That might have sounded rather amusing; however, your daughter's on the right lines. If you suffered from the condition you certainly wouldn't be here like we are."

"Has it got something to do with being naked?" asked Katie's mum.

"Yes that's it. Gymnophobia is the fear of being seen naked, and indeed seeing others naked too."

"It's this true story here about a boy and girl. It starts at the top of page forty-two," said Paul. "James found this magazine on the floor and was reading it while Katie and I where playing badminton. I wondered why he wasn't paying us much attention."

"Paul!" said James abruptly. "You make it sound like I was reading something really seedy and it most certainly isn't."

"Sorry," said Paul. "I didn't mean to suggest it was seedy."

"I thought it was a really nice true story about how those two children over-came their fear of being seen naked."

"Gymnophobia," said Katie.

"Yes exactly. There must be a lot of phobias you can suffer from. Arachnophobia is one of the most common; it's the fear of spiders."

"Wasn't there a film made some time ago with that title?" asked Paul.

"Yes," said the other woman slowly. "It'd be at least fifteen to twenty years ago now I think."

"Did you see it?" asked Katie's mum.

"Yes I did, but if an arachnophobic saw it I think it would have set them back some months if they were trying to overcome their phobia. I don't suffer from arachnophobia myself, but that film made me feel uneasy for a couple of days afterwards."

"Can we have a look for it next time we go shopping mum?" asked Katie excitedly.

"We'll see love. Anyway, you haven't told us how those two children in that magazine managed to overcome their gymnophobia have you?"

"Oh no, sorry."

"Are they brother and sister or just friends?" asked Katie's mum.

"They're like brother and sister in a way, but they're not blood related," said James.

"So they're step brother and step sister," said Katie's mum.

"Yes they are," said Katie. "The boy is twelve and the girl is eleven. They came together when the boy's mum and the girl's dad got married three years ago."

"So how did they come to fear being naked then?"

"It says here they were very 'introverted', whatever that means, and they didn't have many friends either. The girl and her dad moved over eighty miles so they could all be together," said Katie.

"Yeah, the boy and girl were complete strangers until they first met," said James. "It all kicked off when the boy started year seven. He had to get showered naked after playing football. He hated playing football, and rugby; and hated having to shower naked afterwards. He was just like me, until recently of course."

"When the girl heard about this she was scared too because she thought she might have to get showered naked after playing sport when she moved up to year seven as well," said Katie. "The boy's mum and the girl's dad helped them slowly get used to being naked. It started off with simply not getting dressed after bath time and wandering about the house naked for an hour or so."

"Yeah, and after a week or two doing that the boy and girl got to like it, partly because their parents had turned up the heating so much it became uncomfortable to wear more than a skimpy T-shirt and pants! Their parents also decided to get involved and walked about the house naked too. They hoped it would help the kids relax more while they were naked," said James.

"They finally overcame their naked fears, gymnophobia that is, by attending a naturist swim, just like James and I did, but they didn't have to sneak in of course!"

"Oh well, it just goes to show what you can achieve if you're focused," said Katie's mum.

"Quite right," said the other woman. "Anyway, it's nearly nine o'clock now, how are you all getting home?"

"On the bus. There's one down our way just after twenty past nine," replied Katie's mum.

"I think ours is a few minutes later," said Paul.

"Oh don't bother going for the bus tonight. I'll run you all home. By the way, my name's Linda, Linda Barker."

"Sorry, I'm Caroline Finch and of course my daughter Katie. The two boys are Paul Jessop and James Handle, Katie's friends from school."

"Well it's very nice to have met you all," said Linda. "I started coming to this swim about a month ago with my friend Tanya. She's a vet and works a lot which is why she's not here tonight. She found out about this swim back in February, but it took until the first swim in May to actually do it and swim naked for the first time."

It was now nine o'clock and time to get out. Paul, James and Katie went through to the changing room closely followed by Katie's mum and her new friend Linda. All five of them showered for a few minutes then got dried and dressed. They left the leisure centre at twenty past nine and Linda drove them all home in her Range Rover.

"This is a nice car isn't it," said James. "I don't think I've ever been in one of these before."

"It's a Range Rover," said Paul "And they're very expensive! My dad told me."

"They're worth it if you want the ultimate ride," said Linda.

"You must have a good job Linda if you can afford one of these. What do you do then? I don't think you said," asked Katie's mum.

"I'm a doctor."

"Oh, so it's Dr. Barker then is it?" asked Katie.

"If you like, but I prefer to keep things informal with friends. Please feel free to call me Linda." They all kept talking on the way home. Linda dropped Paul and James off first then Katie and her mum.

Paul and James went inside James's house, Paul's parents

being out. James's parents were watching TV when they went in.

"Hi mum," said James.

"Oh, you're home early," replied James's mum.

"We got a lift home with a new friend of Katie's mum," said James.

"She's a Dr. Barker but prefers to be called Linda by her friends," added Paul.

"Yeah, and she drives a Range Rover," said James.

"Didn't she say she lives with a friend of hers, Tanya I think, and she's a vet."

"Really? I bet they're not short of a bob or two," said James's dad who'd just walked in with a mug of tea in his hand. He'd been listening to the conversation whilst in the kitchen. "Helen, is that documentary from two weeks back still on the tape in the video?"

"Yes I think it might be love, why?"

"I just wondered if Paul had seen it. The bit about naturism that is."

"No I didn't," replied Paul quickly. "I saw about a minute or two of it, but didn't really want to watch it in front of my mum. It was on just before we went to that first swim wasn't it and I was scared in case my mum made some connection to James and me." James's dad pushed the tape into the video and pressed play. He had to rewind the tape to get it to the right place. When he had he stopped it and pressed play again. The Handles and Paul then watched the whole section on naturism. It started off on a beach and showed a clothed man talking to a naked woman. Later the TV camera crew did short interviews with willing naturists. They wanted to know why so many people found naturism so enjoyable. Most were saying things like; 'you feel totally released', 'less stressed', 'liberated', and so on. They were on a beach which, according to the signage, prohibits naturism, but the signs are believed to be wrong. This was then followed by interviews with a councillor, a police officer and a local resident. The four of them continued to watch as they all gave differing accounts about the beach. The resident, who'd lived within a couple of hundred yards of the beach for seven to eight years, appeared to be impolite and did not want any form of naturism to take place there despite it being perfectly acceptable for over seventy years! The council's representative, and the police officer, had to admit there had been a few complaints about inappropriate behaviour, but it wasn't seen as a major issue. A short time later the TV camera crew moved on to a large maze, the design of which had been cut into a large field of maize plants. The management here saw an opportunity to make some extra money and once a year for the past nine years there has been a naked night. Most people stripped off in the car park, some even arrived naked! It certainly was a very popular event and further interviews were shown.

After they'd watched this programme they all sat talking for a while. Paul then heard his parents arrive home and go inside, so after a few more minutes he decided to go home too. James got up to see Paul out. "Do you fancy going to the leisure centre on Friday again for a 'textile' swim?" asked James.

"Why do you want to do that?" asked Paul. "I thought we preferred swimming naked."

"Yeah, I know we do, but we might meet Ben and Harry again."

"Oh yeah, I'd forgotten about them."

"So shall we go next Friday," suggested James.

"Yeah sure," smiled Paul quickly remembering what they'd got up to the first time they met Ben and Harry. "OK then, I'll see you tomorrow; night."

"Night Paul," said James.

"Hi mum, dad," said Paul as he went in.

"Hello love," said his mum. "Sorry you had to wait. We got held up coming home. A lorry had overturned and blocked the road completely."

"Aye, we were stuck for over an hour," added his dad.

"Mum, dad, it's fine really. I was with James and his mum and dad. We were watching that programme about naturism which was on a couple of weeks back. James's dad had recorded it by accident. He didn't know how to time set their video so he just pressed the record button and it recorded everything from that moment onwards," said Paul.

"Oh well, I'm glad you got to see what you wanted to love. Even if you were worried about what me and your dad might have thought!" said his mum with a smile.

"Yes mum, I do remember," said Paul clearly remembering the moment he felt very uncomfortable. "Anyway, it's just after half eleven now so I'm off up to bed. I'll see you in the morning. Night mum, night dad."

"Night love," said his parents.

Chapter 7

It was Friday afternoon now and almost three o'clock. Paul and James thought the day was dragging on and couldn't wait to get home. It was three weeks since their first swim of recent and they were looking forward to going again. They specifically wanted to go on a Friday evening so they'd a good chance of meeting Ben and Harry again after they told them they'd be there every Friday until Christmas. Paul and James had enjoyed meeting them before and were looking forward to doing so again, so much so both were finding it increasingly difficult to concentrate on their schoolwork. I absolutely love skinny dipping, Paul kept thinking to himself, and he was wondering if Ben and Harry would be up for an outdoor skinny dip this time. He was going to suggest it to Ben when they next met and hopefully that would be this evening. Where Paul and James went to last time there was nowhere for them to jump in, all they could really do was swim about and Paul didn't do much of that following the near miss with the fish! He was hoping Ben and Harry would have a few suggestions themselves.

Shortly after the final bell Paul met up with James and they walked home together as usual. As they were walking home James asked Paul; "Do you think we can go skinny dipping somewhere tomorrow?"

"I hope so," replied Paul. "I hope Ben and Harry will come with us as well. Maybe they'll know a couple of good places. They did say they'd done it before."

"I think that was only a one off, but who knows, maybe they will. I can't wait to meet them again. I just hope they're at the leisure centre this evening like they said."

"Well we'll find out soon enough," said Paul. They both arrived home and quickly got changed. James's mum had bought him a new pair of swimming trunks like what he'd asked for.

"Hi mum," said James.

"Hello love, good day at school?"

"Yeah, not bad."

"Did you say you were wanting to go swimming with Paul this evening?"

"Yes mum, we were hoping to; do you mind?"

"No love it's fine. You have a good time and enjoy yourself."

"Sure will mum. We're having to wear our shorts this time 'cos it's not a naturist swim."

"So why are you going then if you can't swim the way you like?"

"It's so we can meet the two lads we met three weeks ago. Do you remember me telling you about Ben and Harry?"

"Hmm, yes I think so. I don't remember you telling me their names just that you'd met two boys while you were in the shower before you left and you got chatting with them."

"Yeah we did, and Paul and me are looking forward to meeting them again this evening, hopefully."

"Oh, so is that why you wanted me to get you a new pair of Speedos?"

"Oh, have you got them?" asked James slightly surprised.

"Yes, I left them in a bag on your bed." James quickly went upstairs to his bedroom to have a look at his new swimming trunks. He took them out of the bag and had a good look at them. They were plain dark blue with the Speedo motif on the side. James thought these would be more comfortable to wear than his football shorts and a step closer to being naked. James decided to try them on. I hope these fit, he thought. I know I much prefer swimming naked, but these will certainly be a good second. They fitted perfectly. Brilliant, thought James, and then he took them off. James grabbed his school bag and emptied it out on to his bed. He put his new swimming trunks in along with a towel and a bottle of shower gel.

Meanwhile, Paul was also getting ready next door. He hadn't thought of getting any new swimwear so took his football shorts as before. They both had a bit of tea and left just after six o'clock. Paul and James walked to the bus stop and got there just as a bus was approaching. This bus took a slightly longer route, but as they weren't pushed for time, they got on it and went to the leisure centre. As they were waiting to get in Paul saw Ben through the window. They were part way through their swimming lesson. Ben gave Paul a wave and he took this to mean; 'we'll see you after the lesson'. "Ben and Harry are in the pool," said Paul. "I've just seen Ben."

"Where?" asked James quickly.

"Er, second lane from the left I think," replied Paul. "I didn't see Harry, but I guess he'll be here somewhere."

"I hope so, I can't wait to meet them again," smiled James. The queue to get in was gradually getting longer. Because this was a normal Friday and not a school holiday swimming lessons were taking place. They were due to finish at seven o'clock when the pool would be opened for general swimming along with the slide. Paul and James were here a good twenty minutes early and were having to wait until the lessons ended. "Did I tell you my mum bought me a new pair of swimming trunks like what Ben and Harry wear?"

"Oh yeah, you mean Speedos?"

"Yeah, they're dark blue. Hang on a minute I'll show you." James unzipped his bag and took out his new Speedos to show Paul. "What do you think?" asked James.

"Hey, they look really cool. I wish I had a pair, I'll be the only one of the four of us wearing shorts now instead of swimming trunks," moaned Paul.

"Not necessarily," said James. "Don't they sell them here, in the shop? Why don't we have a look and see?"

"OK, but I've only got about eight quid on me, and I'll need £1:45 to get in won't I." Paul and James went over to the shop and had a look around. James was right, they did sell swimwear and this included Speedos. They also sold other swim related items such as goggles, masks, flippers, swim hats and towels. They continued looking until Paul chose a pair of bright red Speedo type swimming trunks with two narrow black stripes on each side. "These'll do," said Paul. "They're virtually a mirror image of Ben's. His are black with a red stripe."

"How much are they?" asked James.

"Er, oh no, they're £7:95," replied Paul somewhat disheartened.

"That's OK then," said James.

"But what about swimming? If I get these I won't be able to have a swim."

"Don't worry about that; you buy them and I'll pay for us both to swim."

"Are you sure?" asked Paul.

"Course I am," replied James. "I've got a fiver with me, and a bit of change. We'll just have to go without a pizza this time that's all."

"Oh, OK then." Paul took his swimming trunks to the cash desk and paid. They left the shop and rejoined the queue.

Just after five to seven the receptionist started letting people through and it wasn't long before Paul and James were in the changing room getting into their newly acquired swimwear. They had to use separate lockers this time because they both had relatively large bags with them and once changed they went through to the pool. Ben was already sat on the side waiting for them. "Hi there," said Ben.

"Oh hiya," said Paul and James.

"Where's Harry?" asked James.

"He's just gone to the toilet. I'm surprised you didn't pass him coming out actually," said Ben. "Ah, here he is now."

"Hi Paul, hi James," said Harry. "It's great to see you again. How you doing?"

"Great thanks. How was your lesson?" asked Paul.

"Fine," replied Harry. "We've been diving in and picking up rubber bricks this time."

"As well as swimming twenty lengths each," added Ben.

All the swimming lessons had finished now and the staff were gradually removing the plastic lane separators. They also brought the slide into use. Paul, James, Ben and Harry were having a great time together in the pool and were soon on the slide.

Shortly after half past eight the four of them had a rest and were talking to one another in the shallow end of the pool. "I notice you're both wearing Speedos now," said Ben. "Do you think they're better than shorts; to swim in I mean."

"Oh yeah, sure they are. Shorts hold you back and create drag. I much prefer swimming with these on instead of my shorts 'cos it's the nearest you can get to being naked," added Paul with a smirk.

"It's the same on the slide, you go down it much faster with nothing on," smiled James. Ben and Harry looked at each other and were wondering how James could possibly know that. Had he been down the slide with nothing on? They were about to find out. Paul glared at James, and his face dropped. "Sorry, I er..." suddenly realising what he'd said James felt a bit embarrassed and was somewhat stuck for words.

"What did you just say then about going down the slide?" asked Harry slowly.

"You might as well tell them now," said Paul.

"Well, we were gonna tell them, weren't we," said James.

"Yeah, I s'pose so," said Paul. "But I'd have preferred somewhere a bit quieter."

"Well let's go into the small pool so we can talk more privately," suggested Ben. "Come on, I can't wait to hear what this is about." Ben led the way to the small pool and it was empty save for one young mum with her toddler son. Paul, James, Ben and Harry got in and stayed close together in the corner where they'd had their sly skinny dip three weeks earlier. "Well, come on then, what were you going to tell us?" asked Ben showing a keen interest. "Did you er, get into that naturist swim the evening after we first met?"

"Yeah, we did," said James.

"I'm sorry," said Paul. "Perhaps we should have told you we already knew about it."

"We found out about it the day before," said James. "That's why we were here that Friday evening. Not only were we trying to get used to being naked, we were trying to find somewhere to hide after closing time as well, 'cos we knew in advance we needed parental permission to get in."

"I'm guessing you found a good enough place to hide then," smiled Harry.

"Yeah we did," said Paul. "We hid in the group changing room toilet. I checked the time on my mobile phone and at about seven o'clock, after waiting nearly an hour, we heard voices and the sound of people moving about. It was then we opened the toilet door and found the group changing room empty so I went over and opened the main door to check the changing room itself and everyone was naked."

"Yeah, and Paul quickly shut the door while we whipped off our shorts," said James. "All we had to do then was join in with everyone else and make it appear we were having fun!"

"That of course wasn't difficult," said Paul. "'Cos we were having fun. Swimming about in the nude was absolutely brilliant, and so was sliding down the slide."

"I bet it was!" said Ben sharply. "I can't believe you actually managed to pull it off, without er..."

"...being thrown out?" finished James.

"Well, yeah," replied Ben.

"Would you have liked to have been with us?" asked Paul.

"You bet we would!" replied Ben.

"I wish our parents would let us go to a naturist swim, but they won't," said Harry.

"Why?" ask James. "I mean I know your mum can't swim 'cos she's frightened of water and you said your dad's not really into swimming, but surely one of them could drop you off and agree to pick you up later at the end."

"Yeah, that's what we suggested once, but all we got from dad was; 'Don't you two go swimming often enough?' and; 'What's so special about doing it naked anyway? Do you two just want to look at other people naked?' All we could say is; 'No we don't.' and; 'We really like swimming naked'," said Ben.

"And our dad just scoffed at that. I really wish we'd have been with you that night," added Harry looking really disappointed.

"Did they get the inflatable out?" asked Ben.

"Yeah they did," replied Paul. "That was the first thing we had a go on after jumping into the pool naked."

"So did you manage to stay in until the end?" asked Ben. "What I meant was, didn't anyone ask you who you were with?"

"Yeah, they did," replied Paul. "It was a man called Peter Simpkin that first spoke to us. He's the organiser of the naturist swim and he approached us about halfway through. He asked us where our parents were and we lied by telling him they were at the other end of the pool. Thinking we'd been rumbled we got out of the pool for a few minutes."

"But we went back about five minutes later and bumped into a friend of ours from school, which was quite a surprise," smiled James. "And she told us we could play badminton if we liked."

"That was quite good in the nude as well. I don't suppose

you've ever played badminton naked have you?" asked Paul.

"No we haven't," replied Harry a tad surprised.

"So what happened after that? Did you go back into the pool or not?" asked Ben.

"Yeah we did," replied Paul. "And that was when it appeared quite clear we were on our own."

"Mr. Simpkin gave us a lift home and talked to our parents. We thought we'd be in big trouble," said James. "And it did feel quite embarrassing being found out, but although our parents were pretty shocked at what we'd done they didn't mind too much."

"I later found out my parents had enjoyed a quick skinny dip in the sea twenty years ago," said Paul.

"Really?" asked Ben.

"Yeah, well, that's what they said. My mum and dad had a look on the internet later that night after I'd gone to bed and they found out about another naturist swim the next day at Smithfield Water Park. So, after some friendly persuasion from James, both our mums and dads decided to go."

"I bet that was good," said Harry. "I remember us going there last year. I also think I overheard someone say they were building a health spa 'cos we noticed some work going on upstairs."

"Oh yeah, that was good too," said James.

The four of them continued talking together until it was time to get out. At nine o'clock they climbed out of the small pool and went into the shower area. It was somewhat busier this Friday with it not being a holiday and there were only two of the eight showers free when they approached. Paul and James offered the two available showers to Ben and Harry, but they didn't have to wait long and were soon showering with them. There was no mention of showering naked so the four of them kept their swimming trunks on, until they were alone that is. The last person left the shower area a few minutes later. "Well, are we all gonna take off our swimming trunks again and shower naked?" asked Paul.

"Yeah, why not," said Harry and he quickly took his swimming trunks off and dropped them on the floor of the shower by his feet. Paul, James and Ben also took their swimming trunks off as well.

"Oh wow, this feels so much better," said Paul while having a good stretch. I wish we could all swim like this all the time without any fuss."

"Same here," said James.

"I really love showering like this, even here in a communal shower," said Ben. "Like anyone, I could do it alone, but it's great being naked in a small group like this isn't it, where we can just relax and be ourselves."

"I know what you mean," added Paul. "We're in our natural state when we're naked and it feels fantastic."

"Do you think we could get away with another quick skinny dip?" asked Harry with a wry smile.

"Er... I'll have a look, hang on a minute," said Ben. He walked out of the shower area naked for the second time and had a look. Both the main pool and the small pool had covers over them. Damn, thought Ben as he went back to rejoin the others in the shower area. "Can't do it this time guys, both pools are covered," he said.

"Never mind," said James feeling slightly relieved. "It was a bit risky last time with that cleaner, she could've easily seen us."

"Still, there's nothing to stop us being naked in here is there," said Paul.

"True," replied Ben. "But I'd have really enjoyed another quick skinny dip, wouldn't you?"

"Yeah course I would. We could always have a go at skinny dipping outdoors," suggested Paul. "If we all enjoy swimming naked so much why don't the four of us go out tomorrow for the day and find somewhere we can skinny dip safely."

"Yeah, I'd be up for that," smiled Ben.

"Same here," said Harry.

"Do you know anywhere good?" asked Ben.

"Hmm, we were hoping you might be able to help us on that one," said Paul.

"Well there was one place we thought might be suitable," said Ben.

"Where?" asked James keenly interested in a day out skinny dipping. "Where you did it before, in that river?"

"Oh no, we were on holiday then," replied Ben. "This is out in the sticks somewhere, and I think the nearest railway station has a very poor service, only one or two trains call at it each day."

"Well, we might as well check it out," suggested Paul. "We won't know until we get there and it could be really good."

"Right, OK then. Let's leave it until tomorrow," said Ben. "If we agree to meet somewhere, the railway station perhaps, we can take it from there and hopefully spend the whole day together."

"Great," said James. "I'm looking forward to it already."

"I'll have a look at a map of that area," added Ben. "I think mum and dad have the right one, if not I'll check with the OS website."

"What time we gonna meet then?" asked Harry.

"What about nine o'clock," suggested Paul. "Or is that too early?"

"Let's make it nine forty-five so we can get on a train around ten," said Ben. "Our parents will wonder where were going to if we leave that early."

"We don't normally get up on a Saturday till nine as it is," smiled Harry.

"OK then, nine forty-five it is," said Paul.

The four of them continued to enjoy showering together without their swimming trunks on when a man with two young children, aged about seven or eight, entered the shower area. They started to shower without paying any attention to either Paul, James, Ben or Harry until about five minutes later when one of the boys said; "Do we take off our shorts in the showers grandad?" to which their grandad replied; "Well, you can if you want to." This young boy then took his shorts off and continued to shower naked. He was quickly followed by his brother, but their grandad kept his swimming trunks on until they were about to leave. For just over two minutes everyone showering was doing so in the nude. It felt slightly surreal. James in particular felt really at home being naked now and it didn't worry him at all. The two young boys and their grandad left the shower area and went to get dried.

As the time was now nearing quarter to ten Paul, James, Ben

and Harry picked up their swimming trunks and left the shower area. They got dried and dressed and went through to reception where Ben and Harry's dad was waiting. He offered to give Paul and James a lift home which, after the bus incident three weeks ago, they were more than happy to accept. Ben and Harry's dad dropped Paul and James off just after quarter past ten. "We'll see you tomorrow morning then, at the railway station," said Ben.

"Yeah, you will. Night both of you," said Paul.

"Night, thanks for the lift," added James.

"Yeah, see you tomorrow, night," said Harry. Ben and Harry's dad drove off and Paul and James went inside. On arrival home Paul and asked his mum if it was OK to go out for the day on Saturday.

"Do you mind if I go out for the day tomorrow with James?" asked Paul.

"No not at all love," replied Paul's mum.

"It won't be just James and me this time 'cos we're gonna meet up with Ben and Harry again. They're friends of ours now, and we've got similar interests," said Paul.

"Oh have you."

"Yeah, they like skinny dipping too and they'd also like to go to a naturist swim, but..." Paul suddenly stopped, but then continued, "...but they haven't yet done so." He thought it might be best not to mention to his mum the fact that Ben and Harry's parents don't want them to go to a naturist swim. A full and honest explanation for this has not yet been heard.

"So is that what you're planning on doing tomorrow?" asked Paul's mum.

"Well yeah, we were hoping to find somewhere that's safe enough," replied Paul. "Ben's thought of a possibility and he's going to have a look at a map."

"Well, be careful love. Don't just go jumping into water no matter how tempting it may look. I don't want a policeman coming here telling me you've been hurt."

"It's OK mum, we'll be careful. Ben always checks the depth of any river or whatever before he jumps in."

"So where are you going to meet them?" asked Paul's mum.

"We've arranged to meet them at the railway station at quarter to ten tomorrow morning," replied Paul.

"Oh well I can give you both a lift if you like. I've got a ten o'clock appointment with the hairdresser and it's only a stone's throw from the station."

"OK thanks mum. I think I'll get to bed now; I don't wanna be too tired to enjoy tomorrow. Night mum."

"Night love."

Chapter 8

Paul and James were looking forward to their day out with the Ben and Harry and were keen to get to the railway station at quarter to ten which was the time they'd arranged to meet. After breakfast they made a final check to make sure they hadn't forgotten anything. James came round at quarter past nine. "Are you ready?" he asked.

"Yep, sure am," replied Paul.

"Right, come on then you two if you want a lift," said Paul's mum. Paul and James got into the car and they set off. She dropped them off at the railway station at twenty-five to ten, but Ben and Harry were nowhere to be seen. They bought themselves a can of pop each while they waited for them to arrive. At ten to ten Ben saw them from a magazine shop across the road.

"Morning," he called.

"Oh you're there," said Paul.

"We've been here a while actually," said Harry. "Our dad had to go into work today so he dropped us off on his way."

"Oh right; have you decided where we're going to yet?" asked James.

"Yes I have," replied Ben. "We'll have to change trains on the outward journey, but there's a direct train back at 19:28."

"You mean that one that runs just once a week on a Saturday?" asked Paul.

"Yep," replied Ben.

"Well I hope we don't miss it," said James. "I'm not waiting a whole week for the next one!"

"Yeah well, I'm sure we won't, we've got plenty of time. We're taking the train to the next nearest station which is about three and a half miles away. It'll be an easy walk 'cos most of it is fairly flat," said Ben looking at the map. "Have you got your tickets yet?"

"No not yet," replied Paul.

"Well come on then, we don't wanna miss the 10:08," said Ben. Paul and James went over to the booking office and bought their tickets. The four of them then crossed to the correct platform and waited for the train. It turned up spot on time and they got on. It took them a good twenty minutes to get to where they needed to change trains. This was done fairly quickly as they'd only ten minutes between their train arriving and the next one departing, so they were soon on their way again.

After another half hour or so they arrived at the station they wanted. The four of them got off the train in the now very bright sunshine and left the station to walk to Ben's chose location. They walked along the road for a few hundred yards until they came to a level crossing. They crossed the railway line here and immediately turned left on to a footpath which ran alongside. Paul, James, Ben and Harry followed this path which gradually curved away from the railway line. Ben was leading the way and he kept glancing at the map to make sure they we're going the right way. After a good hour they we're well away from any form of human habitation, and Paul and James were wondering if they could go naturist, but neither said anything. James decided to take his T-shirt off so stopped very briefly. He hung it from the side of his rucksack and quickly caught the others up. A few moments later Paul did likewise as it was getting really hot. The four of them continued walking, and about ten minutes later, they came across a relatively large expanse of water. This is what Ben had seen when he looked on Google Earth. As they got nearer to the water's edge they moved a few yards off the path and arrived at the perfect spot. There was a very rocky area here with the water immediately below it. They had found a lake which had formed naturally over a great many years. They could jump in from a number of different points, the highest being about twenty feet above the water. Paul, James, Ben and Harry put their bags down, took out their towels and sat down on the edge of the grass. It was just after one o'clock now and was a very warm day indeed. "Well, what we waiting for?" asked Harry. "Why don't we strip off and jump in?"

"Just hang on a minute," replied Ben. "We don't know how deep it is yet - do we?"

"Yeah, my mum was telling me about that," said Paul. "We could get hurt jumping into water without checking how deep it is first."

"So who's going to check it?" asked James.

"I'll do it," replied Ben. So, after taking off his T-shirt, shorts, boxers, socks and trainers Ben put his sandals on and climbed down. This was fairly straightforward as there were plenty of places to get a good hold. Ben eased himself into the water and swam about. "I can't feel the bottom anywhere, but hang on a minute while I check deeper." Ben took a deep breath and ducked under the water. He swam downwards and still didn't touch the bottom. Wow this sure is deep, he thought as he made his way back to the surface. "Right, we're OK guys; jump in when you want, you won't touch the bottom 'cos it's mega deep."

"Oh brilliant," smiled Harry. Harry quickly stripped naked and jumped in. "Oh this is fantastic," he said after coming up and leisurely swimming about. Paul and James were next, and after quickly stripping off they too jumped in stark-naked.

"What do you think?" asked Ben.

"Brilliant, fantastic," replied Paul.

"Yeah, we've certainly found a good place here for skinny dipping," said James.

"And the water's lovely," added Harry. As they swam about for a few minutes Ben decided he didn't really need his sandals so he got out and took them off. He jumped in again from a bit higher up this time and swam over to the others. The four of them were really enjoying skinny dipping together outdoors.

"Well," said Paul. "Why don't we all get out and stand on the edge, then we can all jump in at once?"

"Yeah, why not," replied Ben. "Come on, let's do what Paul suggested. It'll be great all four of us jumping in together." Ben climbed out first followed by Paul, James and Harry. The four of them stood right on the edge about three to four feet from each other and paused. "After three," said Ben. "One, two, three, JUMP!" Paul, James, Ben and Harry all jumped in at once causing a huge splash and continued swimming about. They kept getting out and jumping back in until they decided to have a break and sit down on their towels. After lightly drying off Paul and James were a bit surprised to see Ben put his boxers back on. They both looked at Ben, "What?" he asked.

"Er, nothing," replied Paul. "I was just a bit surprised at you putting your boxers back on that's all."

"Er, OK then. I'll take them off, if you'd prefer us all to stay naked."

"Well, you've got to admit, it's nice being naked outside in the warm sunshine as well as skinny dipping don't you think," said James.

"Yeah, I s'pose you're right," said Ben. "It's just that Harry and I have never been naked much out of water. We love skinny dipping for sure, but we've never done anything else naked."

"Really?" asked Paul. "Well let's see if we can all stay naked until a few minutes before we get on that train at what-ever-time-it-was."

"19:28," said Ben.

"Right, well that's nearly half seven," said Paul. "So let's try and stay naked until quarter past. If that station has such a poor service I doubt there'll be any other passengers."

"Hmm, OK then," said Ben. "But what happens if someone walks past? Do you think we should put something on if we're not swimming about?"

"Not necessarily," said James. "Most people aren't too bothered about seeing skinny dippers and naturists."

"Oh well, if anyone does walk past I think I'll jump back in," said Ben.

A few moments later Harry climbed out and sat down on his towel between Paul and Ben. Paul and James laid back on their towels face up. "Hmm, this is the life," said Paul as he stretched out his arms.

"Do you like being naked outdoors?" asked Harry.

"Certainly do, don't we James," replied Paul.

"Yeah, sure we do. I love the warm sun on my skin," said James. Ben spread his towel out fully and laid back just like Paul and James.

"Do you know I think you're right, I could get used to this too," said Ben. "It is very relaxing sunbathing in the nude." Looking at how relaxed Paul, James and Ben were it wasn't long before Harry followed suit and laid down on his towel. A sudden and unexpected heat wave was making for a very warm day indeed and was perfect for a day's skinny dipping.

"I think we should all get some sun cream on now," suggested

Paul. "It's very hot and we don't want to end up burning, or worse, do we."

"Worse?" said Ben.

"Yeah, you can get skin cancer from too much sun and not enough protection," said Paul. "Here, get some on both of you."

"...and don't forget to do your privates," smiled James. Paul passed his sun cream around and all four of them slapped plenty on. They soaked up the afternoon sun for a good hour turning over occasionally. After which Paul decided to have his sandwiches and drink. James, Ben and Harry suddenly remembered they'd brought food with them too so decided it was time to have theirs as well. This was followed by another hour or so skinny dipping together.

"Do you want to move on soon?" Ben asked Paul and James.

"Yeah maybe," replied Paul. "I bet we've been here nearly four hours."

"What time is it now?" asked James.

"I'll have a look at my watch," replied Ben. Ben swam to the edge, climbed out and went over to his bag. He looked at his watch; "Ten to five," he called, and then jumped back in to be with the others. "Shall we call it a day here in ten minutes at five o'clock? Or do you want to stay here a bit longer?"

"Hmm, we'll stay here till five," said Paul.

"Well if we're only staying here another ten minutes I'm jumping in a few more times before we go," said Harry and he swam over to the edge and climbed out. Paul, James and Ben also climbed out and the four of them stood on the edge again.

"Why don't we jump in together again, but this time one after the other? I'll start counting," said Paul. "Ben you jump in on 'one', James you jump in on 'two', Harry you jump in on 'three' and I'll jump in on 'four'."

"OK then," said Ben. "Begin the count."

"One, two, three..." Ben jumped in first and was quickly followed by James and Harry with Paul jumping in last. All were swimming about again when James saw a group of people in the distance walking towards them.

"Er, I don't want to alarm anyone, but there's a family heading towards us."

"What we gonna do? Get out?" asked Harry.

"No, let's just stay in the water and calmly swim about," said Paul. "I doubt they'll bother us if we stay in here." This family slowly got closer and stopped about fifty yards away from where Paul, James, Ben and Harry had left their things. Feeling a bit guilty about being naked in the water and having no means of covering themselves up, the four of them kept on swimming about. After nearly ten minutes, one of them, the dad, called out; "Are you four staying in there all day?"

"Er, well. We didn't want to cause you any offence or embarrassment," said Ben slowly.

"It's quite alright. We were hoping to do a bit of skinny dipping ourselves seeing as it's such as nice day."

"Then please, come and be our guests; the water's lovely!" shouted Paul. Paul then suddenly splashed about at the thought of more skinny dippers. This was also a huge 'green light' to this family's three children and they were soon stripped naked. They were twin boys, about Harry's age, and their younger sister. They stood on the edge for a moment before jumping in together. Their parents stayed where they were for a few minutes, but couldn't resist joining in the fun of an outdoor skinny dip. It was now a truly amazing sight. There were nine naked persons all swimming about and enjoying themselves. Harry remembered he'd brought his football with him so climbed out to get it. He threw it into the middle of the mêlée of skinny dippers. One of the twin boys was nearest and swam after it. All nine of them were having a whale of a time playing together in the water with Harry's football. It appeared they'd all forgotten about being naked so much so none of them noticed an elderly couple walk past with faces like stone. Paul, James, Ben and Harry eventually decided to get out and continue their walk. As they dried off Paul said; "Right, shall we all stay naked like we agreed and walk as far as we can in the warm sunshine?"

"Yeah, I'd like that," replied Harry.

"OK then Paul," said Ben. "Let's pack all our clothes and things into our rucksacks and walk naked." It was just after quarter to six when all four of them walked away together in the nude.

They'd only been walking for a few minutes when Harry said;

"Do you know, I quite like walking about like this. It feels really nice in the warm sunshine."

"That's how we feel as well," said Paul.

"We were nervous at first as you know, but I can't get enough of it now," smiled James. "I like to spend as much time as possible in the nude."

"Same here! Have we won you both over yet?" asked Paul.

"Yeah, I think so," replied Ben.

"Harry?"

"Yeah, you've sure won me over."

"Excellent!" said Paul.

A short time later the four of them came to a wood and they followed the path through the trees. It was a wonderful experience walking through the trees naked and neither Paul, James, Ben nor Harry had ever done this before. Although quite dense in places the trees did let in a reasonable amount of sunlight. After ten minutes or so they came to a small clearing which was no more than a hundred yards across. "Why don't we stop here for a break?" asked Ben. "It's only half a mile or so to the station and we've still got well over an hour to kill."

"OK then, let's put our bags down," replied Paul. They put their bags down and Harry took out his football.

"Anyone fancy a nude kick about?" he asked.

"Yeah go on then," replied James. Although he didn't like playing football at school, James was more than happy to participate in a nude kick about in the woods.

"Come on then let's all have a kick about while we're still naked," added Ben. All four of them started by gently passing the ball to each other, but then they decided to go up a gear by moving further apart and putting more energy into it. Ben gave it a really good kick and sent it into the trees where it got stuck.

"Oh no!" exclaimed Harry. "How we gonna get it down?"

"Don't worry," said Paul. "Find a few stones and throw them up at it." This they did but without any success.

"Why don't I try and climb up the tree," suggested Ben.

"Go on then," said Harry. "It was you what kicked it up there."

"OK, I'm having a go!" snapped Ben. So wearing only his sandals Ben began to climb up the tree. He got fairly close but couldn't quite reach it. "Someone pass me a stick, I might just be able to dislodge it." Paul handed Ben a rather large branch and with that he managed to knock Harry's football out of the trees.

"Oh well done!" shouted Harry happy at getting his football back. Paul, James, Ben and Harry continued their nude kick about in the woods a bit longer and it was about ten to seven when Ben called a halt.

"It's just after ten to seven now guys, and I think we ought to be making a move."

"Yeah, we don't wanna miss that train do we," smiled Paul. The four of them each had a quick drink then picked up their bags and headed off.

They got to within sight of the station when Ben said; "I can see the station up ahead. Do you think we should put some clothes on now?"

"Yeah, it might be a good idea to stop for a minute and put our shorts on," suggested Paul. "Let's put just our shorts on and nothing else. We can't really expect to be naked on the station, but this will be the closest we can get."

"OK then," replied Ben. The four of them put on their shorts and continued the last couple of hundred yards to the station.

As they walked onto the platform Harry said; "Blimey, do trains actually stop here?"

"Yes they do, but as I said before it only happens once a week on this side," replied Ben. The platform basically resembled a jungle, and was full of weeds and moss, but there were just a few short yards of clear platform. James found a discarded ticket with a date of nearly two years ago!

"Hey, look at this ticket. It's nearly two years old!"

"Hmm, I wonder how many tickets have been issued since then," said Ben.

"Not many," suggested James. "In fact, I wouldn't mind betting we're going to be next to buy a ticket from here."

The four of them sat down on a bench and waited for this apparent 'ghost' train. While they were waiting a couple of express trains passed through without stopping. Paul got up and had a walk along the platform. "Paul, it's nearly half past seven," called Ben. Paul walked back and stood in front of Ben.

"Are you sure we're gonna get on a train here? We're in the middle of flaming nowhere!"

"I'll ask the signalman in a few m…, hang on," said Ben. The signalman had walked down to open the level crossing gates for another train. "This could be our train." They waited and sure enough a train came into view, but this clearly wasn't what they were waiting for. It was a long train of petrol tankers and it staggered through the station. One locomotive had broken down and the other one was really struggling to pull the train. Once clear of the crossing the signalman opened the gates for the traffic to cross. As he did so he saw them and called out.

"Don't worry lads. It'll be here in about ten to twelve minutes.

"Thanks," said Paul. "We were beginning to worry it being only one a week."

"Tell me about it! You're the first I've ever seen wait for the Saturday train on that side, and I've worked here for nearly eight years."

"Really?" asked James in surprise. "Eight years!"

"Yep. There's a train on this side once a day at 07:28, except for Sundays; but I've only ever seen the occasional passenger use it." There was the sound of a bell in the signal box and the signalman dashed inside.

"Let's get our T-shirts on now," said Paul. "This could be our train coming." The signalman came out again and opened the gates for another train. This one was heading the other way and went through at some speed. After it had gone the signalman stayed where he was.

"This is your train coming now," he said. "Don't forget to stick your hand out, it only stops on request."

"I'll stick my hand out," said Paul. "I don't want to have to sit here a week!" The train arrived about fifteen minutes late and the driver tooted his horn on seeing Paul with his hand out. It stopped with the leading coach in the weed infested part of the platform. Paul, James, Ben and Harry got on at the rear door where the conductor was and once on board he signalled the driver away. The conductor was really surprised at having business at this station.

"I haven't stopped there for ages," he said.

"Then you get four of us at once," smiled James.

"Have you got tickets?"

"No not from here, but we were told we could use them from here on our way back as it's the same price."

"Yeah, that's fine," said the conductor. "Unless of course you'd like to buy a ticket with this station on it."

"How much?" asked Paul.

"It's £1:15 to the next stop, and if all four of you buy a ticket you'll add four points to the annual passenger count."

"Come on then, it'll be a bit of a novelty won't it," said Ben. Each of them bought a ticket from the conductor baring the name of the station they'd joined at. "We should keep these tickets safe. If they ever close that station we can say we used it today."

"Would these tickets have any historical value?" asked James.

"Maybe, but not for some time," replied Ben.

Although it was slow this train took Paul, James, Ben and Harry straight home without them needing to change. "I've really enjoyed today," said Paul. "We must do this again sometime don't you think."

"Sure do, but when?" asked Ben.

"What about tomorrow?" suggested Harry.

"I don't think mum and dad will let us do that so soon after today Harry."

"You could always ask them," said James.

"Yeah, I s'pose we could, but even if we do go out it'll have to be cheaper than today. Today's cost us about twenty quid," said Ben.

"It's cost mum and dad twenty quid," chipped in Harry. "But it hasn't exactly cost us anything."

"Yeah OK, I know," said Ben.

It wasn't long before they arrived back where they'd started, and the four of them alighted from the train and walked over to the bus stop. "I think we'll leave it for a couple of weeks," said Ben. "We've really enjoyed today, haven't we Harry?"

"Certainly have," replied Harry. "I've never spent so long in the nude before."

"Our bus is coming now so we'll have to say good bye," said James.

"Here's my mobile number," said Paul as he scribbled his number down on a scrap of paper.

"Thanks," said Ben. "I'll text you some time, bye for now."

"Bye Paul, bye James," said Harry.

"Bye."

Paul and James were now on their way home after a really enjoyable day out skinny dipping, and walking about and playing football naked in the woods. "I love spending time with Ben and Harry, don't you?" asked James.

"Of course," replied Paul. "I wonder where we'll go next time we have a day out together."

"Well, we'll just have to wait and see, won't we," smiled James.

Chapter 9

Although Paul and James were still relatively new to naturism they knew in their own hearts they loved it and every time there was a naturist swim at their local leisure centre, twice a month, they were there. Usually with a parent or two, but not always. Whilst at one of these swims a few weeks after being found by Peter Simpkin, Paul and James were talking to Alice and Craig Ruston and their mum and dad. The subject of beaches drifted into the conversation and Alice asked them; "Have either of you ever been to a naturist beach?"

"No we haven't," replied Paul quickly. "But we'd love to go to one, wouldn't we James."

"Oh yeah, sure we would. Beaches are great fun, but we've never ever been naked on one," added James.

"Well, we're going camping close to Morfa Dyffryn on the Welsh coast next weekend. Why don't you both come with us?" asked Alice.

"Thanks very much. We'd love to come with you," replied Paul.

"We'll have to ask our parents first, but I don't think they'll mind," said James. Alice then turned to her mum.

"Mum, is it OK for Paul and James to come with us next weekend? Please say yes, please mum."

"Yes of course they can come with us. The tent sleeps six," said Alice's mum.

"What about bedding? Have you both got sleeping bags?" asked Alice.

"Yeah we have," replied Paul. "We'll ask our mums and dads if we can go with you when we get home."

"Great stuff," said Alice. "I really hope you can come with us."

Paul and James were on their own on this occasion. So as soon as they got home they told their parents what Alice had said. It was to be their first visit to a naturist beach.

"Mum, would you mind if I go away for the weekend with Alice and Craig, and their mum and dad?"

"Hmm, I don't see why not. How many nights are you planning on being away?"

"Three," replied Paul. "Friday to Monday. Don't forget it's the last week of term this week and we usually finish early on the last day, Friday. Alice's Dad's not working on Monday otherwise it would have only been two nights."

"Yes OK love. I don't think your dad will mind. We'll see what he has to say when he gets home."

Just after nine o'clock next morning, Sunday, Paul went to see James and to find out if he'd asked his mum and dad about going away for the weekend with the Rustons. James answered the door and let Paul in. "Hi, have you asked your folks about next weekend?" asked Paul.

"Oh yeah, no problem. My mum and dad told me to have a good time and enjoy it. What about your folks?"

"Yeah, they said it's OK," replied Paul. "I'm really looking forward to going now aren't you?"

"Sure am. I just hope the weather doesn't spoil it," said James.

"Yeah, I'll certainly second that," added Paul. "Do you fancy going to our usual spot near the railway line today?"

"Yeah, why not? It's a nice enough day," replied James.

"Right, just hang on a minute while I get a few things." Paul went back to get his sports bag and the usual bottles of water, orange juice, sun cream, a couple of towels and his tennis ball. James got a few thing together as well and they set off just after half nine. This time when they got past the railway crossing Paul said; "I think it's quiet enough here. Shall we go naked here and walk to our usual spot naturist?"

"Yeah, why not," replied James. Paul and James had a good look around. There was no sign of anyone else, so they took off everything they were wearing and put their trainers back on.

"Let's put our clothes in our bags, that way we can't suddenly go 'textile'. If anyone else is walking around and sees us we'll just be honest and tell them we're naturists, OK?"

"Yeah, fine," replied James. Paul and James continued to walk to their favourite spot wearing only their trainers. "Do you know, I really can't get enough of walking around like this, it's just so enjoyable. I feel as free as a bird and I love the warm sun on my skin."

"Same here," smiled Paul. "It's a shame we couldn't have gone naked earlier that day when we were with Ben and Harry."

"Yeah, I was thinking the same thing," added James. "I'm sure we could've gone naked once we were far enough away from the railway line, and they did say they liked being naked didn't they."

"Yeah they did, but that was after we'd all been skinny dipping together. So a naked walk and a kick about in the woods wasn't that difficult for them."

"True, but after skinny dipping together it was great fun kicking a football about in the nude, don't you think."

"Yeah, course I do." Paul paused for moment; "Hmm; well would you believe it!" scoffed Paul. "All this time we've hated playing football and what not at school. Then we kick a football about for half an hour or so while we're naked in the woods and really love it!" James had a sudden thought.

"Paul! We can't do that at school. We'd get the ball kicked right at us." Paul laughed at what he thought James just said.

"Of course we can't do it naked when we're at school. I was just comparing the two different situations that's all. Neither of us likes it when we're part of a full class of kids playing football at school 'cos it's a proper game and it's fast paced and rough. I've also known a few kids get hurt; but when it's informal and just a small group, like when we were with Ben and Harry, it was really enjoyable."

"...and the four of us being naked made it even more enjoyable didn't it."

"Yeah, sure it did."

Paul and James continued walking to their favourite spot and when they got there who should they see - the naked man. He was lying face up on his orange towel. Paul and James wondered if the naked man had come here in the hope of meeting them and they were right. The naked man heard them and looked up from where he was laid. Paul and James stayed where they were.

"Morning," said the naked man. "Are you the two lads I saw here a few weeks back?"

"Yes probably," replied Paul. "How long have you been doing this?"

"You mean how long have I been a naturist?"

"Oh yeah, sorry."

"Just over eight years now. I started when I was twenty nine and I'm thirty seven now. My only regret is I wished I'd started earlier like you two, but I was such a shy child. How old are you two, if you don't mind me asking?"

"We're both fourteen, but we'll turn fifteen in a month or so," said Paul.

"What made you decide to become a naturist?" asked James.

"I'm not sure really. I just took off my clothes one hot sunny day and enjoyed the feeling. I didn't know there was a naturist movement in the UK and private swims you could go to. I found that out later. What about you two, what encouraged the pair of you to give naturism a try?" Paul and James looked at each other and smiled.

"You tell him Paul," whispered James. The naked man looked interested.

"Go on then," he said. "I'm listening."

"Well, it was about two months ago. We saw you walking along a footpath over that way somewhere," said Paul pointing in the appropriate direction. "We didn't realise you were naked at first. It was only when you got closer we found that out."

"We didn't want to scare you so we moved off the path and into the trees while you walked past us," said James.

"...and then we decided to follow you. We stayed within sight of you most of the day," said Paul.

"So at what point did you take your clothes off?" asked the naked man.

"It was when you were lying down sunbathing. James had gone to fetch us both some fish and chips. I stayed and kept watch. After a few minutes I took my T-shirt off then my trainers and socks. I waited a few more minutes and then, feeling somewhat nervous, took off my shorts and boxers. I stood up completely naked. I wanted to feel what you were feeling."

"What did you think?" asked the naked man.

"I felt very exposed and vulnerable at first, but I did like the warm sun and gentle breeze on my skin. It felt really nice." Paul continued to explain to the naked man how he told James about what he'd done while he was away.

"I'm Nathan," said the naked man. "What are your names?"

"I'm Paul."

"And I'm James."

"What was it like the moment you first saw each other naked?" asked Nathan "Were you nervous?"

"Certainly was," said James. "I've never been anywhere naked, except in the showers at school, and I hated having to do that. However naturism is different, it's relaxing and enjoyable. You feel free and unrestricted by clothes. We were here towards the end of May and practiced being naked. We were scared to death initially, but we helped each other overcome our fears. We later found out we were gymnophobic and together we slowly managed to overcome it. We love being naked now, don't we Paul?"

"Yeah, sure we do."

"Oh yes, I remember seeing you walking about naked and throwing a ball. You obviously didn't see me."

"No we didn't!" replied James sharply.

"How did you find out about the swim and actually get in?" asked Nathan.

"We found out about the swim the next day," replied Paul. "While you were clothed did you walk across the railway crossing, check your map and then re-cross?"

"Hmm, yes I do seem to remember doing that. I was going to go naked there and then, but I changed my mind after I saw two lads looking down from the top of the hill."

"Sorry. That would've been James and me. We were wondering if we'd see you again, but when we did see you, you were clothed and we didn't think it was you, as in the naked man we'd seen the previous day."

"Oh right, so I could've gone naked there after all and you wouldn't have been bothered would you, but what's this got to do with the swim?"

"Well, when we got fed up of hanging about, we walked around for a bit and found a flyer for the swim which presumably you'd dropped when you checked your map," said Paul.

"The flyer for the swim! I wondered where I'd lost that. So

how did you both get in without anyone finding out?" asked Nathan. "I'll be honest here, Peter Simpkin is quite strict about who gets in and who doesn't."

"Yeah, we know that now," said James suddenly remembering the uncomfortable moment when they were discovered swimming naked and without permission.

"Well, we went for a normal swim on Friday evening, the day before, and checked the place out. That way we found somewhere to hide after closing time," replied Paul.

"We also met two lads on our way out and they're now good friends of ours," said James.

"Yeah we did," smiled Paul. "After swimming we decided to shower for a few minutes, but as we approached we were quite surprised at seeing a man and a young boy, his son I guess, showering naked. After they'd gone we went in and I felt we should do the same so we took off our shorts and showered naked too. James was a bit nervous at first, weren't you, but we did it and that's when we met Ben and Harry."

"Yeah, they joined us in the shower and weren't a bit bothered about seeing us naked," said James. "It was only a matter of seconds before they took their swimming trunks off too. Showering naked together like that and not being bothered who sees what helped us feel more confident than ever, especially me," continued James.

"Well it's wonderful to hear that. You obviously enjoy being naked now don't you?"

"We certainly do," replied Paul firmly. "There's something else we must tell about before we forget. A bit later that evening while still showering in the nude, Ben, the older of the two lads we met, stepped out of the shower area and had a look at the small pool. He told us the cover hadn't been pulled over it and so suggested a quick skinny dip."

"I couldn't believe I was about to skinny dip for the first time in my life," said James.

"We left our swimwear in the shower area and tiptoed through to the small pool. It was fairly dark 'cos the lights had been turned off. The four of us carefully got in and gently swam about in the nude for the first time in our lives."

"My word you've got some nerve. I wouldn't have dared do that, especially when I was your age," said Nathan.

"Well, it was OK for the first five minutes or so, but a cleaner was working her way along the balcony towards us and she slammed a couple of doors, one of which had a window which smashed. It scared us half to death."

"But after a few terrifying minutes Paul saw she was wearing earphones, so that was when we got out and went back into the shower area."

"So what did you do after that?" asked Nathan.

"We got dried and dressed after that and went home, but we went again on Saturday, the day of the naturist swim, and just after six o'clock we hid in the group changing room toilet."

"Yeah, we were in there nearly an hour, but it was definitely worth it in the long run," said James.

"I checked the time on my mobile phone, and after hearing voices and the sound of people moving about, I carefully opened the toilet door and the changing room was empty. We quickly got out and walked across to the main door. I opened it very slightly and looked through the gap. Not surprisingly, everyone I saw, mums, dads, kids; everybody, were all completely naked! We simply whipped off our shorts and joined in, naked, like everybody else. Looking back it wasn't really all that difficult," said Paul looking somewhat pleased.

"Well I must say, I've never heard of anyone doing that before," said Nathan.

"That's why we were here a couple of days beforehand. We were trying to get used to the idea of being naked so that we'd be as relaxed as possible. We didn't want to draw attention to ourselves. I remember saying to James, if we wanna get in to see what's going on the best disguise is going to be our birthday suits."

"Did it work?" asked Nathan.

"Well it did to start with. We were having a really great time swimming about naked and playing on the inflatable," replied Paul.

"Yeah we did, but I thought the slide was the best bit. You go a lot faster sliding down on your bare bum!" laughed James.

"About halfway through Mr. Simpkin came up to us and asked us where our parents were. We panicked and lied initially, but it was near the end when he finally put two and two together and found our parents were nowhere to be seen. It was a bit embarrassing that, but I thought it best to come clean even though we were worried what might happen. Mr. Simpkin gave us a lift home and talked to our parents together. We thought we were going to be in big trouble, but we couldn't have been more wrong. After all, we did tell our parents we were going swimming; we just didn't mention it was nude," smiled Paul.

"Oh yes I remember talking to you briefly in the changing room. You looked to be on the nervous side, understandable if it was your first time and you'd sneaked in," laughed Nathan.

"Yes, well, perhaps you're right there," said Paul.

"To kill time during the day we went for a walk in the countryside and although it was very cold, we did swim in the river naked," added James.

"Later in the afternoon we walked back to the railway station naked and only got dressed for the last hundred yards or so," said Paul.

"...and we past a girl while we were naked and she didn't even notice," added James quickly.

"Now there's a bit more to that isn't there James? You know why she didn't notice us don't you," said Paul in a way which made James feel about five years old!

"Yeah, yeah I know, she was reading a magazine; but I'll never forget what you said after she'd gone!" giggled James.

"Well it sounds to me like a very positive start you've both made."

"You really think so?" asked Paul.

"Oh I do. It took me a lot longer before I swam naked, and even then it was after dark and I was on my own. I enjoyed it so much I went back to the same place quite a few times."

"Really?" asked James. "Where was that?"

"Stainforth," said Nathan. "It's in the Yorkshire Dales a couple of miles north of Settle. Do you know it?"

"No we don't, but we'll certainly be checking it out," replied Paul enthusiastically.

"Well I'm sure you'll enjoy it. There's at least half a dozen points you can jump into the river from, but if you want to do it naked you'll have to chose your moment carefully. It can get pretty busy at times, especially on a hot day. I couldn't go naked the first time because there were far too many 'textiles' about," said Nathan. "So I went again a week or two later and stayed there till nearly midnight. It was wonderful and so peaceful. Anyway, I'm afraid I'm going to have to leave you alone now. I've got to go to work in just over an hour. It's been nice talking to you both and I'm sure our paths will cross again in the future. All the best then, bye for now."

"Bye Nathan," said Paul and James. Nathan collected his things and walked off leaving Paul and James alone.

"He seems like a decent sort of guy doesn't he," said James. Paul's attention was momentarily distracted. He remembered what his mum had said about adults showing an unhealthy interest in him, but didn't mention it to James.

"Yeah, not bad. If he's been a naturist for eight years he should be reliable enough."

Paul and James stayed where they were for about an hour and a half soaking up the sun. Their all over tans were now quite good and they were enjoying improving them.

"What else do you think we can do while we're naked?" asked James while lying face-down on his towel.

"I'm not sure really," replied Paul. "We've done the obvious, sunbathing, swimming and walking now quite a few times haven't we? It's a pity we haven't got bikes. We could go on a nude bike ride."

"Hey that'd be good, but where could we ride naked? Someone would be sure to see us do that."

"Yes, exactly!"

"Anyway, neither of us has a bike so it's pointless getting worried about something we can't do. Shall we get up and walk about a bit? We could leave our things here and just walk into the trees naked. I doubt anyone will see us," said James smiling broadly.

"Tell you what, why don't we pack all our things away and hide our bags, somewhere where nobody else will find them by accident."

"OK then. Where do you think we can hide our bags?"

"Oh not far. We just have to find somewhere away from any paths," said Paul. Paul and James packed their things away and walked a couple of hundred yards.

"Right, let's put our bags down here behind this bush." Paul pushed his bag and James's out of sight into some thick bushes. "Now then," said Paul stretching his arms wide and smiling. "Now we've just our trainers on and nothing to carry, we can walk about, or run about if you like, completely naked and in the warm sunshine."

"Race you to that gate over there then," said James quickly, and off he sprinted.

"Hey, that's not fair!" shouted Paul running to catch James up. James stopped at the gate and waited for Paul. "That wasn't fair," said Paul. "You ran off before I could catch my breath."

"Sorry, I was only wanting to have a good run round naked. Shall we walk up to the top of the hill and look around."

"OK, go on then," replied Paul. Paul and James began walking up the hillside. There was the remains of a very old building here. They continued to walk slowly up to the top in case there was anyone else about, but thankfully for them, there wasn't. Paul and James walked around and through the old ruined building. There was very little left here of the once extensive house which had been ruined a great many years ago. They stood side by side on a raised point of the ruin and admired the view across the valley.

"Isn't this absolutely fantastic," said James.

"You took the words right out of my mouth," replied Paul. "It's a wonderful view, and standing here naked with the warm sunshine and gentle breeze caressing our bodies - well, it's just so nice."

"I know what you mean. I'd love to stay like this for ages," said James.

After nearly an hour wandering about in the nude, Paul saw someone in the distance who appeared to be heading their way. "James, I think we should move on, look, someone's coming over."

"OK then," said James. Paul and James headed back to the

spot where they'd left their things. They walked passed a large bush only to be greeted head-on by a woman and her son and daughter with their dog.

"W-What on earth are you two doing?" asked the woman with a shock. James ran off closely followed by Paul.

"Sorry, we're naturists," said Paul as he continued to run after James. James stopped as soon as he was out of sight of the woman and her children.

"That was close," he said.

"What do you mean close, she saw us and her kids were laughing," said Paul.

"I bet they've never seen anyone naked before," smiled James.

"Look, let's lie low for a few minutes. I know I like doing this as much as you do, but not in front of clothed people. Come on, let's go and get our bags and go back to our usual spot. I don't know about you, but I feel like relaxing after all that running about." Paul and James walked back to their usual spot, spread their towels out again and laid down.

The sun's heat was cooling down now because it was after six o'clock. They finished off the water and orange juice, then about half an hour later, decided to call it a day and head home. Paul and James, now more confident than ever at being naked outdoors, walked most of the way home in the nude. They stopped just short of the main road and put their shorts and T-shirts back on for the last few yards.

After tea Paul's mum and dad said they were going out with James's parents for a drink and a chat. The Handles came round just after half seven.

"Are you two going to be OK for a couple of hours?" asked Paul's mum.

"Yeah sure. When will you be back?" asked Paul.

"About half nine or just after."

"OK then, have a good evening," said Paul as his parents left the house with James's mum and dad. Paul went back into the front room where James was sat. He was smirking as Paul looked across at him.

"What?" asked Paul.

"We've the house to ourselves till half nine and you can't think of something to do?"

"Well I was thinking we could watch TV or play a game perhaps."

"So was I," smiled James. "But if you draw the curtains we can do it naked, fully naked seeing as we're inside can't we."

"Oh yeah, I don't see why not," said Paul. "Sorry, I was a bit slow there wasn't I." Paul and James quickly took off their clothes. They sat down in the nude and watched TV for half an hour or so after which Paul turned it off. Paul and James then decided to play Monopoly again.

"I suppose this is another 'first'. I've not played nude Monopoly before," said James.

"No neither have I," replied Paul. "I'm really looking forward to next weekend when we go to Wales with the Rustons, aren't you?"

"Sure am. I bet this week goes really slowly for us. Why don't you check your sleeping bag. It'd be better to do it now rather than have to buy a new one on the day." Paul and James put the Monopoly away and went upstairs to Paul's bedroom. They looked through the cupboards and found Paul's sleeping bag to be a little dusty, but perfectly usable.

"I think it needs a wash before I sleep in it," said Paul.

"Yeah, I think so too," added James. "I'll check mine when I get home later. What else we gonna need?"

"A few clothes I suppose, but not too many if we're spending most of the time naked. We'll need toiletry things, you know, shower gel, shampoo, toothbrush and paste, sponge, towels and deodorant."

"Do you think we can get all this stuff by Friday?" asked James.

"I think so. Ask your mum. I'll ask my mum when she gets back." Just then Paul and James heard the front door open. Their parents were back. "Oh no!" said Paul. "Our parents are back!"

"Uh oh," said James. "How we gonna explain being naked again?"

"Paul! James!" called Paul's mum from downstairs. "Where are you?"

"We're up here in my bedroom mum," replied Paul. Paul quickly got out his box of games.

"The cards," said James.

"No, they'll think we've been playing strip snap or something if they come in. Get the Dominoes," said Paul. James quickly took out the box of Dominoes and emptied them out on to the floor. They each took a handful and pushed the rest to one side.

"We should have seven each," said James.

"I know that, I was just trying to make it look convincing if my mum or dad walked in." Paul and James laid a few Dominoes out on the floor to make it look like they were playing the game. They listened intently. Their parents we're talking downstairs.

"Boys, we're just going next door for a few minutes, won't be long," said Paul's mum. The four of them left the Jessop house and went next door.

"That was close," said James.

"Yeah, I think we should go downstairs now and keep our shorts to hand at the very least," said Paul.

"Good idea," replied James. Paul and James went downstairs and into the front room. They'd no sooner got there when Paul's mum came back in unexpectedly, she'd forgotten something.

"Oh my goodness me!" she said in amazement. "Can't you two keep your clothes on."

"Sorry mum," said Paul looking for his shorts. "We really like being naked, don't we James?"

"Oh yeah, absolutely," replied James.

"Well if someone comes to the front door and we're out, please put something on before you answer it."

"What, even if it's Jehovah's witnesses," giggled Paul and James.

"Yes, ha ha very funny," replied Paul's mum. "I'm going back next door for a few minutes now. I think your mum and dad would like you to go home when Paul's dad and I come back James."

"Yeah OK, thanks Mrs. Jessop." Paul and James were alone again and still naked. Mrs. Jessop went back to join the others.

"I think we need to have a little talk about our sons," she said as she went in.

"Oh yeah," said James's dad. "What've they been up to now?"

"Not a lot. When I went back to get my handbag I found them sat in the front room."

"So what's wrong with that?" asked James's dad looking mildly puzzled.

"They were both naked!"

"Oh my word! They seem to have a thing about being naked don't they."

"Were they sat together on the sofa or on separate chairs?" asked James's mum.

"Paul appeared to be looking for his shorts when I walked in and James was sat on the sofa and didn't seem to care."

"I don't think we need to worry. If we ever catch them naked and loved up together we'll certainly talk to them then," smiled James's dad.

Paul and James had gone back upstairs with their shorts and T-shirts. They continued to play Dominoes until they heard the front door again. Paul's parents had come home so they put their clothes on and went downstairs.

"I think it's time for me to go now," said James.

"Right, OK then. I'll see you tomorrow, bye James." Paul saw James out and then joined his parents in the front room.

"Paul love come and sit down," said his mum. "If you're thinking of going away for the weekend with Alice and Craig, you'll need to get a few things together."

"Yes mum, I've already had a look at my sleeping bag. It needs a wash, but other than that I think it should be OK."

"Oh good. You'll need a couple of towels and a toiletry bag as well."

"Yeah, I know. I'm rather tired now mum. I'll sort my other stuff out when I come home from school tomorrow. I'm going up to bed now, night mum, night dad."

"Night love," said his parents.

Chapter 10

The week did seem to go very slowly for Paul and James, but eventually Friday came. With the absence of a lunch break they finished school at quarter to two and went straight home. Both Paul and James wasted no time at all in getting out of their school uniforms. It was now the main summer holiday. Alice and Craig's dad rang Paul and James to tell them he'd pick them up at about half past four. That gave them approximately two hours to pack. James was first and came round and knocked on the Jessop's front door. Paul answered the door and let James in. "Are you ready?" he asked.

"Nearly," replied Paul. "We've still got a good half hour; it's not even four o'clock yet."

"Yeah, I know. My mum always thinks I'll end up being late if I rush at the last minute. I've double checked everything I've got so I don't think I've forgotten anything."

"Good. Right, that's me done as well," said Paul as he zipped up his sports bag. "I've also got a new bottle of sun cream, in case it's very hot. My mum says the forecast is good. 'A mini heat wave' were her words."

"Really, that's excellent," smiled James. "Just what we need."

"Yes, well, we'd better watch out we don't end up sunburnt. A sunburnt bum or a sunburnt you-know-what will be about as painful as it will be embarrassing," said Paul.

Paul and James waited for the Rustons to arrive. They turned up just after twenty past four. Mr. Ruston got out of the car and went across to call for Paul first, unaware of course they were together. Mrs. Jessop answered the door.

"Oh hello. You must be Alice and Craig's dad."

"Yes that's right, I'm Martin Ruston. Is Paul ready?"

"Yes he is. James is here too."

"Oh right, OK. I think we'd better let James's parents know we're here and about to leave," said Mr. Ruston. Paul and James put their bags in Mr. Ruston's car and then came back to tell James's mum and dad they were going.

"Mum, Dad, we're going," said James.

"Right, OK then. Thanks very much for letting us know and have a good weekend both of you," said James's mum as they left. Paul and James got into Mr. Ruston's car, which, by the way, was one of those people carrier type cars. They set off for the Welsh coast at twenty to five. It was a three to four hour drive to Morfa Dyffryn with usually one or two stops on the way, so it was nearly half past eight when they arrived at the campsite. Mr. and Mrs. Ruston took all the camping equipment, including the tent, out of the car and laid everything out on the grass. They were used to putting up the tent, so with a little help from the children, it only took them about twenty minutes or so.

Although the main part of this short holiday was to go naked, the campsite was 'textile'. Everyone settled in and enjoyed a bit of supper. They sat talking for a while until nearly half ten when they all decided to get some sleep.

The next day started very clear and bright and stayed that way. Everyone was awake by half past eight, so after a few more minutes lazing around, decided to get up. Paul was first to put his head out of the tent and get a breath of fresh air. "Hmm, it looks very nice out here," he said. "I think my mum was right; it is going to be a warm weekend," continued Paul as he brought his head back inside the tent. "Have we got time to shower before breakfast?"

"Yes if you like," replied Mrs. Ruston. "I think we should all shower. It'll give us a chance to freshen up before breakfast. Come on you two, get out of bed now and stop messing about," said Mrs. Ruston to her son and daughter.

"Alice, Craig, come on. Let's get over to the showers with Paul and James," said their dad. All six of them walked over to the shower block, showered and then walked back to the tent. They all enjoyed a full English breakfast in the morning sunshine.

After breakfast Mr. and Mrs. Ruston tidied up while Alice and Craig collected a few things to take with them to the beach. Paul and James took their towels, sun cream and a couple bottles of water.

It was quarter to ten when all six of them left the campsite and headed down to the beach. The beach was only a five minute walk directly, but it was a good ten to fifteen minutes to the naturist area. Paul, James and the Rustons walked a good way in and put their things down. All six of them then quickly stripped off without a word. "Race you to the sea!" shouted Alice. Paul, James and Craig ran after Alice straight into the sea. It was pleasantly mild and the four of them were enjoying swimming and splashing about with nothing on. After a few minutes or so they got out and went back to where Alice and Craig's parents had set up their things.

"I think you should get some sun cream on now," said Alice and Craig's mum. "It's very warm and we don't want you to burn do we?"

"No mum," replied Alice. Paul took his sun cream out of his bag, slapped plenty on, and then past it to James. The six of them then spent the best part of an hour lying down on their towels soaking up the sun, but it wasn't long before they were disturbed. An ice cream van drove on to the beach and stopped about a hundred yards away from them in the middle of the naturist area.

"Anyone fancy an ice cream?" asked Mr. Ruston sitting up.

"Yes please dad," said Alice and Craig.

"Paul, James; would either of you like an ice cream?"

"Yes thanks," replied Paul. "Come on James, let's go and help Mr. Ruston with the ice creams." Paul and James accompanied Mr. Ruston to the ice cream van. They came back a few minutes later with an array of ice creams, all of which were enjoyed in the now very warm sunshine.

After relaxing, Alice and Craig's dad joined the children swimming about in the sea while their mum read a book, but she wasn't reading it for very long.

"Cath, Catherine. Come on, come and join us in the sea. It's lovely!"

"Come on mum, dad's right," added Craig.

"OK, I'm coming." Mrs. Ruston put her book down and joined the rest of them in the sea. Paul remembered he had a tennis ball in his bag from earlier so quickly got out to get it.

"Shall we play throw and catch?" asked Paul holding up the ball.

"To me!" shouted Alice. Paul threw the ball to Alice then Alice threw it to her mum. Their mum threw it to Craig who dropped it. He swam after it and threw it to his dad. All six of them enjoyed playing throw and catch and after a few minutes Mr. Ruston went to get his camera. He took some photos of his wife and kids playing in the sea with Paul's tennis ball.

"Dad, can Paul and James be photographed with us?" asked Alice keen to include her new friends as much as possible. Both Paul and James clearly heard Alice say this, and, although they weren't too bothered about being photographed naked themselves, they were wondering if Mr. Ruston would be OK at doing it.

"Paul, James, could you come here a minute please?" asked Mr. Ruston. They walked over to him and he tentatively told them, "Look, this could be a bit awkward. I'm sure you don't need me to tell you that taking photographs of naked children..."

"It's OK, Mr. Ruston, really. I know what you're trying to say. We're OK at being photographed naked on the beach, aren't we James." said Paul turning his attention to James and hoping he'd agree.

"Yeah fine. I can understand why you had to mention it," said James. "Just one thing though."

"What's that?" asked Mr. Ruston.

"Can Paul and me have a copy of the photos when we get back home?"

"Of course you can," smiled Mr. Ruston. "Both of you can have a copy each. How does that sound?"

"Great, thanks Mr. Ruston," smiled Paul.

"Come on, let's go back and join the others in the sea." Mr. Ruston took some more photos of everyone while they continued having fun. He then asked his wife to take a few photos while he played about in the sea with kids. While they were enjoying doing this Paul had an idea. He was wondering if it would be possible to get a photograph with all six of them on.

"Mr. Ruston, can you take a group photograph of us all with your camera? Or would we have to get someone else to take it?"

"Hmm, that's a nice thought Paul, and yes my camera is capable of doing that, but unfortunately I don't have a tripod to put it on."

"Do you think we could ask that old man over there?"

"Yes OK, go on then." Paul and Mr. Ruston went over to the old man and asked him if he'd be kind enough to take a photograph of them all together. He said he'd be delighted to help.

"What would you like as a background?" asked the old man. "The sea or the dunes?"

"The sea I think, with the rocks in the distance," replied Mr. Ruston. The Rustons and Paul and James lined themselves up for the photo.

"Alice, Craig; no silly faces. This is a family naturist photograph with Paul and James, please don't spoil it," said their dad. The old man took about half a dozen photos of them so they could decide which was the best later.

After the photo session the children went back into the sea again. Mr. Ruston thanked the old man for his help and went back to join his wife.

"Martin, it's after half past one. Do you fancy a bite to eat?"

"Yes I do now you come to mention it. I'll call the kids over. Anyone feeling hungry?" called Mr. Ruston. Alice, Craig, Paul and James all came running over. "I'm going over to the shop to get a few things for us to eat. It'll just be something light because we'll be having a main meal this evening."

"OK dad," said Alice.

"Would you like a hand?" asked Paul.

"Yes please Paul, if you don't mind. You'll have to put your shorts on though while we walk over to the shop, we're not in France!" smiled Mr. Ruston. Mr. Ruston and Paul walked over to the shop in the middle of the seaside estate.

"What did you mean when you said; 'we're not in France'?" asked Paul.

"Well, let me put it this way; there are a few places in France where you can go naked from the moment you arrive to the moment you leave, if you so wish. Cap d'Agde on the south coast is one such place. We've not been there yet, but we would very much like to go. Would you and James like to go somewhere like that, where you can be naked all the time?"

"That sounds unreal," said Paul enthusiastically. "You can actually go around naked all the time and no one would mind?"

"Yes, absolutely. That's what the place is there for, and it's been open for over forty years. It's a sort of naturist town; if we were there now we could walk to the shops openly naked and no one would say a word, except for a polite 'bonjour' perhaps. It's also very likely there'd be plenty of other people doing exactly the same."

"I must tell James about this when we get back," said Paul. "It sounds absolutely fantastic!"

"Well, from what I've read about the place it would certainly seem that way," said Mr. Ruston.

When they arrived at the campsite shop Mr. Ruston bought a few packs of sandwiches, some drinks and two large packets of crisps. They got back about fifteen minutes later and immediately removed their shorts.

"Well, what do you think about being on a beach like this?" Paul asked James.

"Brilliant, absolutely brilliant," smiled James. "It's so much better than having to wear shorts or swimming trunks. What about you?"

"Same here, I couldn't agree more. While I was walking over to the shop with Mr. Ruston he told me about a place called Cap d'Agde. It's somewhere where you can go naked all the time and no-one will mind."

"Hey, that sounds like it'll be great," said James. "Do you fancy going?"

"Yes I do, but we can't really go by ourselves because it's in France," replied Paul.

"That's a pity."

"Well not really, the weather's usually like this all summer in France, especially in the south which is where Cap d'Agde is. We'll talk it over with our parents when we get back home. Who knows, they might be up for it as well."

"OK then."

After having their lunch James fancied walking the full length of the naturist area of the beach. "I feel like having a walk along the beach completely naked," he said. "Does anybody want to come with me?"

"Er," Paul pondered but was quickly interrupted by Craig.

"I'll come with you James."

"OK then Craig, anyone else?"

"Er, not right now," replied Paul. "You and Craig go for a walk if you like, I'll stay here with Alice and her mum and dad."

"Right, OK then," said James. "We won't be too long." James and Craig walked off along the beach together completely naked. Neither of them took anything with them, not even a towel, hat or sandals.

Seeing as Craig had been a naturist all his life, and had naturists for parents, James decided to ask him about it. James wanted to know how Craig felt when he was naked. "Craig, can I ask you something, about naturism?"

"Yeah, course you can," replied Craig.

"I've got as I really love being naked now, and so has Paul. I really can't think of anything more enjoyable than walking along the beach like this on a hot day, and I was just wondering how you feel when you're naked."

"Fine. I like being naked too, but I have done it most my life, so I am used to it."

"You've never ever been worried about anyone seeing you naked?"

"No not really, I'm quite happy being naked," replied Craig in a very relaxed way. "I wouldn't want to be naked when it's cold or when everyone else around me is dressed, but like you, I think it's lovely walking along the beach and playing in the sea with nothing on. When we go to my grandparents; that's my dad's mum and dad, we all go naked. They've a nice house and a big garden with a tall hedge so no one can see us."

"That sounds good," said James.

"Yeah, we go there quite a lot. It's best when it's hot and sunny like it is now so we can all play around in the garden naked. Me and my sister have grown up around naked people so it doesn't bother us at all. My mum's mum and dad are naturists too and they sometimes come with us. It's great when there's eight of us all together 'cos we usually play silly outdoor games like throwing wet sponges at each other."

"Now that sounds like fun to me," said James eyes lighting up at the thought of throwing wet sponges about.

"Oh it sure is! We did it with water filled balloons one time and we all ended up soaked, but it was great fun."

"Water filled balloons?" said James barely able to contain his excitement.

"Yep," replied Craig. "But one time last year, when we were all there for over a week, my grandad filled most of them with some sort of slimy blue and green gunge like what you see on kids TV programmes. We all made such a mess we had to get the hose pipe out when we were finished, not just to clean the grass, we had to hose each other down as well. Me and my sister thought it was so funny and were running around all over the garden laughing especially when my grandad got one right in the face from my mum."

"Really? A gunge filled balloon, right in the face?" said James slowly whilst hoping and praying Craig would invite him and Paul to participate next time.

"Yeah, I can remember just how it sounded too - SPLAT! Some of it got me too, then my gran got me right on the bum. If you wanna come with us next time I don't think my mum and dad will mind."

"Come with you next time? I'd love to," begged James. "... and I'm sure Paul would love to come too. We've always enjoyed a daft half hour together and this sounds perfect."

"It usually lasts longer than that, but the time goes very quickly. If you really wanna come with us next time you could always offer to bring a couple of packets of small balloons 'cos we get through quite a lot."

"I bet you do," smiled James.

"There's something else you might like to know about as well," continued Craig. "My grandad set up a long strip of plastic sheeting. I wondered what he was doing at first, but it quickly became clear. Part of the garden has a bit of a slope to it and this is where my grandad set it up. We threw buckets of water on and then slid down it. It was great fun."

"I don't believe it!" said James excitedly. "Did you throw any gunge on to the slide?"

"Yeah, my grandad threw a bit on, but we were already covered in it by then so we just kept on sliding down it and pelting each other with more balloons, but the best bit was when my gran poured some baby oil on. It made the slide so slippy it was impossible to stand up on it. I caught my left knee on one of the pegs my grandad had used to hold the slide in place. It stung a bit afterwards, but because it was so quick it didn't really hurt at the time."

"Is your knee OK now?" asked James.

"Oh yeah; it was a while ago now, but there's still a small scar if you look closely," replied Craig showing James the injury to his knee."

"Do you do anything else when you're at your grandparents' house?"

"My grandad was talking about hiring a bouncy castle one weekend, but was told they'd want it back clean so he's thinking about buying his own now. He's just a big kid at heart my grandad. Having said that, so are most of my family."

"A bouncy castle? Whatever next?" asked James eyes lighting up again at the thought of jumping up and down and sliding about naked on bouncy castle covered in gunge.

"Well, when we've all finished we have a good clean up. We had to hose each other down that time 'cos we were all covered in gunge from head to foot, but even that ended up in a sloppy gunge fight after running out of balloons. We find it hard to stop sometimes 'cos we all enjoy it so much."

"That doesn't surprise me one bit," smiled James.

"When we do finally call it a day and get cleaned up my grandad lights the barbecue and cooks sausages and burgers and whatnot."

"What, a barbecue naked?" asked James.

"Oh yeah. We all go naked as soon as we get there and stay like that until we leave to go home. We only got dressed once so we could go to the swim at Smithfield Water Park," said Craig.

"Have you been to Smithfield Water Park?"

"Sure we have. We've been a few times and it's really good."

"I know it is," said James. "Paul and me went there not that long ago with our mums and dads, and it was great swimming about and going down the slides naked."

"Anyway, when my grandad is cooking the food he wears a

plastic apron so he doesn't get splashed with hot fat from the barbecue."

"Well I guess that's makes sense," said James.

"After the barbecue my grandad turns up the music so we can dance. He has two big speakers which he puts on stands. It's great fun dancing about naked to loud music, and when there's no school the next day my mum and dad let me and my sister stay up really late."

"Wow! That must be absolutely fantastic," said James. "I bet you don't wanna get dressed after spending so long naked."

"Yeah, it is a bit sad when we have to get dressed and go home, but there's always the next time," smiled Craig. "And I'd love to do again what we did last summer."

"What was that?" asked James.

"We stayed there for over a week. We set off on Friday teatime and came back over a week later on Sunday. We had three fights together, one with wet sponges and buckets of water, then one with water filled balloons and the last one was with the gunge filled balloons and slide. We were all naked all the time we were there except when we went to Smithfield Water Park. Even when it rained a bit one afternoon we still enjoying playing about naked 'cos it was fairly warm."

"Do you know Craig, I can't help feeling more than a bit jealous of you, and your sister. You really are so lucky to have such a nice life, and to be able to spend so much time naked as well. I so wish I'd been a naturist all my life," said James, in despair at what he thought were the wasted 'textile' years of his life.

"Well, at least you're one now, and I guess your friend Paul is too," said Craig.

"Yeah he sure is," smiled James. "It was him who started it off actually, and I'm so glad he did now. From what you've told me I can't wait to come with you to your grandparents. I only hope your mum and dad will let me; and Paul."

"Well, I do remember my grandad saying, 'the more the merrier' one time. Someone delivering a parcel to my grandparents' house got quite a shock once."

"Oh yeah, how?" asked James. "Did he see you all naked?"

"Yeah, he did. What happened was, he knocked on the front door, but got no reply so came round the back after hearing us laughing and playing about. I threw a water filled balloon at my sister, but it missed and it hit this man right in his privates."

"What happened? Was he angry?"

"No not really," replied Craig. "He was more shocked at seeing us all naked, I think. I said I was sorry for making him wet and I did get him a towel. He thought what we were doing was really funny and couldn't help but laugh. My grandad offered him a cup of tea, but he said he had to go, he'd too much work on, otherwise he'd have loved to stay for a bit."

"If he'd had time I wonder if he'd have stripped off and got you back!" laughed James.

"Yeah, it would've been good that, but I bet his boss wouldn't have liked it!"

James and Craig kept on talking to each other while they walked along the beach and to anyone casually observing them walk past it was a lovely sight. Seeing two boys their age walk along the beach together naked, and apparently without a care in the world, was the epitome of innocence.

While they were walking along the beach James and Craig past a couple in their early fifties and the woman nudged her husband. "What?" he asked.

"I could have sworn that was one of my pupils who just walked past."

"Which one?"

"The older one, on the left, blonde hair."

"Who did you think it was?"

"He'd a striking similarity to..., b-but it can't be. I know what he's like; he'd have a fit if anyone saw him naked."

"A striking similarity to who? Margaret, who did you think it was?"

"James Handle. He's a pupil in my class, a fairly quiet boy, but works very well. He's got a friend call Paul in the year above. They live next door to each other and they've been friends since they were in nappies."

"Well, wait and see if they walk back. It's only a couple of hundred yards or so to the sign so if they're walking about naked and haven't got anything with them they'll probably be back in five or ten minutes." This assumption was correct. James and Craig walked as far as they could naked and stopped when they reached the sign. After pausing for a minute or two they set off walking back. This woman then got up from her chair to get a clearer view as they approached.

"I don't believe it Stan; it is! It's James Handle! I don't know who he's with 'cos it certainly isn't Paul; but let me say this, he's in for a big surprise!"

"Oh, Margret, leave the lad alone."

"No way! I've just seen James Handle, the most unlikely boy, naked, here, on the beach. I want to see what he's got to say for himself. I'd have put my own sour-faced mother ahead of him."

"Really?" asked Stan. "Seriously, Margaret, are you telling me you'd place your own hard-faced battle-axe of a mother ahead of this boy on a 'who's most likely to go naturist list'?"

"Yes, I am. I've taught him for well over two years and I know him almost as well as our own sons. The PE teacher, Jim Daniels, found him almost in tears once because he didn't want to get showered naked with everyone else."

"Hmm, I suppose I can sympathise with that, especially at his age, but didn't you give him..."

"...a detention, for missing his last lesson; yes I did, and I felt unbelievably wretched afterwards when I found out why he did it."

"My word, this is gonna be interesting then," smiled Stan. "But Margaret, try not to give the poor lad heart failure. Why don't you offer him and his friend a drink."

"That's just what I was thinking of."

As James and Craig walked past Margaret called out to them. "James Handle! What on earth are you doing here without a stitch on!"

"Uh!" James quickly turned to look at who'd just called his name and got the shock of his life. "Waarrhh! M-Mrs. Hemmingway!" James was absolutely aghast and couldn't believe who it was. "W-What are you doing here?"

"Well I strongly suspect I'm doing exactly what you and your friend are doing James. Enjoying the sunshine on the beach without my clothes on," said Margaret opening her arms in welcoming way. "This is a naturist beach James, as I'm sure you're well aware, and it's here for us all to enjoy."

"B-But…" For a few moments James gave the impression of someone with a splinter in their tongue, let alone did he know where to look. Suddenly seeing his form teacher naked while he was naked on a beach was a massive shock, and part of him felt like running for the hills.

"James, James; just calm down and come over here. Bring your friend as well, I'm sure you'd both like a drink."

"Er, er, yeah, er… thanks," stammered James while panting as if he'd just had a coronary, and at the same time struggling to taking this incredible coincidence in. His form teacher, and her husband, naked, on the beach. Could anything be more shocking or embarrassing to a fourteen-year-old boy? And especially one new to naturism.

"Would you both like a J2O or a cup of tea?"

"Er, a J2O would be fine thanks miss," replied James.

"And your friend?"

"Yeah, same for me please," replied Craig.

"There you go both of you, and it's not 'miss' today James. Seeing as we're all naked we're equals, so please feel free to call me Margaret. This is my husband Stan and we've been naturists for thirty years."

"Thirty-two I think you'll find love," said her husband while laid back on a towel. "Hot summer, 1976, south coast, ring any bells?"

"Yes, yes alright Stan. Please don't start nit picking." James thought this quick correction from her husband was quite funny and, with the initial shock of meeting now largely overcome, couldn't help laughing. "But, as I was about to say, we've only ever told people we know and trust. So you've no need to worry James, I won't be telling Paul I've seen you. Now who's your friend?" James and Craig smiled at each other.

"This is Craig Ruston," replied James. "Craig, this is Mrs. Hemmingway, my form teacher at school."

"Oh is that who she is? Now I understand why you were so shocked when you both met. I've never met anyone I know naked on a beach, or at a swim for that matter," said Craig.

"Craig's at junior school at the moment and he'll be in year five in September. He'll be at our school in a couple of years. By the way, if you want to tell Paul we've met on a naturist beach I don't mind, Margaret, 'cos he's over there," said James pointing in the appropriate direction. "Paul and me are staying with Craig, his sister and their mum and dad in their tent. The campsite is about ten minutes walk away over there."

"Oh I see," said Margaret, now looking more interested than ever. "I thought it was a bit unusual you not being with Paul."

"Craig and me decided to go for a walk along the beach, that's all. Paul's with Alice, Craig's sister, and they're swimming about in the sea."

"Oh, right," said Margaret. "Well James, if you don't mind me asking a rather obvious question, and remembering what you were like not long after I first met you, what on earth made you decide to become a naturist?"

"Well, it all started off a couple of months ago, in the May half term."

"What, this year?" asked Margaret.

"Yes," replied James. "Paul and me were out walking and playing about in the woods when we saw a naturist, a naked man. We couldn't quite believe what we'd seen, so after he'd walked past us Paul and me followed him."

"And? What happened next?"

"Not a lot really. We saw him sunbathing in the nude, but after a while I began to lose interest so I offered to go to the chip shop. When I came back Paul told me he'd copied him. He told me he'd taken all his clothes off so he could feel the same feeling."

"And what did he have to say?"

"I think he said he felt vulnerable and nervous, but he also said he liked the warm sun and breeze on his body."

"This is beginning to make some sort of sense now," said Margaret. "I'm guessing Paul persuaded you to join him in his naked venture. Am I right?"

"Yeah you are. We went out together the next day in the hope of seeing this man again, but he was clothed and we didn't think it was him. After getting fed up of waiting we walked about and that was when Paul found a flyer, a letter that is, about a naturist swim taking place in our local leisure centre."

"Hmm, sounds interesting. Carry on."

"Well, when I suggested we go there and look through the windows to see if everyone was naked Paul said; 'I doubt we'll be able to do that 'cos they'll block them out,' which of course they did."

"So what did the pair of you do?"

"We smuggled ourselves in by hiding in the group changing room toilet. We went for a normal swim the evening before and checked the place out. We even had a quick skinny dip after the pool closed that night with a couple of other lads we met in the shower. We went again on the day of the naturist swim and hid there for nearly an hour after closing time. When we heard the sound of people moving about and talking Paul slowly opened the door. The changing room was empty so we quickly got out and went across to the main door. Paul again opened it very slowly and that was when he told me everyone was naked. All we did then was take off our shorts and join in."

"Well I just can't believe it," said Margaret. "How did the pair of you feel swimming about without your shorts or whatever on?"

"Well, I suppose I should be honest here and tell you the truth," said James while smiling, but trying not to laugh.

"Please do, I can't wait to hear this," said Margaret.

"We both absolutely loved it! We had a go on an inflatable first then went on the slide. It was great sliding down on your bare bum and Paul was right, you do go faster naked. We were talking about this the evening before."

James and Craig kept talking to Margaret and Stan as the shock of meeting them had now completely gone. James told his form teacher all about how they'd first got naked and how they'd overcome their naked fears.

After James and Craig failed to return within an hour, Craig's parents, and Paul, were wondering where they were. "Where do you think James and Craig have got to?" asked Paul. "They've been gone quite a while."

"Yes you're right there Paul; I thought it was fairly quiet. I think we'd better have a look for them; it'll soon be time to go. Cath, Paul and I are just going to have a look for James and Craig, back as soon as poss."

"OK love." Mrs. Ruston was sat reading her book again when her husband and Paul decided it was time to look for James and Craig.

"I hope they're not in any trouble," said Paul.

"Me too," said Mr. Ruston. They walked a few hundred yards and found James and Craig still taking to the Hemmingways. "Oh, so this is where you've both been hiding is it?"

"Dad!" said Craig.

"Paul!" said James.

"Mrs. Hemmingway!" said Paul absolutely gobsmacked. "I, I don't believe it!" Paul was equally surprised to see one of his teachers naked on a beach.

"It's a small world isn't it Paul," said Margaret raising a glass.

"Er, yeah. I s'pose it is."

"We've been having quite a nice little chat, haven't we James?"

"Yeah, sure we have, Margaret."

"James! You can't call her that," said Paul with a shock. "It's Mrs. Hemmingway."

"In school Paul, yes, but not here. I believe we're all equal when we're naked, and I was just as surprised as both you and James at us meeting here naked on the beach. If I had to place a bet on meeting a pupil or two from school on a naturist beach you two would have been my last choice. I'd always thought the pair of you were..."

"Gymnophobic," said James suddenly.

"Well, if that means what I think it means, yes."

"It does," said Paul. "Gymnophobia is the fear of nudity, but with some help, we've managed to overcome it."

"So I've gathered from James."

"Yeah, we love being naked now, don't we Paul?"

"Sure we do, especially when the weather's like this." Seeing as they'd so much in common now they were happily talking away together until Mr. Ruston interrupted.

"Look, I'm sorry to interrupt this very interesting conversation, but it's almost six o'clock now and we do have to get back to the tent."

"Oh, OK," said Paul. "We'll have to go now miss, sorry, Margaret."

"Might we see you tomorrow?" asked James.

"We haven't decided what we're doing tomorrow have we? If it's another nice day we could well be here. We'll see."

"OK then, bye for now," said Paul.

"Bye Margaret, bye Stan," said James.

"Bye bye you two."

Just after ten past six Mr. and Mrs. Ruston and the kids collected all their things and walked back to the campsite, stopping briefly at the naturist sign to put their shorts on. "Who've you been talking to all this time?" asked Mrs. Ruston.

"Someone Paul and James knows very well," smiled Mr. Ruston.

"Who?" asked Alice. Paul, James and Craig smiled at each other, but kept quiet. "Have you bumped into someone you know on your first ever time on a naturist beach?"

"Yes, they have. James and Craig were talking to James's form teacher and her husband."

"Seriously?" asked Mrs. Ruston. "James and his form teacher have met on the beach naked?"

"I know it's hard to believe, but it's true."

"Who was the most surprised?" asked Alice.

"Me," replied James. "I nearly had a heart attack."

"I bet you did love, and to think of all the years we've been naturists. We've never ever met anybody we know," said Mrs. Ruston. "Except for one couple we already know from back home."

After walking back to the tent and showering again all six of them got dressed to go out for dinner. Alice and Craig's mum and dad took everyone out for a delicious three course meal at a nearby pub.

"I could get used to this," said Paul. "Thanks very much for taking us with you. It's very good of you, isn't it James?"

"Yes it certainly is, thanks very much."

"You're very welcome. It's nice to have you both with us," said Mrs. Ruston.

"How long have you been naturists?" asked Alice.

"Just over two months now," replied James.

"When we first met you in the leisure centre near home, that was our first time," said Paul. "We sneaked in by hiding in the group changing room toilet, but unfortunately we were found out near the end by Mr. Simpkin. He was OK about it, but he said he had to see our mums and dads."

"Yeah, we thought we'd be in big trouble, but thankfully for us our mums and dads had a bit of a laugh after the initial shock!" said James.

"They joined us for a swim the next day at Smithfield Water Park," added Paul. Paul and James continued to tell the Rustons about how they'd become naturists. "We got over our fears by helping each other. In the run up to that first swim we practiced being naked over by the railway line near to where we live. It was very nerve racking at first because we'd never seen each other naked before, but we gradually got used to it."

"We love being naked now, especially outside when it's nice and warm like today," said James.

"To some extent we're seeing what we can achieve while we're naked. So far we've done swimming, walking and sunbathing. We also had a brief game of badminton that first time back in May just before being spotted by Mr. Simpkin," continued Paul.

"Yeah, we played badminton again two weeks later with Katie Finch, a friend of ours from school and her mum," added James.

"So that's someone else you've met from school then," smiled Mr. Ruston. "I wonder how many more you're gonna meet."

"Well, it's only been two people so far," said James.

"That's two more than us," said Alice.

"Anyway, we were wondering if we'd see you again that evening, but I don't think we did," said Paul.

"Oh no you wouldn't have done that evening," said Mrs. Ruston. "We went to stay with Martin's parents."

"Oh yeah, Craig's told me all about that," smiled James. "Water fights, gunge filled balloons..."

"Craig!" said his dad. "What did you tell James all about that for? He's not going to want to get soaked in a water-filled balloon fight or messed up with gunge is he?"

"Sorry dad," said Craig.

"What's all this about water-filled balloon fights and gunge?" asked Paul.

"Well, when we go to my parents, they're naturists too of course, we tend to play silly outdoor games like throwing wet sponges and water-filled balloons at each other."

"Hmm, that sounds like fun to me," smiled Paul. "But didn't you mention something about gunge as well."

"Yes, I did. Last time we were there my 'kid-of-a-dad' filled most of the balloons up with this gunge. Some were blue and some were green."

"So did you have a fight with those and end up covered in gunge?" asked Paul.

"Yes we did. It was really childish, but I have to admit we all loved it."

"Wow!" said Paul. "I wish..."

"...you could come with us next time?" added Alice quickly.

"Can we? Please," asked James excitedly. "We'll bring some balloons with us, won't we Paul."

"Er, yeah; yeah sure we will."

"OK, OK. It's quite alright you can both come with us. I think my dad will have taken delivery of his new toy by then."

"What new toy?" asked Paul.

"I think I know what that might be," smiled James. "Would it be a bouncy castle?"

"Yes, it is."

"Oh fantastic!" said Paul. "Will we be jumping about on it naked?"

"I'm pretty sure that'll be compulsory knowing what my dad is like. The reason he's bought one is so we can jump about on it covered in gunge after, or during, a balloon fight."

"I don't believe it! When are you going to your parents again?" asked Paul in high expectation.

"Possibly next weekend, or the weekend after. My dad is going to let us know when his bouncy castle arrives so we'll no doubt go the weekend following its arrival."

"I hope it arrives for next weekend," smiled James.

"Well, we'll have to wait and see," said Mr. Ruston. "Changing the subject just a little, I don't know if either of you are aware or not, but when we go to the beach tomorrow it's the day of the BN beach fun day at Morfa Dyffryn."

"What's BN stand for?" asked James.

"BN stands for British Naturism," said Alice showing a keen interest in the conversation between her dad, Paul and James.

"Yes, they're based in Northampton and they organise a number of events throughout the year. Some events are for members only, but some, like the beach fun day tomorrow, are available to all. We've been members of BN for fourteen years without a break, joining shortly after we were married. Catherine and I met at a naturist swim the year before and we've never looked back. We decided to bring Alice and Craig up as naturists because that's what our parents did with us," said Mr. Ruston.

"I wish my mum and dad had brought me up as a naturist," said James. "It would have made my life a lot easier."

"Me too," said Paul. "We were very reserved up until we attended that first swim."

"My mum said it was as if I'd gone from one extreme to the other," said James. "If I'd been a naturist all my life it would have been a lot easier at school with changing for PE, and especially having to shower afterwards which is always done naked."

"Same here," said Paul. "I do so wish I'd been a naturist from birth."

"Still, look on the bright side, you're both naturists now and you obviously enjoy it, don't you."

"Sure we do," said James firmly.

"Yeah me too. I'd hate to have to wear my shorts now to go for a swim. Swimming naked feels so nice and natural," added Paul.

"You're not wrong there Paul," said Mr. Ruston. "Anyway, I think we'd better be heading back to the campsite now. Craig's looking rather tired, aren't you love."

"Dad, I'm OK."

"Well I feel like getting to bed fairly soon, it's been quite a long day," said Mr. Ruston.

Mr. Ruston paid the bill and everyone left. They walked back to the campsite as the sun was setting and settled in for the second night.

Chapter 11

It was Sunday morning now and everyone woke up later than yesterday, nearly nine o'clock. They all enjoyed breakfast cereals followed by toast and tea. After yesterday's evening meal no one could face a cooked breakfast.

Today, of course, was the BN beach fun day which the Rustons had been looking forward to. It also interested Paul and James.

These beach fun days, which BN arrange, are done to help promote naturism. The BN organisers normally set up their tent on the beach in the centre of the naturist area. They are happy to provide information on naturist matters and the associated lifestyle. They also give out free tea, coffee, orange juice and water.

At about ten past ten Paul, James and the Rustons walked over to the beach again. It was another hot day just like yesterday. They set their things up as usual and then looked over to see the BN organisers arriving on the beach as well. Paul, James and Alice went over to help them. It didn't take long and the BN tent was soon set up. They also helped them set up a volleyball net and court.

As the morning progressed it became very busy, no doubt due to the hot weather, and by eleven o'clock there were approximately four hundred people on the beach and virtually all were naked.

"Paul, did you remember to bring your sun cream?" asked James. "I think we should get some on pretty quick. If it stays like this all day we'll be burnt to a crisp."

"Yeah sure, here you are; and make sure you do everywhere," said Paul with a smile.

"Yeah OK; don't worry, I will do." Paul and James both slapped plenty of sun cream on, did each other's backs and bums, and then laid face-down on their towels. "Hmm, I wish we could do this every day," said James. "I love it!"

"Same here," replied Paul. "Let's give it about half an hour and then have a swim in the sea."

"Yeah, OK then."

After soaking up the sun for a good half hour Paul got up from his towel and took a couple of steps towards the sea. He stood still for a few moments facing the sun and the sea while completely naked and reached out with both arms as if embracing it all.

"Are you coming for a swim?" Paul asked James.

"Sure," replied James as he followed Paul into the sea. They were soon joined by Alice and Craig. Swimming about naked in the sea felt wonderful and was so liberating. They were enjoying this so much so that Alice didn't see a jellyfish right beside her and stepped right on it.

"Ow!" she screamed as the jellyfish's tentacles wrapped around her foot and ankle. Craig ran to tell his mum.

"Mum, mum; Alice has been stung by a jelly fish."

"Where is she?"

"Over there," replied Craig pointing to where Alice was. "Paul and James are helping her." Mrs. Ruston quickly went over to see what had happened.

"I-I trod on j-jelly fish," sobbed Alice. "It's stinging like mad mum."

"Well come on, the sooner we get some cream on it the better." Alice was helped back by Paul and her mum and was soon sat down on a chair. "Right, let's rinse and dry your foot and rub some of this cream in. It should take the stinging away."

"Oh dear, what's happened to Alice?" asked her dad.

"She stepped on a jellyfish, but it doesn't look too bad thankfully."

"Oh that's a relief. Jellyfish stings can be quite serious some-times. I've read about people having allergic reactions."

"Well, she seems to be over the worst now Martin," said Mrs. Ruston. "But I think she ought to rest for a while."

"How are you feeling now Alice?" asked her dad.

"It's still stinging dad, but it feels a bit better since mum put some cream on," replied Alice.

"Oh, you'll be OK. You just sit there and relax."

"Thanks dad."

After lunchtime one of the BN organisers was trying to get some players for a game of volleyball. "Volleyball? Anyone for volleyball?" he called. Paul and James had a go at playing volleyball along with Mr. Ruston and a number of other naturists.

This was certainly another 'first' for both Paul and James. They'd never played volleyball before, not even clothed, but playing it naked in the warm sunshine felt fantastic. It took about half an hour for Paul and James's team to win the first game. They played again, but this time the other team were better. Everyone had a break for ten minutes or so then played again. This time Paul and James were joined by Craig, their dad opting out.

Everyone on the beach appeared to be thoroughly enjoying themselves; whether it was playing volleyball, swimming in the sea or just relaxing in the warm afternoon sun. After they'd finished playing volleyball Paul and James returned to their towels.

"Do you know; I'd never have believed living like this could be so enjoyable," said James. "To be so free and unrestricted by clothing is wonderful."

"I know exactly what you mean. I was so carried away playing volleyball I'd completely forgotten I was naked," said Paul.

"Me too," smiled James. "We must try and get our folks to take us somewhere like this for the main summer holiday this year, don't you agree."

"Certainly do. The reason we're enjoying it so much is of course the weather. You wouldn't want to do this if it was cold and wet would you?"

"No, not really. I guess your mum was right about that heat wave."

They all stayed on the beach till quarter past six. It was about this time when Mr. Ruston suggested they all go back to the campsite for a barbecue. Paul and James helped the Rustons carry their things back to the tent. They all stopped briefly at the sign to put their shorts on and go 'textile'. Mr. Ruston said he'd get the food while the others got the table ready. He went to the campsite shop and came back with sausages, beef burgers, steak and chicken drumsticks. Mrs. Ruston prepared some salad as well and everyone thoroughly enjoyed the barbecue. All of them stayed up quite late that night talking about this and that, but mostly about naturism, so just after ten o'clock Mr. Ruston suggested a late night swim in the sea. "Who fancies a moonlight swim in the sea?" he asked.

"A swim? In the sea? Now?" asked Paul.

"Yes," replied Mr. Ruston. "It'll be as quiet as a mouse out there now, and swimming in the sea at this time of night is wonderful."

"Yeah, I'd like to have a moonlight swim in the sea," smiled James. "It'll be like that time when we were with Ben and Harry, remember?"

"Oh yeah, I'll never forget that," said Paul.

"Never forget what?" asked Mr. Ruston.

"We had a sly skinny dip in the small pool with two brothers we met while we were showering in leisure centre the evening before we first met you," said James.

"My word, that was a bit er..."

"...risky?" finished James. "We were only in the pool for ten minutes or so, but ended up being frighten to death by a cleaner who was slamming doors."

"But we can honestly say it was our first ever skinny dip," added Paul.

"Right, OK then. You'll have to tell us more about that later," smiled Mr. Ruston. "Are you coming Craig?"

"Yeah, sure dad."

"I think Alice ought to stay here," said Mrs. Ruston. "And you'd all better watch out for jellyfish too. We don't want any more of us being stung do we?"

"Of course not. Don't worry, we'll be fine," said Mr. Ruston.

"Do you think we could walk over to the beach naked?" asked Paul.

"Hmm, I'm not so sure about that Paul. I know you're keen and we're fairly close to the beach, but there's still the possibility of someone seeing us and getting the wrong idea."

"Oh it's OK," said Paul. "It was just a thought."

"Why don't we take all our clothes off except for our shorts," suggested James. "That way we're down to the absolute minimum."

"Good idea James!" So; Paul, James, Craig and his dad left Alice and her mum playing cards in the tent. "We'll be back in a good half hour or so," said Mr. Ruston.

"OK then, see you later. And be careful walking about out there barefoot."

"We will."

The four of them carefully walked over to the beach again, each taking only a towel with them. They didn't need to go a long way past the sign this time because there was no one else about. They quickly took their shorts off and left them with their towels by the sign. For a few moments they stood side by side completely naked and looked out across a very clam sea with moonlight shimmering on the surface. Then, with Paul leading, the four of them slowly walked into the sea. Considering the time of day the sea was still quite warm and they all enjoyed larking around in the nude and swimming about under a beautifully clear night sky. "What do you think to this then?" Mr. Ruston asked Paul and James.

"Fantastic! I love being here like this, and at this time of day as well. I WANNA STAY NAKED FOR EVER!" yelled Paul flinging his arms wide and jumping up and down in the sea.

"Yeah! Same here," said James. "It's a pity we're only staying one more night."

"Yeah, I know, it is a bit of a shame that. Still, better this than nothing eh? It would've only been two nights if I couldn't have got Monday off work. Anyway, I think we ought to be heading back now. The girls will be wondering where us lads have got to," smiled Mr. Ruston. "Craig, come on, let's head back now." The four of them got out of the sea and walked over to where they'd left their towels and shorts.

"Eh?" exclaimed Paul. "That's funny."

"Where's our stuff gone?" asked James. "I'm sure we left them here."

"We did," replied Paul. "Mr. Ruston, someone's stolen our shorts and towels. They're not here."

"Are you sure?" asked Mr. Ruston. "We left them by the sign didn't we?"

"I know we did, but they're not here now," replied Paul.

"Well let's have a look around. I doubt anyone would steal four towels and four pairs of shorts." They searched as best they could in the moonlight but didn't see any sign of them.

"Dad, does this mean we're going to have to walk back to the tent naked?" asked Craig.

"Yes, I'm afraid it does look as if we're going to have to do that. Unless anyone's got a better idea."

"Do you think someone's seen us here and is playing some sort of joke?" asked Paul.

"Yeah, that's what I was wondering too," added James.

"Hmm, well, if that's true, who could it be?"

"I've no idea," replied James quickly.

"Sorry James, I wasn't suggesting it was you, or any of us for that matter, 'cos we've all been together in the sea haven't we."

"So who do you think it could be?" asked Paul.

"Well, I wouldn't put something like this past Craig's sister."

"Alice? She's back at the tent with mum," said Craig.

"I know that's where we left her, but..."

"Mr. Ruston, if we're going to have to walk back to the tent naked we may as well do it now. If Alice has sneaked over here and taken our things we'll soon find out won't we."

"Yes OK, come on then. Paul can lead the way."

"Er, it's OK, Mr. Ruston, you can lead the way," said Paul.

"Hang on a minute Paul; who was it who wanted to walk over to the beach completely naked in the first place?" Paul suddenly felt a bit embarrassed, but quickly overcame it. Although he'd wanted to walk over to the beach naked he didn't, but he was now naked on the beach and had no option but to walk back to the tent like that.

"OK, fine," said Paul. "I see what you're saying. I'll be firm and lead us back to the tent and if anyone asks us what we're doing I'll just say; we're naturists who have lost everything!"

"Paul! You can't say that. What will they think?"

"James, Paul is just being silly; or at least I hope he is," smiled Mr. Ruston. So with Paul leading the way the four of them began walking back to the tent.

About twenty minutes before they arrived back Alice was laid on her sleeping bag giggling to herself. "Alice, what is it that you are finding so amusing?" asked her mum. "You haven't stopped laughing since you came back from the toilet. Now what exactly is going on?"

"Nothing mum," sniggered Alice.

"That doesn't sound very convincing Alice. Where did you go to when you told me you were going to the toilet?"

"Well, you'll find out mum. I don't really wanna spoil the surprise."

"What surprise? Alice, you're making your mum feel very worried, now what have you done?"

"Mum, it's just a bit of a joke that's all." Mrs. Ruston glared at her daughter and wanted to know exactly what she'd done. "It was 'cos of what Paul said, about wanting to walk to the beach naked."

"But they didn't walk to the beach naked. They were wearing their shorts and they each had a towel."

"I know mum, but their shorts and towels are back here. I followed them to the beach and brought all their stuff back with me."

"I don't believe it! You mischievous little girl. Do you mean to tell me that your dad, your brother and Paul and James are going to have to walk back here completely naked?"

"Yep," smiled Alice. "I'm sorry mum; it was only meant to be a bit of fun."

"Well, don't do it again." smiled her mum. "I'm sure you wouldn't like it if it were the other way around and you had to walk back here completely naked."

"Yeah, OK mum."

"What time is it anyway? It must be after eleven by now.

"It is mum, it's nearly half past."

"Well come on, let's see if we can see them walking back." Alice and her mum unzipped the door of the tent and looked out, but they didn't see anyone. The moon had disappeared behind some thick cloud and, apart from a small light above the shop, was completely dark. Alice switched her torch on and shone it towards the beach.

"I still can't see anyone mum," she said. Just then they heard some laughing and wolf whistling. "What was that?" asked Alice.

"At a rough guess I'd say someone's seen your dad and the boys. Shine your torch over there again." Alice shone her torch right where the noise had come from and glimpsed them walking back naked.

"Mum! It's them! They're walking back naked."

"Alice! I want a word with you!" called her dad.

"Dad, I'm sorry, it was only meant to be a bit of a laugh."

"I know love, it's OK. I might have been tempted to do the same thing myself. What do you think Paul?"

"I s'pose I can see the funny side now and I'm glad our stuff wasn't taken for real."

"And Alice's trick did give us the chance to walk back here naked didn't it," said Craig.

"Yes it certainly did. Alice, where's our shorts?"

"Round the back of the tent dad with your towels."

"Thank you." The four of them retrieved their shorts and put them on. "Oh, I've just remembered, we need some water. Alice, come with us and bring that empty water carrier."

"OK dad." As they walked across to the tap Paul and James were wondering why this couldn't wait until morning. Had Alice's dad thought of something? They were about to find out.

"Right, fill it up," said Mr. Ruston. Alice put the pipe into the water carrier and Paul turned the tap on. They filled it right up and Paul then turned the tap off. "Just hang on a minute. Let's rinse the dirt off the sides and base." Mr. Ruston then turned the tap on again and pinched the end of the pipe so the water came out under a bit of pressure. After rinsing the water carrier Mr. Ruston said; "Who thinks Alice deserves some..., er, recognition, for what she did to us boys?"

"What do you mean?" asked Paul.

"How's about this then?" Mr. Ruston then aimed the jet of water right at his daughter. Alice screamed and ran away soaking wet.

"Dad, that was brilliant! I bet she won't nick our stuff again," laughed Craig. Paul and James had a good laugh too at Alice's quick cold soaking. When they'd finished messing about they walked back to the tent. It was now quarter to midnight and even then the heat was still noticeable. It felt almost tropical and certainly not Welsh.

"Mum, mum! Dad's just made me all wet."

"Well, it was a bit silly love wasn't it, bringing their things back here and leaving them to walk back naked."

"I know, but I thought they'd have liked it. Paul wanted to walk to the beach naked didn't he?"

"Yes love I know he did, but your dad thought it would be best not to. Don't forget love this is a textile campsite. It's only part of the beach that's for us naturists." Alice dried off and got into bed. It was now almost midnight and all six of them settled down for the last night of the holiday.

Chapter 12

Next morning everyone woke to yet another bright sunny day. They all enjoyed breakfast after which came the tidying up and the taking down of the tent. They'd still got most of the day free for fun on the beach, so at around quarter past ten all six of them walked over to the beach for the last time. The Rustons and Paul and James were now looking well tanned. It looked as if they'd all been to Spain or Tenerife instead of the Welsh coast for the weekend.

This turned out to be a much quieter day. There was barely a quarter of the number of people on the beach compared to yesterday, it being Monday and a working day for most. "We need to leave at about half four to five," said Mr. Ruston. "Don't forget we've quite a long drive home." The sun came out even stronger than the last two days and everyone was thoroughly enjoying it.

"Alice, Craig, can you both come here. You need to get some sun cream on," said their mum.

"Have you got any sun cream left?" James asked Paul.

"Oh yes there's plenty, here you are. I'm just going to the toilet, won't be long." Paul walked off into the dunes. He came back a couple of minutes later and rejoined the others.

"Why don't we bury someone in the sand and get your dad to take a few photos," suggested James.

"OK then," said Craig. "Dig a hole and bury me in the sand right up to my shoulders." Paul, James and Alice started digging. They dug a hole about two feet deep then widened it so Craig could sit in it.

"Try that Craig," said Paul. Craig stepped into the hole they'd dug and crouched down. Paul, James and Alice then compacted the sand all around him. Craig's head was the only part of him which could now be seen.

"Dad, Dad. Can you take a photograph of Craig? We've buried him in the sand up to his neck," said Alice.

"Hmm, OK. I'll just get my camera, won't be a moment." Mr. Ruston took a few photographs of Craig buried up to his neck in sand. "Right, why don't the three of you sit by the side of Craig for the next photo."

"Yeah, OK then," said Paul. Paul and James sat on one side and Alice on the other. This made for a really nice naturist photograph. Craig then got up out his hole and went to wash himself in the sea. "Mr. Ruston, can you take a few more photos of us on the beach please?" asked Paul.

"Sure I can Paul."

"Can you take a few photos of me, then James and then both of us together please?"

"Yeah, sure I can. What exactly did you have in mind?"

"I'll sit down here first of all and then I'll lay back." Paul sat down on the dry sand and Mr. Ruston took a couple of photos. He then laid back and moved his arms and legs about creating an angel effect in the sand. Mr. Ruston continued to photograph Paul as he'd requested. "Right, can you take one of me sat in the sea next please?" asked Paul.

"Yeah, come on then. Let's photograph you in the sea." Paul rinsed all the sand off his body in the sea and then sat down so that the waves were just covering him. "Right James, can you rinse yourself in the sea and come and sit with me," continued Paul.

"Sure, won't be a minute." James walked into deeper water and rinsed all the sand off as Paul had asked. "Right, where do you want me?"

"Just sit down here next to me and try to look relaxed." Paul and James were now sat together. They laid back a bit with their hands behind them for support. Mr. Ruston was thinking these were going to be the best naturist photos he'd ever taken.

"Right, I've taken seven photos of you both. Is that OK Paul?"

"Yeah that's fine thanks. Can you take a few photos of James on his own now please?" asked Paul.

"Yes of course. Do you want me to photograph James the same way I did you?" asked Mr. Ruston.

"Yes please," replied Paul. "That is unless James can think of anything better. I'll stand here out of the way." Mr. Ruston began to photograph James on his own. Although James really enjoyed being naked, he couldn't help feeling a tad uneasy at being photographed on his own and at such close range, but he didn't let it show. James was just hoping Mr. Ruston wouldn't get into any kind of trouble for taking photos of naked children.

"Shall I stand up now?" asked James.

"Yeah OK then, face the sun." James did as he was asked and stood facing the sun. Mr. Ruston took a couple more photos.

"Why don't you take one of Paul and me together with our arms around each other," suggested James.

"Oh yes, I think that'll be nice. What do you think Paul?"

"Yeah, fine; come on then let's do it James," smiled Paul. Paul and James now stood really close together and put their arms around one another and Mr. Ruston took a couple more photos.

"Right then, have we finished?" asked Mr. Ruston.

"Nearly," replied Paul. "I was hoping we could finish off with a few group photos of James and me with Alice and Craig."

"OK then Paul. Alice! Craig! Here a minute; I want you both." Alice and Craig ran over to see what their dad wanted. "Paul and James would like a few photos of you both with them, is that OK?"

"Course it is dad," replied Craig. "Can you take one of me with James first please."

"Yes if you like Craig."

"It'll remind James and me of when we walked along the beach and met his teacher."

"OK then Craig. If you really think James needs reminding about that."

"No, I'll never need reminding about that," said James. "I'll remember it for the rest of my life, but if Craig would like his photo taken with me it's fine." James and Craig had a couple of photos taken of them then Paul and Alice joined in. The four of them then had their photos taken together in a number of different poses, in the sea and on the beach. When they'd finished Mr. Ruston put his camera away and sat down beside his wife.

"Martin, I don't know about you, but I think it's time we had some lunch."

"Yeah, me too. Do you want me to go?"

"No it's OK, I could do with a walk. You stay here with the kids." It was just after twelve o'clock when Mrs. Ruston walked over to the snack van to get everyone something for their lunch and while she was queuing up she bumped into an old friend of hers, who she used to work with, and her twelve-year-old son.

"Oh hello, its Rachel isn't it?" asked Mrs. Ruston.

"Catherine Ruston!" exclaimed Rachel briefly covering her mouth. "I don't believe it! How are you?"

"Fine thanks. I haven't seen you for years. How are you?"

"Oh, not too bad considering."

"It must be well over ten years since I last saw you. I do seem to remember you'd just had a baby."

"Yes I did, and he's twelve years old now is Matthew. He's just finished his first year at high school," said Rachel. "Doesn't time fly?"

"How's your husband, Lewis?"

"Oh don't ask, we got divorced. Be about seven years ago now I think."

"Oh, I'm sorry to hear that."

"Don't be," said Rachel. "Lewis got fed up with me and he was away a lot with work and what have you. He didn't seem to care about Matthew and me so we called it a day."

"Oh I see. Whereabouts are you staying then?" asked Mrs. Ruston.

"In a bed and breakfast in Barmouth. It's on the sea front, very nice," replied Rachel.

"We get a nice big breakfast every morning don't we mum," smiled Matthew.

"Yes love we do, but it can be a bit much for me."

"Hmm, sounds nice. Why don't you join us on the beach? It's our last day today, but we might as well make the most of it," said Mrs. Ruston.

"We'd love to, wouldn't we Matthew."

"Yeah sure. Have you got any kids?" asked Matthew.

"Oh yes; I've a daughter age eleven and a son age nine," smiled Mrs. Ruston. After they were served the three of them walked back to join the others.

"Oh you're back," said Mr. Ruston.

"Sorry it took so long," said Mrs. Ruston. "This is Rachel Williams I used to work with at Fox's Biscuits, and this is her son

Matthew. Rachel, this is my husband Martin and our kids, Alice and Craig. The two slightly older boys are new friends of ours, Paul and James. We got to know them when they went for a naked swim, unofficially like! I'll tell you more about that later."

"Well it's very nice to meet you all," said Rachel. "I don't suppose you could be persuaded to stay another night."

"I'm sorry Martin's working tomorrow, aren't you love, and we've taken our tent down already. Everything's in our car ready to go except for what we have here."

"Don't worry then, I'm sure there'll be other times."

Paul and James got on well with Matthew, him being nearer their age. However, they were good friends with Alice and Craig too and they liked the fact that they were naturist friends and they could be open and honest with them and neither would laugh at their desire to be naked.

"Where's your car parked?" asked Paul.

"Haven't got one," replied Rachel. "We came here on the train. It was only one change at Birmingham New Street from where we live at Tamworth."

"Oh, so that's where you move to is it?" asked Mrs. Ruston.

"Yeah, we've lived there over ten years now."

"If you don't mind me asking, how long have you been a naturist?" asked James.

"Hmm, quite a while. A good five years or so I think," replied Rachel.

"Paul and me have been naturists for about two months now, and on Saturday afternoon whilst on our first ever visit to a naturist beach, Craig and me went for a walk along the beach and we only saw my form teacher."

"Really?" asked Matthew. "You met your form teacher on the beach naked?"

"Yes I did," replied James.

"Who was the most surprised?" asked Rachel.

"I was," replied James. "Craig and me were walking past and she just called out. I was so shocked I didn't know what to do or say."

"But you did overcome it fairly quickly James after she offered us drinks," smiled Craig.

"Yeah I know, but that shocking moment will stay with me for the rest of my life."

"Anyway Rachel, you were telling us about how you'd got into naturism," said Mrs. Ruston.

"Oh yeah, I bumped into someone I knew while abroad and simply took to it like a duck to water. I thought Matthew might have resisted, but he joined in willingly. He was only seven back then of course, but he loves every moment now, don't you love?"

"Yeah, course I do. I love playing about on the beach naked, but it's best when there's some other kids to play with, like the four of you. Would you like to play bowls?" asked Matthew.

"Yeah, sure we would," replied Paul.

"Oh no," said Matthew suddenly.

"What's up?" asked James.

"There's only four sets of bowls and there's five of us," said Matthew.

"That's OK. You four boys play the game and I'll act ref," said Alice firmly.

Paul, James, Craig and Matthew all looked at one another and appeared to be thinking the same thing; "We're gonna let a girl referee an all boys game of bowls?" said Paul.

"She'll be fair, and it'll give her something to do," said Craig.

"Right, well let Alice throw the jack," said Paul. Alice threw the jack and it landed about twenty yards ahead.

"Let's go in age order, youngest first," said Alice as she walked nearer to the jack.

"That's you Craig," said Paul. Craig threw his bowls towards the jack one at a time.

"Not bad," called Alice.

"Matthew you're next," said James. "Then it's me, and Paul's last." They continued playing bowls and after Paul had thrown his last one Alice decided who the winner was. This was not difficult to see. There were two of James's three bowls closest to the jack so James won the game and scored two points. They continued playing bowls together and not one of them mentioned anything about being naked even though they were clearly enjoying it.

While the kids were happily playing bowls the adults kept talking. "Seeing as Lewis has left you, do you think you might get married again?" asked Mrs. Ruston.

"Hmm, I'm not sure. I'm not ruling it out, but who knows. It's certainly not a priority at the moment. I work from home mostly these days so looking after Matthew is fairly easy."

"Well, we must exchange details before we go home. It's been really nice seeing you after all this time, and especially meeting you on a naturist beach."

"Well, it's a small world isn't it," smiled Mr. Ruston. "All I need to do now is see someone I know."

"Well I hope you do, and I'm sure you'll enjoy catching up with them if it's someone you haven't seen for ages," smiled Rachel.

"Why don't we all have a swim in the sea together before we go home," said Mrs. Ruston.

"Yeah, come on then; I'll get the kids to join us." Mr. Ruston walked across to were the kids were playing bowls. "How long before you finish?" he asked them.

"Not long," replied Alice. "Paul's about to throw his last bowl now. If he gets this one closest to the jack he'll win. Otherwise Matthew will win. They're neck and neck on nine points each." Paul threw his bowl and it landed right where he wanted.

"YES!" he yelled punching the sky and with a huge smile across his face. "I knew I could do it."

"Well played," said Matthew. "I couldn't have done that at the end. I think you deserved to win with a shot like that."

"Thanks," said Paul.

"Well if that's you lot finished you might like to know we've only got about half an hour left and we were wondering if you'd all like to join us in the sea," said Mr. Ruston.

"Yeah sure we would," said Paul.

"Let's collect the bowls up first," said James. "We'll only be a minute or two." When they'd tidied them away the five of them joined the adults in the sea for the last time. They all enjoyed a final nude swim in the sea before going home.

"Right, come on everyone. It must be after half four now and I'm afraid it's time to go home."

"Aw dad," moaned Craig. "Can't we stay a bit longer? I don't want to have to put my clothes back on yet."

"Same here," added Paul. "I could stay here for ages like this."

"Ten minutes then and that's it we must go," insisted Mr. Ruston. After this final ten minute play about they collected all their things, said 'good bye' to Matthew and his mum and then walked back to the car. They set off home just after five o'clock.

The roads were reasonably clear on the way home so just under halfway back, while still in Wales, Mr. Ruston suggested stopping for a bit. He turned on to a quiet country lane miles from anywhere. It was still very warm even though it was just turning quarter past six. They all had a drink and a biscuit or two, during which Mr. Ruston suggested going for a walk. "Why don't we go for a naturist walk in the Welsh countryside? We can leave our things here in the car and walk down that footpath just there," he said pointing in the appropriate direction.

"Do you mean leave everything here?" asked Paul.

"Yes, that's exactly what I mean. I'd like us to walk down there completely naked, save for our sandals or trainers of course."

"Great, I'm up for that," said Paul as he took off his T-shirt.

"Me too," added Craig.

"Come then, let's all go for a walk in the nude," said Mrs. Ruston.

Mr. and Mrs. Ruston, Alice, Craig, Paul and James all got out of the car. They took their remaining clothes off and left them in the car. Mr. Ruston locked the car and carried the key with him. As this was just a gentle naturist stroll they didn't plan on going very far. The six of them walked a good half mile in the beautiful Welsh countryside and initially didn't see or meet anyone else. They stopped for a few minutes in the middle of a small wood and then slowly walked back. As they walked back to the car in the glorious evening sunshine they saw a couple walking their dogs with their two sons. This family were very similar in age to the Jessops and the Handles, parents early forties and children early to mid teens. As they approached one another there were a few giggles and funny looks from the children.

"Evening; lovely weather isn't it?" smiled the dad.

"Yeah super," replied Mr. Ruston. "I hope you don't mind us being naked. We've been naturists a number of years and really enjoy it. Being here like this, especially in a family group, is our way of enjoying the countryside together. I hope you're not offended."

"Well, I have to say I'd be lying if I said we weren't surprised at suddenly seeing you all naked, but we did see the naturist stickers in the car."

"Oh right, yes. I'd forgotten about those," smiled Mr. Ruston.

"And being offended? I don't think any of us are offended at your being naked, are we?" asked the dad. The rest of his family shook their heads and smiled. "I'm not sure being naked is for us, but if you all enjoy it, keep at it. I don't think anyone should discourage you from doing what you really enjoy, especially out here."

"Thank you we will. I'd love to carry this conversation on, but we do have to get back to the car now, we've a long drive home. I'll leave you a leaflet about naturism on your car when we get back."

"OK then thanks, cheerio."

"Bye for now."

The sun was gradually going down and the sky was turning a deep red colour. It was a truly wonderful scene, and to be naked where they were felt so right. Paul and James looked at each other.

"This feels so nice," said Paul. "To be here and naked like this is just, well it's just…"

"I know what you mean." replied James. "Naturism really is something very enjoyable. I'm so glad we managed to get over our fears of being seen naked."

"You mean gymnophobia?" added Paul with a smile.

"Yeah. I wonder why it's called that. I mean, if I'd come across that word before reading that magazine a month or so ago, I'd have thought it was the fear of going to the gym, working out or something like that."

"Gymnophobia is derived from the Greek words 'gymnos' and 'phobos' which mean 'naked' and 'fear'," said Mr. Ruston. "It's also where the word 'gymnasium' comes from as well. In Greece, and indeed some other neighbouring countries as well, gymnastics were regularly done nude."

"Wow! Could you imagine doing that in the gym at school? Playing on the ropes and climbing on the bars naked," giggled Paul.

"Sounds like fun to me," smiled James. "But if they do that in Greece all the time I don't suppose anyone thinks anything of it, or do they?"

"No not really, it's just us Brits I'm afraid who seem to suffer the worst cases of gymnophobia," said Mr. Ruston.

It was now just after half past seven and Mr. Ruston said; "Come on, I think it's time we all went 'textile' and went home."

"I've just had an idea," said Paul. "Why don't we all stay naked and drive home in the nude?"

"Hmm, we could do," replied Mr. Ruston. "But it would mean stopping again before we drop you off at home, and I really think we ought to get a move on, time is getting on now."

"OK then, may be next time," said Paul. Everyone put their clothes back on. They got into the car and set off home.

It was just after eleven o'clock when the Rustons dropped Paul and James off. "Thanks very much for a great weekend," said Paul. "We've really enjoyed it, haven't we James?"

"Yeah, sure we have," smiled James. "It's been a long time since we enjoyed a weekend away as much as this. Thanks very much for taking us with you."

"It's been a pleasure," said Mrs. Ruston.

"And I'm sure we'll be seeing you both at the next swim won't we?" added Mr. Ruston.

"Sure you will," said Paul. "We'd better go in now, I think our parents are waiting."

"OK then. We'll give you a ring when we fix a date for going to my mum and dad's. I know you and James can't wait!" smiled Mr. Ruston.

"Oh yeah, sure. Thanks again for everything and bye for now, night."

"Night," said James. The Rustons said good night to Paul and James and then went home themselves. Paul and James were now back home and even though it was late they wasted no time at all in telling their parents what a wonderful time they'd had.

Chapter 13

Not much happened during the week following Paul and James's short holiday with the Rustons. They went out every day to their usual place near the railway line to enjoy the sunshine and on the following Friday afternoon, while still busily sunning themselves, Paul received an unexpected text message. Although he didn't know it, it was from Ben and it read: [Wl u b goin swmin 2nite?]. Paul hadn't got Ben's number so he didn't know who it was from and replied with: [Who is this?]. Ben texted Paul again and sent: [It's Ben. U can't av fgt me & Harry!]. "Who's texting you?" asked James.

"It's Ben!" replied Paul quickly.

"What's he got to say?"

"He wants to know if we're going swimming tonight."

"Well why don't we? We haven't seen them for quite a while."

"That's just what I was thinking."

"Text him and tell him we'll be there. I know we've got to wear out swimming trunks when it's not naturist, but we can go naked in the showers at the end can't we."

"Yeah, OK then." So Paul texted Ben again and sent: [Hi Ben. Yeah we'll be there. Is Harry coming too?]. Ben replied again with: [Sure he is. We'll c u about 7 then, OK?]. Paul texted Ben yet again and confirmed they'd meet at the leisure centre at seven o'clock.

"Are we meeting them outside at Seven o'clock?" asked James.

"Yeah why? That's the time what Ben just said," replied Paul.

"What about their swimming lesson?"

"Oh yeah, I'd forgotten about that." Paul was about to text Ben again when he suddenly realised Ben and Harry don't have a swimming lesson in school holidays. "Hang on a minute, I've just remembered, it's the holidays now; Ben and Harry don't have a swimming lesson in school holidays do they."

"Oh yeah, of course; I forgot about that," said James. "So why are they going swimming then?"

"Well, I suppose they're going 'cos they like swimming, and maybe, they want to meet us again," replied Paul.

"Yeah, that's what I was thinking," said James. Paul's phone beeped again. "What's Ben want now?"

"Hmm, he says he's got a surprise for us and will tell us when we meet this evening," said Paul.

"What sort of surprise?" asked James.

"I don't know," replied Paul.

"Well text him back again and ask him," insisted James. Paul did as James said, but Ben didn't give anything away. He just told them to be there this evening at seven and all will be revealed.

"This has got to be something very interesting," said Paul. "Ben's not saying what it is until we meet this evening."

"Well, what do you think it could be?" asked James.

"I haven't got a clue," replied Paul.

"I wonder if he's found somewhere else we can skinny dip," suggested James.

"Hmm, could be, I can't wait to find out for sure what it is."

Paul and James continued to enjoy the sunshine until about half past four when Paul suggested they go home and get ready to go swimming. They left their favourite spot and as usual walked as far as they could naked only getting dressed to cross their road and go indoors. Paul asked his mum if he could go swimming. "Mum, can I go swimming this evening with James?"

"Well I thought we were all going tomorrow when it's the naturist swim."

"Yeah, I know we are, but James and I want to see Ben and Harry again. Don't you remember, they're the two brothers we went out with that day about a month ago?

"Oh yes I remember now. Why don't you invite them over one evening? From what you've told me they sound like really good friends."

"They are, but they do live about twelve miles away. Their nearest leisure centre is closed until Christmas for a rebuild so until then they're coming to ours every Friday."

"Oh I see now why you want to go this evening."

"You don't mind then?" asked Paul.

"No of course not, you enjoy yourself. Me and your dad will join you at the naturist swim tomorrow," replied Paul's mum.

"Right, thanks mum. I'll go get my stuff ready." Paul went

upstairs to his bedroom and packed his new swimming trunks and a large towel into his bag. He also took a bottle of shower gel. As Paul was coming downstairs James knocked on the front door. Paul opened the door and let James in.

"I know it's only ten to six, but if you're ready now my mum's gonna give us a lift. She's going to Morrisons for the weekly shopping."

"Yeah OK then. I've got all I need in my bag. Just hang on while I let my mum know I'm going." James waited on the doorstep while Paul told his mum he was going. "Right then, let's go." Paul and James got into the car and James's mum took them to the leisure centre. They arrived there just before quarter past six and went in. There were a few people milling around in the reception area, some with wet hair who'd obviously just come out and hadn't got full dry. The woman on reception called Paul and James over and told them they didn't have to wait until seven o'clock as there were no swimming lessons taking place.

"Oh brilliant," said Paul. "We can go straight in?"

"Yes, once you've paid," replied the receptionist. "And it's only sixty pence today for unaccompanied children."

"Thanks very much," smiled Paul and James. They paid themselves in and went through to the changing room.

"What about Ben and Harry?" asked James. "They might be waiting for us in reception and we don't want to miss them do we."

"True," replied Paul. "But we can see through the windows when they arrive can't we, and when they see us in here they won't need to wait."

"OK then." Paul and James got changed into their swimwear and were soon in the pool. They were enjoying swimming about and sliding down the slide as usual and the time quickly past. Paul glanced at the clock on the wall and saw it was two minutes to seven.

"James, it's almost seven. Have you seen anything of Ben and Harry?"

"No not yet?"

"Well they should be here pretty soon. I'm going to keep an eye out for them," said Paul.

"OK then," replied James. "I'm just nipping to the loo, back in a mo." Paul kept watch and was hoping Ben and Harry would soon arrive, but for the moment he saw no sign of them. James returned and asked Paul if they'd arrived yet.

"No not yet," replied Paul.

"It's not like them to be late is it?"

"No not really. I hope everything's OK," said Paul as he continued to look out of the window. Just then Ben and Harry arrived. "They're here!" said Paul suddenly and with some relief.

"I'll go and wait for them in the changing room," said James.

"OK, I'll wave them through." Paul saw Ben and Harry walk into the reception area, but although he tried Paul couldn't attract their attention. Upon arrival Ben and Harry were wearing light grey tracksuits which looked clean, smart and very sporty. Paul tried again to attract their attention but failed. Eventually Paul gave up and went over to speak to one of the attendants. "Excuse me," said Paul. "I'm trying to attract the attention of two friends who are waiting in reception, but they can't hear me."

"No problem sunshine. Who are your friends?"

"They're the two lads in grey tracksuits standing by the main entrance and their names are Ben and Harry," replied Paul. On hearing those names the attendant suddenly looked directly at Paul.

"Do you mean Ben and Harry Wetherby?" asked the attendant.

"Er, possibly. I don't know their surname, I just know them as Ben and Harry," replied Paul.

"Well if it's them you'll soon find out; lucky kids. Talk about, 'right place' 'right time'," smiled the attendant as he got down from his high chair. Paul had absolutely no idea what the attendant was going on about, but he had a feeling he would find out soon enough.

James however was still waiting for them in the changing room, but after waiting some time and not seeing them, went back to the pool and spoke to Paul. "Where are they?" he asked. "I thought you said you'd seen them."

"I did," replied Paul. "They're still waiting in reception. By the way, did you know their surname was Wetherby?"

"No, why? What's so special about that?" asked James.

"I don't know," replied Paul. "I asked the attendant to tell them we were here and he started going on about them being lucky kids or something like that. Something sounds very fishy to me."

"Hang on a minute," said James. "Don't you remember Ben say he had a surprise for us?"

"Yes he did, and maybe this has got something to do with it. Let's go through to the changing room." Paul and James quickly went through to the changing room and finally met Ben and Harry. "Hiya," called Paul.

"Hi, how you both doing?" asked Ben.

"Fine thanks," replied Paul and James.

"Is your surname Wetherby?" asked Paul.

"Yep, it sure is," replied Harry.

"Well when I asked the attendant to let you know we were already here and in the pool he started going on about you being lucky kids," said Paul.

"Has this got something to do with your surprise?" asked James.

"Yes it has," smiled Ben. "You see these tracksuits?"

"Yeah, what about them?" asked Paul.

"Well, when we were here last Friday Harry and I got talking to someone."

"In the pool?"

"No, this was in the reception area while we were waiting for our dad to pick us up," replied Harry.

"Yeah, there was this man and a woman and they were from a new sports company. They were trying to find models for their sportswear."

"We couldn't believe our luck," said Harry quickly.

"We had to have permission from our parents and once they'd signed the forms we were treated like superstars."

"Did they pay you?" asked James.

"Yeah, but it wasn't that much. What we liked most of all was the free clothes. We've got all sorts of tracksuits, T-shirts, vests, shorts, socks and trainers," said Ben.

"Yeah, you name it, we've got it!" smiled Harry.

"That's absolutely amazing," said Paul. "No wonder that attendant called you lucky."

"I know just what you mean, it feels like we're living a dream in a way," added Ben. "We've also won lots of sporting equipment for our school." Ben and Harry continued talking while they got changed. Once they were changed all four of them went through to the pool. They all enjoyed the slide for a bit then had a rest. "Why don't we have swimming race," suggested Harry.

"Yeah, OK then. Why not," replied Paul.

"Two lengths, breast stroke?" suggested James.

"Yep," replied Ben.

"Right, well; let's move away from the slide," said Paul.

"If you two go first I'll race Harry," said James.

"Yeah, and then the two winners can race each other," added Ben. So Paul and Ben got out of the pool and stood on the edge. They waited for James's signal then dived in and swam to the shallow end and back. As Paul expected, Ben was the clear winner. James and Harry then got out and stood on the edge ready for Ben's signal. They dived in and swam the same two lengths, and although James won, Harry was only a few seconds behind him. They had another rest for a few minutes then Ben and James raced each other. They stood on the edge of the pool and waited for Paul's signal. This was a very close race. Ben and James were really going for it, and although James swam his best, Ben just managed to beat him. "Yes, I did it!" smiled Ben.

"Er, only; just," panted James.

"We ought to join your swimming lesson," said Paul. "I bet we could learn a lot and improve our swimming."

"Well we start a new set of lessons in September," said Ben. "If you get your parents to fill in the forms and pay you could join us, and it would be here until at least Christmas."

"OK then. We'll talk it over with them when we get back home," said Paul.

It was now almost nine o'clock and time to get out. Paul, James, Ben and Harry carried on swimming about until they heard the final 'all out' whistle on the dot of nine. They were last to leave the main pool, but wasted no time at all in getting into the showers. "I'll just get my shower gel from my locker, won't be a minute," said Paul.

"OK," replied Ben. In the time it took Paul to get his shower gel James, Ben and Harry entered the shower area and immediately took their trunks off. Paul joined them a few moments later with his shower gel.

"Oh, er..." stammered Paul slightly surprised at seeing the three of them naked so soon.

"What's up?" asked Ben.

"Nothing," replied Paul quickly.

"Well come on in then."

"...and take your trunks off," finished Harry. Paul couldn't get his swimming trunks off quick enough and nearly ripped them in the process. "I bet you feel much better now don't you?"

"Course I do!" replied Paul. "I wish we could all be naked and swim naked more often. It's the naturist swim tomorrow evening," continued Paul while stretching out his arms. "Me, James and our mums and dads are all coming this time. It's a real shame you and Harry can't join us 'cos I know you'd love it." Just then Ben and Harry looked at each other and smiled.

"Well, there's something else we haven't told you," smiled Harry.

"What is it then?" asked Paul.

"Our parents have given us permission to attend the naturist swim here tomorrow evening," said Ben.

"Seriously?" asked Paul. "You're coming to the naturist swim tomorrow evening?"

"Yeah we are," smiled Harry. "And we can't wait to slide down the slide on our bare bums!"

"Oh that's brilliant!" smiled James. "It'll be so much fun the four of us swimming about and sliding down the slide naked."

"How did you manage to persuade your mum and dad to let you go?" asked Paul.

"Well, I think you could call it pester power," smiled Harry.

"Yeah, Harry and I were out with our dad one afternoon when we bumped into the guy who organises it."

"You mean Peter Simpkin?" asked Paul.

"Yeah that's right," replied Ben. "Our dad remembered him from somewhere and they got talking."

"So did Peter Simpkin tell your dad about the naturist swim?" asked James.

"Not straightaway he didn't," said Harry. "It was when I noticed him wearing an orange wristband."

"Yeah, it had 'Nothing's Better' on it," said Ben. "Harry asked him what it was for and that's when the conversation suddenly changed."

"Ah, I think I can guess what's coming next," smiled Paul. "But do continue."

"Well, Peter Simpkin then told our dad about naturism and we told him we liked skinny dipping. It was then he said we could attend the naturist swim if we liked but our dad was still not all that happy about it."

"We kept on saying; 'Why not dad?' and; 'It'll be just like skinny dipping, but indoors where it's nice and warm'," said Harry.

"Yeah, it was at that point Peter Simpkin told our dad; 'If the boys want to try it I'll keep an eye on them for you, and they seem keen enough to me'," said Ben.

"So did your dad agree to take you after all that?" asked Paul.

"Yeah he did," smiled Harry. "And we can't wait."

"He did warn us not to get into any trouble or annoy anyone by staring at them or we'd never be allowed to go again," said Ben.

"I can see what you meant by pester power now," smiled James. "I'm really looking forward to the swim tomorrow evening now more than ever."

"So are we," smiled Harry. "Since we went skinny dipping together that day I've got as I really like being naked, but it's best with friends who like it too."

"Same here," said Paul. "I really love it when we can be naked together like this and not be bothered at all."

"That's just what I was thinking too," added James. "Does your dad know about you going naked in the showers here?"

"Er, probably not as we've never told him," replied Ben. "What he doesn't know can't hurt; and it won't matter after tomorrow will it."

"My thoughts exactly," smiled Paul. "It's best to keep things like this on a 'need to know basis'."

"What time is it now?" asked James. "I get the feeling we've been in here well over half an hour."

"I'll check, hang on a minute," said Ben. Ben left his swimming trunks in the shower area and walked openly naked to his locker. He had a look at his watch and was somewhat surprised to see it was nearly five to ten. "Guys! It's nearly five to ten. Harry, bring me my trunks please." Paul, James and Harry left the shower area and walked across to the lockers to get their clothes. They got dried and dressed as quickly as they could and were only a few minutes late. Ben and Harry's dad was waiting for them in reception and offered Paul and James a lift home.

"Would you two be going to this naked swim tomorrow evening?" asked Ben and Harry's dad.

"Yeah sure we are," replied Paul quickly. "We go every time now 'cos we really love it, don't we James?"

"Sure, and both our parents are coming this time as well," added James.

"Why do you ask?" asked Paul.

"Well my two lads have been pestering me to take them ever since they first found out about it three or four months ago."

"Well we've been four times now and we really love it, 'cos everyone's so friendly and it's a great atmosphere."

"Yeah, there's nothing for you to worry about Mr. Wetherby," said James.

"Ben and Harry will love it, I just know they will," said Paul. "If you stopped them from going now you'd break their hearts 'cos they're so looking forward to it."

"Oh it's OK, I wasn't thinking of going back on my word, that would be cruel to do that, but I am warning you both; any complaints and you won't go again."

"Dad, your embarrassing us," said Ben quietly. "Paul and James have told us what to expect so there'll be no problems of any kind."

"Well, we'll see. If you want to keep on going and attend regularly I'll see Peter Simpkin when I pick you up."

"Fine," said Ben. Mr. Wetherby dropped Paul and James off just after twenty past ten.

"See you tomorrow evening then, at the swim," said Paul. "Bye for now."

"Yeah, thanks for the lift. See you tomorrow, bye then," said James. The Wetherbys said goodbye and then headed home themselves.

Chapter 14

It was Saturday morning now, and seeing as the weather wasn't particularly good Paul and James spent most of it indoors. They were helping out at home tidying up their bedrooms and sorting out any rubbish. Paul sorted a few clothes and things he didn't want any more but thought they were too good to simply chuck out so put them to one side in a carrier bag. He remembered his mum saying she'd like to take them to a jumble sale or charity shop.

Just after lunchtime James came round with a couple of bags of similar things he no longer needed. "Hiya," said James as Paul open the front door.

"Hiya, come on in," replied Paul.

"I've got a few things in here for your mum," said James.

"OK thanks. You can leave them just there by the front door with mine. I'll make sure my mum knows what they're there for. Let's go up to my bedroom," said Paul as he closed the front door. James followed Paul upstairs to his bedroom.

"Where's your mum and dad?" asked James.

"My dad's at work and my mum's gone out shopping with a friend of hers."

"So we've got the place to ourselves?"

"Yeah, till about half four; why? You want to go naturist?" smiled Paul.

"Well why not?" smiled James taking off his T-shirt.

"OK, go on then. You strip off first then I will. I'd like to see how you feel being naked when I'm still clothed," said Paul.

"Why?" asked James looking slightly puzzled.

"Well, there's always the possibility we could be naked outdoors when everyone else is clothed."

"You mean like when we saw that woman with her kids and we ran off?"

"Yeah, sort of. I'd like to think we can be strong and stand up in support of naturism. It would've been much better if we could have talked to that woman for a few minutes and helped her understand why we were naked."

"Hmm, you might be right there; but I doubt they'd have

joined us even with carefully chosen words," smiled James.

"Well, it's not going to be for everyone is it. All I want to do is help people understand how enjoyable naturism is. If they then choose to go along with it, all well and good. What I don't want is people looking down their noses at us and thinking we're up to no good."

"Yeah, I see what you mean," said James as he took the rest of his clothes off.

"Right, just stand there where you are." Although James trusted Paul implicitly he couldn't help feeling a tad uneasy at being the only one naked, but he did what Paul asked and stood where he was completely naked.

"Now what?" asked James.

"Well, I'd like to take a photo of you with my phone, and then I'd like you to get dressed again," said Paul.

"Why?" asked James, now more mystified than ever.

"Just trust me on this. I want to see how we both feel when were the only one's naked. When you're dressed I'll strip off and I'd like you to do the same to me OK?"

"Yeah, OK then." James felt a bit better now knowing that he was going to swap places with Paul in a few minutes. Paul took out his mobile phone and switched the camera on. He took two photos of James, one of which clearly showed him fully naked.

"Right, I'd like you to get dressed now," said Paul. James put his T-shirt, shorts and socks back on and waited for Paul's next instruction. "Right, OK. How did you feel being naked on your own and being photographed?"

"Uneasy at first if I'm honest, but when you told me we were going to swap places I quickly felt much more confident."

"Yeah, I s'pose that's pretty much what I was expecting you to say. I could sense you felt uneasy to start with. What I'm trying to do is build up our confidence."

"Oh, I see. You want us to be able to talk to people we meet when we're naked without feeling out of place?"

"Yes, exactly," replied Paul. "I'm going to take my clothes off now and I'd like you to photograph me." Paul took off his T-shirt then his trainers, socks and shorts. Feeling far more confident than James had, Paul stood still completely naked ready for

James to photograph him. "Right, here's my phone," said Paul. "All you need to do to take a photo is press that button there."

"OK fine, you ready?" asked James.

"Yes, I am now," replied Paul. "Take two just like I did of you." James took two photos of Paul as he'd requested.

"How do you feel?" asked James.

"Fine, absolutely fine," replied Paul. "My confidence has never been higher. If anyone asked me to give a TV interview right now I'd jump at the chance. What about you?"

"On my own, naked?"

"Yes."

"Oh er, I'd like to, but..."

"But what? You still not fully confident being naked?"

"Well, it depends on where I am and who I'm with. If I was with you I'd have no problem at all, but on my own, it'd take some guts."

"Right then, let's try something else. I'll get dressed and you strip off again. I'm not going to take any more photos and I'll delete what we've taken now if you pass me my phone. What I'd like you to do is stay naked for about ten minutes." Paul got dressed and James took his clothes off again. "Right," said Paul. "I'm going to lie on my bed. What I'd like you to do now is go downstairs and fetch me a glass of orange juice."

"Yes sir," replied James with a bit of a smirk. James now felt like some kind of naked servant, but did as Paul asked. He went downstairs and into the kitchen. James filled a glass with orange juice and took it up to Paul.

"Thanks," said Paul. "Just stand still over there for a moment while I drink this." Paul slowly drank the orange juice James had brought him.

"Can't we both be naked? I like it better that way," said James.

"It's OK, don't worry, we'll both be naked fairly soon. As I said before I'm trying to build up your confidence. I want you to feel capable of doing anything naked without feeling out of place, worried, uneasy or whatever."

"OK then." James stood where he was for a couple more minutes until he saw two women walking up the path to front door through a gap in the curtains. James moved a step closer to Paul. "There's a couple of women walking up to your front door." Before Paul could reply one of them knocked on the front door.

"OK then, would you go downstairs and answer it please," said Paul.

"What?" exclaimed James. "You want me to go downstairs and answer your front door while I'm completely naked?"

"Only if you feel confident enough," smiled Paul.

"Well I don't; and if you're as confident as you say at being naked on your own why don't you get off your bed, strip off and answer it?" suggested James with a huff.

"Er, well..."

"Paul, don't tell me your confidence slipping," said James with a cheeky smile. Paul and James heard a second knock on the front door. Paul felt distinctly uncomfortable, but then decided to take the bull by the horns.

"OK, I'll do it." He quickly stripped off and ran downstairs. "Who is it?" asked Paul through the letterbox.

"Only Jehovah's Witnesses love; are you going to let us in?"

"Er, let me find my keys." Paul ran back upstairs and told James who was at the front door.

"Seriously? A couple of Jehovah's Witnesses?"

"Yep."

"And are you gonna answer the door like that?"

"Yeah, why not? You coming?"

"Go on then, I dare you to answer the door to then in the nude!" James followed Paul downstairs. Paul unlocked the front door and opened it.

"Good afternoon," said Paul confidently.

"Oh my goodness me!" shrieked the women in surprise while taking a step back.

"It's OK, I'm Paul and this is my best friend James, and we're naturists." The two Jehovah's Witnesses turned round and quickly walked away without saying anything. Paul quickly closed the front door and the two of them simply couldn't help laughing hysterically.

"I bet they'll never call here ever again," laughed James.

"You could be right there," smiled Paul. "Come on, let's go back upstairs." They went back up to Paul's bedroom and Paul sat down on his bed.

"Are we both staying naked for a bit now?"

"Yeah sure; let's play Monopoly." Paul and James played Monopoly again while they were naked. "Would you like a drink?" asked Paul.

"Yes please," replied James.

"Tea or coffee, or would you prefer a cold drink?"

"Tea would be fine thanks."

"OK, I'll be back in a few minutes." While still naked Paul went downstairs and put the kettle on. He came back up a few minutes later with two mugs of tea and a few homemade ginger biscuits.

"Hey, these ginger biscuits are nice; did your mum make them?" asked James.

"No I did actually," replied Paul. "But I did have some of help from my mum. They're not all that difficult to make." Paul and James finished their mid afternoon snack.

By now it was almost two o'clock and it had finally stopped raining. James looked out of Paul's bedroom window. "Hey, it's stopped raining; do fancy going out for a bit?"

"Yeah, I wouldn't mind; but I think we should wait until my mum or dad comes home. They shouldn't be too long. Anyway, we're going to the swim tonight aren't we, so I think we should just stay in until then. It might have stopped raining now, but the grass will be soaking wet where we sun ourselves."

"Hmm, true. Why don't we go downstairs and watch TV?"

"Yeah OK, come on then."

"Well if we're going to stay naked let's at least take our clothes downstairs with us. I'd rather your mum or dad didn't catch us naked together again. They might think we're up to something."

"Hmm, yeah; I s'pose you're right," said Paul. "Come on, let's go downstairs." Paul and James grabbed their clothes and went downstairs. Paul switched the TV on and sat down on the sofa next to James. They watched TV for a good half hour after which Paul suggested they go back upstairs. "Let's go back up to my bedroom now seeing as that's finished."

"OK then." Paul and James went back upstairs, and feeling a little tired, Paul flopped down on his bed. "Can I have a go on your computer?" asked James.

"Yeah sure." Paul plugged his computer in, switched it on and then left it to James. Still feeling a bit tired Paul got into bed and had a brief nap. James was enjoying playing on Paul's computer and didn't notice him fall asleep.

Time swiftly moved on and it was now twenty past four. "Hey, Paul. Paul!" While still half asleep Paul slowly stirred. "Are you getting up? It's nearly half four," said James.

"Yeah, I s'pose so," replied Paul rubbing his eyes. "Don't know why I feel so tired, it's not like we've done much is it."

"Get a cold shower, that should wake you up," smiled James.

"A cold shower?"

"Yeah, you'll feel much better when you get out, trust me, I get one nearly every morning."

"I think I'll have a warm shower first," said Paul getting out of bed. Paul grabbed a couple of towels from the airing cupboard and went into the bathroom. For a few minutes James let Paul shower uninterrupted.

"Would you like me to do your back?" asked James in fun, and not actually expecting Paul to say yes, but he did.

"Yeah, please do," replied Paul. "We can shower together for a few minutes if you like, come and get in."

"Oh er; yeah, OK then," said James. James calmly got into the shower with Paul and both of them showered together for the next fifteen to twenty minutes. Whilst the pair of them were in the shower they failed to hear Paul's mum arrive home. She was in urgent need of the toilet so quickly unlocked the front door and went in leaving the shopping in the car. She heard the shower and initially assumed Paul was showering on his own; strange then considering the time of day and where then were going in the next couple of hours. Paul's mum finished on the toilet, but didn't flush it immediately as this would affect the flow of water to the shower and the temperature. However, while she was washing her hands she heard voices. "Paul? Are you in the shower? Who are you talking to?"

"Oh my word, your mum's back!" said James quietly. "What we gonna do?"

"Stay calm and behave perfectly normal," said Paul quietly. Paul then raised his voice in answer to his mum. "It's OK mum, I've nearly finished."

"Is James up there with you? What are you both doing?"

"Er, nothing mum; just getting a shower." That answer seemed somewhat evasive to Paul's mum so she went upstairs to see for herself exactly what they were doing. She went into the bathroom and was surprised to find her son and James showering together.

"Paul! Why is James in there with you? Just what are you two up to?"

"Nothing mum! We're just getting a shower. James offered to wash my back so I just let him in, what's so wrong with that? We shower together after we've been swimming don't we?" Paul's mum thought for a moment and decided to give them the benefit of the doubt and let them be.

"Well hurry up, your dad will be home soon."

"Yeah, OK mum." Paul's mum went back downstairs and brought the shopping in from the car. After a few more minutes Paul and James got out of the shower and dried off in the bathroom. Realising they'd left their clothes downstairs, Paul put his dressing gown on and went to fetch them. They both got dressed and went to help Paul's mum carry the last few things in from the car.

"I'm just going to make a few sandwiches for tea. We don't want to go swimming after a heavy meal do we?"

"No, I s'pose not," replied Paul.

"Look, I think I ought to go back next door now and get my stuff ready for this evening's swim," said James.

"OK then, we'll see you at the leisure centre." Paul saw James out just as his dad arrived home.

"Hi dad," said Paul.

"Hiya son, you had a good day?"

"Yeah, fine thanks. I'm looking forward to going swimming this evening. It'll be great all six of us together won't it."

"Well I hope so, it's been a while since I've been. Let's go inside, I want to talk to your mum." Paul and his dad went inside and Paul switched the TV on again while his mum and dad chatted in the kitchen. A few minutes later Paul's mum brought some sandwiches and salad through. The Jessops sat watching TV while they had their tea.

Shortly after six James knocked on the Jessop's front door and Paul got up to answer it. "Hiya, I just wanna let you know; we're going now 'cos my dad wants to call somewhere on the way, so we'll see you outside the leisure centre just before seven, OK?"

"Yeah OK, thanks for letting us know. I'll see you later, bye James." Paul closed the front door and rejoined his parents in the front room. "James and his mum and dad are setting off now," said Paul. "They're calling somewhere on their way to the leisure centre."

"OK then, we'll see them when we get there won't we love," said Paul's mum.

"Did I tell you Ben and Harry Wetherby are coming to the swim this evening?" asked Paul.

"Er, no I don't think so love," replied Paul's mum.

"Aren't they the two lads you and James went out with that day not so long ago?" asked his dad.

"Yes they are," replied Paul enthusiastically. "Their dad is taking them to the swim tonight for the first time and they're really looking forward to it."

"Are they indeed," replied Paul's dad.

"Yeah they are. They've been pestering their mum and dad for months and they've finally agreed to take them, but their dad is just dropping them off. Their mum can't swim and has a phobia of water and swimming pools."

"And that's allowed is it?" asked Paul's mum.

"Well that's what's been agreed by their parents and Peter Simpkin. They met by chance last week in town and had a good talk, and the outcome was Ben and Harry could go as long as they behaved themselves. Peter Simpkin agreed to keep an eye on them."

"Oh well, I'm looking forward to meeting these two boys. They sound like very suitable friends," said Paul's mum.

"Yeah they certainly are and they love skinny dipping."

Paul and his dad continued watching TV while his mum tidied up. "Right then," she said. "Are we gonna get ready and go?"

"Sure we are," replied Paul quickly getting up. He went upstairs to his bedroom and grabbed a towel. Paul put it in his bag along with a bottle of shower gel. No need for my shorts or swimming trunks this time, thought Paul with a smile. Paul went downstairs with his bag. "Right, I'm ready," he said.

"OK then. Have you got our stuff, Maureen?"

"Yes love I have," replied Paul's mum.

"Right, come on then let's go," said his dad. The Jessops got into the car and set off just after half six. It took them the usual ten to fifteen minutes to get there and once Paul's mum had parked the car they got out and walked over to the main entrance. The Handles weren't there yet so Paul and his mum and dad waited outside. While they were waiting a number of other naturists arrived including the Rustons.

"Oh hello Paul," said Mr. Ruston.

"Hi, it's great to see you all again. Have you met my mum and dad?" asked Paul.

"Er, just your mum very briefly I think."

"Well it's very nice to meet you er..." Paul's mum paused as she'd forgotten Mr. Ruston's first name.

"...Martin," said Mr. Ruston shaking hands with Paul's mum. "And this is my wife Catherine and our kids Alice and Craig."

"Hiya," said Alice.

"How's your foot now?" asked Paul.

"My foot?"

"Yeah; jelly fish, remember?"

"Oh yeah, it's fine now thanks." They all kept talking to pass the time while waiting and it wasn't long before another car pulled up. Two boys got out and walked across the car park to where the Jessops and the Rustons were waiting.

"Mum, look; it's Ben and Harry; they're here! Oh this swim is gonna be great with so many like-minded friends, I can't wait to get in there," said Paul excitedly. "I wonder where James and his mum and dad are, they're cutting it fine." It was almost seven o'clock when, to Paul's relief, the Handles finally turned up. "Where've you been?" asked Paul. "I was getting worried you weren't coming."

"We had to divert 'cos there'd been an accident," replied James.

"Aye, it looked pretty nasty from what I could make out, ruddy motorcyclists. The way some of them ride anyone would think the 'TT' course is over here."

"Oh I know, it's shocking. A friend of mine was nearly run over by one last Christmas," added Mrs. Ruston. "They think they're indestructible don't they." There were a few nodding heads to this as they all went in. Paul and James were first to strip off and wasted no time at all getting into the pool. They were quickly followed by Ben and Harry with Alice and Craig not far behind them. The adults brought up the rear and everyone was soon in the pool having fun. Ben and Harry thought it was wonderful swimming about completely naked in a normal swimming pool.

"Let's all have a go on the slide," suggested Harry. "I can't wait to slide down it naked."

"Yeah, come on then," said Paul. "Let's have a few goes on the slide." Paul led the way and was followed by Harry, James, Alice, Craig and Ben. None of them appeared to be even slightly bothered by the fact that they were completely naked. Paul stepped aside at the entrance to the slide and let Harry have first go. Harry disappeared down the slide with a whoosh and as soon as Paul got the green light he followed him. Harry swam to the side and waited for Paul. Paul swam over to Harry and asked him what he thought. "Well, do you prefer doing it naked?"

"Certainly do! That was fantastic! I never wanna wear my swimming trunks ever again," smiled Harry.

"Same here; if only it were doable," sighed Paul.

"Yeah I know. This should be the norm for swimming with occasional times when people can wear their costumes." Paul and Harry were soon joined by the others.

"Wow! Going down that slide with nothing on at all is excellent," smiled Ben.

"Yeah, you go a lot faster naked don't you," added Harry.

"I take it you know why," said James fully expecting everyone to know the reason you go down a water slide faster naked.

"Yeah, it's 'cos we're naked," replied Harry.

"And if you wear shorts or swimming trunks it slows you down 'cos they create drag. There's no drag between a smooth slide and a bare bum," said James smiling broadly.

"Let's all have another go then," suggested Craig. The six of them kept getting out and sliding down the slide, and after nearly half hour, a few of the adults joined them.

"Oh my word!" exclaimed Paul's mum. "I don't think I'll do that again, it's far too fast for me."

"What are you saying mum, it's absolutely brilliant," said Paul.

A short time later the staff decided to get the inflatable out. They set it up and turned on the fan which quickly filled it with air. Within just a few minutes it was ready to play on. Paul, James, Ben, Harry, Alice and Craig all swam over to it. They were having the time of their lives; especially Ben and Harry, who'd only ever dreamt of swimming and playing about in the nude.

Everyone was having a thoroughly good time in the pool this evening and the time past very quickly. It was about quarter to nine when the Rustons, Jessops, Handles and the Wetherby brothers all got together in the shallow end of the pool. Mr. Ruston remembered Paul and James practically begging to go with them the next time they stayed with his parents so decided to invite everyone. "Who'd like to get involved in some silly outdoor fun at my parents' house next weekend?" asked Mr. Ruston with a wry smile.

"Me!" replied Paul quickly.

"And me!" added James.

"What exactly do you mean by 'silly outdoor fun'," asked James's mum.

"Well, although my dad is sixty three, he has a habit of behaving like a child. He's recently bought a bouncy castle."

"He's actually got it?" asked Paul excitedly.

"Yes Paul he has, and he's already had it inflated."

"Oh fantastic!" Paul and James's parents had no idea why he was getting so overexcited, and neither had Ben and Harry for that matter.

"Well, when we went to the Welsh coast for the weekend not

so long ago Craig let it slip to James what we get up to at my parents' house. They're naturists too and so are my in-laws."

"So go on then, tell us what you get up to," smiled James's dad.

"Yeah, why is Paul so thrilled by a bouncy castle. He's nearly fifteen and hasn't been on one for years to my knowledge," said Paul's dad.

"Right, well; where do I start. A few years ago my dad saw some programme on TV which was about naturism and naturist activities. A group of naturists were having fun running around and throwing wet sponges at each other. My dad got us to do this one afternoon and we really loved it. However, the next time we went he decided to go one better with water-filled balloons; again, great fun and we all ended up soaking wet."

"What about gunge-filled balloons and that slide?" asked Paul.

"I was just getting to that," replied Mr. Ruston.

"Did your dad fill some balloons with gunge?" asked Harry.

"Yes he did, and we had a whale of time throwing them at each other. My dad also set up a slide which consisted of a strip of plastic sheeting about five or six feet wide by about eighty feet long. We threw water on to it initially, but because we were all sliding down it covered in gunge it became messier and messier as time went on. My mum poured some baby oil on to it which made it really slippy. It was impossible to stand on it after that."

"So where does a bouncy castle come in?" asked James's mum.

"Well I'm guessing they're going to have some kind off gunge fight then jump up and down on the bouncy castle," said Paul's dad.

"Yes, in a nut shell that's pretty much it. After we've finished we all get cleaned up and have a barbecue," said Mr. Ruston.

"This sound like a great way to spend an afternoon," smiled Harry.

"Me too; I'd love to join in," added Ben.

"Well, there's plenty of room at my parents' house so who'd be up for it?" Paul, James, Ben and Harry immediately raised their hands.

"Were you thinking of us staying over for the weekend or just coming for the afternoon and evening?" asked James's mum.

"What we normally do is arrive on Friday evening about eight to half past and then stay until Sunday teatime or early evening," replied Mr. Ruston.

"Saturday's the day we have all the fun and barbecue," said Alice.

"Yeah, anyway; it's time to get out now so let's continue this conversation in reception." Everyone showered for a few minutes then got dried and dressed. They gathered in the reception area and continued talking about next weekend. Ben and Harry's dad came in to collect his sons.

"Ah, there you are. Did you enjoy it then?" he asked knowing full well what the answer would be.

"It was great dad, absolutely wonderful," said Harry. "You must let us come again."

"Yeah too right," added Ben. "I can't remember the last time I had as much fun as this. It was great going down the slide naked."

"Can we come again next time dad? Please," begged Harry.

"Hmm, where's Peter Simpkin?" asked their dad.

"I don't think he's come out of the changing room yet dad," replied Ben.

"Oh he's here, behind you," said Harry quickly.

"Ah, Peter; everything go OK?"

"Oh yeah, fine. Your sons loved it and they're more than welcome to attend regularly if they want to. Why don't you and your wife come too, I'm sure you'd like it once you got used to it," smile Peter Simpkin.

"Hmm, I might come myself next time, but my wife would never come anywhere near the place 'cos she's hydrophobic, and as a result she never learnt to swim."

"Oh I'm sorry to hear that."

"It's not too much of a problem. It just means she has to keep away from the sea, rivers, swimming pools and such like."

"Dad, everyone's going now," said Ben. They followed them outside into the car park and kept chatting. Ben and Harry were trying to get their dad's attention to tell them they'd been invited over to spend next weekend with friends of Paul and

James, but they didn't get chance to say so before the Jessops, Handles and Rustons left.

"I'll text you tomorrow Ben," called Paul as he past by in his dad's car. Ben, Harry and their dad eventually got into their car and headed home.

"Dad, can we go away next weekend with Paul and James," asked Ben hopefully.

"Hmm, possibly. We'll talk it over when we get home."

Chapter 15

It was Sunday morning now, and after breakfast, Paul sat down in the front room with his mobile phone. He texted Ben in order to find out if he and Harry would be accompanying him and James next weekend at Alice and Craig's grandparents' house. Within a matter of seconds Paul's phone rang; it was Ben. "Hiya Ben," said Paul.

"Hi Paul," replied Ben.

"Have you asked your mum and dad about next weekend?"

"Yeah, but we've not really had a straight answer yet. My mum and dad were hoping the four of us could do something together seeing as it's school holidays."

"Oh right, so you can't make it then?"

"No I didn't actually say that. I just overheard my parents talking while they were having breakfast this morning."

"Oh I see; well why don't you and Harry come over this afternoon, we can watch TV, play a few games and have a bit of tea if you like."

"Yeah thanks Paul, I'm sure we can manage that. I'll just ask my dad, hang on a minute." Ben asked his dad if he and Harry could go and visit Paul.

"Yes if you like. You'll have to get the bus there though. Your mum and me are going to the garden centre this afternoon and then were going to see your mum's aunt in hospital, OK?"

"Yeah OK dad, we'll get the bus there; but if you can pick us up about nine o'clock that'd be great."

"Yes, OK whatever."

"Cheers dad. Paul? Are you still there?"

"Yeah, are you both coming?"

"Yeah we are, thanks very much for the invite. I haven't told Harry yet, but I think he'll come. He's not really one for garden centres," laughed Ben.

"Yeah, I heard you talking to your dad," smiled Paul.

"Right then, we should be at yours for about half two to three, OK?"

"Yeah fine, see you when you get here, bye for now."

"OK then, bye." Paul hung up and then went next door to tell

James he'd invited Ben and Harry over.

"Oh good," smiled James. "What time are they coming?"

"Ben said about half two to three so do you wanna come round about twenty past two?"

"Yeah, OK then."

"Right, I'll see you later." Paul left and went back next door. "Ah mum, I've invited Ben and Harry Wetherby round like you suggested last week."

"Oh, have you indeed. You might've given me a bit of notice young man."

"Oh sorry mum," said Paul. "Shall I ring them back and..."

"Oh no don't do that, what on earth will they think? If you want them to come make a start tidying the front room; and your bedroom."

"Yeah OK mum, will do." Paul went upstairs to make a start on his bedroom. He picked up a few items of clothing from the floor and put them in the laundry basket. This isn't too bad, Paul thought to himself as he straightened his bed. Paul emptied his litter bin and took the contents downstairs. "I've done my bedroom now mum," said Paul.

"Right, well when I've finished the dusting you can vac in here and I think that'll do," said Paul's mum.

"OK then; where's dad?"

"He said he was cleaning the car, but that was at least an hour ago."

"Oh right." Paul and his mum continued tidying up and after a good half hour they finished. Paul put the vacuum cleaner away and sat down. He picked up one of the Sunday papers and a thin sportswear catalogue fell out. Paul picked it up and was glancing through it when he got quite a surprise. He instantly recognised Ben and Harry Wetherby. "Mum, come here a minute," called Paul.

"Why, what is it?"

"Look at this," said Paul handing his mum the sportswear catalogue from one of the papers. "Don't you recognise anyone, from the swim last night?"

"Hmm, I don't think so love," replied Paul's mum. Paul pointed out Ben and Harry in the catalogue, but as his mum had only seen them once at the swim last night she didn't recognise them straightaway.

"It's the Wetherby brothers, Ben and Harry," said Paul.

"You mean the two boys that you've invited round this afternoon."

"Yes," said Paul. "They bumped into someone a while back at the leisure centre who was looking for models and they just happened to be in the right place at the right time." Paul told his mum all about Ben and Harry becoming sportswear models. "Ben and Harry told us they were treated like superstars the first time, and they got loads of free stuff like tracksuits, T-shirts, shorts, trainers and whatnot," continued Paul.

"Well, I think you ought to get the vac out again if we're going to have celebrities in the house," joked Paul's mum.

"I'm going to leave it open at the this page; I wanna see if they see it when they arrive," said Paul.

After lunch Paul's mum tidied the kitchen and then went into the front room to speak to her son. "Ah Paul, your dad and I are going to the airport in a few minutes. We've just remembered we agreed to collect Mr. and Mrs. Hope. They're returning from Gran Canaria today."

"Oh, right; but what about Ben and Harry? They should be here in less than an hour."

"It's OK love, you can stay here. If we get delayed I'll give you a ring."

"When do you think you'll be back?" asked Paul.

"At a rough guess about four o'clock, but it could be later," replied his mum. "We should be back in plenty of time to make you and your friends some tea."

"If you're late you could always bring us back some fish and chips; I'm sure Ben and Harry would like that," smiled Paul.

"We'll see young man. Too much fat isn't good for you." Just then Paul's dad came downstairs and into the front room.

"Are you ready, Maureen?" he asked. "If you've got friends coming round you'll have to stay here Paul."

"Yeah I know, it's OK; you and mum go collect the Hopes from the airport, I'll be fine. James will be here soon anyway."

Paul watched his parents drive away then closed the front

door. Paul was now alone and was thinking about going naked again; so, after a brief pause for thought he closed the curtains in the front room and then took all his clothes off. Paul switched the TV on and sat down on the sofa. He kept the sound low so he could hear James when he knocked on the front door. I wonder what James will think if I answer the door to him naked, thought Paul. It was nearing twenty past two. Not long to find out I guess. Paul peeped through the curtains, but didn't see James. Twenty past two came and went and with no sign of James, Paul was wondering where he was. Paul quickly nipped upstairs to the toilet and while he was washing his hands there was a knock on the front door. Ah, James at last, thought Paul. Paul quickly dried his hands and went downstairs to let James in, only it wasn't James. To Paul's surprise it was Ben and Harry! Paul opened the front door to let them in, and in the process, gave them quite a surprise. "Oh, er; I'm sorry," said Paul in shock and at the same time trying to hide behind the front door.

"Wow! I must say you're a keen naturist Paul," smiled Ben.

"I'm sorry, I thought it was James. He said he'd be here by now and I wanted to see his reaction when I answered the door to him naked."

"Well you certainly got a reaction from us alright; no one's ever answered the door to us naked before."

"Well, come on in then," said Paul now a bit more relaxed. The three of them went through to the front room and sat down.

"Does your mum and dad know you do this?" asked Ben.

"Er..."

"No they don't do they," smiled Harry.

"Well, my mum did walk in on James and me watching TV in the nude once, but she didn't say much," replied Paul. "I only do it now again when my mum and dad go out. I like relaxing in the nude; it feels nice and it's really liberating. You remember when we went skinny dipping and then walked off naked?"

"Oh yeah, I'll never forget that day," smiled Ben.

"Well listen, if you were thinking of giving James a surprise why don't we take our clothes off and join you," suggested Harry. "I'd love to see his face when he walks in!"

"Hmm, so would I now you mention it," smiled Paul.

"What we waiting for then?" asked Harry taking off his T-shirt.

"Are you sure your mum and dad aren't going to come back suddenly?" asked Ben.

"They've gone to pick an old couple up from the airport and they said they'd be back about four, but it could be later," said Paul.

"OK then." Ben took his T-shirt off as Harry took off his trainers and socks. Ben took his trainers and socks off too followed by his tracksuit bottoms. Ben and Harry paused for a moment and sat still on the sofa wearing only their underwear. Ben felt slightly uneasy at the thought of actually being naked in someone else's house.

"Oh don't stop there," said Paul. "I've closed the curtains in here and in the kitchen so no one can see us. I'll just nip upstairs and get some towels from the airing cupboard, won't be a minute." Paul disappeared upstairs leaving Ben and Harry alone.

"Come on then, let's take our pants off before Paul comes back down," suggested Harry. Harry stood up in front of his brother and took his pants off.

"Oh what am I so worried about," said Ben. "It's not as if we haven't seen each other naked before." Ben quickly took his pants off and sat on the sofa next to Harry. Paul came back into the front room with four medium sized towels.

"Oh brilliant, you've done it; do you feel OK?" asked Paul.

"As long as your parents don't catch us like this we'll be fine," replied Ben.

"Is James coming or not?" asked Harry.

"Well, he said he'd be here at twenty past two, and it's nearly quarter to three now. I wonder where he could be." Just then there was a knock on the front door. Paul peeped through the curtains to see who it was.

"Can you see who it is?" asked Ben.

"Yeah I can, it's James," replied Paul. "Just before I let him in, would you sit on that chair over there on this towel Ben, and Harry, could you move to the end of the sofa please and sit on a towel too. I want James to see us naked as soon as he walks in," continued Paul. Ben and Harry waited in the front room as Paul went to let James in. "Hi James, come on in."

"Paul, don't you think answering the door naked is a bit risky? I could've been anyone," said James firmly.

"It's OK, I knew it was you I checked; where've you been anyway?" asked Paul.

"I'm sorry, I got watching TV with my dad and forgot what time it was. Are Ben and Harry here yet?"

"Yeah they're in the front room, go through," replied Paul while trying not to smirk. James went through into the front room and was somewhat surprised to see Ben and Harry calmly sat down in the nude.

"Oh! Er,"

"Hi James," smiled Harry.

"Hi. Er, Paul; why are Ben and Harry naked?"

"Because they're naturists now, just like us. My mum and dad are out so we've got the place to ourselves until around four," replied Paul.

"Ah right," smiled James. "Well I might as well take my clothes off then."

"Please do," said Paul. "Can you sit on a towel like Ben and Harry please? It's supposed to be what naturists do."

"Yeah sure," replied James taking off his T-shirt and shorts.

"Hey, James; don't you wear underwear?" asked Harry with a smile.

"Not when I'm wearing my shorts I don't, it feels better without. Paul's the same; in fact, it was him who started it. 'Just put your shorts on and see how you feel'. Wasn't that what you said Paul after our first naked attempt?"

"Yes, I think so; and I stand by it. Would anyone like a drink?" asked Paul. "We've got some lemonade and orange juice or I can put the kettle on if you'd like tea or coffee."

"Orange juice is fine for me thanks," replied Ben.

"Harry?"

"Lemonade please," said Harry.

"James?"

"Yeah, same for me thanks." Paul went into the kitchen and came back with a tray of drinks.

"I know we're indoors, but how do we all feel being naked

and enjoying a drink together?" asked Paul.

"Great, I like it," smiled Harry raising his glass. "Cheers."

"I must admit Harry's right, being naked is very pleasant and relaxing no matter where you are," added Ben.

"If you got the chance to do it at home do you think you would?" asked James.

"Er," Ben thought for a moment.

"Yeah, I would," said Harry. "If our mum and dad were to go out for an hour or two, why not."

"Yeah, but they don't do they; not without us," said Ben.

"Well what about when you come with us next weekend? Did you get a definite answer from your mum and dad?" asked Paul.

"Oh yeah I forgot about that; our mum and dad are fine with it. They've decided to stay in a hotel somewhere next weekend while we come with you. We didn't tell them about the bouncy castle or throwing wet sponges about and whatnot."

"Hmm, perhaps you did right there," smiled Paul.

"Yeah, you can tell them all about it when you get back," added James. There was a brief pause in the conversation which Ben then interrupted.

"Now that we're here, didn't you mention something about playing a game?"

"Oh yeah, do you wanna play Monopoly?" asked Paul.

"I'd love to," smiled Harry.

"OK then, it's in my bedroom, won't be a moment." Paul disappeared upstairs again and came back down with his Monopoly. James helped him set it up and within a few minutes the four of them were enjoying playing Monopoly together naked.

Four o'clock came and quickly went, and because they were so engrossed in playing Monopoly, not even Paul realised. Everything had gone fairly well at the airport; the Hope's flight had landed on time and Paul's parents had collected them and taken them home. They stayed for a while and enjoyed a cup of tea and a sandwich or two, but then decided to head home as their son had invited a couple of friends over for tea. Paul's mum and dad got into the car and drove the short distance home. Paul's dad parked the car, but before either of them got out he glanced across at the house and saw the curtains drawn. "Maureen, did you draw the curtains before we left?"

"No I don't think..." Paul's mum stopped abruptly and looked at her husband. "Are you thinking what I'm thinking?"

"Hmm, possibly," smiled Paul's dad. "Do you think they could be in there watching TV again in the nude?"

"Only one way to find out I suppose," replied Paul's mum.

"Hang on a minute love; if they hear us unlock the front door they'll just grab their clothes. Do you fancy giving them the surprise of their lives?" suggested Paul's dad with a broad smile.

"Tony Jessop! Are you really the man I married?"

"Come on love, let's do it. If we nip in via the back door, strip off and walk in on them while they're naked, their faces will be a picture." Paul's parents walked round to the back door and also noticed the kitchen curtains were drawn.

"Look, the kitchen curtains are drawn too; I bet a pound to a penny they're naked."

"Come on then, let's give 'em a surprise!" Paul's dad carefully unlocked the back door and they crept in without making a sound. He led the way up the cellar steps and peeped through the door at the top. He clearly saw the Wetherby brothers, James and his son playing Monopoly naked. "Maureen, there's four of them," whispered Paul's dad. "Our son is playing Monopoly with James and the two lads who were at the swim last night; and they're all stark naked."

"Well, come on then; let's take our clothes off and join them," smiled Paul's mum. Paul's parents carefully stripped off at the top of the cellar steps and left their clothes in a shopping bag. After slowly opening the door Paul's mum and dad entered the kitchen.

"I'll take some orange juice through to them," whispered Paul's dad very quietly. He carefully took a bottle of orange juice out of the fridge and closed the fridge door. Unfortunately, closing the fridge door made a slight snapping sound. Paul's parents stood perfectly still and waited.

"What was that noise just then?" asked Ben.

"What noise? I didn't hear anything," replied Paul.

"Have your mum and dad come back?" On hearing Ben say this Paul's parents nearly gave the game away by laughing uncontrollably. They almost felt like kids themselves skulking about in the nude.

"No; we'd have heard them come in wouldn't we, and I locked the front door," replied Paul. "What time is it?"

"Twenty to five," said James.

"Hmm, I'll just give them a quick ring and see where they are." Paul rang his mum's mobile, and after just a few seconds, the four of them heard it ringing.

"Oh no, I've left my phone with our clothes," whispered Paul's mum.

"Stay still," whispered Paul's dad. "Let's see what they do next."

"That's funny," said Paul. "I'm sure my mum had her phone with her when they left for the airport."

"Try it again," suggested James. "And let it ring a bit longer." Paul did just that and after half a dozen rings it went to voicemail. "It sounds like it's coming from the top of the cellar steps. Your mum must have left her phone in a shopping bag."

"Hmm, maybe; but I could've sworn she took it with her. She rarely goes anywhere without her phone. It's my dad who forgets his phone most of the time."

"Why don't you try ringing your dad's phone just in case he has got it with him," suggested Harry.

"OK then." Paul rang his dad's mobile, but it didn't ring, it went straight to voicemail. "My dad's phone is switched off, so it could be anywhere; and so could they for that matter," said Paul with a huff. Paul, James, Ben and Harry carried on playing Monopoly. "We'll just have to see if they use a pay phone that's all." Paul felt distinctly uncomfortable and was beginning to worry; something definitely wasn't right.

"Hang on a minute," said James. "I've just had a thought; why don't you have a look through the curtains and see if your dad's car's out there."

"Oh of course, I should've thought of that myself," said Paul. He peeped through the curtains and was shocked to see his dad's car parked up across the road.

"Well, is it there?" asked Harry.

"Oh my word, it is!" replied Paul with a shock.

"We'd better get some clothes on pretty quick," said Ben.

"No; hang on a minute," said Paul. "My dad's car will be there 'cos the Hopes only live down the road. They'll have probably dropped them off and then my dad will have parked his car up here. He'll then have walked back down to help my mum with the Hopes, so it's OK, we can stay naked until we hear the front door."

"Hmm, OK then," said Ben as he stepped out of his tracksuit bottoms.

"Whose go is it then?" asked Harry.

"I think it's yours Harry," replied James. By now Paul's mum and dad had been waiting in the kitchen nearly twenty minutes and couldn't last much longer. Paul's dad finally decided it was time to come out and surprise them. He walked into the front room and was closely followed by Paul's mum.

"Now then," said Paul's dad clearly. "Who'd like some orange juice?"

"Arrrh! DAD! MUM!" Paul was shocked at suddenly seeing his parents walk in on them naked.

"You don't mind if we join your little naturist group do you Paul?"

"Er, er, no I er, suppose not," stammered Paul.

"I'm sorry er, Mr. er," added Ben nervously. "It was Paul's idea to go naked."

"Relax, relax everyone," insisted Paul's dad. "The only difference to last night is the fact we're here and not in the swimming pool."

"You won't say anything to our parents when they come to collect us will you?" asked Ben.

"If you keep quiet about us gate crashing, we'll keep quiet about it all," smiled Paul's dad.

"Thanks Mr. Jessop," smiled Ben.

"Could we have some orange juice now please?" asked Harry.

"Course you can love," replied Paul's mum. Paul's mum shared the orange juice between the four of them while they continued their game of Monopoly. After Paul had won they put the game away and sat still. Paul then asked his parents how they'd got it without them noticing.

"Mum, do you know where your phone is? And how did you and dad get in here without us hearing you?"

"Well, when we arrived home we saw the curtains drawn and assumed you and James were watching TV again in the nude."

"So we just thought we'd come in through the back door and give you a bit of a surprise," smiled his dad.

"A bit of a surprise? Dad, I nearly had a coronary, not to mention what it must have felt like to Ben, Harry and James. Where's your clothes anyway?"

"We stripped off at the top of cellar steps after seeing you all naked. Our clothes are in a Morrisons bag just behind the door," said Paul's mum.

"And I bet your phone's in there as well isn't it," said Paul firmly.

"Yes love you know it is, you rang it twice," smiled his mum.

"I thought it was funny when it rang. I could've sworn you took it with you to the airport."

"Yes I did love, and you're right about your dad..."

"Maureen, I've only lost one phone," said Paul's dad quickly.

"Yes Tony, but let's be honest, you hardly ever take your phone with you when you go out."

"OK OK. I think it's time we made some tea now for our son and his friends," said Paul's dad.

"Yes of course; hands up those who'd like salad and brown bread."

"Mum!" said Paul abruptly.

"What about Beef burgers with chips and beans?" suggested his dad.

"Yes please," replied Harry and James smiling broadly.

"I don't mind a bit of salad with my burgers," said Ben. "But I'm not one for brown bread."

"It's OK, I was only joking; but I'll make you some salad if like, Ben."

"Thanks Mrs. Jessop." Paul's mum and dad went into the kitchen, and for the first time in their lives they prepared a meal while they were naked.

"I don't know about you Maureen, but I could get used to living like this, I feel great," said Paul's dad.

"Hmm; let's stay like this then for the rest of the day and see how it goes. It's not as if we're the only ones is it."

"OK love." Preparing tea didn't take very long and Paul's dad promptly brought through four plates of burgers chips and beans. Paul, James, Ben and Harry all enjoyed their tea together as only naturists know how. Paul's mum and dad weren't that hungry as they'd had a bite to eat earlier at the Hopes. After they'd finished Paul's mum took their plates, cutlery, and glasses from earlier, into the kitchen.

"Right then," said Paul's dad. "What we gonna do for the next couple of hours?"

"We could watch TV," suggested Paul.

"I think your friends might like to do something other than watch TV Paul," said his mum.

"What about a game of charades?" suggested James with a smile.

"Charades! James, I thought you were my best mate," said Paul with a look of mild horror on his face.

"Hang on a minute Paul," said Ben. "I think James's suggestion is pretty good actually. Have you ever played it like this?"

"No I haven't," replied Paul quickly.

"I think it'll be fun playing charades while we're all naked," smiled Harry. Paul thought for a moment about playing charades naked and did quite a U-turn.

"OK then, who'd like to go first?" asked Paul. This was followed by a short pause. "Well, why don't we start with whoever's name's first alphabetically."

"That's me," said Ben. "Thanks very much Paul."

"No it's not," said Paul's dad. "I assume we're all playing, and if we're following what Paul just suggested, I get first go as my proper name is Antony; but if you'd like to go first Ben I don't mind."

"No it's fine Mr. Jessop, you can go first." Paul's mum and dad moved the sofa and two chairs back a bit to create some space. Paul's dad then stood in front of everyone and had first go. There were quite a few guesses, and after a few minutes, Harry guessed the right answer.

"Well done Harry," said Paul's dad. "Who's going next?"

"Ben," said Paul while trying to hide a smirk.

"I'm not surprised you suggested alphabetical order Paul; it means you get to go last."

"I know, I've just worked it out myself; but I swear I didn't know when I suggested it."

"Go on Ben, just do as easy one if you can't think of anything much," suggested James.

"OK, here goes." Feeling a bit nervous, Ben got up and faced everyone. He paused for a moment to think and then began. James guessed it in a matter of seconds. "Yeah, well done James," said Ben. Ben sat down again feeling better after his participation in the game.

"Right, who's next?" asked Paul.

"...C, D, E, F, G, H, it's Harry," replied James, "...and then me."

"Oh great," smiled Harry as he got up off the sofa. Harry was enjoying playing charades naked so deliberately pick a difficult one and it took nearly ten minutes for Paul to guess correctly. They continued playing charades together, and after a while, it appeared they'd forgotten about being naked. James was next followed by Paul's mum and finally Paul. Paul's dad was keeping score and at this stage in the game Harry and James were level on two each. They had a short break and a drink then played another round. At the end of this Paul's dad proudly declared the winner.

"Right folks, I'm pleased to announce that Harry, with five correct guesses, is the winner."

"Oh brilliant!" smiled Harry. "What do I get for a prize?"

"Harry!" said Ben sharply. "This was only meant to be a bit of fun, no one said anything about prizes."

"It's fine, don't worry," said Paul's mum. "He can have a bag of sweets."

"Thanks Mrs. Jessop," smiled Harry.

A couple of minutes later Ben's phone rang; it was his dad and he couldn't quite remember where the Jessop's house was. "Hang on a minute dad, I'll let you speak to Paul's dad." Ben past his phone to Paul's dad so he could better explain where they lived. "I think we ought to get dressed now, our dad will be here soon to pick us up."

"OK then," said Harry. "I've really enjoyed being here today, thanks very much."

"It's been a pleasure," said Paul's mum. "We'll look forward to seeing you again sometime." Seeing as Ben and Harry's dad was due very shortly everyone decided to put some clothes on. He arrived just after quarter past nine and got out of his car to speak to Paul's parents.

"Everything go OK?"

"Yes fine thanks, they can come again whenever they like," replied Paul's mum.

"Thanks again Mrs. Jessop, we've really enjoyed it, haven't we Harry?"

"Yeah sure we have, and I'm looking forward to next weekend when we go away with you."

"Oh yeah, what time are you setting off?" asked Ben.

"About half three, so come for about three to quarter past and we'll take it from there."

"OK then see you Friday afternoon. Bye for now."

"Good night Paul and thanks again," said Harry. Ben and Harry set off home after an interesting day. Paul went back indoors with his parents and James. Together they reflected on the day with fondness.

"Aw no," said Paul.

"What's wrong now love?" asked his mum.

"Ben and Harry never noticed that catalogue I left on the table!"

Chapter 16

Just after quarter to nine next morning Paul got up, and after a quick shower, went downstairs wearing only his slippers and a towel. Following yesterday's naturist evening with the Wetherby brothers, Paul thought he'd have a go at living naked. He put his towel down on a chair in the kitchen and helped himself to some breakfast. His dad had gone to work, but his mum was outside hanging the washing out. She came in to get another load and was somewhat surprised to see her son eating his breakfast in the nude. "Oh!"

"Morning mum," said Paul politely, while behaving as if it was perfectly normal to be naked at the breakfast table. "I hope you don't mind, but I'm gonna to try and live naked; as much as I can anyhow."

"Er, right, OK love."

"I thought you and dad were gonna do the same after last night."

"Well, maybe love, but I can't really hang the washing out in the nude can I."

"No not really, someone might see you," smiled Paul.

"Anyway, I'm staying dressed a while longer while I nip out. I shouldn't be too long, I'm only going to that new Tesco Express just up the road."

"Oh, is it open now?" asked Paul.

"Yes I think so; I saw some people in it on Saturday morning," replied Paul's mum. Paul's mum hung out a few more items of clothing then headed off to Tesco's. Paul put his towel round him and went through to the front room. He closed the curtains and then took off his towel and spread it out on the sofa. Paul sat down and texted James, and within a few minutes James knocked on the front door. Without dressing Paul got up and let James in.

"Morning," said James.

"Hiya," replied Paul.

"Have you er; put any clothes on since last night?" asked James.

"Er, no. Only when Ben and Harry's dad came to pick them up

as you know, I've been naked since then; and I don't intend to get dressed unless I really need to."

"So you're really gonna live naked then?" asked James.

"Yeah; why don't you try it," suggested Paul.

"You actually want me to go about completely naked all the time?"

"Will your mum and dad mind?"

"I think they might; being naked at a swim for two or three hours is one thing, but being naked 24/7 is pushing it a bit don't you think."

"I'm only suggesting we go naked where and when we can. If you're staying for a while go naked now, my mum knows and she and dad are thinking about living naked too."

"OK then," smiled James. James took his clothes off and put them on a chair.

"Fancy a coffee?" asked Paul.

"Please," replied James. Paul put the kettle on and came back into the front room.

"My mum got given one of those cafetière things a while back and some ground coffee; do you fancy trying it?"

"Yeah, as long as your mum doesn't mind," replied James.

"I don't think she'll mind; in fact, I bet she's forgotten all about it," smiled Paul. Paul disappeared into the kitchen again and came back with two posh mugs, a few biscuits, a small jug of milk and a medium sized cafetière full of coffee all on a silver tray. "Coffee in the nude is served sir."

"Wow," said James in surprise. "This is more like er…"

"…coffee in a posh naturist resort?" finished Paul.

"Yeah, something like that."

"All I have to do now is push the plunger down, slowly but firmly, and then pour it into our mugs." Paul did just that. "You can help yourself to milk if you like, unless you prefer 'café noir'," smiled Paul.

"Café noir? What's that?" asked James.

"Black coffee of course. Didn't you learn anything in French?"

"Oh yeah, I remember now," said James.

"We'll need to know some French if we get to that place in France won't we."

"Yeah, I s'pose you're right. What was it called again, I've forgotten?"

"Er…" Paul thought for a moment. "I can't remember now either, but Alice and Craig's dad will know; it was him who told me about it." Paul and James continued talking about living naked while enjoying their coffee and biscuits together. When they'd finished Paul took everything they'd used back into the kitchen and rinsed the coffee grinds down the sink. While he was doing this his mum arrived back with a few items she'd bought at the new Tesco Express. James sat still on the sofa while Paul's mum came in.

"Hi Mrs. Jessop," said James.

"Oh; hello James," said Paul's mum in mild surprise at seeing James naked again. "Would I be correct in assuming Paul has told you about his intention to try and live naked?" Paul heard his mum say this and very quickly poked his head round the kitchen door.

"Yes mum I have, and he's bang up for it, aren't you James?"

"Well, I would like to be naked as much as possible, but Paul; we'll have to put some clothes on to go out won't we," replied James. "What I mean is; we can't possibly go to school naked. If we do we'll end up…"

"Don't be silly James; of course I'm not suggesting we go naked at school, except in the showers after PE, that can be our naked time at school. Let's just take our time in the shower and not rush in and out like we did before we became naturists," insisted Paul.

"Well that's what I've been doing more recently. I've got as I don't mind showering naked at school now. In fact, I quite enjoy it, and I'm usually the last one to get out," smiled James.

"I bet your classmates have noticed a difference James; have they said anything?" asked Paul's mum.

"Some have noticed, but they haven't said much. I wouldn't mind betting a lot of them worry about showering naked too, but try not to let on in case it makes them look weak or small; like it did me."

"Yeah well, we're not like that now, are we James? I could go naked almost anywhere, as long as it's warm enough," said Paul firmly. "And what about the reduction in washing eh?"

"Hmm..."

"Think about it mum; if we go about naked for an entire day there'll be no dirty clothes to wash; or iron for that matter," said Paul. This immediately stuck a chord with Paul's mum as she was the one who did virtually all the washing and ironing.

"OK then you two, you've convinced me," smiled Paul's mum. "We'll all live naked when we're at home and we'll only put on clothes if we have to, to go out." Paul's mum then took her clothes off and joined her son and his friend in living naked. As neither of them needed to go out all three of them stayed naked for the rest of the day, and Paul's dad was a bit surprised at suddenly seeing his wife, his son and his son's best friend naked in the front room watching TV after he arrived home earlier than normal. "Hello love," said Paul's mum.

"Hi dad," added Paul.

"Maureen, have I missed something?"

"Like what? I thought we were all going to try and live naked and see how it goes. I thought you were up for it after yesterday," smiled Paul's mum.

"Oh yeah, course, sorry. I've had a rather hectic day at work and I must admit it slipped my mind." Paul's dad closed the front door and went upstairs. He came down a few minutes later completely naked.

"Feel better?" asked Paul's mum.

"Sure do love."

"I've been like this all day dad and I feel great," smiled Paul. "James is going to try and live naked as well, aren't you James," continued Paul while glancing across at James.

"Yeah, I sure am; I'll go naked as often as I can," replied James.

"Well then, are you staying for tea James?" asked Paul's mum.

"Yes I will, thanks very much Mrs. Jessop," replied James.

"Hang on a minute," said Paul. "If you're staying for tea James why don't you ask your mum and dad to join us, that way we can introduce the idea of living naked."

"Yeah OK, that's a brilliant idea Paul," smiled James.

"Just bob your shorts on James while you go next door,"

said Paul's mum. James quickly put his trainers and shorts on and went to ask his parents if they'd like to have tea with the Jessops. However, James didn't quite know what to say about it being 'tea in the nude', so didn't say much.

"Hi mum, dad," said James as he went it.

"Hiya son," said his dad.

"Where's your T-shirt?" asked his mum.

"Oh, I've er, left it next door," replied James quickly. "I'm going back there for tea with Paul and his mum and dad, and you're invited too, that's what I've come back to tell you. Paul and his mum and dad would like to, er... see you about something."

"Oh, OK son. Do they want us right now?"

"Yes please; come on mum," replied James.

"OK we're coming," said his mum. James quickly went back next door and joined the Jessops in the nude. James's dad knocked on the Jessop's front door.

"Come on in dad it's not locked," called James. James's parents entered and were quite surprised to see everyone, including their son, completely naked.

"My word," said James's dad. "Are you all living naked now?"

"Yes we certainly are!" smiled Paul raising his glass of orange juice. "I've been naked all day and I can't think of a nicer way to live. Didn't James tell you about it being tea in the nude?"

"No he didn't," replied James's mum. "But I don't suppose it matters much."

"Well come on then Helen, are we gonna join our son and our friends and get naked?"

"Well, I don't see why not," smiled James's mum taking off her top. James's mum and dad stripped off and sat down. Paul quickly offered them a glass of orange juice. "Would you like a hand with anything Maureen?" asked James's mum.

"Er, yes thanks; you could lay the table. Paul, would you and James help lay the table for tea please?" asked Paul's mum.

"Yeah OK mum." Paul's mum then brought two bowls of salad through and large cheese and bacon quiche. Paul brought though some bread, butter and pickles.

"Right everyone, if you'd like to sit to the table I'll serve the quiche. Please help yourselves to salad." With the exception of James, this was the first time the Handles had ever eaten a meal in the nude, and they had to admit they enjoyed the experience.

"This is nice Maureen; did you make it yourself?" asked James's dad.

"Yes thanks I did, with a little help from Paul." replied Paul's mum. Everyone enjoyed their tea and kept chatting about this and that until James brought up the subject of next weekend.

"Mum, dad; have I told you where we've been invited to this weekend?"

"Not exactly son," replied James's dad.

"You said we'd been invited to spend the weekend with the Rustons, that family we met last time we went swimming?"

"Yeah that's right." replied James. "We've all been invited over for the whole weekend and we're staying with Mr. Ruston's parents, that's Alice and Craig's grandparents. They're naturists too and they live in a big house. Their garden has a tall hedge all the way round so when we go there we'll be able to go naked straightaway," smiled James."

"Yeah, there could be quite a few of us there," said Paul. "There's the six of us plus Ben and Harry which makes eight; then there's the Rustons themselves which makes twelve."

"So there could be sixteen of us in total if Mrs. Ruston's parents go," added James.

"Well I don't know about anyone else, but I'm really looking forward to it," smiled James's dad.

"Have you any idea what we're going to be doing while we're there?" asked James's mum.

"I think Craig said something about body painting," smiled James. James then looked across at Paul and gave him a nod.

"We'll be playing some games and having a lot of fun," smiled Paul. "Mr. Ruston's dad has bought a bouncy castle, so that's what I'm looking forward to."

"Tut, a bouncy castle at your age Paul." tutted his mum.

"Don't tell me you're not gonna have a go on it mum, it'll be fun, 'cos Mr. Ruston's dad is gonna er… spray water on it."

"…and gunge," said James. Paul glared at James. He didn't really want him to mention gunge until they got there, but thankfully his and James's parents didn't pick up on it.

After tea Paul helped his mum tidy up. When they'd finished they joined the others in the front room. Paul then suggested playing charades again after enjoying playing it naked yesterday evening with the Wetherby brothers. Playing charades naked was definitely a first for James's mum and dad, and everyone had a few laughs along the way. Time seemed to slip away quickly and it was nearly nine o'clock when Paul's mum suggested having a bit of supper. She made some tea and buttered a few scones. Paul helped her carry them into the front room. "So, how do we all feel about living naked?" asked Paul.

"Fine," replied James. "I'll go naked whenever I can, as long as mum and dad don't mind."

"No we don't mind a bit James; you can spend as much time as you like naked at home, can't he Helen?"

"Yes of course he can. I've really enjoyed this evening, and being naked feels wonderful. It makes me realise just how wrong I was when we first found out about it."

"It's a pity we couldn't be outside in the warm sunshine like this," added James's dad.

"Well we can next weekend dad," smiled James.

"Yeah, I just hope the weather doesn't spoil it," said Paul.

"Me too," added James.

At about quarter to ten the Handles decided it was time to go home. James and his parents put the minimum amount of clothing on and went back next door. As soon as they got inside James drew the curtains, removed his clothes and switched on the TV. He sat down on a towel, in accordance with naturist etiquette, on the sofa and waited to see what his parents said if anything. "It'll soon be bedtime James so don't start getting too engrossed in watching TV," said His mum. His dad came downstairs naked and joined his son in the front room. James's mum was still partly dressed and in the kitchen making a bedtime drink. She came into the front room with three mugs of drinking chocolate. "Be careful you two; don't spill any or you'll end up scalding yourselves somewhere er, very sensitive," smiled James's mum.

"We can manage can't we son," said James's dad.

"Yeah sure we can mum," replied James.

"You not going naked love?"

"Yeah OK then," replied James's mum. The Handles were now sat in their front room completely naked. "So, how long are we planning on living naked?"

"For always I hope," said James. "Except perhaps when we have friends round who aren't naturists."

"Yeah, let's see if we can outdo the Jessops when it comes to living naked," smiled James's dad.

"We'll see," smiled James's mum.

It was now Friday, the day Paul and James were looking forward to. They simply couldn't wait to get to Alice and Craig's grandparents' house. To kill two or three hours in the morning they went out together to their usual place as it was quite warm and returned shortly after lunchtime. The Jessops and the Handles then packed a few things to take with them.

At around half past two James and his mum and dad knocked on the Jessops front door. Wearing only a towel Paul let them in. "Hi," said Paul.

"Are you nearly ready?" asked James.

"Yeah, once I'm dressed. My mum and dad have packed what we need to take. They're upstairs at the moment so come on in and make yourselves at home."

"Thanks," said James's mum and dad.

"I think we ought to stay dressed seeing as we'll be going fairly soon," added James.

"Oh that's OK; I'm gonna get dressed myself now anyway," said Paul. Paul went upstairs and got dressed. He came back down a few minutes later wearing a bright green T-shirt, his shorts and socks. His mum and dad followed him downstairs.

"Right, I think we're just about ready," said Paul's mum. "Shall I put the kettle on while we wait for Ben and Harry to arrive?"

"Oh yes please," replied James's mum. "I'd love a coffee."

"Mmm, me too," said James's dad.

"OK then, won't be a moment." Paul's mum went into the kitchen and came back with a tray of six coffees. They chatted amongst themselves while waiting for the Wetherby brothers to arrive. Ben and Harry arrived shortly after three.

"Mum, Ben and Harry are here," said Paul looking out of the window. Paul saw them getting out of the car so immediately put his trainers on and went out to meet them.

"Hiya," said Paul.

"Hiya Paul," said Ben. "Are we going straightaway, only my dad would like to have a chat with your mum and dad."

"No problem come inside. James and his mum and dad are here too," said Paul. Ben, Harry and their dad went inside.

"Hi everyone," said Ben and Harry's dad. "I hope you all have a good time wherever it is your going. Let me know when you want me to pick them up on Sunday evening."

"OK then, we will do," said Paul's mum.

"See you Sunday boys."

"OK, bye dad," said Ben and Harry. Ben and Harry's dad then said good bye and left.

"Right then; if we're all ready we might as well get going," said Paul's dad.

"Ben, would you like to come with us, and Harry; would mind going with James and his mum and dad?" suggested Paul.

"Yeah, that'll be fine," said Ben.

"Are we going straight there?" asked Harry.

"We're meeting the Rustons first at their house, then we're driving on to where Mr. Ruston's parents live a bit later," replied Paul. Everyone put their bags in the appropriate car, and after a few last minute checks, set off. It didn't take more than twenty minutes to get to the Ruston's house and once they'd arrived Paul's dad got out. He went over to ask them what the plan was in regards to getting to Alice and Craig's grandparents' house. Paul's dad came back a few minutes later and informed everyone.

"Right folks, they're almost ready. Once they leave, we'll follow them. It shouldn't take much more than an hour to get there." The Rustons all came out and got into their car. Alice and Craig's dad gave them a flash of headlights which Paul's dad took as the signal to get going.

A good hour later they arrived at Alice and Craig's grandparents' house; they parked up and everyone got out. Mr. Ruston (senior) came out and met them wearing only sandals and what appeared to be a short sarong. "Grandad!" shouted Alice and Craig as they ran over to him.

"Martin, Catherine; it's good to see you again," smiled Alice and Craig's grandad.

"Hiya dad; we've brought a few extra this time, hope you don't mind!"

"Mind! Why on earth would I mind love, the more the merrier I always say!" Paul and James smiled at each other. "I take it we all know why we're here and roughly what we're going to be doing, yeah?"

"Oh yes!" said Paul eyes lighting up in anticipation of a weekend of naked fun.

"How soon can we go naked?" asked James.

"As soon as we get round the back; I'm only wearing this flimsy wrap in case anyone walks past the gate."

"Oh brilliant!"

"Would you be Paul by any chance?" asked Alice and Craig's grandad.

"Yeah I am, and this is my best friend James."

"Hmm, my grandson told me about you two; he says you're keen to get involved in all the fun."

"We are; aren't we James?" replied Paul firmly.

"Oh yeah, sure."

"Well, if you'd all like to follow me round the back and into the garden we can strip off; then, when you're ready, I'll show you to your rooms." Alice and Craig's grandad led the way and was closely followed by Paul and James, and once out of sight of the road, he removed his sarong. "Right, if you'd all like to go naked now you can take your clothes with you to your rooms. If anyone needs a hand just say so." Everyone stripped off and put their clothes in their bags. With the possible exception of a hat no one was wearing anything more than sandals or trainers.

"Right, I'm ready," said Paul promptly.

"Me too," said James.

"And me," added Harry. When everyone was ready Alice and Craig's grandad invited them in and showed them upstairs to their rooms.

"Right, there's four single beds in this room so if the boys would like to choose a bed..."

"Thanks," replied Paul as he entered. Paul, James, Ben and Harry all chose a bed to sleep on and put their clothes and things down by the side of them.

"What do you think of this then?" Paul asked the others.

"Brilliant," smiled Harry.

"Yeah, it is a lovely room," added Ben.

"I think so too, but we ought see what else there is," said James.

"Yeah, James is right; come on guys, let's rejoin the others." Paul, James, Ben and Harry were about to leave their room wearing nothing more than their trainers or sandals. "Hang on a minute, I've just had a thought. I'm gonna to take my trainers off. I doubt there'll be anything we can tread on so I'm gonna go completely naked," said Paul.

"Yeah, I am too," said Harry. In the end all four of them decided to take their footwear off and go fully naturist. They quickly caught up with the others and after seeing where they were sleeping Alice and Craig's grandad showed them a communal shower area similar to that at the leisure centre.

"Please feel free to shower as often as you like; and by the way, the one at the end is cold!"

"Oh great," smiled James. "I can get a cold shower in the morning just like I do at home."

"Do you get straight into a cold shower after getting out of bed?" asked Ben.

"Yeah, most mornings. It wakes you up."

"I bet it does!"

"Right, well that's the guided tour complete so let's all go outside into the warm sunshine."

Alice and Craig's grandparents were used to entertaining and had plenty of garden furniture in the form of chairs and tables with large parasols. He held a glass of white wine in his hand and welcomed them in an almost official way. "Right; to all regulars, and newcomers, my I welcome you to our naked paradise."

"Thanks very much," said Paul.

"Please help yourselves to a drink and a few nibbles. Catherine; did you say your parents were coming over this weekend or not,

I can't remember?"

"Oh I'm sorry, I forgot to tell you. They've gone to the south coast for a long weekend, and they've had it booked for a couple of months."

"Oh don't worry love. They can come next time. I expect they'll enjoy Studland beach."

"Studland beach?" said Paul after overhearing what was just said. "Is that a naturist beach?"

"Yes, part of it is. It's usually regarded as the best naturist beach in the UK," replied Alice and Craig's grandad.

"Really!" Paul looked at his mum and dad, but didn't need to say anything 'cos they too heard what had just been said.

"We'll see Paul. The south coast is quite a long way away," said his mum.

"OK then. Would someone like to give me a hand setting up? I'm sure you'd all like to dance the night away while you're naked." Paul and his dad offered to help and the music system and speakers were soon set up. Alice and Craig's gran had also been busy preparing food and drink. "We'll be having the barbecue tonight as the weather forecast for tomorrow evening isn't too good," said Alice and Craig's grandad. "Oh, before I forget I've a couple of surprises for you all. Paul; would like to remove that green cover."

"Sure, what is it?"

"Just remove the cover and you'll soon see," smiled Alice and Craig's grandad. Paul did as he'd been asked and underneath the cover was a fairly large jacuzzi.

"Oh wow!" exclaimed Paul. "And it's lovely and warm. Can I get in?"

"In a minute Paul, I'd like to show you all something else. Craig, would you like to remover the other cover down there."

"I'll give him a hand," said James. Craig and James pulled back the cover together to reveal a beautifully clean swimming pool.

"Well, what do we thing to these little additions then?" asked Alice and Craig's grandad.

"Grandad they're brilliant," replied Craig.

"Can we have a swim please?" asked Alice.

"Yes of course jump straight in." Alice did just that and was quickly followed by Paul and Craig, but before James jumped in all three of them very quickly got out.

"Ah! Grandad, it's freezing!" screamed Alice.

"Yeah, it is pretty cold," added Paul. Unfortunately, when Alice and Craig's grandad had switched the pool heating on a few hours ago it blew the main fuse, so consequently the pool had not been heated.

"That's odd; I switched the pool heating on just after lunchtime. Just bear with me while I check that out." Alice and Craig's grandad disappeared inside and found the offending fuse in a matter of minutes. Who the hell put a five amp fuse in this, he said to himself; no wonder it blew, it should've been a thirty amp, and I bet I haven't got a spare one. They waited for Alice and Craig's grandad to sort out the swimming pool and after a few minutes he came back outside and told everyone what the problem was. "I'm sorry about the pool, a fuse has blown and I haven't got a spare one."

"Well, couldn't we use it as a cold plunge pool after we've been in the jacuzzi?" suggested James.

"I suppose we can," replied Alice and Craig's grandad. "I won't be able to do anything with it until tomorrow."

"Can we have a go in the Jacuzzi now grandad?" asked Alice.

"Yeah go on then, but be careful you don't slip. Oh, just one more thing everybody; after the balloon fight tomorrow please shower before getting into the jacuzzi. I've hired it for the weekend and it's 'cost me almost £300 so I don't want anyone getting into it covered in gunge, clear?"

"Yeah OK grandad," said Craig.

"Wouldn't it be a good idea to cover it tomorrow afternoon while we have our balloon fight," suggested Paul.

"Yes I will do that now you come to mention it Paul. Well, please do make yourselves at home and help yourselves to a drink if you haven't already, I'll get the barbecue going in half an hour or so." Paul, James, their mums and dads, and Ben and Harry helped themselves to refreshments. They were really enjoying being naked in Alice and Craig's grandparents' garden. They had quite a large area to play and relax in and save for the patio next to the house, all of it was grass lined with a tall thick hedge and a few of those infamous Leylandii trees, which in the past have been known to cause neighbour disputes; but in this case the absence of them would probably be the cause of any dispute!

Just after half six Alice and Craig's grandad lit the barbecue. He struggled with it for a few minutes but it took hold soon enough. Alice and Craig's gran brought out a couple of large trays mostly of meat. There was steak, burgers, sausages, pieces of chicken and a few skewers containing mushrooms, onions, peppers and tomatoes. Looking across at all the food Paul had the distinct feeling the barbecue was going to be fantastic. James glanced across at the food too and then at Paul. "Looking at all that meat is making me feel really hungry," said James.

"Me too," smiled Paul. "I can't wait to try a sausage 'cos they're usually the best."

"Mmm, I like most things you can cook on a barbecue, even veggie burgers."

"Veggie burgers!" snapped Paul pulling a face.

"Yeah, my mum bought a pack by mistake last year; we grilled them and they didn't taste too bad, but my dad didn't care for them."

Paul thought for a moment and smiled; "You bought veggie burgers by mistake and you ate them?"

"Yeah, so what? Mum didn't want to throw them away."

"Well, I was just wondering how many veggies would eat normal burgers if they happened to buy them by mistake," smiled Paul.

"Oh yeah, good point that," smiled James.

"I doubt a veggie, a true veggie that is, would eat normal burgers even if they did buy them by mistake," said Ben. He'd been listening to what Paul and James were saying while enjoying a drink with Harry. Ben and Harry moved their chairs nearer to Paul and James. They sat talking together for a few minutes when Ben said something that made the rest of them snigger.

"What are you four finding so funny?" asked Paul's mum.

"Nothing much. Ben just told us about a friend of his who claims to be a veggie, but she can't resist sausage rolls from Greggs!"

"And that's funny is it?"

"Well we thought so," smiled James.

"Don't you like Greggs's sausage rolls then Mrs. Jessop?" asked Ben.

"Yes of course I do; and I'm looking forward to the barbecue here, aren't you?"

"Sure we are mum," replied Paul.

Alice and Craig's grandad soon called everyone over; "Right folks, there's a few things ready to eat if you'd like to come and help yourselves." Paul was first but was quickly followed by everyone else. He helped himself to a couple of sausages, a bit steak, a couple of onions and mushrooms, a piece of tomato and some chips and salad. Everyone sat down and enjoyed their food in the warm sunshine.

"This is really nice Mr., er Ruston," said Paul. "Thanks so much for inviting us."

"My pleasure Paul," smiled Alice and Craig's grandad. "But just you wait until tomorrow when we really have some fun!"

"Grandad, do you think you could put some music on while we eat?" asked Alice.

"Yeah sure; I thought I'd forgotten something." He went inside for a moment and switched the music on. "I'll keep the volume down for a bit while we finish eating."

As the time past everyone kept helping themselves to a bit more food from the barbecue, and it was nearly half past eight by the time all the meat products had been eaten. Alice and Craig's grandparents then tidied up and made some coffee. "Can I turn the music up now grandad?" asked Craig.

"Yes OK go on then, but not too loud Craig." Craig went inside and turned up the volume.

"Oh wow! This is great," smiled Paul getting up from his chair.

"You gonna dance the night away then Paul?" asked Harry.

"Yeah why not? I feel like a bit of exercise after scoffing all that food."

"Well come on then, are we gonna have a dance or what," said Ben. Paul, James, Ben and Harry got to their feet and moved to where there was some space. They started to dance and it wasn't long before they were joined by Alice and Craig.

Moments later Paul shouted across to his mum and dad.

"Mum! Dad! Come and join us; it's great dancing about it the nude." Paul's parents looked at each other and smiled.

"Our son does know how to enjoy himself doesn't he," smiled Paul's mum.

"Come on then, let's join them." Paul's parents joined in and were soon enjoying themselves immensely. After a couple more minutes, and unable to resist it, James's parents joined in as well. Everyone was having a whale of a time dancing to music in the open air and it felt so liberating doing it naked.

As darkness came Alice and Craig's grandad switched on a number of garden lights and a powerful flood light. They carried on dancing till way past eleven o'clock it being a warm clear night. At ten to midnight Paul was starting to feel somewhat tired and so sat down to rest. It wasn't long before everyone else decided they'd had enough of dancing so just after midnight Alice and Craig's grandad went inside and switched the music off. Paul's dad helped take down the speakers and put everything away while the rest of them helped tidy up. "It doesn't matter too much about the lawn," said Alice and Craig's grandad. "It'll need a good clean tomorrow after you-know-what!"

"Oh OK then," replied Paul.

"When are we going to have our balloon fight?" asked James.

"Mid afternoon, I think," replied Alice and Craig's grandad. "I've got some special body paints for us to use in the morning if you like. Have any of you had a go at body painting before?"

"No we haven't," replied Paul quickly.

"I like the sound of body painting," smiled Harry.

"Me too," added Ben.

"What about us adults?" asked Paul's dad. "Do we get to have a go too?"

"Of course you do, no one is ever left out here."

"That's true," said Craig. "When we've finished painting each other, dad takes photos of us so we can look back. I've lost count how many times I've been painted now," continued Craig with a broad smile.

They carried on talking about body painting while taking the rest of the garden furniture and the barbecue inside; and by the time they'd finished it was nearly half past midnight which meant it was way past Paul and James's normal bedtime; even the adults were feeling tired. After a wonderfully entertaining evening everyone went to their rooms. Alice and Craig's grandad locked all the doors and then headed off to bed himself.

Chapter 17

With not getting to bed until after midnight it was no surprise everyone was late up. It was nearly quarter to ten when Paul woke up. He sat up, rubbed his eyes and looked across at James, Ben and Harry; neither of them made any sort of movement. The adults however had all got up and were showering together before breakfast. While they had a private bathroom and shower, Alice and Craig's grandparents also had a communal shower area as mentioned before which featured seven showers, six warm and one cold.

After showering Paul's mum decided to check on her son and his friends. She walked round to their room, knocked on the door and then slowly opened it. Paul was awake and was half sat up in bed. "Morning mum," he said.

"Are you lot getting up, we're about to have some breakfast?" Just then Ben woke up too and looked across at Paul's mum.

"Oh er, morning Mrs. Jessop," said Ben sleepily.

"I think it's time you boys got up, we'll be having breakfast shortly," said Paul's mum.

"Yeah, OK Mrs. Jessop." Ben then looked across at his younger brother; "Harry; Harry! Come on, get up!" Harry turned over in bed and rubbed his eyes, meanwhile Paul woke James up.

"Come on guys let's get up," said Paul. Paul and Ben got out of bed first but it wasn't long before Harry and James dragged themselves out of bed and into the shower area.

"Hey, this is great," said Harry on entering the shower area. "It's just like being at the leisure centre."

"Yeah, I was thinking the same thing," smiled James. "But when we've finished showering here, we stay naked."

"Of course. I'm really looking forward to today," said Paul. "Spending an entire day naked is gonna be great and I can't wait for the balloon fight to start."

"Same here," smiled Ben. After ten minutes or so showering together the four of them grabbed their towels and went downstairs for breakfast.

"Morning all," said Paul.

"Morning, you all sleep well?" asked Alice and Craig's grandad.

"Fine thanks," replied Ben.

"Yeah fine," added James.

"I wish I could live like this all the time," smiled Harry. "I've never come downstairs for breakfast naked before, it's brilliant."

"Well then, help yourselves to some cereal and orange juice. If you'd like something cooked, like bacon and eggs, I'll see to it in just a moment," said Alice and Craig's grandad. Paul, James, Ben and Harry helped themselves to a glass of orange juice each, and some cereal, and then sat down outside with everyone else in the midmorning sunshine.

"This is just so nice," said Paul. "Eating breakfast in the nude in such a lovely garden is fantastic."

"Yeah, same here," smiled James.

"It's like being on holiday, but even better," added Harry smiling broadly.

"I agree," said Ben. "Harry and I have never spent so long without our clothes, and I have to say we both absolutely love it."

"Right then; who's for something cooked?" asked Alice and Craig's grandad. Paul, James, Ben and Harry all asked for pretty much the same thing; a full English breakfast. Alice and Craig's grandad went inside and started grilling bacon and sausage, the smell of which wafted outside making a few mouths water. It only took ten or fifteen minutes to cook some more food for breakfast and Alice and Craig's grandad soon brought out four plates of bacon, egg, sausage, mushrooms and baked beans.

"Where's Alice and Craig?" asked James while cutting a sausage in half.

"There in the jacuzzi," replied their mum.

"Oh I just wondered with them not being here."

"Have they had their breakfast?" asked Paul.

"Yes, they just had some cereal 'cos they weren't feeling all that hungry," replied their dad.

"Hmm; well that was delicious," said Paul. "Thanks very much."

"Tea or coffee?" asked Alice and Craig's grandad.

"Tea please," replied Paul.

"James, Ben, Harry; is tea OK with you?"

"Yes thanks," replied James.

"Yeah same for me thanks," said Ben.

"And me," added Harry.

"Right, OK then. If you'd like any toast or croissants just help yourselves." Alice and Craig's grandad went inside and made a pot of tea while Paul and Ben went over to the toaster. They helped themselves to what they wanted and were soon followed by James and Harry. Alice and Craig's grandad then brought out a large tea pot full of tea.

By eleven o'clock everyone had finished breakfast and helped by taking all the plates and things into the kitchen. "Are we gonna start body painting soon?" asked Paul. "Or have we got time for a swim first?"

"You can have a swim if you like Paul, but I haven't fixed the heating yet so it'll still be on the cool side," replied Alice and Craig's grandad.

"Oh that's OK," said Paul. Paul headed over to the pool with James, Ben and Harry not far behind. He dipped his foot into the water; "It's not all that cold."

"Go on then, jump in," said Ben.

"OK then," replied Paul. Paul stood on the side momentarily pausing for breath and then jumped in; but instead of just jumping in Paul decided to make a big splash and did a brilliant 'John Smith's' style bomb!

"Paul! Did you have to do that?" said James with a huff after getting a bit of a soaking.

"That was brilliant Paul!" shouted Harry as Paul emerged. Harry quickly ran forward and did likewise. Ben and James looked at each other and then jumped, or rather, bombed into the pool. The four of them spent a few minutes splashing about in the pool. Alice and Craig saw them so went over to join them and all were having fun getting out and jumping back in.

After half an hour Alice and Craig's grandad called them over; "If you lot would like to get out of the pool now we're about to start body painting."

"Oh great," replied Paul. Paul got out and grabbed his towel as did the rest of them.

"If you'd all like to dry off first, it is much easier to paint on dry skin."

The children all dried off and readied themselves for a spot of body painting. Whilst waiting for them to get dried Alice and Craig's grandparents made a start. Their gran began to paint Paul's mum and their grandad began by painting James's dad. This was certainly something the Jessops and the Handles had never done before, and neither for that matter had Ben and Harry; however, the Rustons were all use to it and enjoyed being painted up in various guises.

After fifteen minutes or so Paul's mum and James's dad were finished and looked quite good. Alice and Craig's gran had painted a number of white flowers with green stems. This stretched from Paul's mum's waist to just above her breasts and was surrounded by a few light blue and yellow wavy lines on her arms and shoulders. James's dad was considerably different; he'd opted for a more macho look and sported dark green, black and brown camouflage. He could've easily hidden in the shrubbery and no one would have ever know he was there. "Right, who'd like to be painted next?" asked Alice and Craig's gran.

"Me please!" replied Paul enthusiastically. Paul stood in front of her.

"What would you like me to paint on you Paul," she asked.

"Er, oh; I don't know," replied Paul. "Can you do one of the others while I have a think?"

"OK then," smiled Alice and Craig's gran. Harry stepped forward while Paul thought about what he wanted painting on his body. Meanwhile Alice and Craig's grandad made a start painting Craig.

"Is there some spare paint brushes?" asked James.

"Yeah, sure there is," replied Alice and Craig's grandad. "If you'd like to paint each other go ahead; it'll certainly speed things up."

"Paul, can you paint something on me?" asked James.

"Yeah, I'll have ago. Anything in mind?"

"Er... start with a black bow tie on my neck and then paint the outline of a suit on my body."

"Right er, OK then," replied Paul with some surprise at what James just asked him to paint. Paul did as he'd been asked and painted the shape of a bow tie in black paint on James's neck.

"Right, use white paint now and paint the outline of a jacket on my body and arms." Paul continued to follow James's instructions and after a good ten minutes it looked like James was ready to go out for evening dinner!

"Can you paint me now?" asked Paul.

"Sure. Have you decided what you want yet?"

"Just paint me white from the waist up my neck and partway down my arms. Make it look like I'm wearing a white T-shirt."

"OK then." James swapped the brush for a small sponge. This was better for painting larger areas and after only five or six minutes James had covered Paul's chest in white paint. James then moved on to Paul's shoulders and upper arms. When he'd finished James decided to add a bit of colour and painted the end of Paul's 'sleeves' red.

"Hey that looks good," said Paul while watching James paint red rings round his upper arms. "If you paint a pair of blue shorts on me it'll look like I'm ready for PE at school," smiled Paul. Coincidently or not, that was what their indoor PE kit was; blue shorts and a white T-shirt.

"OK then," replied James. James was getting quite good at body painting now, but what Paul just asked him to do presented a problem; how was he going to paint a pair of shorts on to Paul's body without touching his privates. James thought about this as he reached over for the blue paint and a clean sponge. He was rather expecting Paul to paint his own privates blue, but for the moment James didn't say anything. James dipped the sponge into the blue paint and applied it to Paul's waist. James initially painted the area immediately below the white of Paul's painted T-shirt. He then applied more blue paint to the top of Paul's thighs and was within inches of his privates, but Paul never said a thing nor did he suggest taking over to paint his own privates blue! When James had got as far as he could without painting them Paul did say something.

"Don't forget to paint my privates. I don't want my 'shorts' haven't got a hole them."

"You what?" said James looking up at Paul. "You actually want me to paint your privates blue?"

"Yes I do," replied Paul calmly and with a perfectly straight face. "I won't be able to do it properly myself 'cos I'm not facing them." James thought this answer was somewhat odd. He felt sure Paul could paint his own privates perfectly well.

"OK then, if you're sure you can trust me," smiled James.

"Well if I can't trust you to paint my privates who can I trust?"

"Hmm, good point," said James in agreement. "Well, here goes." James carefully took hold of Paul's penis and gently dabbed blue paint all around it. When he'd done this James continued to paint the rest of Paul's private area blue. "Would you like me to paint your feet and ankles?" asked James. "It'll look like you're wearing socks then."

"Yeah sure, please do," replied Paul quickly. James swapped the blue paint for white and painted 'socks' on to Paul's feet and ankles. Finally, James used a slim paint brush to paint two coloured bands around the top of Paul's 'socks'; one red, the other dark blue. Paul then turned round and faced the others.

"Hey mum, look at Paul," said Alice pointing directly at him. From a distance it now looked like Paul was wearing his school PE kit.

"What do you all think of James's handy work?" asked Paul.

"Pretty good," smiled Alice and Craig's grandad.

"I'm not sure you'll be able to get away with a painted PE kit at school Paul, but nice try!" smiled his dad.

"Who painted your 'shorts' Paul?" asked Craig with a smile.

"James did, why?"

"Paul! Did you have James painting all your bits and pieces?" asked his mum firmly.

"Yeah, why? James did OK and it didn't hurt," replied Paul very honestly. "I'd have done the same for him if he'd asked." James's ears pricked up on hearing Paul say that and he wondered how he might have felt if things had been the other way round, but he didn't say anything. Paul's mum tutted at what he'd let James do to him.

Approaching one o'clock the body painting session came to an end. Everyone looked very different after being painted. Craig had been painted very elaborately from head to toe in a number of different colours. Paul's dad had a black and white diamond pattern painted on his chest similar to a chess board. Alice looked really good as wonder woman. It wasn't all that obvious what the rest were. Ben and Harry had just painted various different lines and blobs on each other 'cos they couldn't make up their minds what to paint. A few more lines on Harry and he'd have looked like a map of the Underground!

With everyone now stood in line it was time for a quick photo session. Mr. Ruston and his dad took photos of everyone individually and as a group. At the end Alice and Craig's grandad set his camera up on a tripod so he could get a photograph with everybody in it. "Right! Now comes the fun part," said Alice and Craig's grandad.

"Are we gonna have the balloon fight now?" asked Paul in high expectation.

"Yes Paul very shortly. I want to set up the bouncy castle now and the slide."

"Would you like a hand?" asked Paul.

"Please; it is rather heavy." Paul and his dad helped set up the bouncy castle. Alice and Craig's grandad then turned on the air pump and it soon inflated. Paul simply couldn't resist the temptation and climbed on to it. Meanwhile, Alice and Craig's grandad had walked away in order to set up the slide.

"This is great!" shouted Paul while bouncing up and down.

Alice and Craig's grandad then spoke quietly to everyone else; "I've just had an idea which I think you'll all like. If Paul asks anyone to join him on the bouncy castle please say, 'in a minute'.

"Why?" asked James.

"Well, Paul appears to be very keen on this balloon fight so why don't the rest of us throw a gunge filled balloon at him while he's on the bouncy castle," replied Alice and Craig's grandad with smirk.

"Oh wow! He won't know what's hit him," smiled James.

"Right then; the balloons are all ready in these large plastic boxes." With the exception of Paul, who was still bouncing away, everyone took out a gunge filled balloon and walked over to the bouncy castle. Paul wasn't aware of what was coming until the very last second.

"GUNGE HIM!" shouted James; and everyone threw their balloons at Paul. Paul immediately stopped bouncing and slithered about on the bouncy castle covered in gunge.

"RIGHT! Where's those damn balloons?" growled Paul wiping gunge away from his face. "I'm gonna get you all back for that!" Paul slid off the bouncy castle and walked over to where the balloons were. He picked one up and immediately threw it at James, then one at his mum, which unfortunately missed. Paul threw a third at Ben, but ended up getting Harry full in the face. Everyone then quickly helped themselves to balloons and within a matter of seconds it was complete and utter mayhem. Balloons were being thrown from every possible direction and it wasn't long before they'd emptied the first box. Alice and Craig's grandad then opened the lid on the second box of gunge filled balloons and battle resumed. The balloons in this box were all filled with black gunge and after only a couple of minutes everyone was virtually covered in it!

"Can we have a go on the slide grandad?" asked Craig.

"Of course."

"Let's all throw balloons at Craig as he slides down the slide," said Paul. Paul, James, Ben, Harry and Alice all readied themselves with balloons. Craig took a run up to the slide and slid the full length of it while the others pelted him with balloons.

"My turn now," said Paul. Paul simply swapped places with Craig and slid down the slide while being pelted with balloons full of black gunge.

"Craig, do you think your gran can pour some baby oil on the slide like you said she did last time?" asked James.

"I'll ask her, just a minute." Craig walked over to his gran and he asked her to pour some baby oil on to the slide like she did before. She obliged straightaway and everyone had a go on the slide which was now incredibly slippery. Alice and Craig scooped up as much gunge as they could and placed it at the bottom of the slide.

"Go on dad, slide down it," said Paul encouragingly. Paul's dad did just that and covered himself in gunge at the bottom of the slide.

Everyone was larking around and having fun especially the children. After a good half hour the balloons had all been used up and the garden was a slimy mess, but that didn't stop Paul from slinging handfuls of gunge about the place and on to the bouncy castle, along with the rest of the children. While still mostly covered in gunge Paul, James, Ben, Harry, Alice and Craig all climbed on to the bouncy castle. There wasn't really enough room for all six of them to bouncy about at once so it was more of a messy slide about instead, but still great fun. While they were doing this the adults hosed themselves down. Pleased with the way things had gone Alice and Craig's grandad went inside and made a few flour bombs with some flour that had past its use-by date. The adults took a couple of these each and headed over to the bouncy castle. With a few light thuds the children were now covered, not only in gunge, but in flour as well. To make things even more interesting Alice and Craig's grandad then turned on the hose pipe and sprayed them with water. Paul felt like he was in schoolboy heaven with so much mess, and being naked added to the brilliance 'cos he knew his mum couldn't tell him off for getting his clothes all messed up!

While the adults cleaned themselves up the children carried on messing about mostly on the bouncy castle, but occasionally getting off to slide down the slide. At about five o'clock Alice and Craig's grandad decided it was time to call it a day. "Right kids, come on. I think you've all been on there long enough now."

"Aw grandad," said Craig.

"Can't we have a few more minutes Mr. Ruston please? James and me have never had so much fun before," added Paul.

"OK then. Half five and that's it. Dinner will be ready by then and I'd like you all to get cleaned off before you come into the house."

"Can you spray water on us again please Mr. Ruston?" asked James.

"I could, but I'm going to help with the dinner, so you'll have to do it yourselves. The hose is over there and I'm sure you know how a tap works." Paul slid off the bouncy castle and turned the tap on. He aimed the jet of water directly at James. Paul wanted revenge for earlier. He thought it was James's idea to gunge him first. James and the rest of the children were now sliding about on a bouncy castle in a few inches of water, and although they weren't initially aware of it, the water was thinning the gunge and flour, and cleaning them up.

After a few minutes Paul let Craig take hold of the hosepipe while he climbed back on to the bouncy castle. "Craig, spray me!" shouted Paul. Craig aimed the jet of water at Paul who was enjoying it to the full.

"Dinner's nearly ready kids. Can you clean any remaining gunge off the bouncy castle and hose yourselves down now please?" asked Alice and Craig's grandad.

"Yeah OK grandad," replied Alice.

"Let's sweep all the gunge off the bouncy castle on to the grass," said Paul. "Then we can hose each other down."

"I'll help you," said Harry. This didn't take very long and the bouncy castle was soon clean enough to be taken down and put away once dry. The children then hosed each other down, dried off and went inside.

"I take it you all enjoy that then?" asked Alice and Craig's grandad.

"Sure we did," replied Paul smiling broadly.

"I've never done anything like that before in my life," said Ben.

"Same here," added Harry. "Thanks so much."

"What we gonna do after tea?" asked James.

"Well I think we should tidy up outside first and then perhaps a bit of relaxation in the pool or jacuzzi," replied Alice and Craig's grandad. Everyone continued to make polite dinner conversation and after they'd finished the children went outside and jumped in the pool. The adults came out a few minutes later and Alice and Craig's grandad removed the cover from the jacuzzi. He turned the bubbles and water jets on and then climbed in. "Hmm, my word this is lovely," he said. After a couple of minutes Paul's parents joined him. When Paul saw his mum and dad in the jacuzzi with Alice and Craig's grandad he thought he fancied a warm up with them, 'cos the pool was still on the cool side; it not being heated. Seeing as the jacuzzi could only take six at a time, and even that was a bit of a squeeze, everyone took it in turns to have a relaxing warm up.

After a good couple of hours relaxing Alice and Craig's

grandparents made a bit of supper. A large box of cheesy crackers and other savoury biscuits was brought out by Alice and Craig's gran. Alice then brought out a wooden board with no less than five different types of cheese on it. "Please help yourselves to biscuits and cheese," said Alice and Craig's gran. "I'll bring some buns and cakes out a bit later." Paul was impressed by the array of biscuits and cheeses that were on offer, and not wanting to appear greedy by being first, he held back and let James, Ben and Harry go ahead of him. After everyone had helped themselves to what they wanted they sat down and enjoyed their supper. A few minutes later Alice and Craig's gran brought out a large tea pot. She let it stand for five minutes or so before pouring it into mugs. "Alice, would you like to bring out the buns and cakes please?"

"Yeah sure gran," replied Alice. Alice nipped into the kitchen and brought out a tray of sweet tasty treats. These all went in a matter of minutes after which everyone sat chatting until around half nine.

"I think we ought to head indoors now," said Alice and Craig's grandad. "I think it's about to start raining." There was then a brief flash of lightning, but the thunder which followed wasn't particularly loud. Less than a couple of minutes later it started to drizzle.

"Damn weather!" said James in mild annoyance at the rain making things miserable and wet.

"Still, look on the bright side," said Paul. "We did manage to have the barbecue and the balloon fight in bright sunshine."

"Yeah, s'pose you're right."

"Well come on then, let's help take the tables and chairs inside." Paul and James helped the rest of them take things indoors out of the rain. It continued raining and rapidly became a downpour.

"Why don't we go outside now and run about naked in the rain," suggested Harry.

"Hmm," Paul thought for a moment about doing just that. "OK, come on then. Are we all gonna go outside in the rain?"

"I think we'll stay here," replied James's mum and dad.

"And so will we, but you kids can go out in the rain if you

like," smiled Paul's dad. Paul went outside first and stood with his arms outstretched. The rain was second only to being in the shower and it was still fairly warm considering the time of day. James went outside next followed by Ben, Harry, Alice and Craig. For a few minutes they all ran around the garden naked.

"I take back what I said about the weather," said James. "This is pretty good."

"That's just what I was thinking," said Ben. The six of them were actually enjoying running about in the rain while they were naked. Paul simply had to climb on to the bouncy castle again and was soon accompanied by the others. After a while Alice and Craig's grandad suggested they come back inside. The six of them went back in and after drying off went upstairs to their rooms. It'd been quite a good day even with the weather. Paul, James, Ben and Harry talked away together until they fell asleep.

Sunday morning soon arrived and after breakfast everyone was sat outside in the warm sunshine. Following last night's heavy rain the day was warming up nicely. "What can we do today?" asked Paul.

"Well, if you were thinking of another balloon fight Paul I'm afraid you're out of luck 'cos we've none left," replied Alice and Craig's grandad.

"What about the sponges Ken? They can play with them if they want to," suggested Alice and Craig's gran.

"Oh yes. I'd forgotten about them. Craig, would you be a love and go and get them; they're in the usual place I think."

Paul and James smiled at one another across the table while Ben and Harry looked on mildly puzzled. "Why would we want to play with sponges?" asked Ben.

"You'll find out," smiled James. While not quite as much fun as throwing gunge-filled balloons at each other throwing wet sponges about was certainly going give its participants some fun.

Craig came back after a few minutes dragging a large plastic bag full of sponges. "What we gonna do?" asked Harry.

"You'll soon see," replied Paul. With some help Craig emptied all the sponges out on to the grass.

"Right, let's fill a few buckets with water," said Alice and Craig's grandad.

"Ah; are we gonna throw wet sponges at each other?" asked Harry.

"Yep, sure we are," smiled Paul.

When they'd enough buckets of water the children divided up the sponges and split into two teams. Paul, Ben and Alice stood opposite James, Harry and Craig. They'd a bucket of water each and, although things seemed orderly right now, it was to be any but in the following minutes. They all picked up a couple of sponges, dipped them in their buckets and then began throwing them at each other. In a matter of seconds wet sponges were being thrown in all directions! They were absolutely loving this and it wasn't long before all the buckets were empty. Alice then decided to get the hosepipe out again. She unwound it and turned the tap on fully. She sprayed all five of them and sent them running for cover all over the garden. However, while running around Paul had had an idea. He quietly crept behind Alice to where the tap was without her seeing or hearing him. Paul then grabbed hold of the hosepipe and kinked it to stop the flow of water. Alice couldn't understand why the water had stopped so looked into the hose. At that point Paul relaxed his grip. Water, under some pressure, hit Alice right in the face. Paul had never laughed so much. "That was brilliant Paul," laughed Harry. "I was watching you from behind that tree. I thought you'd turned the tap off at first."

"No, I just twisted the pipe," smiled Paul. Alice threw the hosepipe down in disgust at being outsmarted. "Oh Alice, don't be like that. It was only meant to be a bit of fun."

"I know it was. I'm just going to the toilet, back in a minute. Get Craig and James for me." Paul picked up the hosepipe, but instead of aiming it at anyone else he hosed himself down. His feet were dirty as a result of running around the edge of the garden. Just then James walked up, his feet covered in soil as well.

"Hold your feet out James, I'll rinse the dirt off for you."

"Thanks," replied James. After Paul had done this he quickly aimed the jet of water straight up and twisted the nozzle to give a finer spray.

"Hey that looks good," said Craig walking over.

"It's just like taking a shower, but outdoors; pity it's cold though. I fancy a warm up in the jacuzzi, anyone else coming?" asked Paul.

"Yeah, go on then," replied Craig. "Let's turn the hose off."

After Craig had turned the water off he coiled up the hosepipe. He and Paul then took the cover off the jacuzzi and climbed in. A few minutes later Alice came back outside to find all five boys in the Jacuzzi. She walked over and stood on the side. "Come on guys make a bit space for Alice," said Paul.

"Thanks guys," said Alice as she climbed into the jacuzzi.

"Are you OK Alice?" asked Ben.

"Yeah, fine. Why do you ask?"

"We thought you looked a bit er, tired that's all," replied Paul.

"Yeah well, I s'pose I am," said Alice. "It's all that running around."

"You are OK being in here with the five of us aren't you?" asked Ben cautiously.

"Yeah course, why wouldn't I be?"

"Well, er, you are the only girl," said Paul. "And we didn't want to..." Paul stopped mid sentence.

"It's OK Paul. I know I'm the only girl, but it's no problem. Don't forget, I've been brought up as a naturist along with my brother, so we're used to being in the company of many naked people," insisted Alice.

"OK OK," said Paul.

"How would you feel Paul if you were the only boy among five girls? Would you feel embarrassed; 'cos there's no reason to feel like that."

"Yeah, I can understand what you're saying now Alice, and no I don't think I would be embarrassed at being naked among five naked girls."

"Hmm; is that ever likely to happen?" smiled James.

"Doubtful," smiled Ben.

"It could do," insisted Paul. "And I'd be the perfect gentleman."

The six of them carried on chatting about this and that until Alice and Craig's grandad came looking for them. "Oh, so this is where you're all hiding is it?"

"We fancied a warm up grandad after our sponge fight," replied Craig.

"It's OK, you can all stay there a bit longer if you like. Your gran's making some potato soup for lunch and it'll be ready in a few minutes. She was whizzing it in the blender as I came out."

"Oh right, we'd better get out now then and dry off," said Alice. Paul and the others gave it a couple more minutes then got out too. James helped Ben replace the cover over the Jacuzzi then followed the others indoors.

"Let's all use the cold shower upstairs by our room," suggested Paul. "It'll give us a chance to freshen up."

"OK then," said Ben from behind. They showered together for a few minutes and took it in turns to freshen up with the cold one. After lightly drying off the six of them joined the adults in the living room.

"Lunch is about to be served," said Alice and Craig's gran. Everyone got up and sat to the table. Having said this was lunch it was more like afternoon tea it being nearly four o'clock. The day had gone pretty quickly. While the kids were play fighting with wet sponges the adults had been playing games; Chess, Scrabble, Monopoly and Back Gammon to name but four.

"This soup is very nice Mrs. Ruston. You must let my mum have the recipe," said Paul very appreciatively.

"Thank you very much Paul, but why don't I give you the recipe then you could make it for your mum. It's not all that involved," smiled Alice and Craig's gran.

"Er, yeah OK then, but I think my mum will want to oversee things; I'm not sure she'll want to leave me alone in the kitchen just yet."

"I'll let you do the biggest part of it Paul so don't worry," smiled his mum.

After they'd eaten the adults sat outside in the evening sunshine while the children watched TV, but they weren't watching it for very long. Harry noticed that Alice and Craig's grandparents had got quite a few games and one of them was Twister. "Has anyone ever played this?" asked Harry.

"Played what?" asked Paul.

"Twister," replied Harry pulling the game from under a few others.

"Is it a board game?" asked Paul.

"Not exactly," replied Harry.

"What do you have to do?" asked James.

"I'm not exactly sure, but I seem to remember seeing a couple of kids playing it at school. It was the last day before we finished for Christmas last year. You have this mat with coloured circles on and some kind of spinner thing."

"Yeah, the one spinning the spinner tells you what colour of circle to place your hand or foot," said Craig suddenly showing interest.

"Have you played it Craig?" asked James.

"Yeah, a while ago. We all kept falling over 'cos we weren't very good at it."

"Why don't we give it a try," suggested Harry.

"Go on then," said Craig. "I s'pose it'll be interesting playing it while we're all naked." Paul helped Harry spread the mat out on the floor.

"Right, I'll spin," said Craig.

"What do we have to do start?" asked Paul.

"Just stand on the side and wait for my instructions," replied Craig.

"So who's playing then?" asked Paul.

"I will," replied Harry.

"I don't mind giving it a go," said James.

"Ben?"

"OK then, if I must." Although Ben fancied playing Twister he was a bit apprehensive at playing naked, but decided to give it a go.

"Right, I think we're ready," said Paul. "Where's Alice disappeared to?"

"She's sat outside with mum and dad," replied Craig.

"Well come on then, let's play." With Paul now stood opposite James, and Ben and Harry similarly positioned, Craig spun the spinner.

"Left foot; green," he said. The four of them each placed their left foot on a green circle. "Right foot; red."

"Easy," said Paul. Although this was a fairly easy move the result of it left the four of them standing on the mat with their legs apart because the red and green circles were on opposite sides, the yellows and blues being in the middle. Craig then gave them their third instruction.

"Left hand; blue." This was a little trickier, but they all managed it without falling over. However, it was Craig's next instruction that moved the game up a gear. "Right foot; yellow." Craig was smiling as he said this because he could see it was going to be pretty difficult for the four of them to do it, however, they did. "Right hand; red," was Craig's next instruction. This was quite straightforward and resulted in all four players now having both hands and feet on the mat. After a short pause play continued. "Right hand; green."

"Craig that's impossible. There aren't enough green circles," said Paul.

"It's OK, you're allowed to share a circle when there's more than two players on the mat." The four of them tried to reach round for a green circle, but in the process of doing so Ben slipped and fell.

"That's you out Ben," said Harry with a cheeky smile.

"Hmm!" Ben tutted at having to leave the game so soon, but decided to sit next to Craig and give the instructions.

"Left foot; blue." This made the three of them turn round and face the opposite direction. While they were doing this Ben whispered something to Craig which caused him to giggle. This made Paul feel uneasy, but he didn't say anything and play continued. Craig and Ben were now in charge of the spinner, but instead of spinning it and calling out the correct instruction, the two of them collaborated and deliberately called out difficult instructions. "Right hand; red," said Craig. Paul, James and Harry struggled to get their right hands on a red circle, but managed it after a minute or so. The three of them were now in a precarious position with their legs crossed and their hands behind them. "Left foot; green," smiled Craig. This really did make things difficult and caused James to abandon the game. He sat down on a chair and watched Paul and Harry battle it out.

"Come on then, what's next?" asked Paul.

"Left hand; red, and you can't share any more 'cos there's only two of you playing now." Paul and Harry did their best and were now in very awkward positions indeed. "Left hand; yellow." Neither Paul nor Harry wanted to give in and both placed their left hands on a yellow circle. Even though Craig and Ben were trying to make it as difficult as possible, Paul and Harry somehow managed to keep going. After a few more successful moves Ben suggested changing the rules slightly and giving Paul and Harry separate instructions so they wouldn't be moving the same part of their body to same coloured circle at the same time.

"That's fine with me," said Paul. "I'll take the next instruction, then Harry, you can take the one after."

"OK, go on then," said Harry. Craig and Ben carried on calling out instructions and it wasn't too long before Paul ended up almost on top of Harry with his legs splayed. Whilst Paul was in this precarious position his mum decided to look in on them; and was shocked to see her son in the position he was.

"Paul! What on earth do you think you're doing?"

"We're playing Twister mum," replied Paul calmly. "And I'm determined to beat Harry.

"B-but Paul; I really don't think you should be playing that game naked."

"Why ever not Mrs. Jessop?" asked James. "It's great fun!"

"Well, er," Paul's mum found James's question somewhat awkward to answer so finished by saying; "You might slip and hurt yourselves, so please be careful." Paul's mum tutted as she walked away. Tut, naked Twister, she thought to herself; what on earth will they think of next? Paul and Harry continued to play Twister with Craig, Ben, and now James, all calling out separate instructions to the pair of them. James suddenly started smirking to himself because he'd had the same idea as Ben. He whispered it to Craig and Ben making them smirk too.

"That's what we've been doing James," whispered Ben.

"What are you three joking about?" asked Paul indignantly.

"Nothing," smiled Craig.

"It doesn't feel like nothing to me," snapped Paul.

"We were just thinking about what your mum said that's all," smiled James. "Now are you ready for your next instruction?"

"Yes I am." Craig, Ben and James continued with the instructions, and Paul and Harry continued to obey them. What Paul and Harry didn't know was they were being set up. Craig, Ben and James were gradually working the game so that Paul and Harry ended up in the most compromising position they could think of. When they'd achieved this James whispered to Craig he should get his dad to take a photo. Craig agreed and made an excuse.

"I'm just nipping to the loo, back in a minute." Craig went outside and asked his dad to take a photo of them playing Twister naturist style.

"OK then, if you like. Hold on a minute while I get my camera." Alice and Craig's dad nipped upstairs and came back down with his camera. He walked over to where they were and got quite a shock. However, because of his son's polite request, and apparent innocence (Craig wasn't laughing), Mr. Ruston took a couple of photos of Paul and Harry on the Twister mat with Craig, Ben and James sat close by. "How long before you finish?" asked Alice and Craig's dad.

"I don't know," replied Paul quickly.

"I hope it's not too much longer, the backs of my legs are starting to ache," said Harry.

"Yeah, so are mine for that matter," moaned Paul. "Now will one of you give us the next instruction."

"Paul, left foot; yellow," said Craig.

"Harry, right foot; green," said James. Craig, Ben and James were continuing to make Paul and Harry's battle for naturist Twister champion an interesting one. After a further twenty minutes of play Harry had no option but to give in. Cramp in his left leg forced him to quit.

"Arrrh! My leg," screamed Harry.

"Sorry Harry! I never touched you, honest," said Paul in mild panic. Paul and Harry sat down with the others and Harry stretched out his leg. Harry's pain eased relatively quickly. "You OK Harry?"

"It's not too bad now."

"Do you wanna keep going?"

"Paul, I think we ought to call it a draw and put the game away now," said James. "If anyone's to blame for what just happened to Harry it's probably us."

"How do you mean?" asked Paul.

"We were giving you difficult moves to do on purpose, but only for a bit of fun," replied Ben.

"Yeah, that's why we were giggling earlier," said James. "I'm sorry Harry, we never thought anyone would get hurt."

"You mean to say you weren't spinning the spinner, you just called out whatever looked most difficult at the time," said Paul.

"Well, yeah," smiled Ben.

"I thought it was funny," said Paul. "...and when you had us stop for a photo my feet were on opposite sides of the mat and my legs were wide open!"

"So were mine!" snapped Harry. "No wonder I got cramp."

Paul and Harry now realised they'd been tricked by the other three and were wondering how to get them back, but whatever it was they were thinking of, it would have to wait. It was now nearly eight o'clock and was, unfortunately, time to get dressed and go back home.

Paul, James; their parents, and Ben and Harry got dressed. They packed all their things away and took them downstairs. The Rustons had also packed up and were dressed ready to leave.

"Thanks very much Mr. Ruston. It's been an absolutely brilliant weekend, hasn't it James," said Paul.

"Yeah, I've really enjoyed it. Thanks so much for having us over, it's been great."

"Our pleasure," smiled Alice and Craig's grandad. "Ethel?" Alice and Craig's gran got up and stood next to her husband. "We'd like to thank you all for coming. We've both enjoyed having you over and you're more than welcome to come again sometime next year."

"Oh thanks," said Paul his eyes lighting up. "Mum, dad; can we come again next year?"

"I don't see why not," smiled Paul's dad. "Thanks again for a great weekend." The rest of them said thank you and good bye to Alice and Craig's grandparents.

At nearly nine o'clock the weekend of fun packed naturist activities, in which clothes had not been worn for well over fifty hours, finally came to a close. The Jessops, the Handles, the Wetherby brothers, and the Rustons all said a last 'thank you and good bye' as they drove out on to the main road and headed home.

Chapter 18

After having a fantastic time at Alice and Craig's grandparents' house last weekend Paul was now thinking about his fifteenth birthday which was in just ten day's time. His last birthday party was five years ago when he was ten so Paul felt like having a few friends round to mark the occasion, and, because he was now a naturist, Paul wanted to do it all without clothes.

Midmorning Paul put his shorts and trainers on and went next door to see James. James answered the door wearing only a towel. "Hiya," he said.

"Hi," said Paul stepping inside. "It's nice to see you're still living naked."

"Oh yeah, we all are, aren't we mum," said James turning to look at his mum and closing the front door.

"Oh yes; it's not something I'd ever give up now I've discovered how wonderfully liberating it is. James's dad and I really enjoy it."

"Excellent," smiled Paul taking off his shorts and trainers.

"Any thoughts about your birthday Paul?" asked James's mum.

"Yeah, that's what I've come to see you about actually," replied Paul.

"What you got in mind?" asked James.

"I'm not quite sure at the moment," replied Paul. "What I'd really like is a party where everyone we invite goes naked."

"You could invite the Rustons," suggested James.

"...and Ben and Harry, I'm sure they'd come and I bet they'd enjoy being naked again," smiled Paul.

"What about Katie Finch and her mum. I know we haven't seen them for a while, but I reckon they'd come." Just then James's mum came into the front room with a pad and a pen.

"It sounds to me like you're going to have to make a few notes as to who you're inviting Paul."

"Oh yeah, thanks Mrs. Handle." Paul and James discussed plans for Paul's birthday and Paul wrote down the names of who he planned to invite.

"Do you think Peter Simpkin would come?" asked James.

"Er, possibly. I s'pose he has been good to us since we first met," replied Paul. "I'll put his name on my list."

"How many is that now?" asked James.

"Nine," replied Paul. "But that's not counting any of us. It'll be fifteen with the six of us."

"That sounds like a very good number considering it's your fifteenth birthday Paul," said James's mum.

"Yeah OK. I'll talk it over with my mum and dad; I hope everyone can come. It'll be great fifteen of us all together in the nude," smiled Paul.

"Yeah it would; and we could play party games as well couldn't we," added James.

"You mean charades?"

"Yeah, it was fun doing it naked," smiled James. "And Ben and Harry seemed to enjoy it when they were here that time."

"Hmm, I s'pose musical chairs would be good fun too, but I doubt we'd have enough chairs to do it, unless we borrowed some from somewhere." Whether or not it was Paul's intention that James's mum over-heard his last sentence, she did.

"If you need to borrow a few chairs Paul it's no problem," smiled James's mum.

"OK Mrs. Handle, thank you," said Paul. Paul then turned to James. "Do you wanna come next door for a bit? My mum and dad are out shopping at the moment, but they should be home soon."

"Yeah why not," replied James. "Mum; I'm just going next door for a bit with Paul."

"OK love." Paul put his shorts and trainers on and James put a towel round him while they nipped next door. As soon as Paul had shut the front door both of them went fully naturist. James placed his towel on the sofa and sat down. They continued to talk about Paul's birthday party and Paul made a few more notes.

"We can ask the Rustons and Ben and Harry this evening at the swim can't we," suggested James.

"Sure; and Peter Simpkin. I'm not sure how we'll contact Katie and her mum if they not there 'cos I never got there phone number," said Paul. Just then Paul's parents arrived back home. "Hi dad, hi mum," said Paul.

"Hiya son," replied his dad.

"Hiya," said James.

"Oh hello you two," replied Paul's mum. "Everything OK?"

"Yeah sure," replied Paul.

"Well, seeing as you're both here we might as well tell you where we've been," smiled Paul's mum.

"Morrisons wasn't it?" suggested Paul while wondering where his parents might actually have been to if it wasn't Morrisons.

"Yes love we did go to Morrisons for the usual shop, but on our way back we called in at the garden centre."

"So? What's so special about that?" asked Paul looking puzzled.

"For goodness sake Maureen just tell them," said Paul's dad firmly.

"We popped into the garden centre, Hatley's that is, on our way home and got quite a surprise. They were holding a naturist day. The owners are naturists and I seem to remember seeing them at Smithfield Water Park that time."

"Really? You went round Hatley's garden centre naked?" asked Paul enthusiastically.

"Well, we didn't actually go naked because we were only there a few minutes," said Paul's dad.

"...and that's when we thought of you two," finished Paul's mum.

"Can we go? Now - Please?" asked Paul impatiently.

"Yes of course, but there's no great rush as it's on until it closes at half six. We'll put the shopping away first and then get our things ready for the swim this evening."

This rather sudden discovery of a naturist day at Hatley's garden centre, only three miles away from where Paul and James lived, was too good an opportunity to miss. After the shopping had been dealt with Paul and James nipped back next door to tell James's parents where they were about to go. James entered the house all excited, his towel dropping to the floor in the process; "Mum, mum! Where are you? And is dad home?"

"I'm in the kitchen love, and what's with all the rushing around?"

"Paul's mum and dad have been to Hatley's garden centre and it's a naturist day today, right now!"

"What? A naturist day at Hatley's garden centre?"

"Yeah; my mum and dad have just been there, but they came back after only a few minutes 'cos they knew we'd probably like to go too," said Paul.

"Where's dad?" asked James.

"He said he was helping a friend of his clear out some rubbish," replied James's mum.

"Where?"

"Only a few doors down love. Why don't you go and… look for him." James very quickly put his shorts on and darted out of the house with Paul before James's mum had finished speaking. They quickly ran down the road and found James's dad sat down on the grass drinking a mug of tea with the friend he'd been helping.

"Oh hello you two. What's with all the running about?"

"Can you come, quick?" asked James.

"Er, yeah sure. What's happened? Is it your mum?"

"No, no she's fine," replied James.

"Are you OK if I…"

"Yeah, sure. I can sort the rest myself, thanks for your help Andy."

Paul, James and James's dad walked back up the road fairly quickly. James's mum was waiting for them on the doorstep. "Have they told you?" asked James's mum with a smile.

"They haven't told me anything Helen, are you OK?"

"Never better," replied James's mum who'd just been on the phone to Hatley's garden centre to confirm what she'd been told by her son and his friend.

"Will someone please tell me what it is that's so interesting."

"Well, you know that big garden centre on the edge of town?"

"Oh yeah, you mean Hatley's?"

"Yes that's the one. They're holding a naturist day right now. I've just been speaking to a supervisor on the phone to enquire, and not only can you go round the place completely naked you also get ten percent off all your purchases, if you're naked; and by all accounts it's attracting quite a lot of interest."

"Wow, I bet it is," smiled James's dad.

"It's ten to twelve now, so if we get our towels and whatnot ready we can go straight to the swim from there," suggested

James's mum. "Would you and your parents like to come with us Paul?"

"Er, yeah I should imagine so. I'll nip next door and ask them."

While still wearing nothing more than his shorts and trainers Paul nipped back home and spoke to his parents. "Mum, dad; James's parents have offered us a lift," said Paul.

"Oh fine," smiled Paul's mum. "I've got all we need, towels and shower gel, so I think we're ready."

"Where's dad?"

"In here son," replied Paul's dad from the front room.

"Mum and me are ready," said Paul.

"Well come on then, let's go."

The Jessops, now dressed, but only minimally so, left their house and waited for James and his parents. "I've just been thinking," said James's dad. "I know we offered you a lift, but would you mind going in separate cars; it's just that if we buy anything from the garden centre we won't be able to fit it in with all six of us in one car."

"No problem," replied Paul's dad. "In fact I was thinking the same thing myself actually." Paul's dad nipped back inside briefly to get his car keys. They set off for Hatley's garden centre just after quarter past twelve. During the journey Paul texted Ben to see if he'd like to attend with his brother Harry and possibly his mum and dad.

There was a large car park at Hatley's garden centre to the rear of the main building and this is where the Jessops and the Handles parked. There were quite a few people naked in the car park so as soon as Paul got out of his dad's car he quickly whipped off his shorts and left them on the back seat. James did likewise and the pair of them walked over to the main entrance. Their parents were not far behind them after they too stripped off leaving their clothes in their cars. They had no choice but to carry their keys, wallets and mobile phones in their hands 'cos no one had thought to bring any bags.

The six of them paused for a few moments to read the sign above the main entrance. It read; 'NATURIST DAY - 10% OFF ALL PURCHASES IF SHOPPING NAKED!' "Oh my word!" said Paul in surprise at stepping inside and seeing a garden centre almost full of naked people.

"What we gonna buy?" asked James.

"I don't know really," replied his mum. "There's not much we need. I thought you just wanted to come here for the atmosphere, and some lunch perhaps."

"Why sure we do," smiled Paul. Just then Paul's phone beeped. He'd received a text message from Ben which read: [Y do U want us to come to Hatley's GC?]. Paul replied straightaway with: [Trust me, U won't wanna miss this! Get the bus if U have to and tell Harry.].

Ben was intrigued as to why Paul wanted him to attend Hatley's garden centre. He spoke to his younger brother; "Harry, have you any idea why Paul might want us at Hatley's garden centre?"

"No, why?"

"Well he tells me there's something going on that we wouldn't want to miss," replied Ben.

"Well let's find out what it is then. They're bound to be in the phone book," smiled Harry.

"OK then." Ben looked in the phone book and soon found the number for Hatley's garden centre. He dialled it carefully and a woman answered. "Oh er, hi," said Ben. "Are you holding a special event today?"

"Yes we are. It's a naturist ten percent off day. Put simply; if you shop in the nude you get ten percent off all your purchases, including what you spend in the café."

"Oh right, OK then, thank you." Ben hung up.

"Well?" asked Harry.

"Paul was right, we don't wanna miss this event they're holding. It's a naturist day and to encourage it you get ten percent off if you shop naked!"

"Why don't we see if mum and dad wanna go?" asked Harry.

"OK then." Ben and Harry spoke to their parents and asked them if they were thinking of going to Hatley's garden centre.

"Well, we were thinking of going tomorrow boys," said their dad.

"But dad it'll be er, busier tomorrow, Sunday."

"Why don't we go now?" suggested Harry.

"Yeah, we can take our towels with us that way we can go

straight to the swim afterwards," suggested Ben. "It's not far from the leisure centre."

"Hmm, OK then. I fancy a bite to eat actually and the food's really good there."

"Well, what we waiting for?" asked Harry.

"Er, let me speak to your mum. What's the rush anyway?"

"Paul's just told us there's a special event on right now and we shouldn't miss it," replied Ben.

"Like what?"

"Ten percent off everything if er...," Harry suddenly stopped mid-sentence. He didn't want to spoil what could be a nice surprise for his mum and dad!

"If what?" asked his dad, looking directly back at his younger son.

"If you er, get there now," replied Ben quickly.

"Hmm; it sounds to me like you two are hiding something. Now what is it, or do I have to ring them to find out?"

"Oh no don't do that dad, please; it'll spoil the surprise," said Harry.

"Hmm..." Ben and Harry's dad pondered. He was in two minds whether or not to trust his sons, but in the end he did. "OK then you two, I'll trust your judgement for once, but I'm warning you, if this is some sort of prank you won't be going swimming tonight." Just then Ben and Harry's mum came downstairs and into the front room.

"What are you three rabbiting on about?" she asked.

"Nothing much," replied Harry quickly.

"We were thinking of going to the garden centre," said Ben.

"Oh yeah, Hatley's? I thought we'd planned to go there tomorrow and then to my mum's."

"Yes love I know, but apparently they're holding a special event there right now; ten percent off everything." This caught Ben and Harry's mum's attention as she was wanting a new lawn mower plus quite a few other items.

"Really, ten percent off? Everything?"

"Yes mum, everything, including the café," replied Ben.

"If we take our towels with us you could drop us off at the leisure centre then go on to nana's for a bit and pick us back up on the way home," suggested Harry.

"Hmm...don't you want see your nana then?" asked their mum.

"Yeah, but we can see her anytime can't we and it'd be better if we'd more time 'cos we could always stay for tea," said Ben.

The Wetherbys continued talking about what they'd planned to do, but in the end all four of them had to agree they couldn't miss a 'ten percent off everything day'. They got in the car and set off just before one o'clock. When they were about five minutes away Ben texted Paul so he could be in the car park as they arrived.

"James; Ben and Harry are almost here," said Paul checking his phone. "Mum, Dad; Ben and Harry are almost here. James and me are gonna meet them when they arrive. Do you wanna come too?"

"Er, yes OK, go on then. I'll come with you both to meet them," said Paul's mum.

So; Paul, James and Paul's mum left the main building and walked outside into the bright sunshine. They'd no sooner stepped outside when the Wetherby's car pulled into the car park. Then, wearing nothing but their trainers Paul and James ran over to meet them. Ben and Harry's parents got quite a shock seeing them naked. "Oh! What on earth are you two doing?" asked Ben and Harry's mum with a shock. "And where's your clothes?"

"We've left them in the car," replied Paul. "It's a naturist ten percent off day today."

"Yeah, you get ten percent off all your shopping if you shop naked," smiled James.

"Didn't Ben and Harry tell you?" asked Paul.

"No, they didn't let on about that part did you," said Ben and Harry's mum firmly while turning to look at her sons.

"I'm sorry mum, we didn't wanna spoil the surprise," said Ben trying to make light of it.

"Paul, are you saying we only get the discount if we shop naked?" asked Ben and Harry's dad.

"Yes Mr. Wetherby. That's exactly what I'm saying." Ben and Harry then got out of the car and started to undress.

"Er, j-just wait a minute you two, we haven't decided whether or not we're going in yet."

"Oh, haven't we; I think our sons have love. It'd be a shame to spoil their fun and it's not as if we're pressuring them to do it; is it? I kind of get the feeling it's the other way round."

"Sean, if you want get your kit off and join them feel free. I'm staying right here." After their mum said this Ben and Harry took the rest of their clothes off and put their trainers back on. Their dad stripped off as well and the three of them left their clothes on the back seat. Now that they were naked they walked into the main building and rejoined the others.

Mr. Wetherby coughed as he went in. "I don't believe it. I've never seen anything like this before in my life! Even the staff are naked." Before anyone responded to this a female voice made an announcement over the public address system.

"Ladies and gentlemen; the management and staff of Hatley's garden centre would like to welcome you all to this special naturist ten percent off day. There's only one polite request for the discount, which applies to all your purchases, and that is you join in the fun and shop naked. Where else in the UK could you do this? Only at Hatley's!"

"Dad, is this brilliant or what?" smiled Harry.

"Well it's certainly different, I'll say that much."

"Same here; I think it's great," added Ben. "I wish mum was with us. What's she got against being naked?"

"I don't know love; but I must admit, after seeing all these people here naked this lifestyle is kind of growing on me. Maybe I can persuade your mum to join in sometime."

The next hour passed by very quickly. Paul's mum and dad decided to buy a few plants, a couple of garden ornaments and a pack of garden lights. While moving on into the outdoor part of the garden centre, where larger plants, garden sheds, fence panels, plant pots and dustbins were on display; Ben and Harry's dad received a text message. It was from his wife who was still sat in the car in the car park and it read: [How much longer r u lot gonna b?]. Ben and Harry's dad replied with: [Not sure luv, we cud b a while cos there's lots to c! I thought u wanted a new lawn mower. Y don't u come and join us and buy one!]. On receiving this message Ben and Harry's mum called back;

"Sean, I told you I'm not taking my clothes off in public; I'd feel exposed and grossly out of place!"

"Don't worry love, I'll come out and see you in a few minutes."

"OK then."

Mr. Wetherby hung up and then said; "I'm just gonna nip out and see Amanda, she's still waiting in the car."

"Oh my word! I'd forgotten all about mum," said Ben.

"She must have been waiting over an hour by now," added Paul with a slight smile.

"I won't be long. I'll let her have the car key so she can drive on somewhere else if she wants to," said Mr. Wetherby.

"OK, no problem," replied Paul's parents.

"We'll see you back here in five minutes or so, OK," said James's mum.

"Yeah, OK."

Mr. Wetherby left the others looking at the various water features and such like while he went back out to the car. He gave the car key to his wife with the suggestion she might like to drive on somewhere else to kill time. This she agreed to do. "What time do you want me to come back for?"

"It closes at half six, so; come back for about quarter past to twenty past then we can drop the kids off at the leisure centre."

"Fine. I'll see you all later - dressed I hope!"

Mr. Wetherby then headed back inside and soon rejoined the others. "I think we've got all we want," said Paul's mum.

"So have we, I think," said James's dad.

"Are you buying your wife a new lawn mower Mr. Wetherby?" asked Paul.

"I'm not sure actually. I really think Amanda should be here herself if she wants to get ten percent off the price," replied Mr. Wetherby. In the end Ben and Harry's dad gave in and bought his wife a nice new lawn mower with a durable metal blade, which was just what she wanted. After paying for their purchases they wheeled them outside to their cars and put them in. Paul's dad offered to take care of the Wetherby's new lawn mower seeing as Mrs. Wetherby had not yet returned.

"Right then; are we all gonna have something to eat and drink in the café?" asked Paul's dad with a smile.

"Yes please dad," replied Paul enthusiastically.

"Let's all go together then," said Mr. Wetherby. "The drinks are on me!"

"Oh thanks dad," smiled Ben. All nine of them headed back inside to the café where food and drink was plentiful.

While they were enjoying their afternoon tea in Hatley's café Mrs. Wetherby had driven the relatively short distance into town. As she was due a visit to her hairdresser she thought she might as well go now. She parked the car in the main street not far from the salon and got out. She didn't have very long to wait and was soon in the chair receiving the full works.

About twenty minutes into Mrs. Wetherby's hair care a car transporter carrying about ten cars slowly past the salon. Nothing was said and both Mrs. Wetherby and her hairdresser carried on chatting. However, no more than five minutes later there was the sound of an almighty crash! This car transporter had knock into the side of a building and in so doing it dislodge a good hundred yards of scaffolding about a hundred and fifty feet high. Following the crashing sound there was a few moments of quiet and a cloud of dust wafted past the salon window. The hairdresser paused for a moment to listen. "What do you think has just happened?"

"I don't know, but it sounds serious to me," replied Mrs. Wetherby. "Stick your head out the door and have a look." This she did and seeing what she saw made her scream at the top of her voice!

"Arrrh! Oh my word! I, I don't believe it!"

"Karen, what the hell... what's just happened?"

"You know all that scaffolding outside the shops just down the road?"

"Yeah, what's wrong with it?"

"Well it's virtually all fallen down. It looks like the aftermath of an earthquake out there!" said Karen while panicking wondering what to do. Just then there was the sound of more scaffolding falling into the street. People were shouting and running about all over the place, then came the sound of emergency vehicles which grew louder as they approached. The police immediately cleared the area and closed the road fearing further falling debris and scaffold poles. In a matter of minutes the whole area looked like a scene from Casualty. There were at least five fire engines and a number of ambulances. Several police vehicles were also in attendance due to the severity of the situation.

"Karen, can you finish my hair fairly quickly? I want to see what's going on out there 'cos it's close to where I left the car. I hope it's not damaged."

"If it's under all that scaffolding it'll be a complete write off."

Karen worked as swiftly as she could and Mrs. Wetherby's hair was soon finished. She left the salon and walked back to where she'd parked the car. No surprises then to find that the police had cordoned it off. Mrs. Wetherby then attracted the attention of the nearest police officer. "Excuse me," she said politely. "I parked my car round here and I was wondering if I can get to it. It's a dark blue Ford Focus '06' reg."

"I'll have a look for you madam, just wait there." Mrs. Wetherby waited for the officer to come back and when he did his face said it all. "I'm afraid your car's been seriously damaged. Was there anything in it you need urgently?" asked the officer.

"Well, no not really; I've got my handbag and my phone, so I suppose I can sort it out later once you've cleared everything away."

"OK then, we'll be in touch."

Thankfully, as this had happened just short of four o'clock on a Saturday afternoon, all the workers had gone home so no one was working on the scaffolding when it fell. However, there were a few people walking past in the street at the time of the collapse. These people were now being attended to by the emergency services.

Mrs. Wetherby decided to walk back to Hatley's garden centre to meet her husband, her sons and their friends. While she was walking back she texted her husband: [Sean, I'm on my way back to Hatley's. R u all still there?]. Mr. Wetherby replied straightaway with: [Yes we r. We're in the café and I've got a surprise for U! C u soon.]. Mrs. Wetherby texted her husband again: [And so have I!]. Ben and Harry's dad wondered what this surprise might be. They all sat in the café talking about it.

"Dad, what do you think mum's surprise is?" asked Harry.

"Haven't got a clue son."

"Maybe she feels like joining us and is coming back," suggested Paul.

"I doubt that Paul, although it would be nice," replied Mr. Wetherby.

"Perhaps she's bought a lawn mower somewhere else and wants to boast about it!" smiled Ben.

"I hope not," said Mr. Wetherby sharply.

They kept on chatting until Mr. Wetherby received another text message from his wife which read: [I'm almost back. R u still inside?]. He replied straightaway with: [Yes we r luv.]. Mrs. Wetherby responded by phoning her husband.

"Hello love," he said answering the call.

"Would you like to come out side for a few minutes, I've got something to tell you."

"OK love, see you in a minute then." Mr. Wetherby told the others his wife wanted to see him outside. "Back soon," he said as he left the café.

"Dad, wait. I'll come with you," said Ben.

"And so will I," added Harry getting up from the table.

"Me too," said Paul. "I wanna see what this surprise is your mum's got. Come on James."

"Can I go with them?" James asked his mum and dad.

"Yeah, go on then. In fact we've all finished so why don't we all go and see what this surprise is," said James's dad.

Everyone left the café and headed for the car park. Mrs. Wetherby was waiting for them not far from the main entrance. "Oh, hello love," said Ben and Harry's dad.

"Your hair looks nice mum," said Ben.

"Thank you very much Ben," replied his mum.

"Well, what's your surprise love?" asked Ben and Harry's dad.

"Hmm; you first love," replied Ben and Harry's mum cautiously.

"OK then. I got you a lawn mower, like what you wanted."

"Oh Sean thank you."

"My pleasure; and I saved a good twelve quid by buying it naked!"

"Yeah, he did," said Paul. "It's a real shame you couldn't have joined us Mrs. Wetherby."

"Yeah mum, Paul's right. It's been great being here like this," smiled Harry.

"Well I'm sorry about that, but I didn't feel confident enough to walk about naked in a garden centre."

"Right, where did you park the car Amanda, I can't see it anywhere."

"Well, that's my surprise actually," smiled Ben and Harry's mum.

"Oh Amanda, it's not been stolen has it, and with all our things in the back as well?"

"Have you had an accident mum?" asked Ben.

"No, no, it's not been stolen and I haven't had an accident, but I'm afraid our car has been seriously damaged. On a scale of one to ten it's probably nine or ten," said Mrs. Wetherby.

"So what's happened to it mum?" asked Ben worried about what they were going to do about their clothes.

"Well, while I was having my hair done a lorry carrying cars knocked into the side of a building and sent, well, quite a lot of scaffolding crashing to the ground. When I left to walk back here it looked like something out of a film."

"And our car is?..."

"...virtually buried underneath it all, I'm afraid," finished Mrs. Wetherby.

"What we gonna do about our clothes?" asked Ben. "We left them on the back seat."

"Yeah, does this mean we're gonna have to go naked to our naturist swim?" asked Harry.

"Don't worry," said Paul's dad. "We always bring a couple of extra towels."

"Dad, can't we nip back home and get Ben and Harry something to wear. I'm sure most of my things will fit Harry, and if James doesn't mind lending Ben a T-shirt and a pair of shorts or whatever we should be fine," said Paul.

"Good thinking Paul; and I'll let their dad borrow a few of my clothes."

It was now five past six and it was less than half an hour to closing time at Hatley's garden centre. Most had gone around half five, but there were still a good twenty to thirty nude shoppers about plus a few members of staff. Paul, James and their dads and quickly got dressed. Ben and Harry's dad put a towel round himself and went with them while the others waited inside Hatley's garden centre. Ben and Harry wandered off together leaving the three mums to get better acquainted. While Paul and James's mums were still naked Ben and Harry's mum was fully dressed. They talked about this and about naturism in general. "How do you both feel being here naked?" asked Ben and Harry's mum.

"Fine," replied Paul's mum. "I've got to admit, I did feel nervous at first, but I love it now just as much as my son does."

"Same here," smiled James's mum. "Look, there's not many people about now so why don't you take the first step and slip off that top and your bra?"

"Oh, I'm not so sure about that. What will Sean think when he comes back? I gave him and our sons quite a hard time over it."

"That won't matter," said Paul's mum. "Trust us, this is the best and most liberating feeling in the whole world."

"Yes absolutely, Maureen is right there. It took me a bit to get my head round the idea of going naked, but I'm so glad I did now."

"OK then, but promise me you won't laugh."

"Why on earth would we laugh?" asked Paul's mum. "We want to help you." Mrs. Wetherby slipped off her top and undid her bra. To say she'd had two children her breasts were on the small side one in particular looked noticeably smaller than the other and it was something she felt embarrassed about.

"How do you feel now you've done that?" asked James's mum.

"I don't know, perhaps a bit er, vulnerable and exposed. It's my breasts; I don't like the way they look.

"They look OK to me," smiled Paul's mum.

"You really think so? My left breast is a 'B' cup size and my right is almost small enough to be an 'A'. I've had to pad one side of my bras for ages."

"Well if that's your only concern about going naked you should be able to overcome it fairly soon," said James's mum somewhat sympathetically. "Last time we were at the swim we saw a middle-aged man who's had a colostomy and he doesn't let it bother him."

"You're joking! A naturist with one of those er, 'bags'?"

"Yes, as sure as we're sat here," said James's mum.

"Why don't you take your trousers off next and walk about a bit," suggested Paul's mum.

"Hmm, OK then. I've no worries about anything else it's just my breast I'm not all that happy with. I've always wondered if I let my sons feed on one side more than the other when they were babies."

"Hmm, that could a possibility," said James's mum. Mrs. Wetherby took off her shoes and her trousers, and then stood up in just her underwear.

"Feeling better?" asked Paul's mum. Mrs. Wetherby smiled and looked at them both.

"I have to admit this is kind of growing on me. Oh to hell with it, I'm gonna take my underwear off as well!"

"My word," smiled James's mum. "You've done it!"

"And it only took you a good ten minutes," added Paul's mum. "How do you feel?"

"Good," replied Ben and Harry's mum. "I actually feel quite good and pleased with myself."

"How do think you'd cope if your sons saw you naked?" asked James's mum

"Why? Where are they?"

"Over in the far corner running about in the shrubbery," said Paul's mum.

"We could go over and surprise them if you like; the three of us together that is," suggested James's mum.

"Just a minute." Mrs. Wetherby took a deep breath. "I think I need a drink before I face my family."

"Well come on then," said Paul's mum. As the café had closed their only option was from a drinks machine. They each had a quick coffee then walked over to where Ben and Harry were last seen. They went through to the outside area where garden sheds and fence panels were. Harry was first to spot his mum and was pretty shocked to say the least.

"Mum!" said Harry suddenly seeing his mum naked. "Is, is that you?"

"Yes love, it is. Where's your brother?"

"I, I don't know. He's round here somewhere I think. How come you've stripped off?"

"Paul and James's mums talked me into it, and I'm glad they did now, 'cos it does feel quite good."

"I know it does," smiled Harry. Harry then shouted for Ben. "Ben, Ben! Where are you? Mum's stripped off and joined us!" Mrs. Wetherby suddenly felt a tad embarrassed by her youngest son's use of the words 'Mum's stripped off', but she tried not to let it show. Harry soon reappeared with Ben.

"Mum! I don't believe it, I thought Harry was joking at first."

"Well he wasn't. I've managed to undress and go naturist with the help of Paul and James's mums."

"Are you gonna let dad see you naked?" asked Ben.

"Yes I am," replied Ben and Harry's mum.

Meanwhile; Paul, James, their dads and Mr. Wetherby returned to Hatley's garden centre. Paul's dad parked the car not far from the main entrance. "Are we gonna strip off again and go back inside naked?" asked James.

"Well I am," replied Paul. "It's not quite half six yet."

"OK then, let's all get out and strip off again," said Paul's dad. This they all did and Paul was first back inside closely followed by James. Mr. Wetherby brought up the rear and when he saw his wife naked with the others it almost reduced him to tears.

"Oh Amanda! Come here." Ben and Harry's parents gave each other a hug.

"Aw, isn't that nice," said Paul. "How did you and James's mum get her to do it?"

"We just had a nice little chat about naturism and how we feel when we're naked," replied Paul's mum.

"I strongly suspect it's what you and James did when you first went naked; hmm?" smiled James's mum.

"Yeah, OK. I get the message," smiled Paul.

It was now half past six and Hatley's garden centre was about to close. The public address system crackled into life once again;

"Ladies and gentlemen; Hatley's garden centre is about to close. The management and staff would like to thank you all for attending today. We hope you've enjoyed it and we look forward to seeing you again in the future. Good bye."

With everyone now dressed and ready leave for the swim they had to decide how best to split up because the Wetherby's car had been seriously damaged in the scaffolding collapse. Ben and his mum went with James and his parents while Harry and his dad went with the Jessops. They arrived at the leisure centre just after quarter to seven. Everyone got out and walked over to the main entrance. "Sean, how are we going to get home?" asked Ben and Harry's mum.

"Oh don't worry about that," smiled Paul's dad.

"It looks like we'll have to stay for the duration of the swim love. It's only a couple of hours." Sure enough that was the Wetherby's only option, but it did give them the chance to see their sons and friends swim about in the nude.

At seven o'clock Mr. Simpkin let through those which had paid while he continued to collect money from those which hadn't. Paul, James, Ben and Harry wasted no time at all and were soon naked in the pool. Paul and James's parents soon followed, but because Mrs. Wetherby was hydrophobic Ben and Harry's parents stayed where they were. "If you'd like to try it for a few minutes free of charge I don't mind," smiled Mr. Simpkin.

"You go if like Sean, I'll wait here."

"No way Amanda, I'm not abandoning you again. It would be nice though if we could do it together."

"No, no; I couldn't Sean. You know how I feel about water and swimming pools."

"I know love; but if you overcame that fear the sky's the limit." Ben and Harry's mum and dad carried on talking about this until she finally decided face her fears and give it a try. Mrs. Wetherby was shaking like a leaf as she got closer to the pools. She'd no problem with going naked now; it was the fear of water which now took priority. "Just sit on the top step love and put your feet in the water." With some help from her husband and Paul's mum Mrs. Wetherby managed to do this. Progress was slow for very obvious reasons, but after half an hour, during which time the Rustons arrived, Ben and Harry's mum found herself in a swimming pool for the first time in nearly thirty eight years, even though she was only forty four!

She held her husband's hand throughout. "Where are our sons?" she asked. "I think they should see this." Paul's mum said she'd go and fetch them. Ben and Harry quickly came across from the main pool into the small pool after hearing their mum was in there.

"Mum! What are you doing!" yelled Harry.

"I don't believe it," said Ben in amazement. Seeing their mum in a swimming pool was something Ben and Harry had only ever dreamt of. They went over to her immediately and both of them gave their mum a hug.

"Mum, I'm so proud of you," said Ben almost in tears.

"Yeah, same here," said Harry. "You must let us teach you to swim."

"Let's just take it slowly boys. Your dad and Mrs. Jessop have given me a lot of support. I'd have never have done it without them." The Wetherbys stayed together for a while and talked privately.

Meanwhile in the main pool, Paul and James were chatting with the Rustons. Paul was keen for them to attend his birthday party. "It's my fifteenth birthday a week on Tuesday," said Paul. "And I'm planning a party; a naturist party that is."

"Hmm, sounds good," smiled Alice.

"It should be," said Paul. "I'm inviting quite a few people."

"What we gonna be doing?" asked Craig.

"Er, I'm not exactly sure at the moment, but I guess we'll play some party games naked and have a dance naked too," smiled Paul. Alice and Craig then asked their mum.

"Mum, mum; can we got to Paul's birthday party?" asked Alice.

"It's a week on Tuesday," added Craig.

"Yes I should think so."

"Mrs. Ruston, the invite includes all four of you," said Paul.

"Oh, thank you Paul. That's really nice of you to invite Martin and me to your birthday party."

"Can you come?"

"I'm sure we'll be able to come Paul." Mrs. Ruston then called over to her husband; "Martin, Martin! Here a minute."

"Yes love."

"Paul has very kindly invited the four of us to his fifteenth birthday party a week on Tuesday; please say you can come, and by the way, it's a naturist party."

"Oh great, thanks very much Paul."

"What time do you want us to arrive?" asked Alice.

"I'd guess about half five," replied Paul. "I'm not sure just when we'll be eating."

"Who else is coming?" asked Craig.

"Well, James will be there."

"Sure will," smiled James.

"And so will your mum and dad I hope. Then there's the Wetherbys," said Paul.

"It looks like you might get all four of the Wetherbys now seeing as Mrs. Wetherby doesn't mind going naked," smiled James.

"Well, I'll ask them and they can decide what they want to do. I was also gonna invite Peter Simpkin seeing as he's been good to James and me," said Paul. "Where is he?"

"Hmm, I'm not sure; I don't see him in the pool," said Mr. Ruston looking around.

"Maybe he's playing badminton," suggested Alice.

"Oh yeah, who fancies a game?" asked Paul. The Rustons all fancied playing badminton for a bit so, after letting their parents know where they were going, Paul and James followed them to the gym.

On entering the gym Paul and James got a nice surprise. They saw Katie and her mum playing badminton. This was only the third time they'd met because Katie and her mum hadn't been for a few weeks. Paul and James noticed another girl who appeared to be three or four years older than Katie playing alongside her. As soon as Katie saw Paul and James she went over to see them. "Hi Paul, hi James. Haven't seen either of you for a while, how you doing?"

"Fine thanks," replied Paul.

"Same here," smiled James.

"Who's that playing badminton with your mum?" asked Paul.

"Oh that's my sister, Jenny," replied Katie. "You haven't met her yet have you?"

"No we haven't," said Paul. "But I thought you said your sister didn't like being naked."

"I did, but things have changed since then, and for the better," smiled Katie. "My sister came home from university about three weeks ago and she's staying with me and mum for the summer 'cos dad's place is well, er, not very clean and tidy."

"Go on," said Paul encouragingly.

"Well, mum and me decided to go naked at home, mostly in the evenings, but these days we're naked at home all the time unless we go out," smiled Katie.

"So where does your sister come in?" asked James.

"Well, when my sister came to live with us mum made it clear her and me were not going to wear clothes in the house unnecessarily. She told Jenny we were naturists and if she didn't like it she should go and live with dad."

"So what did she do?" asked Paul showing a keen interest.

"Not much. She didn't want to go and live with dad for two reasons; one, his flat is untidy; and two, he works long hours so is hardly ever there."

"Seems reasonable enough to me," said James.

"Yeah it does to me," added Paul. "I think your sister made the right choice."

"Yeah, so; after a week or two living with mum and me Jenny kind of got used to seeing us naked. In the evenings, after showering, she started wearing only panties and her dressing gown. Then, last Monday evening when mum and me were out Jenny went fully naturist. Mum gave me her house keys while she had a quick chat with a friend who was waiting at the bus stop. I unlocked the front door and when I went in I saw my sister fully naked in the front room watching TV."

"And, what did she do?" asked James.

"Yeah, did she make a quick exit for some clothes?" smiled Paul.

"No, surprisingly she didn't really do anything. I took my clothes off and sat down next to her, but all she said was; 'nice this, isn't it sis.' I was quite surprised at suddenly sitting next to my sister watching TV while we were both completely naked. Mum came in a few minutes later and saw us both. She had to do a double take to make sure she wasn't mistaken. While she was naked Jenny got up to make mum and me a cup of tea."

"I bet your mum was really surprised at that," smiled James.

"Sure she was. When mum joined us naturist we switched the TV off and had a long talk. After trying naturism again Jenny said she felt different. She told us she felt free and liberated. This is what I was trying to tell her two or three years ago, but she wasn't really interested. She said she felt as if everyone was looking at her."

"So is this her first time here since then?" asked Paul.

"Yes it is and she loves it," replied Katie.

"Are you gonna introduce us then?" asked James.

"Sure, come on over." Paul and James walked over with Katie to meet her sister Jenny. "Jen! Jenny, there's two friends of mine who'd like to meet you," smiled Katie.

"Oh yeah," replied Jenny pausing for a moment.

"Paul, James; this is my sister Jenny. Jenny this is Paul and this is James."

"Please to meet you," smiled Paul and James.

"How long you known my little sister?" asked Jenny.

"Well she's in my year at school," replied James. "But the first time we met here was at the end of May when Paul and me sneaked into this swim."

"Really? You both sneaked into a naturist swim?"

"Yeah we did, but it wasn't exactly trouble free," said Paul.

Paul and James carried on talking to Jenny, Katie and their mum and it wasn't long before Paul invited them to his birthday party. They agreed to come and were looking forward to it even more so when Paul told them it was to be a naturist party.

Realising they'd left the Rustons to play badminton by themselves Paul and James made their excuses and left. They walked over to where the Rustons were and Paul said; "Sorry about wandering off like that. We saw Katie Finch and her mum, and her sister."

"Yeah, we haven't seen them for a while so we felt we had to say something," said James.

"Oh don't worry," said Mr. Ruston. "You obviously know quite a lot of other naturists now you've been coming for about three months." Paul and James were very happy with this and it was true, they had made a number of new friends through naturism. Paul eventually saw Mr. Simpkin and he asked him if he'd like to come to his naturist birthday party a week on Tuesday. "Oh Paul, your so kind; and yes I'd love to come to your party, but I'm afraid I can't because I'll be in Croatia," said Mr. Simpkin.

"Oh it's OK, there'll be other times," said Paul. "I hope you enjoy your holiday."

"I'm sure I will," smiled Mr. Simpkin.

After another half hour or so it was time to get out. Paul and James had gone back to the pool for another quick swim and to see there mums and dads. "Mum, you might like to know that apart from Peter Simpkin everyone can come to my birthday party."

"Oh good. What time did you tell them to come for?" asked Paul's mum.

"I suggested about half five, is that OK?"

"I should think so. Have you told Ben and Harry and their mum and dad?"

"Er, no I don't think so," replied Paul. Paul immediately corrected this and invited the Wetherbys to his party. They were thrilled to be invited to a naturist birthday party as it was something neither of them had ever done; even their mum agreed to come!

Now that everyone was dried and dressed they left the leisure centre and walked over to their cars. Paul's dad gave the Wetherbys a lift home. Paul and his mum went home with the Handles.

With the visit to Hatley's garden centre lasting all afternoon and then going swimming in the evening this had been quite a long, but none the less enjoyable day. Paul was now looking forward to his birthday a week on Tuesday.

Chapter 19

It was now was Tuesday the nineteenth of August and was Paul's fifteenth birthday. Paul got up fairly early to see what his mum and dad had bought him for his birthday. He put his slippers and dressing gown on then went downstairs and into the front room. His parents were already there when he walked in. "Happy birthday son," smiled his dad holding out a card and what looked like a rather small gift-wrapped box.

"Thanks very much," replied Paul. Paul opened his birthday card and checked the inside. He then placed it on the mantelpiece next to two other cards he'd received through the post yesterday morning.

"Happy birthday love," said his mum. She too held out a gift-wrapped parcel, but this one was much bigger.

"Thanks very much mum, what on earth it is?"

"Open it love and find out." Paul opened his presents in front of his mum and dad. Both presents and the card were from his parents as a whole even though his mum and dad had given him a present each. Paul ripped the paper off in a matter of seconds.

"Oh wow! A rucksack, thanks very much," said Paul in grateful appreciation.

"Have a look inside son," smiled his dad. Paul did just that and inside was a bright orange towel with the '100% off' BN logo in the corner.

"Oh brilliant dad, I can't wait to show it to James."

"Well, I think we ought to tell you; we've joined British Naturism," said his dad.

"Oh great! Does James and his mum and dad know?" asked Paul.

"Yes love they do, 'cos we all joined at the same time," smiled Paul's mum.

"This is brilliant news," said Paul. "I'll tell James and show him what I've got as soon as I see him."

"OK then, but don't forget your other present love that your dad gave you."

"Oh sorry mum. Where did I put it?" asked Paul.

"It's right here son, but be careful how you open this one,

it's not for throwing around," smiled his dad. Paul carefully tore the wrapping paper off and was pleasantly surprised to discover that his mum and dad had not only bought him a rucksack and an orange BN towel, but a digital camera as well.

"Mum, dad; I don't know how to thank you."

"You're our only child Paul, and we both love you dearly," said his mum softly.

"Come on then son, try your rucksack for size."

"OK dad." Paul put his new digital camera back in its box and placed it next to his birthday cards on the mantelpiece. He then removed all the packaging, slipped off his dressing gown and tried his rucksack on for size. Paul thought it was brilliant. When he and James had gone out walking in the past they'd always used James's rucksack to carry their things, but now Paul had one too. This meant they could take more equipment with them and it wasn't going to be down to one person to carry it all.

Just then there was a knock on the front door. Without thinking Paul quickly answered it - while still naked, apart from his slippers and rucksack! Fortunately enough it was James and he'd come round to give Paul his birthday card and present. "Paul! What you doing answering the door completely naked again? Have you gone mad?"

"Oh er, sorry; I just forgot. Look at what my mum and dad have bought me," smiled Paul closing the front door. "And they've just told me we're members of British Naturism now as well."

"Hmm, great. We've joined BN as well," smiled James. "Nice rucksack by the way Paul."

"I guess it'll be as big as yours," said Paul.

"I think it looks bigger," said James. "Next time we go out for a walk you'll have to bring it with you."

"Sure will. It'd be great if Ben and Harry can come too. It'll be just like that day when we all went skinny dipping," smiled Paul. Paul took off his rucksack and followed James into the front room. Once there James slipped out of his shorts and T-shirt and sat down opposite Paul.

"Well here you are then Paul, happy birthday," smiled James handing over his card and present.

"Thanks very much," replied Paul. Paul opened them

straightaway. James had bought Paul a pack of fifty blank CDs. "Thanks James, these are just what I need; my mum and dad have also bought me a digital camera."

"Really? Can I have a look at it?" asked James.

"Yeah sure, but please be careful with it, it's not a little kid's toy."

"I know that, I'll be careful," insisted James. Paul took his new digital camera out of its box and past it over to James. "What's the pixel rating?" asked James.

"It's a ten point five mega pixel camera," replied Paul. "We'll have to go out later and take some photos with it."

"Sure. It looks like it's gonna be a nice day for your birthday Paul."

"Yeah, I was thinking the same thing."

Paul and James carried on talking while Paul's mum and dad finished their breakfasts. "I don't think you've had any breakfast yet have you Paul?"

"No I haven't mum, I thought I was feeling hungry," replied Paul. "Would you like a bit of brekky with us James?"

"Yeah, what about a full English?" suggested Paul's dad with a smile.

"Oh er, thanks, but I couldn't face a full English breakfast Mr. Jessop. I've just had a bowl of cereal and scrambled egg on toast before I came over."

"That's OK James. Would you like a tea or coffee?"

"Yes please; tea would be fine thanks Mrs. Jessop," replied James. Paul's dad got busy in the kitchen cooking himself and his son a hearty English breakfast. In the meantime Paul helped himself to a couple of Weetabix and a glass of apple juice. While waiting for his dad to finish cooking breakfast Paul took James his mug of tea. "Thanks," said James. "I must admit it smells nice what your dad is cooking."

"Hmm, I know it does," smiled Paul.

"Is your dad wearing an apron or something while he's cooking food?" asked James.

"Yeah, course he is. He wouldn't want to get hot fat spattered on his bare skin would he," laughed Paul.

A few minutes later Paul and his dad sat down to enjoy their full English breakfasts. "Hmm, my word, this is delicious mum," smiled Paul while scoffing down his sausage, egg and bacon.

"Yes, well when you finished you can help your dad tidy the kitchen. I'll make a start in the front room shortly."

"Can I help at all?" asked James.

"Yes if wouldn't mind James, that'll certainly speed things up," replied Paul's mum.

After breakfast the four of them tidied up and got things ready for Paul's birthday party. By one o'clock the tidying up was largely done; that only left the food and drink to be got ready. Paul's mum had suggested a buffet style party rather than trying to sit everyone at the dinner table; which, given the number of guests attending, would be rather difficult. "Mum, do you mind if I go out for a bit with James? I wanna take a few photos with my new camera."

"Yes OK then, but don't be much more than a couple of hours. I'd like you to help me with preparations for your party."

"Yeah, OK mum. Paul and James got dressed and put their trainers on. Paul packed his orange BN towel into his new rucksack along with his camera and then left with James.

They walked to their usual spot by the railway line and once past the crossing Paul just had to take his clothes off and go naturist. James wasn't far behind him in getting naked and very soon both of them were enjoying the fresh air and warm sunshine as only naturists know how. "Come on James we're almost there."

"Yeah, I know; what's the rush?"

"Nothing," replied Paul. "I just wanna put my rucksack down somewhere safe and take some photos." Soon enough Paul and James arrived at their favourite sunbathing spot and Paul took off his rucksack. "Hmm, this is the life," said Paul slowly while taking a deep breath of fresh air.

"Well, you gonna take some photos then or what?"

"Sure, just let me get my camera out." Paul took his new digital camera out of its box and switched it on. He took a few photos of the surrounding countryside and of the tree they'd used as their initial target when they first got naked together, but what Paul really wanted to take photos of was James; while he was naked. Paul thought James would be happier doing this if he initially reversed the situation and let James photograph him, so he did. "Could you take a few photos of me, here, in the nude?"

"Er, yeah, if you like," replied James. James wasn't expecting Paul to say this, but he was more than happy to oblige; after all, it was his birthday and his camera. James took a few photos of Paul in the nude where they were, but after only a few minutes Paul wanted to stand over by the ruins like they did before with their arms outstretched.

"Do you mind if I take some photos of you?" asked Paul.

"No not at all," replied James. "Where's best?"

"Just stay there where you are for now." James stood still and let Paul photograph him.

It was interesting, in an artistic sort of way, to see them do this out in the open. James had already photographed Paul, now it was Paul who was photographing James; and neither of them were the least bit bother by the fact that they were naked. "Right, let's move on. I want to take a few photos of the ruins and of us standing by them."

"OK then. Shall I carry your rucksack for you?"

"Yeah, if you like." James followed Paul towards the ruins, but they stopped short as Paul had seen someone walking close by. Paul and James waited a few minutes and then continued when the coast was clear. They couldn't see or hear anyone else at all. "Right," said Paul clearly. "Put my rucksack down just there and come over here." James did what Paul asked. "I'm gonna stand over there by the ruin and I'd like you to take a few photos of me."

"No problem," smiled James. Paul walked across and positioned himself next to the ruin. He leant to his right resting his arm on the ruin itself, and while primarily standing on his left foot Paul positioned his right leg across his left and pointed his toes downwards to give a somewhat relaxed carefree look.

"OK, when you're ready." James took five or six photos of Paul stood by the ruin. "Now take a few of me on this mound with my arms outstretched," smiled Paul. James did so and was beginning to enjoy being the 'David Bailey' of the pair of them.

"Paul!"

"What?"

"I've just had a thought; why don't you take your trainers off and go totally naturist. I think it'll make for a better, more natural looking photo; what do you think?"

"Oh yeah, you're right there," replied Paul enthusiastically. "That's a brilliant idea James." Paul quickly removed his trainers and threw them down by his rucksack. He then retook his original pose by the ruin minus his trainers.

"This definitely looks more natural Paul without your trainers. Could you move to your right a bit and step forward slightly, you're in the shade just there."

"Yeah sure." Paul moved into a better position, and with the sun now shining directly on to him James took a few more photos.

"Right; I've taken twelve photos of you by the ruin, do you wanna stand on the mound again?"

"Certainly will," replied Paul. Paul stood on the raised part of the ruin overlooking the town and stretched out his arms. James continued to photograph him in the bright sunshine. "This feels fantastic. I remember when we were both here a month or so ago. We were stood side by side with our arms outstretched weren't we?"

"Sure we were," replied James. "But we'll need a tripod or something to put your camera on if we're to get a photo of us both together won't we?"

"Yeah I s'pose so, but we could improvise in the short term."

"How do you mean?" asked James.

"Well, I could stand my camera on a wall or litter bin perhaps. It just depends what's available to us at the time."

"Oh right."

"Anyway, would you like to change places now? I'd like to take a few more photos of you by the ruin and on the mound," said Paul. "And we haven't got much time left. My mum wanted us back about half three and it's nearly three now."

"OK then," replied James. Paul put his trainers back on while James took his off. James stood by the ruin completely naked just as Paul had done. Paul took a few photos of James where he was then asked him to stand on the what he called 'the mound'.

"Right, stretch your arms out," said Paul. "Brilliant James; this is absolutely brilliant!"

"Thanks," said James. "Tell you what; why don't I try and climb up on top of the ruin. That should make for a good photo."

"You're gonna try and climb on top of the ruin barefoot?"

"Yeah, it doesn't look too difficult. I'll sit down once I'm up there."

"Go on then, but be careful," said Paul. James carefully climbed up the side of the ruin and sat down on top.

"Well, what do you think?"

"Great." Paul carried on taking photos of James while he was sat on top of the ruin, after which James got down. "Right, you can take a few more photos of me now," said Paul. After removing his trainers once again Paul sat down on the ground by the ruin. For the next few photos Paul decided to adopt a more discreet pose, one where it was clear he was naked, but his privates where hidden from view by the position of his legs and/or body. As James began to photograph him again a middle-aged couple walked past. Paul and James failed to notice them as they were busy photographing each other. On seeing them this couple suddenly stopped and stared.

"What do you think they're doing?" asked the woman softly, so as not to be overheard.

"How should I know?"

"Perhaps it's an art project or something. You know, life modelling?"

"Yeah, but don't you think they're a bit young for college or university. I wouldn't put them much over thirteen or fourteen. What do you think?"

"Hmm, I guess you could be right." Just then Paul looked across and saw them.

"James! Behind you!" said Paul suddenly running forward.

"Steady on! I'm sorry if we startled you," said the man.

"We were just wondering what you were doing, that's all. Is it some kind of art project?" asked the woman.

"Er; yeah, that's exactly what it is," replied Paul quickly. "I've just been given a new digital camera for my fifteenth birthday, which is today. Pass me my camera James." James handed Paul his camera. "What do you think?"

"Hmm, it looks like a very good camera to me," replied the man.

"Thanks," said Paul. James felt a bit out of place standing about naked, but didn't say anything. He remembered Paul's confidence building exercise from not so long ago and as a result stood his ground as did Paul. James was hoping Paul would be able to sort this situation out; which, of course, he did.

"I'm an artist myself," said the woman. "And I teach art at college. I've painted quite a few nudes in my time."

"And you've posed naked a few times as well haven't you love," smiled the man.

"Yes of course I have. I don't see anything wrong with the naked human form, male or female. It does unfortunately have a tendency to be link with sex which is not always the case."

"I know exactly what you mean," smiled Paul. "Would you mind taking a few photos of James and me by the ruin 'cos I haven't got a tripod with me."

"No problem." Paul and James were both equally stunned at how accepting this couple were about what they were doing. This woman took a few photos of them both together by the ruin and on 'the mound'. "Why don't the pair of you stand one behind the other like Leonardo DiCaprio and Kate Winslet did in 'Titanic'?"

"Oh yeah! That's a brilliant idea! James, you stand behind me 'cos you're taller." Paul and James thought these photos would be the best yet and couldn't wait to see them.

"Thanks very much for your help," said Paul. "We really should get going now, we're late as it is."

"Same here actually; we've a train to catch in just under half an hour. Here's your camera, I hope you like the photos," smiled the woman.

"I'm sure we will," replied Paul. "Thanks again, see you later, bye."

This couple walked off leaving Paul and James alone. "I don't believe it! How on earth did we get away with that?" asked James.

"Oh, you know; there's nothing wrong with the naked human

form, male or female," smiled Paul.

"Well, come on, I think we should be going home now, it must be well after three," said James. Paul and James wiped their feet in the grass then put their trainers back on and began to walk home. They stopped briefly just before the foot crossing and put their shorts on as well because they could see someone ahead walking a dog. They arrived back just after quarter to four and went naturist as soon as they got indoors.

"Where've you two been all this time?" asked Paul's mum. "I was expecting you back half an hour ago. There's still quite a lot to do for your party, Paul."

"Yeah I know mum, I'm sorry," replied Paul. "We've been over by the railway and the ruin again, and got talking to someone."

"Yeah, it was great Mrs. Jessop. We took quite a few photos."

"Yeah we did mum," smiled Paul.

"Oh, OK then. We'll have to have a look at them later when everyone's here." Paul suddenly froze.

"Er, I'm not sure about that mum. No one's gonna wanna see my photos. They'll think they're boring."

"Why should anyone thing that? What have you been taking photos of?" asked his mum suddenly showing quite a lot of interest. As his parents were now naturists themselves Paul decided to be honest about what they'd taken photos of.

"I took a few photos of the landscape and the ruin, but what we really enjoyed doing most of all was taking naturist photos of each other stood next to the ruin.

"It looks quite artistic in a way Mrs. Jessop," said James.

"Oh, does it indeed," said Paul's mum. "I hope the pictures tasteful; I don't want the police getting involved and seizing your camera, or your computer for that matter."

"Relax mum they're fine, I'll show you if you like." Paul showed his mum a few of the photos they'd taken.

"Hmm, I suppose they're OK," said his mum. "Well, would you like to put your camera away now and come and help me get the food ready? Oh, and wash your hands first." Paul put his camera back in its box and took it upstairs.

"Mum? Have I got time for a quick shower; only my feet are dirty from walking about outside?" asked Paul calling down to his mum.

"Yes OK, go on then, ten minutes."

On overhearing this James said; "If you're gonna get a shower, why don't we do it together again? It'll be quicker that way." It didn't take Paul long to think about this.

"Yeah OK, come on then; before my mum realises." Paul grabbed a couple of towels and followed James into the bathroom. The pair of them stepped in and Paul turned the shower on.

"Would you like me to do your back first?" asked James.

"Yes please, that'd be great," replied Paul. Paul stood still and let James wash his back. However, while James was doing this he'd had an idea he thought Paul would like. He finished washing Paul's back, but instead of stopping James carried on and washed Paul's bottom, legs and feet.

"Would you like me to wash the rest of you?" asked James.

"Please do; I'm enjoying this," smiled Paul.

"OK then, turn round." Paul turned round and faced James. James now turned his attention to Paul's front and washed his arms and torso. When James had finished Paul thoroughly washed and rinsed his privates himself; but without realising it, Paul did this in James's full view giving him quite an eyeful! Suddenly seeing Paul's penis at such close range rapidly caused James to become fully aroused.

"Would you like me to wash you now?" asked Paul.

"Oh, er…, yeah OK. Do my back first if you would," replied James feeling more than a bit embarrassed about it.

"Are you OK?" asked Paul. "Only you seem…"

"I'm fine thanks," snapped James. Paul didn't bother saying anything else and continued washing James's back then moved down to wash his bottom, legs and feet. James was finding it very difficult to control his feelings and was dreading the moment when Paul would ask him to turn round. However, unbeknown to James, Paul found himself in pretty much the same position after catching a glimpse of James's penis in the mirror beside the bath. Paul smiled to himself after quickly realising why James felt uncomfortable.

"Right then; do you wanna turn round?"

"Er…, just a minute, I…"

"James," said Paul softly. "It's OK, really; don't worry about it, it happens. Mine's pretty stiff as well."

"You serious?"

"Yeah, honest. Turn round and have a look if you don't believe me; I'm not embarrassed." James initially looked over his shoulder and then slowly turned round and faced Paul.

"Oh wow! You weren't joking," smiled James.

"Hmm; not bad eh?" smiled Paul.

"Yeah; nice. What do you reckon to mine?"

"Pretty good. I wish mine was as big as yours!"

"I'm not much bigger," said James moving closer to Paul.

"You really think so?"

"Yeah. I think you've got a few more pubes than I have, but…" James paused but then continued. "Why don't we put our penises together and compare them?"

"Hmm, go on then," smiled Paul. Paul and James placed their penises close together and compared them. "See - yours is bigger than mine."

"Yeah, but it's only a bit bigger; and yours will get bigger in time."

"So will yours won't it?"

"Yeah, I s'pose so. Why don't we compare them again on your sixteenth birthday?" smiled James.

"OK then. If you think we can remember," smiled Paul. "Would you like me to finish washing you now?"

"Yeah, go on then; and make sure you do everywhere." smiled James placing one foot on the side of the bath.

"OK then, if you insist," smiled Paul.

James was now feeling somewhat proud after they'd 'compared' themselves, and had gone from being quite embarrassed about his aroused state to virtually flaunting it openly in front of Paul. "I think we'd better get a cold shower and chill for a couple of minutes before we go downstairs," said Paul.

"Yeah, I think so too," added James. "If your mum sees us like this she'll have a fit!"

"Yeah well, come on then; we must have been in here well over ten minutes."

While Paul and James were in the shower Paul's mum was

still preparing party food in the kitchen. She was beginning to wonder where James and her son were after saying they'd only be ten minutes. "Paul? Have you finished in the shower yet?"

"Yeah, I'm just getting dried mum. I'll be down in a minute. James is having a quick shower too, I hope you don't mind."

"Fine. Just come down as soon as you can."

"We will." Paul then spoke to James. "Stay in my bedroom for a few minutes and then come down. I don't want my mum to think we've been in the shower together again."

"OK then," said James. Paul went downstairs to help his mum. "What would you like me to do?" asked Paul.

"You can make a start on the sandwiches please. There's five loaves of bread there; get buttering." Paul sat to the table and began buttering bread for sandwiches. While he was partway through the third loaf he was beginning to wonder where James was.

James eventually came downstairs with a rather sheepish smile on his face. "Is there anything I can do to help?" he asked.

"You can help Paul with the sandwiches if you like James, there's still quite a lot to do," replied Paul's mum. Paul and James continued buttering bread.

"What are you looking so pleased about?" Paul asked James.

"Er, n-nothing," smiled James. "I s'pose I'm just looking forward to your party, that's all."

"Really?"

"Yeah, it won't be long now will it."

"You've got something planned haven't you? Some kind of prank?"

"No I haven't!" said James firmly. "I'm not gonna spoil your party by playing some silly prank."

"I'm glad to hear it James," said Paul's mum.

"So what's so funny then?" asked Paul.

"Nothing," replied James. "I don't know why you're making such a fuss." Paul continued to look at James. He felt sure James was up to something, he just didn't know what. "What would you like us to put in the sandwiches Mrs. Jessop?" asked James.

"Oh er, just a minute James." Paul's mum took a few things out of the fridge and a couple of tins from a cupboard next to it. "Right, there's a couple of cheese spreads, some egg mayonnaise, some ham, cucumber and tomatoes. There's also a tin of salmon and tin of sardines."

"Sardines? What are they?" asked James.

"They're a small sea fish similar to pilchards and herring," replied Paul's mum.

"Oh right. I've only ever hear the word 'sardine' when I've been on a train with mum or dad and it's been really busy."

"That's why people use the phrase 'packed in like sardines'," smiled Paul. "That small tin will probably be packed with thirty or forty sardines."

"Let's open it and find out," smiled James. Paul got the tin opener out of the draw and opened the tin of sardines so James could see for himself what they looked like. In this particular tin they were packed in BBQ sauce.

"Try one," said Paul. "I think there quite nice, especially in BBQ sauce."

"Hey, don't eat too many you two; there supposed to be for your party," said Paul's mum firmly.

"Sorry mum, I just wanted to see if James liked them." On the whole James did like them and the sauce which they were in. Paul then tipped them out into a small serving bowl and put them on the table with the rest of the food.

"Paul, I thought we were gonna put those sardines in sandwiches," said James.

"Oh yeah, I forgot."

"Leave them where they are now Paul it's fine. Open the tin of salmon next and mash it up in a dish please," said Paul's mum. Paul did as his mum asked and opened the tin of salmon. He mashed it up in a cereal bowl and then spread it on a few slices of buttered bread.

"Mum, shall I put a few slices of cucumber or tomato in with the salmon?" asked Paul.

"Er, you can if you want to love," replied his mum. Paul sliced a good half of a cucumber, but thought slicing a tomato was too intricate so didn't bother.

"I'll just put cucumber in mum 'cos I think tomatoes will be a bit messy."

"OK then."

As time progressed so did the amount of food being put on the table. Paul and James took the last couple of plates of sandwiches through and came back into the kitchen. "I'll take the warmed up food through just before we eat," said Paul's mum. "That way it'll be fresher." It was now just after quarter past five and Paul's dad arrived home from work. He'd arranged to leave earlier than usual because it was his son's birthday.

"Hi everyone," said Paul's dad as he came in.

"Oh hello love," replied Paul's mum. "I'm glad you got away in time for Paul's party."

"Well, I couldn't let my only son down now could I?"

"Hi dad, hi Mr. Jessop," said Paul and James.

"I'm just gonna go upstairs, won't be long. I'll be back down in the buff after a quick shower," smiled Paul's dad.

"OK love." A few minutes later there was a knock on the front door. It was Katie Finch and her mum and sister. They were on the early side as they'd managed to catch an unexpected bus which was running late. Paul grabbed a towel and answered the door.

"Hi, happy birthday Paul," smiled Katie.

"Oh thanks," replied Paul very grateful at receiving their card and present. "I'll open them later when everyone's here. Please do go through and undress, we're naked already."

"Thanks very much, we will," smiled Katie. Katie and her mum and sister didn't waste any time in getting undressed.

"Have you got anywhere where we can leave our clothes?" asked Katie's mum.

"Yeah sure. Let me get a few shopping bags for you that way they won't get mixed-up with anyone else's," replied Paul.

"Oh thanks very much Paul," said Katie's mum.

"If you wanna write your names on I'll take them upstairs and put them on my mum and dad's bed so they're out of the way."

"That's a good idea Paul," said Katie.

"Have you brought any towels with you at all?" asked Paul.

"Oh sorry, we haven't no," replied Katie's mum.

"It's OK, it doesn't really matter. I'll get a few from the airing cupboard," said Paul. Paul took the Finches clothes upstairs and came back down with a few towels. "Right, so that we're following naturist etiquette we'll all sit on towels." Paul placed a towel on each chair and on each part of the sofa.

After showering and freshening up Paul's dad came downstairs and into the front room; and, save for a pair of novelty slippers was completely naked. "Oh hello; I thought I heard the front door," said Paul's dad.

"Dad, this is Katie Finch, she's a friend from school; and this is her sister Jenny and her mum."

"Pleased to meet you," smiled Paul's dad. "Come on then Paul, offer your guests a drink."

"Oh sorry, what can I get you?"

"I'll have a coke please," replied Katie.

"Same for me please," said Jenny.

"I wouldn't mind a glass of orange juice please Paul," said Katie's mum.

Paul dealt with the drinks and took them through on a silver tray. As he did this there was another knock on the front door. "I'll get it mum," said Paul putting the tray down and quickly grabbing his towel. It was the Rustons which arrived next.

"Hi Paul, happy birthday," said Alice and Craig.

"Thanks, thanks very much," replied Paul at being given another card and present. "Please go through and join everyone else. James; can you get the Rustons a few bags for their clothes while I get each of them a drink?"

"Yeah sure," replied James.

Paul and James were now in the thick of things. His naturist birthday party was steadily coming along as more and more guests arrived. Next to arrive was James's parents from next door, and then the Wetherbys. Following the incident with the scaffolding the Wetherbys had received a courtesy car, which incidentally, just happened to be another Ford Focus.

Now that everyone was here and naturist Paul decided it was time for the first game. "How long we got before we eat mum," asked Paul.

"About twenty minutes or so love, why?"

"I was just gonna start the first game," replied Paul.

"OK love."

"Right everyone; we've about twenty minutes to kill before we eat so I suggest we play a quick game of charades. Any volunteers for first go?"

"Oh can I have first go Paul, please?" asked Harry.

"Sure you can Harry." Paul sat down on the floor in front of James and his parents. Last time Harry played this game he won and was given a bag of sweets as a prize. This time, however, the game was to be played a little differently. It was decided that whoever guesses correctly would have the next go. So, Harry got up from his chair and stood in front of everyone. He liked playing this game and playing it naked added to the fun. After five minutes or so James guessed correctly.

"Yeah, well done James; your turn now," smiled Harry. Harry sat down again and watched James act out what he'd chosen. He hoped he'd get another go fairly soon, but this didn't happen as it was Katie who knew what James doing and guessed the right answer.

"Well done Katie, your turn now," said James. James sat down again by his mum and dad and watched Katie closely. Katie was finding this game interesting, especially as it was her first time playing it naked. She chose a fairly easy one to allow her sister the chance to have a go and sure enough it worked. Jenny guessed the right answer in less than two minutes.

"Right, your turn sis," smiled Katie.

"Oh er, OK then." Jenny was perhaps a little nervous at getting up and standing in front of everyone while completely naked, but she remained strong minded and didn't let it show, and after just a few minutes, Jenny was giving the impression she'd been a naturist most of her life. In the end Ben guessed correctly, but as it was now time to eat Paul's mum suggested a break.

"Right everyone, please help yourselves to food, there is plenty." In order to cut down on washing up Mrs. Jessop had bought a pack of paper plates. James had placed these on the table along with a pile of napkins. "Please be careful eating the vol-au-vents, sausage rolls and pork pies," said Paul's mum. "I've only just taken them out of the oven." Everyone queued up to the table and gradually helped themselves to what they wanted.

In addition to the vol-au-vents, sausage rolls and mini Melton Mowbray pork pies there was heaps of salad, cubes of cheese and onions on sticks, mini sausages on sticks, three or four types of crisps, bacon fries, a bowl of sardines and a wide variety of sandwiches. Paul and James felt they should hold back and not appear greedy by being first.

After ten or fifteen minutes most guests had helped themselves to what they wanted and were sat down eating. "Mmm, Mrs. Jessop; the sausage rolls and vol-au-vents are absolutely divine! Did you make them yourself?" asked Ben and Harry's mum.

"Please call me Maureen, and yes on the whole I did make them, but James helped make the sauce for the vol-au-vents, didn't you love."

"Yeah sure. They taste really nice." With everyone now eating conversation between them reduced.

"So what have you got for your birthday Paul?" asked James's dad.

"I've got a rucksack, an orange BN Towel and a digital camera from my mum and dad," replied Paul. "James bought me some blank CDs as well so I'll be able to store my photos on them."

"Anything else Paul?" asked James's mum.

"Yeah, but I haven't opened them yet. I'll wait until we've all finished eating."

About twenty minutes later Paul's mum took a few empty plates and things into the kitchen. To say there was quite a lot of food on the table to start with there wasn't much left. Paul's mum returned from the kitchen carrying a few sweet things. There was trifle, fruits of the forest cheesecake, fresh fruit salad and a few buns and cakes. "Please help yourselves, I'll be back shortly." Paul's mum went back into the kitchen to get her son's birthday cake. As she only had five candles Paul's mum placed all of these on the cake; two in the 'one' and three in the 'five'. She lit them and then took the cake through. "Right everyone; Paul, please be upstanding. Happy birthday to you, happy birthday to you, Happy birthday dear Paul; happy birthday to you!" Paul proudly stood up while everyone sang 'happy birthday' to him. He felt a warm glow inside him.

"Thank you, thank you all very much," said Paul blowing out the candles.

"Speech! Speech!" shouted James.

"Er, yeah, OK then James." Paul paused for a moment to gather his thoughts. "Well, I'd like to thank you all for coming here this evening and for the cards and presents you've given me. I haven't opened them yet, but I will do."

"Why don't you open them now?" asked Katie.

"You might as well Paul, it's your birthday love," said his mum.

"OK then." Paul sat down on the floor and began to unwrap his presents in front of everyone.

First up was the Ruston's present. It felt soft to Paul's touch, but inside something felt like a book. Paul ripped the wrapping paper off to reveal an orange BN towel and a book about naturism. "Thanks very much," said Paul while looking at the Rustons. "I've already been given a BN towel by my mum and dad so as we're all BN members I'll let James use one of them. The book looks interesting as well."

"It is; it tells you all about the history of naturism and the best places to go today," said Alice and Craig's dad.

"Thanks very much. I promise I'll only read it when I'm naked," smiled Paul.

Next up was the Wetherby's present. This felt like a box of some kind. Paul ripped the wrapping paper off to reveal a DVD compilation of one of his favourite TV shows; 'One Foot in the Grave'. "Thanks very much," said Paul while looking across at the Wetherbys. "I've been wanting this on DVD for ages."

"You enjoy it Paul, it is very funny," smiled Ben and Harry's dad.

Next up was the Finch's present. Paul had absolutely no idea what this could be. It was fairly flat and stiff. It turned out to be another DVD, but Paul got quite a surprise when he opened it because this was no ordinary DVD. It was a naturist film and was titled 'Body Art Nudists'. Katie's mum had bought it online. "Oh my word; this looks great," said Paul. "And there's a booklet with it."

"I think you'll enjoy watching it Paul," said Katie's mum.

"It's all about body painting," added Katie. "And there's loads more films you can buy in the booklet."

"Thanks very much. I can't wait to watch it." With his presents now dealt with Paul was about to suggested another game when Harry chipped in.

"What about pass the parcel Paul?"

"Er, yeah I s'pose so. Mum, have we got anything we..." Paul stopped as his mum brought out a large parcel which she'd wrapped earlier.

"Here we are," smiled Paul's mum.

"Thanks mum." Paul's dad put some music on and stopped it every few minutes to allow a layer of paper to be removed. After ten to fifteen minutes Harry tore off the last layer of paper to reveal a chocolate orange.

"Aw brilliant, choccy orange," smiled Harry showing everyone what the parcel contained.

With the music still on from playing pass the parcel Paul's dad turned the sound up. Even though space was limited most of them, Paul included, got up to dance. After a good half an hour or so dancing Paul had a rest and sat down and with Katie. They talked for a while mostly about naturism, but they also discussed something else. Katie asked Paul if he'd consider going out with her. Paul was more than a bit surprised to say the least, but he did have a soft spot for Katie and he and James always got on well with her. "Hmm," Paul pondered. "Let me think about this. What have we got in common?"

"We're both naturists," replied Katie quickly.

"Yeah; that's what I was thinking," said Paul. "And I s'pose I'd like a naturist for a..., but..."

"But what?"

"I'm not sure..." Paul paused for thought, but didn't really have long enough to considered his feelings for Katie.

"Well? What about it then? I quite like you Paul," smiled Katie.

"Er, OK then. I like you too Katie, and I think it'd be nice if we formed a relationship with naturism as our common interest."

"So do I." Katie paused for a moment then leant over, and without saying anything, she gave Paul a brief kiss. Paul had very mixed feelings indeed. Although he thought this was sweet he couldn't help feeling as if James would disapprove. James and him had been best friends all their lives and Paul did not want to spoil this.

"Let's tell James. I want him to know that while we're gonna start going out with each other I won't be abandoning him."

"OK then, he's over there with Harry Wetherby." Paul and Katie went over to talk to James.

"James; can I talk to you for a minute please?" asked Paul.

"Yeah, what about?" asked James.

"Well, er, not to beat about the bush; Katie has asked me out and I've agreed," replied Paul nervously.

"You what? You and Katie? I thought we w..." James stopped very abruptly.

"...best mates?" finished Paul quickly. "We are James, and that'll never change. I like Katie, and she likes me, so we've decided to give it a go, haven't we Katie."

"Yeah we have. James, I like Paul, he's a really nice looking boy," said Katie. Paul could see tears were starting well up in James's eyes, and in spite of what Paul just said, James thought he was about to be abandoned.

"B-but Paul, we've been best mates for ages; why do you suddenly wanna go out with Katie?"

"Well, as I've said James, I like her and she likes me," replied Paul as sympathetically as he could.

"Don't worry James I'm not gonna take him away from you. I've got other friends too and I'll be seeing them just as much as Paul will see you," added Katie. James couldn't help it. His eyes were now full of tears, but it was what Paul and Katie said next that pushed James over the edge. "Come on James, you're making us feel awful."

"Yeah you are, and it's still my birthday so please cheer up James."

"You'll get a girlfriend one day," said Katie. This was just too much for poor James and he burst into tears.

"I don't wanna girlfriend! I want Paul!" James pushed through everyone and went upstairs crying his eyes out. Paul's dad turned the music down low and everyone sat down. They were looking across at Paul and Katie. There was a brief moment of quiet until Paul's mum spoke.

"Why has James run away crying like that? What on earth have you said to him Paul?"

"Er, well I." Paul was close to tears himself now, but he told his mum why James ran away upset. "Well, Katie has asked me out and I've agreed to go out with her. When we told James he couldn't handle it. I think he thought I was abandoning him, but I told him there was no way I'd do that 'cos we're best mates. When Katie suggested he'd get a girlfriend soon he just burst into tears and ran off."

"Is that it?"

"Yes mum, I swear it. I'd never do anything to hurt James, 'cos..." Paul was getting quite upset himself now. He thought his decision to go out with Katie might not have been such a good idea.

"'Cos what?" asked his mum.

"'Cos he's my best friend and I like him a lot." Just then Alice and Craig's dad interrupted.

"Look, would you like us to go? I'd hate us to get in the way of any family problems, and it's nearly nine o'clock now as it is."

"Yes OK then. We'll let you know what happens if anything," said Paul's mum.

"I really hope Paul doesn't fall out with James over Katie 'cos they're really good together," said Alice. Paul's mum went upstairs to get the Ruston's clothes and saw James in Paul's bedroom still crying. This must be something serious, thought Paul's mum. I've never seen James so upset before.

"Right, there you go." Paul's mum gave the Rustons their clothes. They got dressed and left. "James is sat in Paul's bedroom and he's still crying. I think it might be a good idea to have a word with him."

"Shall I come too?" asked Paul.

"If you like," replied James's mum. The three of them went upstairs to Paul's bedroom and found James sat on the floor. He still appeared to be upset but had stopped crying. His mum was the first to speak to him.

"Come on love, what's wrong?"

"P-Paul's going out with K-Katie," sobbed James.

"Well, it is Katie's decision who she goes out with love. If you wanted to go out with her perhaps you should've said something sooner," said James's mum while wrongly assuming they both wanted to go out with Katie.

"What?" said James firmly. "I don't wanna go out with Katie! She's just a friend, nothing more. It's P-Paul I want." James burst into tears again. Paul and James's mums looked at one another and then at Paul.

"What?" asked Paul getting slightly worried the finger was being pointed at him.

"Tell me again exactly what it is that you and James have been doing when you been out together," said Paul's mum.

"We just walk around and sunbathe, that's all; I swear it mum!" Paul then thought a bit more about what they'd got up to in the past few months. "Well, er..." James was still crying while they were talking.

"Yes Paul? Is there something else you'd care to share with us?" asked James's mum.

"Well, we had a swim, I mean a skinny dip, together, the day before that day we sneaked into the leisure centre and then we went skinny dipping again that day with Ben and Harry Wetherby. Other than that we just enjoy the sunshine outside going naked where and when we can."

"Did you take any sun cream with you?" asked Paul's mum.

"Yeah, course we did," replied Paul. "We'd have been burnt to a crisp if we hadn't." Just then Paul had a sudden thought. He remembered the times they'd rub sun cream into each other's backs, and other areas, but never thought much of it at the time. Why should he? Paul cast his mind back to the days before that first swim and things seemed to fit together. In addition to that Paul thought about the times they'd showered together and especially this most recent time which was only a few hours earlier. "Mum, I think I might know why James is so upset."

"Well, come on then, let's hear it."

"Well I'm not certain, but I think it's a possibility. Just before James came up here in tears he said he didn't want a girlfriend; he wanted me."

"Go on," said James's mum a bit surprised.

"James and me have always been best mates, but I'm kind of

getting the feeling that James was wanting us to be more than just friends."

"Is this true James?" James nodded his head and started crying again.

"I-I c-can't help it m-mum," sobbed James. "I like P-Paul so much." James continued sobbing, but if the truth be known, James had feared this moment of rejection for some time.

"Let's go back downstairs and have a drink, it'll help us feel better. I think we ought to put some clothes on while we discuss this situation," said Paul's mum. The four of them got up and went downstairs to an almost empty room. Paul and James put their shorts and T-shirts on while their mums got suitably dressed.

It was just after half past nine now and the Wetherbys and the Finches had gone home. James's dad had also disappeared. Paul's dad was in the kitchen making a hot drink.

"Oh, there you all are. Everything OK? How come you're dressed?"

"I'm afraid we've got a bit of a problem Tony, that's why we're dressed. If you're making tea put a drop of whisky in mine, I need it."

"Oh, right. This sounds serious." Paul's dad put a towel round him and sat down on the sofa with his wife and son. James sat opposite with his mum. He'd stopped crying, but was still clearly upset. "Well?" asked Paul's dad. Paul and his mum explained as best they could why it was that James was so upset. "Oh James, James; you poor thing. To feel rejection like that must have been absolutely heartbreaking; and from your best friend as well."

"It was s-such a s-shock Mr. J-Jessop," sobbed James. "I like P-Paul a lot, and I was worried this might happen one day, but I'd have thought if it had it would've been at least five or ten years from now." Just then James's dad came back in.

"Oh; what's wrong with James? Why did he scarper in tears like that?"

"Sit down Andrew and I'll tell you." James's mum told her husband everything.

"Well I; I don't believe it," said James's dad. "I mean, you read about things like this in magazines and such like, b-but it seems so unreal when it's your own family." James's dad was struggling to take in what he'd just been told, but then he looked across at his son and couldn't help shedding a tear. "Come here James," he said. James sat next to his dad and they both had a cry together. "If you like other boys James, it's fine with your mum and me, so whatever you do don't worry son."

"Your dad's right there James. You're our son; we love you dearly and we'll stand by you."

"Look, it's getting late now. Let's get home and we'll talk about this later."

"OK-K then," sobbed James. Music was still playing in the Jessop's front room as James's parents got up to leave, but as James was about to follow them through the Jessop's front door Paul suddenly had a change of heart. Paul had only seconds in which to think, but think he did, and he felt a lot better with himself because of it. Paul had now made up his mind what he wanted in life. He liked Katie, but wasn't fully sure about a long term relationship with her, and that's when he thought about James; his best and most loyal friend in the whole world.

"James! Don't go," said Paul quickly. "Come here a minute." Hoping his parents would be as accepting as James's were, and with Abba's 'Dancing Queen' now playing, Paul flung his arms around James and burst into tears.

"I'm so s-sorry James," sobbed Paul. "I'm so very sorry to have put you through this."

"Put me through what?" Paul then looked directly into James's eyes.

"I've changed my mind; I'm not gonna go out with Katie."

"So, w-what does that m-mean?" asked James, who was on the verge of crying again.

"It means I'm gonna stay with you, if you can forgive me," sobbed Paul.

"Seriously? You and me? You and me, together, for always?" sobbed James.

"Yes! I like Katie, but I love you!" yelled Paul. Paul and James were both in floods of tears, but these were now tears of joy and of happiness. Paul had narrowly averted making the biggest mistake of his life. James was now not only his best friend he was the person he'd fallen in love with.

"Well, I don't know about anyone else, but I need one hell of a stiff drink," said Paul's dad.

"So do I," added James's dad.

"Me too, come back in everyone," said Paul's mum. Paul's dad opened a bottle of strong brandy and poured some out into four glasses.

"Would you two boys like a nip of brandy to help calm you down?"

"Yes please dad."

"Yes thanks Mr. Jessop." Paul's dad handed the drinks round and then sat down.

"Well, where do we go from here then?" asked James's dad.

"Not exactly sure," replied Paul's dad. "It looks like our boys are pretty much inseparable doesn't it." Paul and James were sat together on the sofa with an arm around each other in a warm embrace, and both looked physically drained.

"Well, I take it we're all going to support our sons in the choice they've just made," said Paul's mum.

"Yes, we should, very much so," said James's mum. "This is 2008 and we live in a modern civilised society."

"Here, here," said Paul's dad raising his glass. "We can't possible stop them from being together, it would break their hearts if we did. I know this has come very unexpectedly, but we must stand by them and give them all our love and support."

"Yes, absolutely," said James's dad in agreement. "I'm with you one hundred percent."

It was now almost eleven o'clock, and after unanimously deciding to stand by their son's decisions James and his mum and dad left and went home.

Chapter 20

After last night's emotional rollercoaster Paul and James both slept in; but at around ten o'clock Paul got up. Now that everything was out in the open he wanted to see James and have a long talk.

Paul went downstairs and got some breakfast. His mum came in while he was eating. "Morning love; did you sleep well?"

"Not too bad mum, considering," replied Paul. "I do hope James is OK."

"I'm sure he will be love. Your dad and I have known his parents a long time."

"Yeah, course." Paul finished his breakfast and got dressed. Just after half ten he went next door to see James. While still feeling the emotional scars of last night Paul knocked on the Handles front door. James's mum answered it.

"Morning Paul, how are you feeling?"

"Not too bad thanks, considering; how's James?"

"Oh he's fine, come on in love." Paul went inside and sat down in the front room. "I've just put the kettle on if you'd like a coffee Paul."

"Yes please," replied Paul. Just then James's dad came downstairs and into the front room.

"Oh, morning Paul. Feeling better after a good night's sleep?"

"Yeah, not too bad thanks. Where's James?" asked Paul.

"He's in his bedroom, hang on, I'll give him a shout." James's dad went to the bottom of the stairs and called up to his son. "James!"

"What?" called James from his bedroom. "Your boyfriend's here and he wants to see you!" Paul was a bit surprised at James's dad using the word 'boyfriend', but he smiled at him as he came back into the front room. As soon as James heard those words he knew it was Paul that had called, so quickly went downstairs to see him.

"Hi; are you OK?" asked James.

"I'm fine thanks," smiled Paul. "What about you?"

"OK, I guess." Paul and James looked across at James's dad.

"Yes?" he asked. Paul and James didn't say anything. "If the pair of you want to be alone feel free to go upstairs."

"OK dad." Thinking they ought to keep their clothes on for the moment Paul and James went upstairs to James's bedroom. They sat on opposite ends of James's bed and talked.

"I still can't believe last night," said Paul. "I nearly made the biggest mistake of my life."

"Do you mean Katie?"

"Yeah I do. When she asked me to go out with her I was pretty surprised and I said 'yes' almost straightaway without really thinking about it."

"I'm so glad you did."

"I'm glad I did too. I don't dislike Katie, and she's fun to be around when we go swimming, but if I'm honest, I don't feel as if I actually love her."

"Who do you love then?" smiled James knowing full well what the answer would be.

"Hmm…, you'll have to let me think very carefully about that," replied Paul. James's face dropped slightly when Paul said this because he was expecting a quick answer; however, Paul didn't keep James waiting too long.

"Well?"

"Well; the love of my life would have to be someone I've known for a long time."

"Yeah; and?"

"And; would have to be a similar age."

"And?"

"And; should ideally live quite close."

"And?"

"And; enjoy being naked."

"Yeah; and?" James was now smiling 'cos he knew Paul was just messing about.

"And; he; should have blond hair, fair skin and, er…, be circumcised."

"Eh!" James looked at Paul in horror! "I'm not circumcised!"

"Well; how painful do you think it would be?" asked Paul picking up a pair of very sharp scissors.

"No! Paul, Please! I'd rather have it done properly if you'd prefer me to be circumcised." Paul looked across at James and smiled.

"Ha ha! James; relax," laughed Paul. "I'm only joking. I'd cut my own foreskin off before I let anyone circumcise you."

"I'm glad to hear it," said James firmly. "Everything you said was fine until that last bit."

"I know, I was only teasing. Of course you're the love of my life; come here," smiled Paul holding out his arm. James cosied up to Paul and Paul put his arm around him.

"I like it when we can be together like this," smiled James.

"Me too," smiled Paul. While still wearing their T-shirts, shorts and socks, Paul and James cuddled up together on James's bed. They stayed like this for a few minutes and James began gently stroking Paul's bare leg. They loved each other very much and it was clear to see.

"If you ever wanted us to be circumcised, I'd go along with it as long as we did it properly," said James.

"Well..., what do you think it would feel like?" asked Paul.

"I don't know; but I s'pose we could always ask Lee Scott when we get back to school," suggested James with a smile. "I showered next to him just before we finished for the holidays."

"And is he circumcised?"

"Yeah he sure is, and believe me, he left nothing to my imagination that afternoon!"

"Well, that's not really all that surprising is it? 'Cos he is a bit of a show off; but we can't really go up to him and say; 'Hi Lee, what's it like being circumcised?' can we?"

"No course not. We'd have to see a doctor I guess," said James.

"Yeah, I s'pose so."

"Anyway, you remember yesterday when you were accusing me of being up to something?"

"Yeah, what about it?" asked Paul cautiously.

"Well, I sort of couldn't help it really, and I am sorry; but I..., you know..., I did it, on your bed."

"Did what on my bed?" asked Paul looking directly at James. "Did you pee on my bed?"

"No! I didn't pee on your bed!" snapped James.

"So what are you trying, to…" Paul suddenly cottoned on to what James was hinting at and gave him a very sly smile. "I wondered why it took you so long to come downstairs, and no wonder you were smiling."

"Look, Paul, I said I'm sorry so can we just forget about it?"

"Why? I wish I'd have been with you; it would've been great sharing an experience like that."

"Yeah, but that was before we ended up falling for each other; and I thought you were straight when you agreed to go out with Katie."

"Well I'm not, I'm just like you; which is why it didn't feel right to go out with Katie, and, it's also why I got a stiffy in the shower same as you."

"OK, I get the message," smiled James. "Maybe we could shower together again one day when our parents go out."

"We'll see," smiled Paul.

While Paul and James were in each other's arms James's mum came upstairs and into his bedroom. "Oh, sorry you two." James's mum was a bit surprised to see them the way they were.

"It's OK mum. Paul and me love each other and we wanna be together for always."

"OK love, it's your life; and as your dad and I said last night it's not a problem."

"Thanks Mrs. Handle, it's nice to know approve," said Paul. "I've had feelings for James for quite a while, but I didn't really understand them until last night. I felt awful when he got so upset, and it made me think hard about whether I should go out with Katie. I decided not in the end because I'd much stronger feelings for James. That's why I started crying, 'cos I knew then that I was in love with him." As Paul finished speaking he was close to tears, but didn't actually start crying. James comforted him and gave him a hug and a kiss. Paul responded by kissing James.

"Alright you two; I'm going back downstairs now to put the kettle on again. Come down if you'd like a coffee and biscuit."

"Thanks mum, we'll be down in a few minutes." While they were alone Paul and James hugged each other and, for the first time, they shared a passionate kiss. They went downstairs about ten minutes later and had quite a long chat with James's mum and dad over coffee and biscuits. They were interrupted part way through by a knock on the front door. James's mum got up to answer it. It was Paul's mum and dad. They were carrying a couple of holiday brochures and were smiling as James's mum invited them in.

"Hiya," said Paul's mum and dad.

"Oh hello; come on in, Paul's here," said James's mum.

"Thanks, we knew he'd be here seeing as he wasn't at home," smiled Paul's mum. The three of them joined the others in the Handles front room and sat down.

"We've been looking through these holiday brochures and we think you might like Gran Canaria and Fuerteventura," said Paul's dad.

"But I thought we we're gonna go to that place in France for a holiday this year dad," said Paul.

"You mean Cap d'Agde?"

"Yeah that was it," replied Paul quickly.

"Well, I'm afraid we'll have to leave Cap d'Agde until next year 'cos we've left it a bit late; that is if you want hot sunshine."

"Yeah we do," said James firmly.

"Right, well, Gran Canaria and Fuerteventura are just as naturist friendly and have a hot climate virtually all year round."

"Hmm, that sound nice," said James's dad.

"Well it should be," said Paul's dad. "I got these brochures from the Hopes down the road and they said it was really hot all the time they were there."

"Dad, that sounds great! What else is there?" asked Paul.

"Well, er, you and James might like to check Gran Canaria and Fuerteventura out for yourselves. I think you'll be well catered for when you get to eighteen," smiled Paul's dad.

"How do you mean Mr. Jessop?" asked James.

"I think I know," smiled Paul. Paul then whispered something to James which made his eyes light up.

"Really?" asked James.

"I think so," replied Paul. "If we go with our mums and dads before we turn eighteen we won't be able to drink or go into any of the bars, but we should be able to soak up some of the atmosphere; and it'll be nice knowing there are many other people with similar interests to us."

"When can we go?"

"Hmm, what do you think about the October half term?" asked James's mum.

"Yeah, I think I could get that week," replied Paul's dad.

"Andrew?"

"Go on then, let's do it. I'm owed a few favours at work."

As usual Paul and James got quite excited about going on Holiday together, but this holiday would be extra special because they would be spending most of it naturist; not only that their parents, having previously agreed to stand by their sons in their choice of relationship, agreed to take them to a few bars so they could safely see for themselves what life was like for gay people.

Chapter 21

* Three Years Later *

Following their holiday to Gran Canaria in 2008 the Jessops and the Handles considered the possibility of emigrating. They enjoyed their holiday so much they went again in 2009 and twice in 2010. It was towards the end of their second holiday there that year they became aware of a bar which was up for sale, so; in February 2011 Paul's parents and James's dad flew back out to see what was involved in buying and running it.

The name of the place is what caught their attention. It was called P&J's Bar after the current owners Pascal and Joel. They had run it together for the last thirty one years and, following their sixtieth birthdays in 2010, were looking to retire. Pascal had also suffered a mild stroke the year before.

"This would be great for our sons," said Paul's dad.

"That's just what I was thinking," said James's dad in full agreement. "It's in a great location in the centre of Maspalomas."

"And we wouldn't need to do anything with the name would we," smiled Paul's mum.

The three of them got talking to Pascal and Joel and were shown exactly what was involved in owning and running a bar.

If the Jessops and the Handles were to join forces they could easily afford to buy the place, which also had spacious accommodation combined. In addition to that it had four other things going for it; one, location; two, the name; three, it was a well-known gay bar with a usually pleasant clientele; and four, it was within walking distance of the beach and the centre of town.

Upon their return to the UK Paul and James's parents contacted all the relevant people with a view to moving out there as soon as the practicalities would allow. They'd agreed a price with Pascal and Joel so expected the sale to go through as soon as they'd sold their properties in the UK. This was, of course, much easier said than done; however, towards the end of April the Jessops found a buyer who was keen for them to move out quickly. He was one of those wealthy property experts and was the sort of person you might see driving a Lamborghini one day and then a Bentley the next. His wealth was a godsend for both families and when he became aware the Handles house next door was also up for sale he made them an offer which James's parents accepted immediately.

The Jessops and the Handles both made a packet selling their homes in the UK, and because of the swiftness of this, they had to move out into temporary accommodation and place all their furniture, and most of their belongings, into storage.

Towards the end of July the sale of P&J's bar in Maspalomas went through. Paul, James and their parents made arrangements to move in shortly afterwards. By the middle of August everything had been arranged; they'd booked their flights, sold their cars and arranged furniture transfer.

So, on the afternoon of Paul's eighteenth birthday they set off. There were lots of people gathered at the airport to see them off and they were waiting in the bar. The Jessops and the Handles were to get quite a surprise as neither family knew of this. Peter Simpkin had arranged a good send off. He'd always had a soft spot for Paul and James ever since they successfully smuggled themselves into the leisure centre at the age of fourteen just so they could experience swimming naked. He was going to miss both of them and their parents a lot.

Just after 13:15 the Jessops and the Handles checked in for their one-way flight to Gran Canaria and then, as they walked over to go through security they heard an announcement. "Your attention please; would Mr. Paul Jessop and Mr. James Handle, and their parents, please go upstairs to the bar. Thank you." The Jessops and the Handles wondered what was going on, but as they'd nearly two hours to go through security they thought they'd better check the bar out as requested. As they walked in everyone stood up and called out; "Surprise!"

"Oh my word!" said Paul. "Is this all for us?"

"Yes Paul it sure is; and happy eighteenth birthday as well," said Mr. Simpkin. "I'm really gonna miss you and James, and your parents."

"Thanks very much Mr. Simpkin," added James.

"Your very welcome, all of you. And I think Craig Ruston has something for you over there." Sure enough Craig did. It was a big leaving card signed by virtually everyone at the swim. Craig handed it over to Paul and James as the cameras snapped away. Everyone was all smiles, but there were a few tears as well.

Katie Finch in particular was disappointed about Paul choosing James over her, but at the time she didn't feel as if it was what Paul really wanted.

Alice and Craig, now fourteen and twelve, wanted their photos taking one more time with Paul and James before they jetted off to pastures new as did the Wetherby brothers Ben and Harry, who were now nineteen and sixteen.

The leaving party lasted a good hour and after three cheers, a few burst balloons and another announcement the Jessops and the Handles left. "Thanks very much everyone, it's been great. Bye for now," said Paul.

"Yeah, thanks; thanks very much everyone," said James. "Bye."

"We hope to see some of you out there before too long," smiled Paul as he disappeared through to security with James and their parents.

The Jessops and the Handles arrived in Maspalomas and made their way to their new home. It was warm when they left the UK, but it was scorching in Maspalomas. Neither of them had experienced it quite as hot as this, but none of them complained.

With some help from their staff, all of whom they were keeping on, everything was on schedule for a quick opening. On Thursday the first of September 2011, two days short of James's eighteenth birthday, the Jessops and the Handles opened P&J's bar for business. They'd had it specially decorated with rainbow flags, banners and balloons. Pascal and Joel were also there for the inaugural opening and wished them well. They were glad they had sold their bar to two families who had sons just like them.

Pascal and Joel were both only children and had pretty much grown up together, but they were well into their twenties before they declared their love for each other. Things were very different in their younger days, and to a large extent they envied Paul and James.

Paul and James were now setup for life. Their parents were the current landlords, but in time this would change. P&J's bar would soon be Paul and James's bar.

Two days later, on James's eighteenth birthday, James asked Paul to be his legal partner. Paul accepted without any hesitation and both were over the moon.

Paul and James had it all in Maspalomas; they enjoyed year round sunshine, they could go naked on the beach whenever they liked, they lived and worked in what would one day be their bar and they were soon to be civil partners.

"Here's to the next thirty-one years of P&J's bar," said Paul raising his glass.

"I couldn't agree more love," smiled James. "Give us a kiss!"

* *

www.ingramcontent.com/pod-product-compliance
Lightning Source LLC
Chambersburg PA
CBHW070833250626
47159CB00003B/755